Emily Carmichael
Touch of Fire

WARNER BOOKS

A Warner Communications Company

WARNER BOOKS EDITION

Copyright © 1989 by Emily Krokosz
All rights reserved.

Cover art by Dave Gatti

Warner Books, Inc.
666 Fifth Avenue
New York, N.Y. 10103

 A Warner Communications Company

Printed in the United States of America

First Printing: May, 1989

10 9 8 7 6 5 4 3 2 1

They Looked at Each Other for a Moment That Seemed Suspended in Time.

◆ ◆ ◆ ◆

Logan loomed above her, so overpoweringly masculine that Kit's breath caught in her throat.

"Maybe one little goodbye kiss," she said in a soft voice.

It was surrender. Kit knew as well as Logan that one little kiss wasn't possible between them. His mouth came down on hers in a gentle exploration that soon became a savage demand. She yielded, opening her mouth to his thrusting tongue and arching against his hard body with a silent plea of her own.

"Don't go tomorrow." There was pleading in her voice. She hated it, but it was there just the same.

"There is no tomorrow, Katarina." The low, husky voice was laced with passion. It vibrated through Kit's body and set every nerve aquiver. "There is only tonight," he whispered. "And when you remember tonight, remember that you are mine, completely, and I am yours."

His lips grazed on the satin of her skin, recognizing no boundaries and no limits to their wandering caress, devouring the heat of her desire...

◆ ◆ ◆ ◆

"Sensitive...fresh...a wonderful romance. HIGHEST RATING."
—***Romantic Times*** on ***Autumnfire***

"An excellent romance author. Her fresh style and sprightly humor turn this high seas adventure into a delightful tale for a winter's night. SPICY."
—***Romantic Times*** on ***The Devil's Darling***

Also by Emily Carmichael

Surrender
Autumnfire
The Devil's Darling

Published by
WARNER BOOKS

ATTENTION: SCHOOLS AND CORPORATIONS

WARNER books are available at quantity discounts with bulk purchase for educational, business, or sales promotional use. For information, please write to: SPECIAL SALES DEPARTMENT, WARNER BOOKS, 666 FIFTH AVENUE, NEW YORK, N.Y. 10103

**ARE THERE WARNER BOOKS
YOU WANT BUT CANNOT FIND IN YOUR LOCAL STORES?**

You can get any WARNER BOOKS title in print. Simply send title and retail price, plus 50c per order and 50c per copy to cover mailing and handling costs for each book desired. New York State and California residents add applicable sales tax. Enclose check or money order only, no cash please, to: WARNER BOOKS, P.O. BOX 690, NEW YORK, N.Y. 10019

December 1654
The island of Barbados

Prologue

The girl was an illusion. She had to be an illusion—a mocking vision born of starvation and weakness and intolerable heat.

Logan Steele, late of Somerset Manor, and more lately of Newgate Gaol, squinted against the blinding light of day. Five long weeks in the fetid, dark hold of a convict ship had made him a creature of the night. His eyes ached from the glare, and burning red spots danced across the dark of his eyelids. He could feel his fishbelly-white skin crisping under the relentless tropical sun.

He opened his eyes once again, slowly bringing into focus the glittering backdrop of Carlisle Bay, the dusty Bridgetown marketplace, the milling, sweating crowds—and the girl. Was she real, then? Logan let his eyes cling to her, not caring if she was real or imagined. Anything to divert him from the thought that soon he would be auctioned off like a hog bound for slaughter.

The girl was tall and slender, dressed in a white muslin costume that owed much more to comfort than to fashion. The clean white of her simple gown set off the smooth golden tones of her skin. Her head was unfashionably bare of cap or hat, and the afternoon sun shot blue sparks off the midnight black of her hair, which was caught smoothly back from her face and fastened at the nape of her neck in a severe, unflattering knot. Logan had to acknowledge that she was not really beautiful, this vision of his. But she was arresting, fascinating even—an elegant swan amid a crowd of garish peacocks.

A grating voice brought Logan back to the unpleasantness at hand.

"Stand back, there. Give way, ye swine." Two burly militia guards grabbed a frightened Negro and pushed him to the center of the platform. The auctioneer began his pitch, his voice rising above the clamor of the crowd. The black, his eyes showing wide and white against his ebony skin, was soon sold. Another was pushed into his place.

Logan stood with his fellow convicts, wondering how long before all the blacks were sold and the whites would be pushed to center stage. He felt the sun beat down upon his uncovered head and tried to chase away the spots that swam before his eyes. Once he had prided himself on his strength. Now he despised his weakness. He could smell his companions, and he could smell himself. The rank odor of fear mixed with the stench of hot, steaming, unwashed bodies.

He took refuge once again in his vision. The sight of the girl in white evoked memories of a more pleasant time. Images of gentle green Kent and the rolling meadows, pleasant gardens, warm sunshine, and soft rains of his home washed through his mind in bitter contrast to his present circumstances. Most likely he would never again see Somerset Manor, his brothers, or his friends. The British admiralty had no mercy for a naval officer who committed the high crime of mutiny. For Logan Steele there would be no reprieve from the fate he had brought upon himself.

The last group of blacks stepped up to the block—a family fresh from the Guinea coast, the auctioneer explained, in case anyone wanted to bid them as a unit. Interest had died down. Most of the buyers had already purchased what they needed. Only one party bid, in a voice that was high, musical, and sweet, a melodic contrast to the raucous clamor of the marketplace.

Logan's attention jerked away from his bitter reverie and back to the girl in white. She might look like an angel, but apparently she had no qualms about dipping her hands in the filth of this travesty. His narrow lips twitched in a faint grimace of disgust. Had he thought she was some vision sent to comfort him in his pain? More fool he!

As if drawn by Logan's intense gaze, the girl looked up. Her eyes rested momentarily on his, then quickly dropped, as if she had been burned by that brief contact. Logan saw the look of disgust that flashed across her face. It matched the similar expression on his own.

The girl turned to leave as the auction of blacks came to an end. She spoke a few words to a man who stood beside her, a man who closely resembled her in appearance, for all that his skin was fairer and his dress resplendent with the garish satins and velvets that she apparently disdained. He took her by the arm and gestured toward the convicts who were now being moved closer to the auction block. She shook her head vehemently, but the man prevailed, and she stayed beside him.

The convicts were prodded into a line where the buyers could see them. Logan gazed out at the swarming crowd, straightened his shoulders, and stood tall in his lice- and flea-infested rags. A foolish gesture, he told himself. But he was what he was, and pride had been bred into him from the cradle. There was no escaping its demands now.

The auctioneer tried valiantly to incite the buyers' interest as the convicts were prodded toward the center of the platform. Fine laborers all, he declared, and the Lord Protector Cromwell had generously decreed that the loyal colonists on Barbados could have these fellows for only 1,550 pounds of sugar apiece.

A catcall interrupted his monologue. "Lord Cromwell would do better to hang the lot of them. We'll get precious little work from a shipload of walking corpses."

"Fifteen hundred fifty pounds of sugar for those wretches?" another buyer commented in a loud voice. "They're naught but scarecrows."

A murmur of agreement swept through the crowd of planters. Still, as the auctioneer persisted with diligent enthusiasm, he found those who would foot the price. One by one, the convicts marched off with their new masters.

As his own fate drew ever nearer, Logan turned his

attention back to the vision in white. The girl declined to buy any of the convicts, but the man beside her bought one and then another.

Finally Logan stood alone on the platform. Here was a rare buy, the auctioneer exclaimed. He extolled Logan's supposed strength, pointing out his height and the width of shoulder. Feed this one up, and you might even get the full ten-year sentence out of him. To add to the bargain, this was a man who could read and write and keep accounts, for before the infamy that sent him to this isle, he had been an educated gentleman.

A silence settled over the crowd. Most of the buyers had by now drifted away. Then a voice called out in a bored tone.

"He's worth the price, I suppose."

"Was that a bid, Master St. John? This one's a generous bargain, sir."

Master St. John sighed wearily. "All right, my man. Have him brought along to my wagons."

Logan had allowed his eyes to sweep over the crowd in unfocused disdain. Now he swung them toward his new master's voice as he was led down from the block. A crooked smile twisted his mouth.

He had been purchased by the man with the girl in white. He wondered if the lady and her companion realized how bad a bargain they had made.

Chapter 1

Katarina Isabella Christina St. John postured saucily in front of the gilded parlor mirror and slanted a mischievous look toward her brother.

"And just what qualities do you see, brother mine, that would draw suitors to my door?" She cocked one brow in flippant disdain. "Except of course my wealth, and that's not reflected in the glass."

Oliver St. John snorted with exasperation and thanked God he was not often required to keep company with this sister of his. Usually he was at sea captaining the flagship of the family shipping line and safely away from her sharp tongue and biting wit. But he had crushed his left arm in a recent gale, and now he was sentenced to two or three months ashore at the mercy of his sister's changeable humors. Lord above! All he had done was mention a few times that it was well past time that she marry, and before he knew it he was greeted with this blast of female sarcasm!

Oliver grimaced in disgust. "You amaze me, Kit. One would think that a woman of your sensibilities would have more insight into the reasons a man takes a wife."

Kit laughed irreverently, refusing to match his grave demeanor. "I well know why most men take a wife, Oliver. And I have no intention of falling into that trap!"

"You have many fine qualities that a man seeks in a wife."

"Indeed I do!" Kit agreed, turning back to the mirror and regarding her own face and form with a frown. "I have the finest qualities of all—half interest in the richest three hundred acres in Barbados and half interest in one of the most prosperous shipping lines plying the seas between Mother England and this fertile island colony. I would say that adds up to the whole interest that my suitors have in courting me."

Oliver shook his head in resignation.

"Dear Oliver," Kit offered in a more placating tone, "I know you have my best interests at heart. But I am not willing to put my future into the hands of some man who is interested only in my wealth, just to have a husband. I can do very well without one, thank you!"

"You do men a disservice, Kit," Oliver persisted. "Fortune can never be ignored, it's true, but there are other things men consider in pursuing a woman. You place too high a value on beauty. You have deeper qualities..."

A cynically raised brow from Kit stopped his dissembling. He grinned disarmingly. "All right. All right. Here I am home for the first time in a year and we're fighting like cats and dogs."

Kit moved to sit beside him on the velvet settee and gave his arm an affectionate squeeze. "Of course we're fighting like cats and dogs. We always have."

"We have at that," Oliver agreed with a smile. "But if you weren't so cursed stubborn..."

"And if you would stop trying to run my life."

Oliver chuckled. "Big brothers are supposed to look after their sisters—even half sisters."

"This sister is doing quite well on her own," Kit pointed out with a confident grin.

"Yes, I suppose you are at that." Oliver patted the hand that still rested on his arm. "And I'm supposed to be resting so my arm can heal, not battling with a stubborn she-cat." His tone softened. "But truly, it is good to be home again, Kit. I've missed you."

"Rubbish!" Kit stood and, taking her brother's hand,

pulled him up beside her. "You don't think about me at all when you're at sea! All you think about is making money."

He laughed and followed her toward the French doors that led onto the veranda. "And I suppose so much of your time is spent thinking about me!"

She shrugged and threw him a mischievous smile over her shoulder. "The plantation does keep me very busy."

"Indeed! We're two of a kind, sister mine. It's fortunate I'm such an understanding fellow. What other man would tolerate a sister who insists on running the family plantation by herself?"

"That was our agreement, was it not?" Kit's voice became cautiously defensive. "I keep my hands off our shipping line and you keep your hands off our plantation."

Oliver raised his arms as though in defense. "Now don't jump all over me again. I swear, Kit, you're as touchy as a wet cat!"

She smiled in apology. "I suppose I am at times."

They leaned against the veranda railing and looked down at the spacious lawns that stretched out to a placid palm-lined lake. The two of them made a handsome pair. Anyone looking at them standing together would have no doubt that they were brother and sister. Though Oliver's skin coloring was more pallid, they had the same midnight-black hair and the same deep brown eyes. The St. John features that stamped the brother's face and made him handsome made the sister's face far too strong to be beautiful.

"It never fails to move me, this view," Oliver said. "Sometimes I wonder why I don't spend more time here."

"The sea is your home," Kit reminded him. "You would never be content to stay ashore."

Kit looked out over the acres of green that stretched out from the house in all directions. In the distance, almost hidden in the lingering morning haze, the glinting waters of Half Moon Bay stretched out to the horizon and faded into the soft blue tropical sky. This was more than her home. It was her very life. The coral-stone house with its broad verandas and large sunlit rooms that caught every cooling breeze, the acres and acres of cane fields, the sugar mill, the slave village, the streams and ponds and lakes, the tangled jungle—she knew every inch of the land and the name of every slave who worked it for her. There was nothing else in her life, and it appeared there never would be. She was content with what she had.

Kit's grandfather, George Harold St. John, had been with the first English colonists who settled the island in 1627. Being a clever man with his eye to the future, he had appropriated some of the island's most fertile and beautiful acreage for himself. At first he had tried cultivating tobacco to sell to the mother country, but when sugar cane had been introduced to the island in 1637 he'd been among the first of the planters to switch to the new crop. Other smaller planters who continued the struggle with tobacco, cotton, and indigo finally either went broke or gave up. St. John expanded at their expense. He ended up with Greenhaven—not the largest plantation on the island, but certainly one of the most profitable.

George St. John passed Greenhaven down to his son, Roger, who in time passed it on to his son, Oliver—and his beloved daughter, Kit. He left half interest to each of his children, with the stipulation that the plantation be managed as a single unit. But Kit regarded the plantation as wholly hers. Oliver took no interest in it, other than as a place of refuge when he was not off adventuring on the sea. Greenhaven was her own little niche. And she was not about to share it with some fortune-hunting man who would only regard it—and her—as an easy source of money.

"It certainly is beautiful," Oliver commented, still contemplating the view.

"It certainly is!" Kit agreed heartily.

"Don't you get lonely here with only Mandy and the house slaves to talk to?"

Kit gave her brother a warning look. "Are we about to fight again?"

"I don't want to fight. I only have your welfare in mind."

Kit snorted in disbelief. "Are you sure about that?"

"Yes, I am. My God, Kit, you're becoming a veritable spinster. You are wasting your life, and I'm concerned for your happiness."

"I don't regard my life as a waste."

Her voice rang with a quiet undercurrent of anger. But Oliver wasn't listening.

"There's at least half a dozen worthy fellows who would be glad to pay you court if you would just give them a bit of encouragement."

Kit sighed. "Name one 'worthy' fellow."

"Nicholas Basey."

Kit shouted with unladylike laughter. "Nicholas Basey? That gaudy-feathered popinjay! He's prettier than I am!"

Now it was Oliver's voice that was tinged with anger. "There you go again!"

"What do you mean, there I go again?" Kit demanded.

"You make much too much of your plainness. You wear it like some badge of honor and use it as a shield to fend off anyone who might dare to be interested in you."

Kit puffed herself up for a haughty reply, then on further reflection relaxed and shrugged with unconcern. "Perhaps I do, but it is really none of your concern, Oliver. I'm a woman grown, and I know what I want. You may as well stop railing at me."

Oliver's lips drew into a tight line of exasperation. How was he to deal with this obstinate, saucy-mouthed sister? Ever since childhood she had been too proud and independent for her own good. That was the real reason that suitors went away feeling as if they had tried to assault the Rock of Gilbraltar. Kit wasn't really as plain as she thought herself, Oliver acknowledged silently, running a practiced eye over his sister's slender frame. Certainly no man of discernment would call her beautiful, but there was a striking quality to her looks that caught and pleasantly held the eye. She was much too tall, of course—as tall as most men, and taller than some—but she had a slender grace that compensated for her height. Her face had none of the delicate beauty so fashionable in Europe, but the combination of large almond eyes and the winged brows that slanted above them gave her a gypsyish charm. The nose was too small and too pert to be truly pretty, the mouth too generous, the chin too determined. And the olive-tinged skin she had inherited from her mother was definitely a flaw, even though it was smooth as fine silk. No, Oliver concluded, Kit was not so much plain as she was different—almost exotic. Many a man might find her attractive if she were not so damnably outspoken, independent, arrogant, strong-willed, and spoiled. That was the rub.

And what was he, her brother, to do about it? Oliver had come to realize that Greenhaven could be making them much more money if it were run by a man more like himself, a man with a more ruthless turn of mind than Kit would ever have. His sister wasted money on nonessentials. The slaves were outrageously overfed and underworked, and sheltered and clothed much more cosily than was needed in this mild climate. The sugar mill should be working the day around instead of just two shifts, and the drivers needed to get the slaves to cut faster. So much could be done, but Kit seemed content with things just as they were. A husband was the answer—someone who would listen to Oliver's directions and place the same value on profit that he did. They would all benefit, Kit included. But Nick Basey was Oliver's last hope. Where else would he find a man willing to take on such an independent-minded, unconventional woman?

"What of love, Kit?" Oliver was nothing if not persistent. "Are you willing to live your life without children, without a man's love?"

Kit chuckled tolerantly. "I have children enough that I can visit in the village."

"Black children?" he scoffed.

"Children are children."

"Then love. What of that?"

Kit laughed and shook her head. "You can speak to me of love? You who have probably dishonored every planter's daughter from here to Bridgetown, and no doubt plied each of them with words of undying love—you can stand there and bleat of love?"

Oliver had the grace to flush at the unexpected gibe. "What I do has nothing to do with it," he insisted. "I am a man. A woman needs the comfort of a husband's affections."

"Bah! Love is a pleasant fantasy for poets and children, and I am neither. Really, Oliver, give up. We've had this argument so many times, and I'm tired of it. Stop meddling in my life or I'll start trying to arrange yours in revenge." Kit's eyes twinkled in merriment as she shot her brother a wicked smile. "Did I tell you I saw Lucie Nelson the other day in town? She's still unmarried, you know, and since her complexion cleared up she is really quite fetching. Now there's a girl who would make you a very suitable wife. It might do you good to settle down, big brother."

"Heaven help me!"

Oliver conceded defeat, for the time being. But not for good. Something needed to be done about Kit's damnable stubbornness, and soon. He would talk to Nick Basey about the plan that was hatching in his mind. He had put up with this farce much too long.

Poor little sister, Oliver thought with a smile. She really wasn't so much different from other women. A bit of romance would get her mind back to proper female pursuits. He and good old Nick would give her just what she needed, and they would all three be the richer for it.

"Hold still, me love. Stop yer squirmin'. I'll never finish if ye don't stop dancing like ye've ants in yer petticoats!" Mandy Carpenter took another pin from her pursed mouth and tacked the last seam in place. "There now, love. It's done. Let me 'elp ye out now."

Kit climbed out of the heavy satin brocade with a sigh of relief. She cared little for fripperies and lace, and she absolutely hated dress fittings, but Mandy had made up her mind that Kit needed a new ball gown for Mavis Edmond's ball. And when Mandy Carpenter set her rudder and bent on sail, not even a hurricane could blow her from her course. Kit rarely even tried.

Oliver had been outraged when Kit had bought the woman's indenture, an understandable reaction in view of Mandy's past. But Kit had never been sorry. The plump redhead was a fine companion as well as a good servant. And she cared for Kit much better than any fancy lady's maid, even if she did get a bit bossy at times.

"It's goin' t' be a beautiful gown," Mandy assured her. "Ye'll be the envy of every fine lady at the ball."

Kit smiled. "I'm sure the gown will be lovely, Mandy. You are very talented."

Mandy preened herself. "Aye, that I am. If ye'd let me 'ave my way with this plain wardrobe o' yours, ye'd have every man on this island pantin' at yer heels."

"You and Oliver should join forces." Kit chuckled wryly.

"'Ow's that, miss?"

"Oliver seems to think I should marry. He's quite determined on it, actually."

Mandy shrugged philosophically, sat her plump body down on the window seat, and set needle and thread to a seam. "Most ladies do marry sooner or later, love. Proper ladies, that is."

Kit shook her head. "I suppose I'm not quite proper, then. I see no advantage to it."

The redhead sniffed. "Ye've got my sympathy, for one. Men are a bother. Learned that in my former profession, ye know."

"So you've told me." Kit was no longer embarrassed to be reminded that her tire-woman had once been a London whore.

"Aye, well, so I 'ave. But ye must admit, love, that whether or not ye marry, ye could still try t' be a bit more of a proper lady. Ye go about a man's business, talkin' like a man, actin' like a man. I vow if ye 'ad yer way ye'd dress like a man as well."

Kit threw up her hands in disgust. "You too? Heavens, why can't anyone leave me to live my own life?"

"Everyone loves ye, dear," Mandy replied, unruffled by her mistress's anger. "that's why we be concerned."

"Well, you needn't be!" Kit shot the servant a haughty glare. "Just let it go."

Mandy raised an offended brow. "If ye insist."

"Where's my riding habit? We're going up to look at the fields. I want to see how the cutting is progressing."

Mandy looked up in alarm. "We?"

"Yes, we." Revenge was a petty thing, Kit mused, but at times it was sweet. She would teach Mandy to meddle in her affairs! "You are coming with me. Since you're so concerned with my being a lady, surely you wouldn't want me to ride out unaccompanied."

"God above, miss! Ye know 'ow I feel about 'orses—those awful beasts!"

Kit shot her a look of pure mischief. "Indeed I do!"

Kit began to regret her peevish insistence on Mandy's company when she observed the contortions the servant endured to stay on the back of the placid nag she rode. Her plump face was white as a sheet, and her abundant freckles stood out in unsightly blotches. She clung to the fat little nag's mane with a desperation born of terror, and every time the beast moved at a pace faster than an ambling walk, she gave a groan of abject misery.

"Why could we not take the carriage?" the redhead moaned.

"Because these paths are not suitable for a carriage," Kit replied with a grin. "Come now, Mandy. Relax and you'll do much better. A child of two could stay on Lady Sheba."

"I am not a child of two! I am a woman 'oose body was not meant to fit around an 'orse, I tell ye! An' this nag is bound t' throw me into t' bushes an' break me poor neck!"

Kit reined her spirited little mare to a halt. She turned a saucy smile on the miserable servant. "I'd tell you to get off and go back, but what of my ladylike reputation? Were you not just telling me I should mend my behavior?"

Without invitation Mandy allowed herself to slide ungracefully from the nag's back. She breathed a sigh of relief as her feet encountered solid ground.

"Trust me, miss! Ye're as ladylike as ye're likely t' get. Never will another word on 't pass me lips. Ye can depend on 't."

Kit shook her head. "Poor Mandy! I do abuse your good nature. I'm a spoiled brat, aren't I?"

Mandy rubbed her bruised posterior. "That ye are, love. An' a vengeful one at that!" The color slowly returned to the woman's face, and good humor to her soul. "But I'd not trade ye fer another, an' a truer word I've never spoken, beggin' pardon fer the impertinence. Ye go about yer man's business, love, an I'll get this beast back t' where it belongs. Then I'll get meself back where I belong.''

Kit watched as Mandy hobbled around the bend and disappeared, mumbling curses at poor Lady Sheba all the way. Mandy bore Kit's piques with constant good humor. Not that the indentured woman had a choice, but Kit vowed to be especially nice to her to make up for this latest prank. Oliver had gotten her riled, but she had no right to take it out on poor Mandy.

Her little mare whinnied in impatience.

"All right, Windy," Kit soothed. "Let's go visit a field or two. And on the way back you can have your run."

The cutting and milling season had just begun, and cane that had taken sixteen long months to ripen was finally being harvested. Kit was counting on a good harvest this season, for the mill needed expansion and the big house needed some repairs. And Oliver was constantly after her for higher profits. She shook her head at the thought of her brother. He had a passion for gambling, horses, and, she ventured to guess, expensive women. His share of their profits always dwindled unbelievably fast, and he was always scheming for more.

How fortunate, she thought, that her father had seen fit to leave half of his extensive plantation holdings and shipping business to her. Kit still remembered the day when she had turned eight years old. Her father had told her frankly—he had always been frank with her, sometimes painfully so—that he saw already that she would not be a beauty with suitors banging down her door. She had best learn to do for herself. Learn to use your brain, he had advised her, instead of flipping your eyelashes like other useless females. He had promised to provide for her well if she would only promise to learn.

And Kit had learned, eagerly drinking in the knowledge that her father offered her. She had always been Roger St. John's favorite—his little kitten, he had called her, insistently shortening the name her Spanish mother had given her to Kitty and then to Kit. He had delighted in taking her with him everywhere he went, teaching her the intricacies of running a sugar plantation—the planting and cutting and milling, marketing and profits, management of slaves and servants. And in the end he left her an equal partner with her older half brother.

Early on she and Oliver had discovered they could not manage their businesses together, so they had reached an agreement. Her domain was Greenhaven, and his was St. John Shipping. They split the profits of each, and neither intruded on the other's territory. Until now, Kit thought with a grimace.

The slave driver in the first field tipped his hat courteously as she rode up.

"How goes it, Geordie?"

"Well as can be expected, miss."

"Is there a problem?"

"No, miss. Not exactly. But I don't much like these fellows your brother put to work. They cause more trouble than they're worth."

"What fellows?"

"The convicts."

Kit made a very unladylike comment under her breath. She had warned Oliver about buying those white convicts, and insisted that they were his own personal purchase, not Greenhaven's. And here he was sending them out under her drivers.

"Where are they?" she demanded.

"Most of 'em are in Simon's crew, next field over. I've only got one. He's not causing any trouble, but he's so old I doubt he'll get through the week."

Geordie pointed, and Kit made out a white back bending over among the black ones. Red, rather, not white, for the sun had taken a dreadful toll. When the man straightened, she could see he was gray-headed and narrow shouldered. Kit's face tightened in anger.

Without another word she spurred her mare to the margins of the second field, which was being supervised by the plantation overseer. Here were the other four of her brother's purchases. She cursed soundly and mentally reviewed the tongue-lashing she would give Oliver when she got back to the house. Time and time again she had told him she would not use whites in the cane fields. They were not fit for the work, and died like flies even with the best treatment.

Abruptly, one of the closest convicts straightened and looked toward her, as though he had felt the weight of her eyes upon him. Kit recognized him at once, for in height and in breadth of shoulder he exceeded even the largest of the blacks working beside him. Surely no other slave could boast such size. He was the convict who had somehow caught her eye at the auction two days before.

Kit's nose wrinkled in an involuntary grimace of distaste at being confronted with such a one. His reddened skin was blistered and peeling, his dark hair a matted tangle that hung down beyond his shoulders. So little flesh padded the slave's broad-shouldered frame that he seemed a caricature of an overlarge scarecrow. But worst of all, there burned in his sun-cracked face two crystalline-blue eyes that glinted with pure insolence. They caught Kit's gaze in a hypnotic spell she couldn't break. A mocking smile twisted the slave's face, and with a gesture of practiced ease, he swept her a courtly bow that was ripe with impertinence.

It took only moments for the overseer Simon Brownlow to come to Kit's rescue. He had been standing halfway across the field when she first appeared, and moved promptly to join her. Then, seeing his mistress confronted by an unruly slave, he hastened his stride and loosened the braided leather whip that was coiled at his hip.

The lash that fell across Logan's back took both slave and mistress by surprise, so absorbed were they in their own private drama. Logan grunted as the whip bit into his tender skin and left a raw and bloody gash in its wake. Instinctively he turned on his attacker, only to be met by another agonizing cut across his chest and the business end of a primed pistol pointing directly at his face.

"I'll teach you, scum!"

The overseer raised the whip for another vicious stroke.

"Mr. Brownlow! Stop!"

Kit's curt order abruptly stopped the man's arm, but he didn't lower the whip. The mocking smile returned to

Logan's lips, and it infuriated Brownlow almost past the point of control.

"This piece of slime has to be punished, Miss St. John. Let this kind of behavior go unanswered, and next minute this scum will be at your throat. Especially this one." The overseer sneered in contempt. "Master Logan Steele. His papers say he's a mutineer seaman. Just barely escaped the hangman's noose. Believe me, miss, I can't give this wretch anything he doesn't deserve."

"Why are these men out here?" Kit's face clouded with an ominous frown that Brownlow recognized all too well. "These convicts are in no condition to be working the fields."

The overseer finally lowered the whip. "Back to work, dog!" He shoved Logan toward the line of blacks who were diligently ignoring everything but their own task. His eyes said plainly that he would conclude the incident in his own way at a later time. Then he turned to Kit and pasted a subservient smile on his lips. "Master St. John sent them out yesterday morning, miss. Said they was to work out here till he figured something else to put them to."

"Send them back to the stockade. All of them. And I don't want to see them in the fields again."

"Beggin' your pardon, Miss St. John, but I wouldn't want to go against your brother's direct orders."

Kit fixed him with a haughty and entirely unladylike glare. "I'll remind you, Mr. Brownlow, that I manage Greenhaven. My brother does not. These convicts are my brother's property, and he can do with them what he wants. But I will not have them dropping dead in Greenhaven's fields. So you can do exactly as I tell you, and I will worry about what Master St. John says about it. Do I make myself clear?"

"Yes, miss!" The overseer touched his hat in deference, his face a blank mask. "Very clear."

"Then do it!"

Kit whirled her mare and cantered back the way she had come. Brownlow eyed her receding figure with distaste. Then he turned back to the work at hand, scanning the field for the slave who had caused all the trouble. He had a knot of fury in him that needed untying, and he knew just how to do it.

Chapter 2

Horace Raleigh was a butler of the old school, and he prided himself on bringing the niceties of British tradition to the backwater island colony of Barbados. He ran the St. John household at Greenhaven in a manner emulating the finest houses in the mother country, demanding that every person and thing always be in its proper place. It was a source of constant amazement to this bastion of British domestic service that Miss St. John did not profit more from his example. In her colonial ignorance she tolerated a host of social irregularities which never would have plagued a butler in Raleigh's native Surrey. And because of Miss St. John's misplaced tolerance, the impertinence of the plantation's social inferiors was a burdensome cross that Raleigh was forced to carry.

It was therefore with a suitably disdainful expression on his countenance that Mr. Raleigh announced that Bradford Cartwright was at the front entrance seeking a word with Miss St. John. The butler had endeavored to put the slave driver in his place and send him around to the servants' entrance in the rear, but the fellow had simply brushed his objections aside and insisted on seeing the mistress. And much to Raleigh's dismay, the lady of the house seemed most willing to receive him.

"Send him in, Raleigh." Kit let her volume of Shakespearean sonnets drop to her lap and wondered what could bring poor Cartwright to see her at such a late hour. She always thought of the old man as "poor Cartwright," even though he was one of the more fortunate of the thousands of whites who had lost their small farms when the island's economy had turned to sugar cane. When his small holding had been gobbled up by a neighboring planter nine years ago, Roger St. John had taken him on as driver of Greenhaven's third slave gang. He was temperamentally unsuited to the job, for he was softhearted and sympathetic by nature. But since the third gang was composed mostly of children and old people who did light work and odd jobs, a terribly stern driver was not needed. He had served the St. Johns well in return for the opportunity that Roger had given him.

Cartwright cleared his throat awkwardly as he stepped through the parlor archway, hat in hand and looking highly uncomfortable among the finely carved furniture and rich Turkish carpets.

"Mr. Cartwright." Kit smiled a welcome. "What is amiss to bring you here at this hour?"

The driver fixed his eyes on the sweat-stained hat that he turned nervously in his hands. He had talked to Kit many times when she made her rounds of the plantation. In fact, he had spun her stories of giants and fairies when she was a child tagging along at her father's heels. But this was the first time he had ever visited the big house, and seeing her sitting in the midst of the parlor's quiet elegance made her seem much more the unreachable lady.

"In . . . in truth, miss, I'm sorry to disturb you at such an hour. I . . . I came to see Master St. John."

Kit's eyes flashed a sharp inquiry. "Did you indeed?" She waited patiently. There had to be a reason he had demanded to see her instead of Oliver.

"It's about one of your brother's slaves . . ." Cartwright ventured.

"I see." At least she was beginning to see. Brad Cartwright had unofficial charge of the stockade, where the convicts were housed. In any matter concerning them, he was obligated to consult Oliver. But there was no love lost between the two men. He probably hoped she would consent to take the matter out of his hands.

"Is there a problem?" Kit urged.

"One of the fellows is pretty tore up, miss. I'll need Mr.

Brownlow's permission to get old Oona from the village to tend him, and I figure Brownlow won't move without word from Master St. John himself."

Left unsaid was that Oliver St. John would not want to be bothered with such a matter, so Simon Brownlow would simply give Cartwright a flat no. Knowing Cartwright, Kit guessed that he wanted to see the man treated, and he thought she was the only one who would order it.

"Which one is it?" Kit asked, a sudden suspicion growing in her mind.

"The big one. Darkish hair. Cocky fellow."

"I know the one," Kit assured him with a grimace. Her suspicion became certainty. Devil take that insolent Simon Brownlow! In spite of her direct orders to send the convicts immediately back to the stockade, he must have taken time to vent his rage on the slave who had dared to provoke him.

"Didn't seem worth botherin' anyone about this afternoon, miss. But now his back is lookin' ugly, and the fellow was right out of his 'ead for a time. He's calmed down some now, but I still think he needs tendin'."

"Oona's in no condition to be tending others tonight," Kit said. "She's sick herself. And there's no use in disturbing my brother or Mr. Brownlow." That brute Brownlow would just as soon the wretch die, Kit thought, and her brother simply wouldn't care. "I'll get my things and see what I can do."

"No need for that, miss!" Cartwright objected. But from the satisfied gleam in his eye Kit could tell he had accomplished his purpose.

Kit had not been in the stockade since it was first built, for it was constructed to house unruly slaves who were isolated from their village as punishment. Discipline problems were rare among the slaves at Greenhaven, and the stockade had been used only twice or three times in all of Kit's memory. She was shocked by the meanness of the flimsy palmetto huts that afforded the only shelter in the place. They were hardly more than a loose network of fronds piled against an A-frame of timbers that would certainly come tumbling down in the least bit of wind. The water barrel that stood against one wall of the palisade was foul with dirt and windblown leaves and sticks. Since it hadn't rained in more than a week, the barrel was less than half full, and even in the pale light of the moon, Kit could see that an unappetizing scum was beginning to form on the surface of the water.

Cartwright led silently to the hut farthest from the gate, then preceded her into the flimsy thatched structure. Two men squatted in the narrow space, and one lay facedown on a crude pallet of filthy straw.

"Light the lantern," Kit told the driver.

The dim light etched the haggard faces of the two who squatted. The younger glared at her with green eyes that burned in a pinched, hostile face. When Kit returned his glare with a level gaze, he rose awkwardly and sketched a mocking bow.

"Michael Carmody, at yer service, yer ladyship." The little man's twisted, insolent grin clashed with his lilting Irish voice.

As the older slave got slowly and painfully to his feet, Kit's mouth tightened in pity. The man was sixty if he was a day, and his face was lined and drawn with pain.

"Are none of these fellows fit to work?" she asked sharply.

Cartwright shrugged.

"Get them out of here," Kit ordered with a disgusted grimace, turning toward the injured man on the pallet. "I'll tend to this one."

"The old one claims t' be a doctor, miss."

Kit swung around and fixed the older convict with an accusing gaze. "Then why haven't you done anything for this man?"

"Begging your pardon, mistress"—the old man's eyes shone with an intelligence that had not yet been dulled by hopelessness—"but the gent here wouldn't permit it. Besides, I've nothing but that foul water out there to work with. It would only have made him worse, I fear."

"Why did you not permit him to treat this man?" she asked Cartwright.

"I didn't have permission, miss."

"Mr. Cartwright, since when have you needed permission to do what compassion demands?"

He shrugged in sad resignation. "Yer brother's home, miss," he explained, as if those words were sufficient. "These slaves are his."

Kit sighed. "Get some clean water. Take these two to help you, then send this so-called doctor back in. Then you go back to the gate in case Mr. Brownlow is making rounds tonight. I'm in no mood to argue with him."

Kit had some knowledge of healing from her old nurse Oona, whom the plantation slaves revered as a witch, an "Obeah woman" who could cure or curse at will. But little skill was required in this case. There was not much to be done other than wash the festering slashes that cut the slave's broad back and apply an herb salve to ease his pain and clean the infection.

The old convict doctor had no skill to supplement what Kit herself could do, and he was tottering from weakness himself. Kit sent him to his own hut before she was half done with her job. When her patient woke from his swoon, cursing the pain she was causing him, Kit was sorry she had sent the old man away. Being alone in the hut with an unconscious convict was one thing, but being alone with one fully awake and angry was quite another case.

Kit lost no time in putting the slave in his place.

"Lie still, fool, or I'll hurt you worse. You brought this on yourself, so act like a man and take what's coming to you."

"Goddammit, woman!" Logan was in no mood to be scolded. "What are you doing to me?" He thrashed around and managed to sit up as she applied the last of the salve to his lacerations.

"Hold still!" she commanded again.

"No! Damn! That stuff hurts like hell!"

"I imagine it does," Kit replied. "But you'll be grateful in the morning."

Logan twisted around to look at his tormentor and a flash of recognition lit his eyes. His face rearranged itself from a grimace of pain to a stare of disbelief, then contemptuous amusement. Under his insolent gaze Kit felt increasingly uneasy.

Too proud to admit to even a glimmering of fear, she placed a firm hand on Logan's shoulder and pushed him back down. Then she added the last touches of medication with more than necessary vigor.

"Ouch!"

"Keep your mouth shut!" Kit ordered. "Do you want the overseer in here asking questions?"

Logan twisted toward her as she rose to leave. He shrugged, then grimaced in pain. "What concern could you have for what your overseer does or thinks? Does he not do what you order him to do?"

"Sometimes he does." Kit gestured to his back. "Sometimes he doesn't. Not that you didn't deserve a beating, mind you."

The slave sat up and glared at her through eyes that were a startling blue contrast to his sun-scorched face. "You think you're a qualified judge of what I deserve?"

"I can judge well enough that you're a fool!" Kit shot back. "I'd advise you to keep a civil tongue in your head. You were witless enough to provoke Brownlow. Don't provoke me as well!"

Logan got shakily to his feet. His height made Kit want to shrink back. Being tall herself, she was not accustomed to anyone towering over her. And this slave did indeed tower. Thin and bony as the man was, his size still made the hut seem far too small for the two of them.

"Do I provoke you, mistress?" He attempted a stiff bow. "Accept my most humble apologies." His voice was anything but humble. In fact, his whole demeanor was incongruously haughty, given his appearance and position.

"I can see there was no need for me to disturb myself by coming to your aid," Kit replied stiffly. "Good Mr. Cartwright feared for your health, but you appear to have recovered quite enough to resume your foolishness. Are you so lacking in brains that the stripes across your back taught you nothing?"

Logan ignored her taunt. "What kind of plantation mistress doctors her own lowly slaves? Are you sure you didn't simply come to gloat?"

Kit's eyes narrowed dangerously. She wondered why she didn't just give the slave her back and walk out the door.

"You are not *my* lowly slave," she corrected in a taut voice. "You are my brother's lowly slave. I did him the favor of seeing that you will mend. But unless your attitude mends as well, no doubt you will be stripped to the bone before many days have passed."

"No doubt that would please you."

"It might at that," Kit replied with growing anger. "I'm sure the crimes that sent you here merit these stripes and more."

"Perhaps so." Logan's crooked smile mocked both her and himself. "But I wonder if they were as great as the crime of trading on human misery and misfortune to line one's own pockets."

Kit's eyes blazed. She began to understand why Brownlow had disobeyed her and carried out his punishment. Her own hand itched to strike out in retribution. She controlled her temper with difficulty. "You forget your position, I think."

He had the effrontery to laugh softly. "It would be passing difficult to forget my position. Believe me, I would if I were able."

"You'd best guard your memory, then," Kit snapped, "or you'll not survive long enough to realize how very foolish you are. Be grateful I'm a tolerant person, or I'd end this discussion by giving you another lesson like the one you had this afternoon."

Without giving the slave a chance to reply, Kit grasped the lantern, turned abruptly, and stalked out of the hut. She'd had enough of this man's mocking eyes and too-easy smiles. The very idea that this overlong stick of a slave with his matted, dirt-colored hair and tangled beard would dare to speak to her in such a way made her angrier with every passing second. He should have offered meek gratitude for her generosity in helping him. Instead, the ungrateful villain acted as if her very presence was an affront to him. And what was worse, she, Kit St. John, who had never bent to her father—bless his soul—or her brother, or any other man, had actually felt intimidated by a scraggly, worthless convict whose life and death rested in the palm of her hand.

She stopped in her tracks and whirled indignantly back to face the little hut, which was now a dark silhouette against the stockade wall. Somehow she felt that the rascally slave was standing unseen at the entrance, staring back at her and silently laughing. What kind of a man dared to put on such a demeanor of assurance and command in spite of being a convict and slave? Those blue eyes of his burned with a spirit that should have been beaten out of him long since. Suddenly Kit was very glad this man was Oliver's slave and not her own.

"Miss St. John?"

She jumped in alarm.

"Sorry, miss," Cartwright apologized. "I didn't mean t' startle you."

"You didn't startle me," Kit replied testily. "If you'll just open the gate, I'll be going now."

"Yes, miss." He nodded to the hut from which she had emerged. "Is that fellow goin' t' mend?"

Kit snorted. "He's already well enough mended for his vicious tongue to be wagging. The kindest favor anyone could do for him would be to cut that unruly appendage from his mouth."

"Did he offend ye, miss? If so, I'll—"

"Leave it!" she ordered abruptly. "He's not worth the trouble."

Cut, toss. Cut, toss. Cut, toss. The rhythm never ended. It had become a part of Logan's brain. The long cane knife he wielded seemed an extension of his arm, swinging in measured cadence from sunup to sundown, with only a two-hour midday break to give his weary muscles rest.

It was hard to believe that only three weeks had passed since he first set foot on this wretched plantation. Christmas had come and gone, and the new year was one week old. Three weeks or three years—Logan had learned it made little difference. Hell was still hell, no matter how long you stayed.

Logan continued the rhythm and tried to ignore his misery. Sweat stung his eyes and burned in the innumerable little skin slices that were the price of working in the cane. His back was on fire from the constant bending. His shoulders cramped and his hands bled. He had blistered and peeled and blistered again in the sun's hot glare. Now his skin was browned and tough, but the sun was still the constant enemy, beating down upon his bare head, making his brain swim and spots bounce crazily before his eyes, wringing every drop of moisture from his body.

But he was surviving. Logan told himself that surviving was the only thing that mattered right now. Later he could groan and rail against the twisted scheme that had sent him here to this hell in paradise, but now he must survive. Just survive. That was all he could ask of himself.

He paused a moment in his labors, straightening his stance to push the sweat-soaked hair out of his face. In the adjacent row, a huge black looked up and grinned at him. The bastard had a right to grin, Logan thought bitterly. He lived in a cozy thatched hut, ate twice as much as Logan, and had sturdy sandals and two extra sets of clothes.

The slaves at Greenhaven considered themselves well treated. Four times a week they ate red meat or salt fish. Each hut in the slave village was allowed its own small plot of land to grow vegetables. Some of the slaves even grew extra produce and raised chickens or pigs to take into the Bridgetown market on Sundays.

But while the blacks lay comfortably in their hammocks at night, protected from rain and wind by the walls and roofs of their sturdy shelters, Logan and his four convict companions slept on filthy straw pallets in huts that admitted even the lightest rain. They ate spare rations of potatoes and water, rarely supplemented with fish. Each worked and slept in one set of clothes that was worn already to rags, and no sandals protected their feet from the stony ground.

A whip cracked and Logan felt the fire of it on his back.

"Back to work there, sluggard! Or I'll lay a few more of those on yer back!"

Logan bent once more to his task. He should have known better than to pause for even a second. The drivers had singled him out as a troublemaker and were more than anxious to prod him along with extra flicks of the whip. In the three weeks since Brownlow had beat him, his back had almost healed. But it was still tender enough that the slightest touch of the lash set him burning from shoulder to buttocks. One more misery to add to cramped muscles and unbearable heat. Once more Logan told himself that all he had to do was survive just a few days more. Maybe not even that long.

It had been a mistake to make trouble so soon. He had bought himself a cartload of misery by being such a jackass. But that black-haired witch was a target he couldn't resist. Something had moved inside his very soul when he first saw her at the slave auction, and then when two days later she had ridden so casually among the human chattel that were her property. So close she had been, almost close enough for him to touch, to smell the fresh scent of her skin that contrasted so sharply with his own rank odor, to feel the weight of those eyes that rested on him without really seeing. What else could a man do besides stand up and let the slave mistress see his contempt?

Then there had been that night. Having the opportunity once again to taunt the haughty Miss St. John was almost worth the beating he had received at Simon Brownlow's hand. Logan almost grinned at the memory. Her face had been white with outrage, and her eyes had blazed in sable-brown radiance in the dim lanternlight. He could still see the stiff, angry set of her shoulders as she had stalked out of the hut, her skirts swishing indignantly behind her. She was easily riled, that one. It made the game more fun, and more dangerous.

A bell clanged insistently across the fields—the bell that hung outside the sugar mill and sounded to divide the day into morning, midday, and afternoon. As though controlled by one giant puppeteer, the slaves straightened from their labor, stretching sore arms and aching backs. Most drifted off the fields to seek shelter from the sun while they ate their small ration. Some dropped wearily in the same spot where they worked.

Logan followed the blacks into the forest that bordered the cane field. But he didn't stop where they gathered to sit and chatter in groups. The convicts were not fed a noon meal, so there was no reason for him to stay, and no one detained him. Few slaves escaped the plantations of Barbados. There was no way off the island for those who tried. In the end, escapees were always brought back for a punishment that discouraged their fellows from indulging in the same foolishness.

No one gave Logan a second glance as he made his way away from the group of slaves. Five minutes' steady walking brought him to the lively stream that bounced and danced down the hillside beside the sugar mill. Another two minutes of climbing upstream and he reached a pool of deepest jade, screened from casual view by the heavy brush and tangle of vines that had grown up around its grass-covered banks. The surface spread out like cool green glass below overhanging palmettos, bullywood, and tamarisk trees. A ripple of water over a small cascade at the pool's upstream end was the only sound that, together with the occasional call of a bird, disturbed the perfect peace that surrounded the little glade.

Logan had found this spot the first week he had come to Greenhaven. It was one of the few things that kept him sane. Here for a brief time he could forget his slavery and be a whole man once again.

Logan wasted no time in stripping off his sweat-stiffened rags and diving cleanly into the deepest part of the pool. A long moment passed before he reappeared, matted hair and beard streaming with water. He wished briefly that he were allowed a razor, or soap, or at least a comb. Once a friend in England had accused him of being a clotheshorse and paying more attention to his garments than his mistresses. Logan wondered what that friend would say if he could see him now. He felt like a wild animal—almost as much as he resembled one.

The threadbare shirt served as a washcloth, then was dunked and scrubbed in its turn, along with the crude trousers that were almost too ragged for modesty. Logan laid his clothing out to steam in the sun, then took himself once more into the heavenly cool refuge of the crystal-green water. He rolled onto his back, moving only enough to keep himself afloat in the sluggish current. The frustrations and bitterness that had plagued him the whole morning long began to loosen their grip on his mind. Today of all days he needed this peace. His temper was shredded to ribbons. The setbacks of the week past were taking a nasty toll of his never too abundant patience.

Every night for the past five days Logan and his four convict companions had plotted escape. Every night they had been foiled by ill luck. First old Doc had taken sick and lay coughing up his very innards all the night long. Then the always impatient Carmody had gotten himself thrown into the hole—a cramped, tin-roofed excavation in the scorched dirt outside the slave village. He had baked for six long hours, and by the time Brad Cartwright had dug the little Irishman out and, over Brownlow's objections, dragged him back to the stockade, the fierce little banty rooster had been in no condition to do anything but collapse in his hut.

And then last night Brownlow had gotten wind of something brewing. Maybe he had believed Carmody's carelessly shouted curses of vengeance as he had been stuffed into the hole. But for whatever reason the overseer had posted a guard on the stockade for the first time since the convicts had been confined there. Tonight they were prepared to deal with the guards, but what else would happen to keep them here?

Logan turned over and stroked for shore. His respite was almost ended. Soon he would go raving mad if he couldn't gain his freedom. When this task had been set for him, he had given little thought to the time he must spend as a slave. He had been full of faith in his own cleverness. How could he have guessed at the forces that worked to destroy a man, making him less a man and more an animal? How could he have known that he, who had ever fancied himself as mild in temper as any man could be, would learn to hate, would start to harbor a thirst for vengeance that could sear a man's soul? Logan's dreams were plagued with images of revenge on the man who had beat him, on the man who thought he owned him, and on the woman who had dared to mock him in his misery and call him a fool. His soul was seeking out the level of his physical existence. He was becoming as much of an animal as he looked, God help him. And if he didn't escape soon, the transition would be complete.

Logan thought back to his time in Newgate, to the bargain he had made for his life. Sir Thomas Modyford had been all glib phrases and persuasion, and at the time any course had seemed better than hanging. But now Logan was beginning to wonder if escape from the noose was worth the price he was paying.

Kit gave Windwalker a fond pat on her lathered neck as she reined to a halt in front of the mill. Already it had been a long day. She had paid an early morning visit to her old nursemaid, Oona, who lay sick in the slave village, then spent sweltering hours riding the fields. The morning's work would be concluded when she had talked to Samuel, the slave who supervised the sugar mill.

"Samuel!" Kit stepped lightly down from the mare's back.

Instead of Sam's familiar black face, the visage that appeared in the mill's open doorway belonged to none other than her brother, Oliver. She greeted him in a friendly fashion. The last two weeks had seen an uneasy truce spring up between them. They had compromised on his convict purchases. Kit had agreed that after a few days of rest the whites could be put to work in the fields, as long as Oliver sold them elsewhere before he left once again for the sea. In return Oliver left off his complaining about her openhandedness with the blacks.

"What brings you up here?" Oliver asked, walking out to greet her.

"I wanted to inspect the sugar coming out of the knocking house," she answered. "This is the first run this season, you know."

"I know. It's quite nice. And the molasses looks good, too. It should be a good year."

Kit shot him a dubious smile. "Since when do you take such interest in Greenhaven?"

He shrugged. "Perhaps it's time I did. I never realized what a money-maker this place could be before I took a close look at it."

Kit was in no mood to argue with her brother about their management agreement. And neither was she in a mood to spend time with him going through the mill.

"Since you've inspected the pots," Kit said, "I think I'll head for the house. It's a terribly hot day."

"Yes, you do that. Tell Mrs. Simpson to have some of her rum punch waiting. I'll be along shortly."

Kit remounted her mare, but instead of turning directly onto the path for the house, she headed for the pool up the hill. There she could water her thirsty horse and have the privacy to wipe some of the sticky sweat from her body.

Logan looked up in annoyance as the screen of vegetation parted and the girl led her horse into his private refuge. He recognized her instantly—the unfashionably tall, slender frame in an equally unfashionable plain riding habit. Even here she came to plague him, robbing him of the only moments of privacy he could snatch during the day.

The mare dipped her muzzle into the clear green water, and the girl loosened the tight, stiff bodice of her riding habit, exposing softly contoured curves Logan never would have guessed were there. As she dipped a kerchief into the water and proceeded to cool her bared skin, Logan stood up abruptly.

Kit gasped and jumped back from the pool. At the sound of her alarm, the mare also jerked back, rolling her eyes in fright.

Logan smiled and casually stepped out of the shadows, his trousers dangling from one hand. "No need for alarm, mistress. It's only one of your lowly slaves, as you can see."

Kit's eyes widened. She saw entirely too much. The slave was clad only in the brief loinpiece that he wore under his trousers. His bones seemed to poke through his skin, so thin was he, and she could count every rib in his chest. But there was still enough masculinity in that tall figure to bring a hot flush to her cheeks. She stared in dismay for a moment before remembering that she herself was displaying a good deal too much skin to be proper.

"What are you doing here?" she demanded, hastily closing her bodice.

"Swimming," Logan admitted without remorse.

"Swimming?" Kit regarded him in disbelief. "Swimming!" The idea of a slave taking leave of his duties for a leisurely swim left her speechless.

"It's the midday break," he offered in the way of explanation.

"Then you should be eating and resting."

"Convicts eat only at dawn and sundown."

Another surprise, but Kit didn't pursue it. "Then you should be resting... or whatever. But you should not be here lurking in the forest."

The frown she gave him would have sent any of her servants scurrying for cover. But Logan merely smiled.

"I was not lurking, mistress. I was merely swimming. I just as well might say that you were the one lurking, you came so quietly through the brush. But then, well-bred young ladies do not lurk, do they? They may buy and sell human flesh. They may enslave a hundred miserable souls. But they may not lurk."

Kit bristled with outrage. She took a step in Logan's direction, her hand closing convulsively on the handle of her braided riding quirt. Once again this infuriating villain had broken through her guard and put her on the defensive. Her usual calm poise fled.

Logan felt Kit's fury break over him in invisible waves. It struck a responsive chord. His own cynical amusement swelled to anger, and to something even more elemental that he did not care to define. He could not help but admire how her dark sable eyes sparked like lightning against the light gold of her skin. It was a crime, he thought, that those striking features should hide such an insensitive heart.

Logan's smile grew broader, and less than pleasant. Most men would have had the sense to flee before the look of that smile. But Kit blundered on heedlessly into harm's way.

"You're right," she hissed, slapping the quirt against her heavy skirts. "Well-bred young ladies do not lurk. Murderers, mutineers, and slaves lurk. The scum of humanity, the dregs of mankind—like you—they lurk." She sucked in a deep breath. "Now put on your clothes and get out of here. Next time you take your insolent tongue to me I'll lay your backbone bare myself, I swear I . . . !"

Logan's control snapped. His ragged sanity deserted him, driven away by starvation, overwork, and finally the humiliation of this stonehearted bitch screaming insults in his face. In three rapid strides he was confronting the infuriating witch, his hand grasping her, his mouth grinding down upon hers in a brutal attack that silenced her evil tirade. Her one strident scream was quickly swallowed into struggling silence.

Kit raised the quirt and managed a vicious swipe to the side of Logan's head. In the next instant Logan twisted the whip from her grasp and brutally forced her arm behind her back. She continued to fight, but he held her in an unbreakable grip, his whipcord-hard body pressed insistently against hers. Ruled by the chaos of fury, he forced his mouth against hers in a raw and violent passion.

Long months had passed since Logan had touched a woman. Once they had been his for the asking, lightskirts and gentry alike. He had taken the cream of the lot with casual acceptance of his due. But those dainty ladies had never roused the hunger fired by this arrogant hellcat who was struggling and kicking in his arms. Desires that had been ignored in his long celibacy woke to life with abrupt fury and clamored for attention. His anger melted in the heat of a gentler passion, and his brutal kiss softened and deepened with new demands.

Kit felt the savagery fade. The slave's mouth moved against hers now in gentle supplication, then in passionate demand. His grip eased its painful pressure, but she had somehow lost the will to escape. Deep in the core of her a fire burst to life and spread a delicious warmth through her veins. Against her belly, hot, hard, and insistent, rose the evidence of male desire. Of their own will Kit's hips pressed closer to Logan's and a spear of primitive longing shot down her last defense.

Suddenly she was free, her mouth burning from Logan's brand and her body aching from his grip. Crystalline-blue eyes were all Kit could see, burning blue eyes that seared their way into her soul. Her own eyes widened in surprise and dismay at her reaction to this scraggly beast of a slave, but she didn't pull back when his mouth found hers again. She closed her eyes and let herself escape into the dizzying world of passion that was fast closing around her.

The vicious sound of the lash brought Kit sharply back to earth. The arms that had supported her were abruptly jerked away. Bereft, she stumbled and dropped to her knees.

The whip cracked again. Kit looked up, and reality washed over her in a cold and sickening flood of humiliation. Her brother stood purple-faced with rage over the bleeding form of her erstwhile attacker.

"You cursed dog!" Oliver promised as the whip lashed out again and again. "I'll see you in hell for this!"

Chapter 3

"Stop, Oliver! My God! You're going to kill him!"

"Damn right I'll kill him!"

Logan lay half-conscious in the bloodied grass by the pool. Taken unawares and with his mind locked firmly on to other things, he'd had no chance to fight back when Oliver's whip cut across his back. He struggled to rise, but pain muddled his head and made the ground tilt under him.

Oliver shook the whip out to strike out again, his face flushed with anger.

"No! I said stop!"

Kit grabbed her brother's wrist in both of her hands. Impatiently Oliver shook off her grip and flung her back. With a desperate lunge she came at him again, this time grabbing the whip instead of his arm.

"Oliver! I will not have this!"

"You'll not have this? My God, Kit, the man was . . . !"

"I know what he was doing! Do you think I don't?" She tried to slow her breathing to its normal rhythm, but she could do nothing about her heart, which raced at a dizzying pace—from Logan's attack or Oliver's violent retribution, she knew not which.

"You'll not punish him out of hand like this!" Kit insisted in a calmer voice. "You're so angry you've no reason left. The man is helpless, Oliver!"

"Helpless?!" Oliver sneered. "He's—"

"Yes, helpless! He's a half-starved bag of bones! Do you think he could stand up to you and defend himself?"

"He seemed to stand up to you fairly well, sister!" Oliver's eyes narrowed. "Or maybe . . ."

"You keep a civil tongue in your head, brother mine, or I promise you'll regret it! The man will be punished, but not until your head is cooled and sitting straight on your neck again."

For a moment brother and sister glared at each other in silent battle. Then Oliver smiled and relented. He turned hard eyes on Logan.

"You're right. He should be punished so that all these cocky slaves of ours can benefit from his lesson." He went over to the prostrate figure by the pool and delivered a hearty kick to his ribs. "Get up, you craven dog. Get up and face what's coming to you." Logan stirred and received another kick for his efforts.

"Oliver!" Kit warned.

He waved her away. "Go back to the house and make yourself presentable. Then meet me at the village."

Kit looked stubborn.

"Go on, for God's sake! Can't you ever do something

without arguing about it? Do you want everyone to see you like that?"

Kit looked down and noticed for the first time that the lacings on her bodice were ripped apart and her lacy, sheer chemise was all that covered her from the eyes of the world. When had that happened? she thought in a panic. Had she been so carried away? Had he actually touched...? Embarrassed speculation brought a hot flush of shame to her cheeks. Without a word she turned, mounted her mare, and spurred the horse out of the glade.

Satisfied that his meddlesome sister was gone, Oliver bound Logan's wrists behind him and tied another rope around his neck. Then he mounted his own horse and moved out at a brisk trot, pulling his prisoner behind. The pace was fast, and when Logan stumbled, he was dragged until he somehow managed to regain his feet. By the time they reached the cane fields, his chest and arms were as bloody as his back.

Kit met them at the slave village. Her face was ashy pale, but outwardly at least, she had retrieved her usual calm poise. Anger, resentment, remorse, and pity surged in a confusing tide back and forth across her mind. Her emotions were staging a violent tug-of-war. But none of this showed on her face. She had learned while still a child that one never showed weakness in front of slaves or servants. She had always been true to this maxim—until, that is, she had met the loathsome rogue who was being tied to the whipping post even as she rode up to where her brother sat astride his mount.

"This crude display isn't necessary, Oliver." Her sable eyes were dark with dismay. "Why don't you just sell the rogue and wash your hands of him? Let someone else deal with him."

Oliver's mouth tightened in fury. "After what he did to you? Do you think I'd let him escape my revenge?"

"I was the one attacked, Oliver. I should decide the revenge."

Oliver lowered his voice to a furious whisper. "Like hell you will! You are my sister, Kit, and I will avenge your honor as a brother should!"

"I assure you my honor is unsullied," she snapped.

"It would have been sullied as hell if I had come along a moment later! God's light, Kit! You of all people should be grateful to see this cur's back cut to ribbons!"

Kit's eyes narrowed. "You're the only member of this family who likes that kind of show."

"Precisely," Oliver agreed in a frosty voice. "Which is why we need a man to run this plantation. You wanted the rogue fittingly punished. This is as fitting as it gets! The fellow's lucky I didn't strip him to the bone there by the pool. I would have, had you not starting your mewling."

"That is not the way things are handled at Greenhaven."

"So we'll do it your way. I trust you will not object to the fellow receiving a just number of lashes."

Kit was sickened by the whole business, but she knew that Oliver was right. She had been attacked by a slave—an incident without precedent at Greenhaven. The villain had to be punished. And she had to put on a strong countenance.

"He's your slave," she said coldly. "Do what you want."

Oliver smiled. "I plan to. I'm grateful to you for staying my hand earlier. This will be so much more instructive to the other slaves, don't you think?"

He jerked on the bit and his mount sidled away before he dismounted.

"Hold there, Brownlow."

With determined stride Oliver pushed through the circle of uneasy Negroes who had gathered as they were commanded. He took the vicious length of braided rawhide from the overseer, who was waiting on his command to start punishment.

"I'll deal with this villain myself."

Oliver stripped off doublet and hat and put them carefully aside. Then he hefted the whip in his hand and turned toward Logan, who stood stiffly upright against the post to which he was bound, back bared and awaiting the bite of the whip. The throng of Negroes grew silent.

Kit winced as the whip whistled through the air and landed with a sickening crack on the convict's back. It left an oozing line of red as it was snapped back. The sight was all the more painful because her brother was the one who held that crude instrument of torture, and he appeared to be enjoying his task to the utmost.

She and her brother had squabbled since they were children together. After their father had died, the fighting had become more than squabbling. But in spite of their differences, Kit had always loved Oliver as only a sister can worship an older brother. Today was the first time she had seen him unleash the dark side of his nature in full view of her and anyone else who cared to watch. This, almost more than the whipping, made her sick inside.

The whip cracked again. Logan jerked, but no sound escaped his mouth. He bit his lip to stifle the cry of pain that welled up in his throat. Trickles of scarlet coursed down through the dirt-brown beard and mixed with the sweat pouring off his face. On the third crack of the whip he turned his head toward the slim figure that sat her mount so tall and proud just outside the circle of blacks. Crystalline-blue eyes unerringly locked on to that uncaring countenance. His gaze stayed there as the whip sang through the air again and again—until his eyes could no longer see for the waves of black and red that were snuffing out his consciousness.

Kit sat with stony calm while her brother vented his rage with strokes ever faster and harder. She saw Logan's head turn her way, felt his eyes, those terrible ice-blue eyes, bore into hers. She couldn't tear her gaze away from the fury of his look. The blood chilled in her veins, such was the raw anger in those eyes. Then abruptly she was free of that frightening regard. Logan was no longer looking at anything or anyone. He hung in his bonds, jerking grotesquely when the rawhide, now slick with blood, fell on his back. One guttural cry wrenched from his lips. Then he was silent.

Kit felt sour bile rise up in her throat. Oliver's slave or not, this was going to stop! She spurred Windwalker through the wide-eyed blacks and halted the mare between her brother and his victim.

"That's enough, Oliver."

Oliver started, as though waking from a trance. With difficulty his eyes focused on Kit's face.

"You're killing him."

Oliver shook the whip out again. Droplets of blood flew out from its glistening length.

"I mean to." He laughed almost drunkenly. "Indeed, dear sister, that is my purpose. So move out of the way."

"No."

Oliver's face began to darken with anger. "The wretch is my property. At your insistence, I might add. I'll do with him as I please."

"Not here you won't," Kit insisted, her voice a quiet counterpoint to his almost frenzied pronouncement.

She motioned to the overseer. "Mr. Brownlow, cut the prisoner down."

Brownlow hesitated and looked to Oliver.

"Cut him down!" The force of Kit's voice carried a threat, and the overseer hastily remembered that it was Miss St. John, not Master St. John, who paid his wages. With a look of apology to the master, he drew his knife and hacked at the rope that bound Logan to the pole. The prisoner collapsed onto the ground in a bloody heap.

"Get the slaves back to work," Kit ordered the overseer. She gave her brother a stern look, and he sullenly coiled the whip he still held in his hand. "Do you want to argue here," she asked coldly, "or shall we wait for the privacy of the house?"

Oliver glowered, then turned on his heel, mounted his horse, and spurred the poor animal so that it squealed and rose on its hind legs before galloping off in a flurry of dust.

Kit stared after him, then shrugged and dismounted. She motioned to one of the convicts who was shuffling along with the other slaves.

"You're the doctor, aren't you?"

The old man gave her a bitter look, then nodded.

"See what you can do for this poor man."

"Your brother's already done it for him, I'd guess."

"Do as I say." Kit's eyes narrowed. "I've had my fill of impertinent slaves today. You two!" She motioned two muscular blacks over to where Logan lay. "Carry him to the stockade. And you"—a grinning black youth stopped at her command—"you get some clean water, and whatever else this man tells you."

Kit turned to Doc, who knelt beside Logan's inert form. "Will he live, do you think?"

She was surprised by the fear that stabbed through her when Doc sighed and shook his head. Why should she care what happened to the wretch? After what he'd done to her, why had she made a fool of herself in front of the entire plantation and precipitated what promised to be the granddaddy of all arguments with her brother? The convict was a criminal—a mutineer and God knew what else. And he had forced on her an intimacy she would allow no man, not even a suitable man from her own class.

She followed as the slaves carried Logan back to the stockade, then sat and watched Doc tend him until the old man could tell her that his patient would most likely live. It was concern for her brother that kept her there, Kit decided—concern that he had not killed a helpless man in a fit of temper. But there was another reason, also, that she stayed. With characteristic honesty she admitted to a stupid and misplaced admiration for brave and rebellious fools, even if they were the scum of the earth. Whatever this man had done, he owned a courage and audacity that was hard to beat down. She didn't want to see him die.

"He'll mend," Doc finally pronounced. "If the heat and flies and foul food don't kill him before he can heal."

"I'll have him brought extra rations," Kit offered.

"Your brother won't like that."

Kit raised a haughty brow. "My brother and I differ somewhat on how slaves should be treated, but he'll not want to lose a valuable piece of property. The rations will be sent."

Doc snorted in irreverent disbelief. Kit whirled on him with a glare.

"You forget your place." She'd had enough disrespect piled on her head for one day, and her temper was close to being frayed past repair.

Doc was unshaken by her show of ire. "Begging your pardon, mistress. But it doesn't seem to matter anymore, to tell the truth." He looked at Logan and shook his head. "The world just seems turned upside down somehow, and I can't say it would grieve me to leave a world where something like this could be called justice."

Kit raised a cynical brow. "You think yourself and this man unjustly treated for your crimes?"

The old man laughed. "My crimes? My crimes consist of disagreeing too strongly, and too vocally, with my Lord Cromwell's policies in England. And this man... I know not what crimes they lay at his feet. But I traveled through hell with Logan Steele on board the convict ship that brought us here, and I've borne the next best thing to hell with him here on your plantation, mistress. I'll vow there's no finer man—no man I'd sooner live with, or die with, than this man right here."

"You don't know what he did, so how can you judge?"

"I judge by the man, not by what people say of him. I'm an old man, and I've seen enough of the world to know its hypocrisy. I don't know what the poor wretch did to merit this beating, but whatever it was, I'd still take him over your brother, mistress, who I know for sure is a piece of offal. But then, no doubt you already know that."

Kit's mouth opened and shut several times without a sound. Angry words boiled to get out, all crowding into her mind so fast that none could be coherently spoken.

"You're a fool!" she finally managed to spit out. "How dare you mouth such lies! You're fortunate I don't have you whipped and laid beside him!"

Doc smiled. "No, mistress, good fortune has naught to do with it. You see, just as I know that Logan Steele is a good man and your brother a villain, I know about you, too."

"You know about...! Dash it! I'll see you...! If you weren't old enough to be somebody's great-grandfather I'd...!"

Kit sputtered into ragged silence, then lofted her nose arrogantly into the air and stormed out of the hut, leaving the old man shaking his head in resignation.

* * *

Kit would not have believed it possible, but the day continued downhill for the rest of the afternoon and evening. The servants and house slaves became more sullen with each passing hour. Punishments at Greenhaven were rare enough that the convict's whipping became the gossip on every tongue, and Kit suspected she had suddenly been cast as a wicked witch who whipped her slaves on a mere whim.

As if her household was not sufficiently uneasy, Oliver's temper added enough fuel to bring the caldron of resentment to an angry boil. He loosed his ire on any domestic within range of his tongue, leaving the parlor maids in tears, the cook beating at the bread dough with angry fists, and even staid Raleigh daring an offended scowl. Kit was the primary target for Oliver's anger, though. The day closed with the resumption of the argument that had begun when Kit ordered Logan Steele cut down from the whipping post that afternoon. Oliver railed at Kit for embarrassing him in front of the overseer and undercutting his authority with Greenhaven's slaves, calling her a spineless, naive fool. Kit followed suit by naming Oliver a brute. The yelling escalated until the very walls seemed to vibrate, but nothing was resolved. When Oliver left the library, his frown was even more thunderous than when he had entered.

Kit stayed in the library for a few moments after her brother stormed out, telling herself that Oliver was not really a brute, just a hot-tempered fool. Still quivering with the aftershocks of her own temper, she sat and stared unseeing out the dark window, very glad that this day was finally ended. She hoped another one like it would not come along any time soon.

The day was not quite over, though, as Kit discovered once she had doused all the lamps and climbed the stairs to her chamber. She had unpinned the heavy mass of her hair and was brushing it with long, vigorous strokes when a shy tap sounded on her bedroom door.

The black child who stood at the door cast her eyes shyly downward when Kit opened it.

"Little Rachel."

"Yes, ma'am." The little girl studied her toes.

Kit knelt down to place her face on a level with the child's. "What is it, Rachel?"

"It's Oona, ma'am. She sent me t' gits ya."

Kit's heart skipped a beat with fear for her old nurse. "Is Oona . . . is she all right?"

Rachel shook her head, started to shove a finger in her mouth, then thought better of it. "She's 'bout gone, ma'am. She wants t' see ya."

Kit closed her eyes in a wave of pain. She had known this moment was near, but hadn't expected it quite so soon. Death was a thing that could not be stopped or even slowed, and it didn't take heed of loved ones not ready to face its coming.

"Run on, Rachel," she sighed. "Tell Oona I'm coming."

The night was drenched in a warm rain that soaked Kit through before she had gone a hundred yards from the house. The soaking fit her mood, and the steady effort of walking up the steep path toward the village kept her warm.

Rachel was waiting for Kit in front of Oona's hut. With a solemn face the little girl ushered her mistress into the pitch-black interior. Kit produced candles from under her cloak, grateful that she had remembered to bring them. Slaves were not allowed lanterns, candles, or flints.

She struck the flint and lit the first candle, giving it to Rachel to place on the crude table that was the only item of furniture in the hut. The wavering glow lit the black faces of the mourners who had come to watch out the old Obeah witch's last earthly hours. They squatted on the dirt floor and gazed up at Kit with expressions ranging from welcome to hostility.

"Leave us." The dying woman's voice was a dry whisper that barely carried above the sound of rain pattering on the palmetto-leaf roof. "Leave us, my friends. I would talk to our mistress alone." Her voice seemed to gather strength. "You too, Rachel, child. Go out now."

Kit hastened to kneel beside Oona's pallet.

"You came," the dry old voice said.

"Of course I came. How could you think I would not?"

The old woman sighed. "Those are my children and grandchildren who came to see me die. Rachel is my great-granddaughter, I think. Sometimes I can hardly remember." Rheumy eyes turned up to Kit's face. "But you are the child of my heart. I had to see you once again before I left this world."

"Oona... don't talk like that."

Oona gave a raspy chuckle. "I am not afraid to die. Those fools believe I am a witch—an Obeah. I know the old ways. But I wanted to tell you, Katarina. I am Christian, just like you."

Kit smiled and took the old woman's withered hand. Christianity was forbidden to the slaves of Barbados, for it was against the law to enslave a Christian—except, of course, as punishment for crimes. So the blacks must remain heathen. And the priests preached that they had no souls.

"Then I'm glad for you," Kit said softly.

"All these years," the slave woman continued, "I've known about Jesus. The priests say you can't be a Christian unless they sing over you, but that's not true." She looked at her mistress with uncertain eyes. "That's not true, is it?"

"No," Kit smiled. "It's not true."

"And I'll go to heaven, just like all the other Christians."

"Indeed you will. I've never known anyone more likely to go to heaven than you."

Oona's wrinkled face smiled in relief. "I knew that."

For a moment the old woman seemed to sleep, and Kit checked fearfully to make sure she was still breathing. But when the old eyes opened they seemed brighter and clearer than before.

"My baby Katarina." Oona spoke very softly, so Kit had to lean forward to catch the words. Her unbound hair fell forward like a veil around her face. Oona lifted a shaky hand and ran her fingers through the black silky cascade, then touched the cheek that was wet with tears.

"Don't cry, my baby. I'll tell you something before I die, though perhaps by telling I prove myself a witch in truth, for sometimes I see things a Christian shouldn't."

"Oona... don't."

"I see trouble for you, little Katarina. Uncertainty, danger. Brought by a man. Though I don't see his face, I see his soul. His spirit is like the great turtles that came to the beaches when I was a child, before the ships came—a hard shell covering the soft heart. He is a rebel, and a conqueror. He brings destruction. No. Listen to me."

The old nurse gestured impatiently as Kit would have bid her stop.

"You must know that you will win through, my Katarina. This man who is a destroyer—he will also bring you something you never thought to have. Take it, my baby girl. It is worth more than everything you will lose."

With that the old woman's strength seemed to fade. No more words were spoken between them, but each saw in the face of the other the special love that had buoyed them throughout their time together on this world. Finally life faded from the tired old eyes. The old woman had slipped the bonds of her enslavement. Choking back her tears, Kit turned and left the hut as the mourners' moans began to rise into the wet night.

Logan squatted in the scant shelter of the stoackade wall, trying to ignore the agony of the rain dribbling down his torn back. On one side of him sat Doc, on the other side, Michael Carmody.

"You're a fool if you think you can make it over the wall in your condition," Doc hissed at Logan. "What difference will another day make, or two?"

"There have been too many delays already," Logan whispered. "We're going tonight."

"You'll end up killing yourself."

Logan shook his head, then winced as the movement started new knives of pain carving on his back. "I'm harder to kill than you think, especially when I have something to live for. Oliver St. John is going to pay for being what he is, and I'm just the man to collect the debt."

"I'm with ye, m'lord!" Carmody chimed in. "We'll make the bloody bastard sorry he ever messed with the likes o' us!"

Logan shushed them all to silence as they were joined by

the other two convict slaves who shared this sorry corner of hell. They had all decided that they would either succeed in this night's work or die trying. Death was far preferable to living like a whipped dog under the tender mercies of Oliver St. John.

"Quiet!" Logan warned them in a low whisper. "The guards won't be looking for trouble after what happened this afternoon, and the rain will hide most of the noise we make. But get too careless and we'll all end up in chains."

In a prearranged choreography that had been rehearsed over and over again in their minds, the convicts moved stealthily around the stockade and easily disposed of the two unwary guards by means of crude clubs. Once the two unfortunates were securely tied, gagged, and stashed in one of the huts, a rope ladder fashioned from woven grasses and vines was flung over the stockade wall. On the very first throw the ladder hooked itself on the sharply pointed logs.

Carmody was the first to go up and over, scrambling up the ladder like a monkey and jumping off the top to land with a soft, wet thud on the other side. Doc was next, not nearly as agile but almost as fast. Gabriel Potter and Jud Smythe followed in quick order. Then finally it was Logan's turn. He had purposely waited until last, fearing that when the moment came he might not live up to his boast.

He grasped the crude rope and willed himself to think only of the freedom to be had on the other side of the wall. Logan's back screamed in protest at every tiny move. His head swam and his vision became blacker even than the starless night could account for. But he climbed with determination born of desperation, and after an excruciating eternity he felt the pointed top of a log under his fumbling hand. With the last of his strength he heaved himself to the top of the wall and unhesitatingly launched himself into the wet darkness. He had barely touched the ground before helping hands and arms of his comrades pulled him onto shaking legs and helped him onto their path to freedom.

* * *

Kit ignored the rain that blew in under her hooded cloak and dribbled in cold runnels down her back. Her mind was full of old Oona and a childhood filled with the love and caring of her dear black nanny. Although she had been robbed of her beautiful aristocratic mother at the age of three, Kit never lacked for maternal love. Oona had more than filled the rent that a mother's death had torn in the young girl's life. But now the old woman was gone, and Kit felt the last of her childhood go with her.

Darkness was no hindrance to her progress down the path from the village. Almost every day of her life Kit had walked or run or ridden up and down this trail, and her feet automatically picked their way around stones and roots and washouts. But she walked slowly all the same. The rain and darkness suited her mood. She was in no hurry to return to the comfort of the house.

Finally she stopped and, sitting down on a flat rock, cradled her head in her hands. It was almost as if she could hear the passing of Oona's spirit in the patter of the rain and the soft rustle of the wind. She hadn't said a proper good-bye, she thought sadly. Oona had been too anxious to say those last words before she gave up her life.

Kit shivered, though the air was warm. Long ago she had accepted the fact that her old nurse saw things that other people did not. Kit had never doubted her truthfulness. But what an unlikely pronouncement had been those last faltering words. No man was likely to bring Kit trouble or destruction or anything else. She was a woman alone, and that was what she wanted. Plain spinster Kit St. John, with a manner much too forward and a brain much too sharp for any man's taste. Not to mention a face and form that would fail to turn even the most desperate bachelor's head. Oona must have been addled in her last hours, seeing nightmares that wouldn't come true. No man would bring Kit St. John anything she would ever want.

An unexpected sound brought Kit sharply back from her thoughts. Was that a voice carrying through the sound of the rain, or simply a fancy of her overtaxed imagination? No one would be out at this hour of the night, not in this foul weather.

She started down the path again, walking faster now. The

voice did not come again, but it seemed that there were other rustlings that did not belong in this familiar night forest. Suddenly Kit regretted walking instead of riding. She halted again and cocked her head to listen. Nothing. The patter of rain, the whisper of a breeze. Other than that, nothing.

Kit had about decided that her imagination was working overtime when a man-sized shadow separated itself from the forest and moved toward her. Her heart leapt into her throat. Without pausing to discover what or who the shadow was, she whirled, picked up her skirts, and started to sprint back the way she had come. But hardly a step had she taken before two wiry arms wrapped around her and pulled her kicking and screaming to the ground. A horny hand clamped down over her mouth.

"Quiet, bitch!" ordered a voice in high-pitched tenor. "Quit squirmin' or I'll break ye in two. Don't think that I won't!"

The Irish cadence struck a familiar note. Kit had heard that voice before. But where?

The next voice banished all doubt.

"What goes on here?"

Logan Steele. Unmistakable. Kit would never forget that voice as long as she lived—what he had said to her, what he had done to her by the side of that pool.

"Look'ee what I found right in the middle of the path," the tenor voice chortled. "If it isn't the lady mistress herself, takin' in the night air."

"Let her go." Logan's voice was quiet, but held a ring of command that most men would obey without thinking. Not so Michael Carmody.

"What d'ye mean let her go? D'ye want her to go screamin' all over the plantation that we're loose? God's eyes, m'lord! Ye'd have us all hanged, drawn, and quartered in no time!"

There followed a silence in which the only thing Kit could hear was the desperate pounding of her own heart.

"Give me a rock," Michael offered. "She won't tell no tales with her head caved in. And no one'll find her till morning. By that time we'll be well away."

Doc's familiar voice spoke softly in Kit's defense. "Good God, man! You can't murder an innocent woman!"

"Innocent my arse!" Carmody hissed. "She's St. John's sister, ain't she?"

"Give her to me," Logan finally commanded. "Go on down to the beach as we planned. I'll take care of this."

Carmody shoved Kit into Logan's arms with a nasty, knowing cackle. "Don't be long about it, m'lord. We've got to get t' Carlisle Bay before the dawn."

Kit struggled in silent protest as Logan forced her back up the path toward the village. His grip was weaker than she remembered, but it was strong enough to hold her prisoner.

"Thought I remembered this was here." Kit's captor shoved her through the doorway of a deserted hovel on the edge of the slave village. She immediately lunged for the door and freedom, but found herself knocked unceremoniously to the ground.

"Don't try it," Logan warned, "and don't make a sound, or I might take Carmody's advice."

Kit started at the sound of cloth ripping, then struggled as Logan grabbed her wrists and bound them with the remnants of his shirt. With every passing second she felt more helpless.

"You'll never get away from here," she said with an angry hiss. "They'll catch you and make sure you never run again."

"They certainly will if you go running up to your brother with the tale that we're gone."

"He'll find you anyway."

"Could be," Logan agreed in a level voice. "But either way, we're not coming back."

He lifted her wrists above her head and tied them to the center post of the hut.

"I wouldn't bother to struggle, if I were you," Logan advised. "You might bring this hovel down around you. I doubt anyone would find you before you smothered."

"I wouldn't think a man like you would care," Kit said sourly.

"A man like me?" Logan laughed softly. "You have no

idea what a man like me is like, Miss St. John. Maybe if you're lucky you won't ever find out."

Kit couldn't see through the inky darkness, but she could imagine his mocking smile. Somehow it wasn't a surprise when she felt his hands on her waist.

"Your meddling brother interrupted me before I had finished this afternoon. But he's not here now, is he?"

His lips came down on hers and his body pressed her against the post. Kit stiffened and clenched her teeth against his assault, but one hand moved from her waist to her jaw, forcing her mouth to open to his questing tongue. The insidious fire ignited once again in the pit of Kit's belly. The slave's gently probing tongue and the intimate press of his body against hers fanned the flame still higher. She couldn't find the strength to object when his hands slipped down to her buttocks and pressed her even more closely against him. The world of reality was washed away in a flood of wanting and the shame of knowing exactly what it was she wanted. When he finally released her, the darkness was alive with the current that had passed between them, and she could hear him breathing just as hard as she.

But Logan's voice was icy calm as he checked her bonds and stuffed a foul-tasting gag into her mouth. "That should finish it, then. Good-bye, Miss St. John."

Without another word he was gone.

Chapter 4

Tea at the Governor's Mansion in Bridgetown was usually a dull undertaking, but on this warm day in late February Kit found the gathering less tiresome than she expected. The usual sampling of planters' wives and daughters was in attendance, and here and there a sprinkling of husbands fulfilled their social obligations. Two of Governor Searle's higher ranking government officials sat drinking tea and eating biscuits with several naval officers from the fleet anchored in the bay. One guest, however, retrieved the party from incurable tedium. Sir Thomas Modyford had returned from England some weeks ago and was making a rare social appearance in Lady Searle's parlor.

Sir Thomas was a prominent planter who had his finger in a political pie much larger than the provincial intrigues found on Barbados. In 1652 he sensed that the Royalist cause on the island was about to fall. Expediently switching his support to Parliament, he quickly became a man who was much heeded by Oliver Cromwell. Cromwell's ambitions against the Caribbean holdings of Spain were at least partially inspired by Sir Thomas, and the British fleet that had been anchored in Carlisle Bay these two months past were proof of his influence with the ruling powers of the mother country.

Kit had never found Sir Thomas Modyford to her liking. He was a man of whom other men were cautious, and for good reason. An air of ruthlessness about him shone through his polite smiles and small talk. But Kit had to admit the man's presence at Lady Searle's tea added spice to the usually bland gathering. His mind was sharp as the edge of a well-honed knife, and his eyes and ears seemed to miss nothing that was done or said. Kit enjoyed watching Sir Thomas watch other people, and when he finally made his exit, the life seemed to go out of the gathering.

"Such an unexpected honor to have Colonel Modyford attend tea this afternoon." Lady Searle's acid tone gave lie to her polite words.

"An interesting man," Kit replied.

"Isn't he, though," Elizabeth Rogers chimed in. "Charming gentleman. Absolutely charming."

Kit thought privately that Elizabeth Rogers would find charming any man with a title and wealth to go with it. Then she mentally scolded herself for being a shrew. She was no doubt jealous, for Elizabeth's peaches-and-cream complexion and honey-blond hair made Kit feel like a plain brown mouse. In penance for her rude thoughts, she gave the girl a warm smile. "You may be too generous in your estimation, Elizabeth. I suspect that all that amiability and charm overlie a scheming heart. I understand Sir Thomas is the one responsible for those warships in the harbor."

"Yes." Lady Searle was now frankly disapproving. "General Venables has been recruiting every ablebodied white man he can lure aboard those ships, and Admiral Penn has been helping him, all with Colonel Modyford's approval. They're even taking indentureds. Do you believe it? I can't imagine what Sir Thomas is thinking. The number of decent Christian whites on this island has been decreasing for years, and here he's robbing us of the few we have left. General Venables and Sir Thomas certainly do not have the good of this island in mind with this silly expedition of theirs."

Kit agreed, but she had no desire to follow where Lady Searle was leading. The good woman was convinced that Modyford was plotting to replace her husband as governor of Barbados, and would harangue endlessly on the subject to anyone willing to listen.

"I do wish those supply ships would arrive and Admiral Penn would get his expedition on its way," the lady continued. "There are other English colonies that they can rob of men just as well as this one. I can't imagine why my Daniel stands for General Venables's meddling. I really can't. And you can depend that Colonel Modyford is watching to turn all this to his advantage."

"I'm sure you're right, my lady." Kit smiled blandly. Elizabeth also saw what was coming and wisely engaged herself in conversation with the lady seated at her right. Smart girl, Kit acknowledged.

"This has been very pleasant," Kit said, forestalling Lady Searle's lecture on her favorite subject. "But I'm afraid you must excuse me now. I must return home this afternoon, and if dark is not to catch me on the road, I should be getting started."

"Oh, of course, my dear." The governor's wife was all concern. "It has been so pleasant having you. You really should get into town more often, you know. You must be bored to tears on Greenhaven with your brother gone so often. I can't imagine what you find to do!"

Kit smiled and made a polite reply, thinking as she made her farewell that Lady Searle and the other matrons and misses in the parlor knew exactly what she found to do at Greenhaven, but chose to ignore the fact that a lady of good breeding could possibly turn her hand to such an inappropriate, masculine task as managing a plantation.

As it turned out, Kit did not leave quite early enough, for the sudden tropical nightfall did catch her still on the road. Usually she didn't mind being out after dark, but in the past few weeks an unusual number of slaves had been running. No doubt they were holed up in the mountains somewhere, for there was no way for them to leave the island. Eventually they would be rounded up and punished, but in the meantime, there was no guarantee they wouldn't band together and come swarming down to the coast to get revenge for imagined wrongs that had been dealt them.

Kit leaned forward and spoke to the young indentured man who drove the carriage. "Keep a sharp lookout, Adam. You never can tell what you might meet along this road, and there's no moon tonight."

"Yes, miss."

"And keep that pistol o' yours 'andy," Mandy added. "If the master 'ad known we'd be 'home this late, 'e'd have come with us, I'd wager. No telling what sort of evildoers are 'aunting the roads these days. I 'ear that just last week the Edmonds' overseer saw a loose gang o' slaves crossing the road down by the eastern 'eadland. By the time 'e'd rounded up the dogs to give chase, they'd disappeared. Some o' the blokes was white." Mandy lowered her voice. "Could've even been those fellows 'oo escaped an' left ye in that 'ut."

"Not likely." Kit's eyes flashed a warning at the talkative redhead. It had been Mandy who found her in the early morning hours after the convicts' escape at the beginning of the year. Kit had spent an uncomfortable night struggling with her bonds and imagining appropriate punishments for the arrogant slave who had left her there. Had the early-rising Mandy not grown concerned over Kit's unslept-in bed, had she not remembered the ailing Oona and thought to search for her mistress in the village, Kit might have had to endure the embarrassment of being discovered in such an awkward position by one of her own slaves.

She had forbidden the maid to speak so much as a word of the incident to anyone. Kit had endured enough humiliation as it was. Logan Steele was gone for good. He and his convict friends could run to the mountains, escape to the sea, or descend to hell itself for all she cared. And after nearly two months she certainly didn't want the subject brought up again. "All the same," Mandy continued, "I wish Master Oliver 'ad come with us. It's not safe to travel this late at..."

Her remark ended abruptly as their horse shied, jerking the carriage to the side of the road and landing one wheel in a ditch.

"Whoa there!" Adam shouted. "Easy now! Easy now!"

But the horse spooked again, and now the reason was apparent. Four shadows detached themselves from the forest and ran toward the carriage. Fresh in her thoughts, Logan Steele's face flashed through Kit's mind. It couldn't be. Not him. It couldn't be.

It wasn't. The men who had materialized out of the dark were burly and broad. Even the tallest did not approach Logan Steele's height.

Before Kit could breathe a sigh of relief, two of them grabbed the bridle and brought the horse to an uneasy standstill while the other two clambered aboard the carriage.

"'Ere now!" Adam shouted. He fumbled for the pistol that lay under his seat, but before he could raise it, a blow to the head sent him sprawling to the ground.

Carelessly confident, the attackers grinned at the two women. Kit wasted no time in feminine hysterics. She was more angry than frightened as she doubled a fist and smashed it into the closest head.

"Ow!" The man she had struck staggered back to the ground, swaying dizzily. "Damn vicious hellcat!" He surged forward again. "I'll teach you a thing or two!"

Kit reached for the carriage whip perched by the driver's box, but before her hand could close on the weapon, she was grabbed from behind by two long, encircling arms.

"Come wit' me, darlin'! What the..,! Ouch!"

This second assailant had no sooner grabbed Kit than Mandy rushed to the rescue, raking her nails down the villain's face, then sending her knee with painful precision into his groin. Kit twisted away as her captor doubled over in agony. She lunged once again for the whip, just in time to lay it across the first man's face.

"That's enough o' that, miss!" The third man had left the horse to his companion and joined in the fray. He grabbed Kit's arm and twisted it painfully. "Drop it now."

Kit's numbed fingers did as he commanded. Behind her she heard Mandy screech.

"Attack a couple o' helpless women, will ye, ye 'orse's arse. I'll teach ye t'mind yer manners."

Kit aimed a kick at her captor's knee. He deftly avoided her foot and delivered a sharp cuff to her head. She stumbled to her knees, her vision swimming with red spots.

"Mandy, run!" Her voice echoed painfully in her throbbing head. "For God's sake, run!"

"Git off o' me, ye old hag!"

Mandy was on her assailant's back, legs wrapped around his waist and hands and arms thumping him enthusiastically on the head. No matter how he swatted and whirled and bounced, the poor man couldn't rid himself of the screeching she-devil who rode him.

Kit's captor hauled her to her feet and pulled her against him in a firm grip. "Let the baggage go, Tom me boy." He chortled in appreciation of his comrade's pained cursing.

Kit struggled to escape the grasp that held her and was rewarded with another sharp blow for her pains.

"Behave, darlin', or I'll put yer lights out. Indeed I will."

"Mandy, go!" Kit pleaded. "Run! Get Oliver!"

The maid stopped her pummeling and jumped nimbly from the man's back. Avoiding a vicious swipe from his arm, she scurried into the forest. Her panting victim made a lunge to follow her, but was stopped short by a sharp command.

"Let 'er go, I said!" Kit's captor laughed in a snide voice. "That's right, ye old witch. You run. Run get Mr. Oliver. See what good it does ye."

Kit was trussed and gagged and thrown across a beefy shoulder. The indignity of her position was made worse by the swat that was delivered to her rump every time she made an attempt to struggle. So she stopped struggling and tried to plan just how she was going to get out of this mess. But panic was eating away at her reason. Who these ruffians were and what they intended Kit didn't know, but she didn't want to be in their company long enough to find out.

The conversation of her captors was not very informative.

"We're almost to the beach. Where are they?"

"How in hell am I supposed to know?"

"Keep quiet!" a third commanded. "D'ye want to spoil it all?"

"Let's stop fer a rest. This ain't no dainty miss, ye know. Like carryin' a load o' bricks!"

Kit kicked out indignantly at this. She connected with something soft which she hoped was some delicate and sensitive part of the man's face.

"Ow! Goddammit!"

She was rewarded with a horny hand coming down on her backside.

"Quiet, dammit! There they are."

"S'about time."

Their little procession stopped. "Are ye sure that's them? That don't look like them t'me."

"Who else could it be?"

"Whoever, we're goin' t' find out soon. Here they come."

Kit's captor bounced her into a firmer position on his shoulder.

"What the...?" a voice close by whispered. "That's not...! What in hell? Run!"

They ran. The point of a shoulder pounded painfully into Kit's middle with every jarring step her captor took. But the man ran only a few yards before deciding he could make better time without Kit. She landed with a jolt on the hard sand of the beach. But it was too late for her abductor. A flying tackle from his pursuer sent him sprawling to the ground, head smashing against a rock with a dull thud. He twitched once, then was still. His comrades fled into the forest, not bothering to look back.

When her rescuers gathered around her, Kit was not certain she was any better off than before. In a few moments she became quite sure she was not. She lay bound, gagged, and mumbling curses to herself while they gawked and grinned as though she were some prize fish that they had landed. It was too dark for her to discern faces. But the Irish lilt in one of the voices carried her back to that horrible night weeks ago—the night of Oona's death, when she had stumbled into the grasp of an angry-eyed Irish convict who had offered to smash her skull, and had been saved by an equally angry Englishman who had smashed her pride with a kiss.

"God's eyes! What have we here?" the Irish voice mocked. "If it isn't the slave mistress of Greenhaven Plantation! What d'ye suppose so fine a lady is doin' in such a place?"

"Stow it, Carmody," a clipped voice ordered. "We've got passengers waiting. Release the woman and let's be on our way."

"Stow it yourself, Van Halen! You don't tell me what to—"

"Someone's comin'!" a frightened voice called.

"Release her!"

"She's seen too much!" The Irish lilt sounded like a knell of doom. "She knows me, goddammit!"

Carmody unsheathed his knife. The edge caught the faint gleam of starlight and seemed to fill Kit's whole vision. She knew the knife was not intended to cut her bonds. It descended with nightmarish inevitability toward her throat.

A hand closed around Carmody's wrist. "I said release her!" Van Halen's voice snapped. "Now!"

"Dammit, Van Halen! I told ye . . . !"

"Then bring her, if you're afraid she's seen too much. The captain can deal with the problem."

Kit's bonds and gag were swiftly cut and she was pulled ungently to her feet by the seething Irishman. As he pulled her toward the water where a boat was being launched, Kit looked behind her to see three men standing atop a low dune, frantically waving their arms and shouting for them to stop. One of the voices she recognized. It belonged to Nick Basey.

The beach was certainly crowded tonight, Kit thought with a hint of confused hysteria. Then she was pushed into the boat among a crowd of sweating bodies. She could smell the stench of fear, and it wasn't only her own.

The hull they eventually bumped against was merely a darker blot in the velvet-black night. Not a light was showing, and the only sound to greet them as their boat came alongside was a soft hail from the deck above. Boarding nets were lowered, and Kit watched while a dozen figures clambered awkwardly up the side of the ship. The night was dark, but not so dark that she couldn't see that at least eight of those figures were black men, and two more were black women. She had little time to ponder what she saw before she was pushed up the side herself.

Kit was hustled down a companionway and thrust into a spacious stern cabin. She heard the click of the lock as the door was shut behind her. A quick, desperate examination of the stern windows showed them to be locked as well. She pounded against them in frustration, but they refused to give.

"Break one of my fine windows, Miss St. John, and I'll take the price of new glass out of your hide."

Kit's heart quickened its pace as she turned. The voice was hauntingly familiar, but the face and figure of the man who stood in the doorway was not. He stepped in and shut the door firmly behind him.

The cabin had been roomy before. Now it seemed small. The man's broad shoulders seemed to span completely the distance between desk and wardrobe, and surely the four-poster bed, big as it was, was not long enough to accommodate that towering height. He wore no doublet or jerkin, only a silk shirt which did nothing to disguise the width of his chest or the ripple of taut muscle in his arms. Fashionably wide knee-length breeches and polished black boots only served to emphasize the power of his long legs.

Arms folded across his chest, the man leaned back

against the door and smiled at her. Something about that satisfied smile, Kit thought nervously, was not very friendly.

"You don't recognize me, do you?" he said.

Once again her memory stirred. She had heard that voice before. But where?

"Should I know you, sir?" Kit's voice was cold, her tone as haughty as she could make it. It would not do to let this arrogant fellow think that she was some swooning miss who could be easily intimidated.

His smile broadened. "Indeed, you should."

There was something familiar... but no. Kit was positive she had never seen that face before. She would have remembered it. Lean and sun-bronzed it was, with boldly sculpted features reflecting humor, intelligence, and a measure of ruthlessness. The jaw was angular and prominent, the mouth wide and framed by narrow, chiseled lips. The nose was straight and only slightly flared at the nostrils. Deep-set clear blue eyes burned beneath a slash of level dark brows. Mahogany-colored hair was cropped unfashionably short, curling around neck and ears and falling in errant tendrils over a wide brow.

All in all, it was a devilishly attractive face, a dangerous face, a face that might make any woman catch her breath and look again. No, Kit thought, she wouldn't have forgotten this man. No woman past the age of puberty would have forgotten that face and figure.

"You're quite mistaken." Kit's voice quavered in spite of her effort to keep it firm. "I do not know you. I've never seen you before. Are you someone of consequence?"

The man's smile grew broader. "Maybe this will help your memory, my lady."

In three long strides he was in front of her. Kit's heart skipped a beat. She retreated a step, only to find the bulkhead at her back. Then a hard masculine arm circled her waist. Lips came down on hers in a fierce kiss that snatched the very breath from her lungs.

Kit writhed and kicked and pushed against the hard body that pressed so insistently and so intimately against her own, but her struggles only brought her more firmly into the man's grasp. The more she fought, the deeper and more voracious the kiss became. But for all the intense hunger of that plundering mouth, there was a quality of frigid, passionless contempt that jarred her senses, and her memory. A face swam into her mind's eye—bearded, gaunt, filthy.

With a surge of strength she pushed her assailant away. "You!" she choked incredulously.

In contrast to the kiss, his face was almost amiable. "Do you know me now, then?"

"I know you indeed, you blackguard!"

His courtly bow was ripe with sarcasm. "Captain Logan Steele, madam. Your servant. Or perhaps I should say, your slave."

"Captain, is it?" She let the title roll off her tongue in sarcastic disdain. "A fine title for an escaped slave and criminal. How many men did you kill to get this fine ship?"

"As it happens, none. The night we left your kind hospitality this lovely frigate was anchored in Carlisle Bay—very conveniently within swimming distance of the shore. The few fellows standing guard were only too happy to hop overboard—after a little gentle persuasion."

"How fortunate that you were able to sail such a vessel." Kit's voice was sharp with irritation. "I'm surprised your talents extend beyond abusing innocent women."

Logan refused to rise to the bait. "After eight years in the British Navy, I can sail anything afloat, given a few willing fellows to man the yards. And a visit to Tortuga provided me with plenty of those. Faith! This is the first time that service to my country has paid off."

"Ah, yes," she continued, unable to resist flinging one more barb. "I remember now. Mr. Brownlow told me you were involved in some sort of mutiny at sea. No doubt you're well suited to piracy."

Kit recalled dimly that soon after his return from England, Sir Thomas Modyford had complained that one of his ships had been stolen. He had influenced Governor Searle to demote the commandant of Wallenghby Fort for letting a band of audacious pirates slip into Bridgetown's harbor and steal a ship from beneath his very nose. At the time, Kit hadn't thought to connect the incident with the convicts' escape.

"I have an idea your pirate's career will be short-lived, though, Captain Steele. If this is Sir Thomas Modyford's stolen ship, then you've made yourself a formidable enemy."

Logan's mysterious smile made Kit wonder what he was hiding. "I think Sir Thomas might forgive me. Or he'll find that I'm a fairly nasty enemy myself."

Kit stiffened indignantly as those startling blue eyes regarded her in cool assessment. "Are you indeed? I take it you consider me your enemy as well." She schooled her voice to icy calm. "Is holding me here your idea of revenge?"

"Certainly not, my fine lady. You are here quite by chance. Believe me, I relish the idea as little as you do."

Kit snorted her disbelief. "You expect me to believe that? I saw the look of hatred you gave me that day you were whipped."

Logan strolled over to the cabinet beside the desk and poured two glasses of wine. A devilish gleam sparkled in his eyes as he handed her one. "You mistake the look I gave you, Miss St. John. That wasn't hatred. That was merely lust." He smiled. "An effective diversion from pain—up to a point."

Her eyes grew wide and her fingers tightened dangerously around the fragile stem of her glass. Was it to be rape, ending with a slashed throat? Kit wished she could gather the courage to throw the wine into that arrogant face.

"I'll let this be a lesson to me. Next time I won't stop my brother from meting out punishment to a rogue who deserves every stripe he's getting."

A flash of memory turned Logan's eyes to blue ice. "Ah, yes. You are much too softhearted, my lady. Obviously, you should have let your brother kill me. Then my men would not have been there to rescue you from those worthy gentlemen who were carting you toward the beach."

"Rescue me, indeed! Only to deliver me into your rapacious hands." Kit tilted her chin at a defiant angle, trying to speak with a courage she didn't feel. If only the scoundrel weren't so big. If only she didn't remember so clearly the feel of his hands, his mouth. "I warn you, villain, your revenge will not be easily accomplished. I'll scratch out your very eyes before I submit."

"Submit?" Logan rolled the word over his tongue as though he didn't know the meaning. Then he laughed. "Ah yes, submit."

Kit flushed. "I am not a sheltered, simpering maid, Mr. Steele. I know how vile creatures of your stamp treat women. You forget, I've had a taste of your vengeance already. But I warn you...!"

"Miss St. John." Logan waved her to silence, his smile a pure taunting insolence. "I beg your forgiveness. I am quite new at being a vile creature, and obviously I am unfamiliar with some of the finer traditions. It was my intent to leave you in peace, but if you feel the need to be raped, I'm sure I can find someone among my crew to oblige you. I myself, unfortunately, am otherwise occupied."

Leaning casually back against the bulkhead, Logan sipped his wine and regarded her with a mocking smile. Kit met his regard with a gaze that could have frozen the heart of a volcano. She glared at him in seething silence for a moment, then with lips pressed into a furious line and jaw clenched in anger, she whirled and gave the pirate a ramrod-stiff back. When Logan finally broke the silence, all the mocking humor had fled from his voice. "Be grateful I'm such a mild-tempered and forgiving gentleman, mistress. For if I were truly bent on vengeance, my revenge upon you and your brother would surely be worse than anything your imagination could concoct." He studied her stiff back. Not a single quiver met his pronouncement. "As it is, I will set you ashore as soon as I may. For now, I've pressing business to attend to, and I've no time to inconvenience myself further for your sake. I will guarantee your safety aboard this ship only as long as you follow my commands. I suggest you resign yourself to obedience."

A loud crack from the sails was audible even below deck. The cabin's single lantern swayed and creaked and the deck beneath their feet tilted to starboard as the canvas caught the wind.

"As I said, I have pressing business." Logan started toward the door. "We are under way. I suggest you drink your wine and try to get some rest. You're not to leave this cabin without my permission." He gave her back a chilling smile. "If you do I will take great pleasure in tying you to the center post. So behave, Miss St. John. Don't try my patience. Ever since you stepped aboard my ship, it has been wearing dangerously thin."

The door shut on the unladylike epithet Kit hurled after him. Of all the insufferable nerve! The man insulted her, threatened her, and was carrying her off to God only knew where, and he had the effrontery to tell her he cared not a whit for revenging himself on her. Did he think she was some gullible schoolgirl to believe his words?

Kit started to pace. Her ire blossomed brighter the more she thought about it. He couldn't use her as he had twice—no, three times—use her in such an intimate and insulting manner and then prate about his noble forbearance and promise she would not be molested. How dare he! How dare he behave as he had and then pretend he had no interest in pressing himself further upon her.

Kit kicked at the massive oak bedpost, and then realized with chagrin where her thoughts were straying. She was as angry about the filthy pirate's lack of attention to her feminine charms as she was about being kidnapped. She had never longed for men to go drooling after her as they did Mavis Edmond or Elizabeth Rogers, but this confirmation on her lack of womanly appeal was just one thing too much to be borne on this terrible night. How humiliating that not even the lowest scoundrel of a pirate paid her any mind, even after he had so casually and heartlessly sampled her charms. Kit suddenly wished she were devastatingly beautiful and could break the rogue's heart to pieces after casually toying with his emotions. She pictured him kneeling before her, begging for mercy, humiliating himself for the sake of her favors, and all the while she wrinkled her nose in disgust and turned her back in heartless rejection. That would be the very thing. She kicked at the bedpost again and stubbed her toe.

"Dash it all!"

Kit flounced on the bed, close to tears. Even the furniture was out to humiliate her.

Before long, Half Moon Bay had been left in their wake and the frigate was beginning to plow through the rolling swell of the open sea. The first qualms of seasickness added to Kit's misery. She had never been a good sailor, and with an empty stomach already churning in distress, the symptoms came on heavy and hard. Frantically she looked around the cabin for the chamber pot. She found it just in time.

An hour later Kit looked up from her retching to notice that she had an audience. Logan didn't look at all concerned that she was turning herself inside out with every roll of the ship.

"I thought I heard the telltale sounds." He offered a steaming cup. "Drink this. It's Doc's remedy for the heaves."

Kit turned her face away, but he lifted her to her feet and forced the concoction to her lips. She had to admit that the hot liquid did feel good going down her raw throat, and her stomach almost instantly settled into uneasy quiescence.

"Now come with me. You'll be better off on deck in the fresh air. You've turned my cabin into a sour-smelling privy."

She did feel better when the cool night wind hit her face, and on deck the rolling rise and fall of the ship seemed not quite so malevolent. All eyes seemed to turn her way as she followed Logan across the main deck. Some were merely curious, others were blatantly hostile.

"Where are we headed?" Kit asked abruptly.

Logan shook his head. "Nowhere you need to know about."

They climbed the companionway to the quarterdeck and Logan escorted her to the rail, his big hand firmly on her arm. Quickly Kit turned her eyes away from the dark and heaving sea that raced along the hull. She was unpleasantly reminded that if she pushed this renegade too far, he could easily toss her into the vast and empty ocean and no one would say him nay. In fact, it might give him a great deal of satisfaction to do just that. She tore her eyes from the waves and instead fastened her gaze on the bright cloak of stars that spangled the sky.

"I was just curious," she explained. "You needn't snap my head off. After being kidnapped and threatened and carried halfway across the ocean, it seems I might be permitted some curiosity."

"You've hardly been carried halfway across the ocean," Logan replied dryly. "And curiosity can get you into a great deal of trouble."

"Just as kidnapping a St. John can get you into a great deal of trouble."

Logan chuckled. "Ever spoiling for a fight. I have to admire your spirit, girl, if not your sense. You should be nicer to me, Kit St. John. I'm your only defender among these cutthroats of mine."

Kit felt her face grow hot. How dare the man use the pet name her father had given her! He shouldn't even know it, though she supposed among Greenhaven's slaves it was common knowledge.

"My name is Katarina Isabella Christina St. John," she corrected proudly. "You may continue to call me Miss St. John."

"Katarina. . . ." The syllables rolled languidly off Logan's tongue as he savored her annoyance. "It fits you better than Kit. Kit brings to mind kitten, and you're anything but soft and cuddly. But how did such an English miss come by such a Spanish name?"

"My mother was Spanish. In fact," Kit said proudly, "she was the youngest sister of the Count of Penalva, who is now the Governor of Hispaniola. My father was English."

"The Governor of Hispaniola. . . ." For a moment Logan stared at her, frowning. "That fat pig in the *palacio* at Santo Domingo is your uncle, then. A most unusual connection."

Kit glared. "My uncle is not a fat pig."

Logan lifted a brow in surprise. "You are actually acquainted with this relative of yours?"

"Of course. My mother was his favorite sister. And I am his favorite niece, even though we cannot often see each other. Uncle Juan is a decent and honorable man, and I will not stand by while you slander him just because he is Spanish."

Logan smiled indulgently. Kit could see his face only

dimly in the starlight, but there was a look about him that she'd seen before—a warmth of regard that seemed to be his prelude to humiliating passion. Her heart skipped a beat. For a moment she imagined he was about to kiss her again, right here in front of his crew of smirking pirates. She backed up a step. He reached out and stopped her with a hand on her arm.

"What are you afraid of, Katarina?"

"I'm not afraid of anything... or anyone."

He chuckled, a rich sound from deep in his chest. "I think I believe you. I also think, for a number of reasons, that you are a singularly unusual woman."

He didn't mean that in a complimentary way, Kit guessed. Miffed, she shook his hand from her arm. "The air up here is growing stale," she said pointedly. "I prefer it down below."

"As you wish." Logan watched with thoughtful eyes as she strode stiff-backed to the hatch.

"Katarina."

She tossed him a look of annoyance over her shoulder.

"Sometimes, Katarina, it is permissible even for the bravest to be afraid. Sometimes it is only the foolish who are not."

The tropical breeze suddenly felt cold. Shivering, Kit gathered up her skirts and hurried below.

Chapter 5

"Sail off the starboard bow!"

The shout from the watch aloft broke the peace of the slowly graying dawn. Kit heard and sat up in her rumpled bed. For a moment she was disoriented. Then she remembered. She was aboard an outlaw ship and in the power of an arrogant renegade. All the night before she had paced the deck of her locked cabin while the crew of the ship had busied themselves in some barbarous pirating activity. Kit didn't know what the rogues had done during those dark hours. She had stood at the stern windows and watched as the longboat plied back and forth between the ship and a little shadow of an island, but she could glean no clue as to their purpose.

The cry from the watch came again, accompanied by the pounding of feet on the deck above. Poor little ship, Kit thought. Doubtless it would fall prey to the beast who commanded this villainous vessel.

Kit reluctantly climbed from bed, splashed her face with cold water from the pitcher on the washstand, and pulled chemise and gown over her head. A comb from the washstand served to smooth the tangled skein of her hair. She pulled back the ebony mass, deftly twisted it into a knot at the nape of her neck, and pulled a few wispy tendrils from the severe bun to curl around her face. Her hands stopped abruptly in the middle of their task. What did she care how she looked? There was certainly no one on this ship she cared to impress.

By the time Kit emerged from below, the first molten sliver of the sun was peeking over the horizon. For a moment she was transfixed by the beauty of the morning. The rolling swells of the sea were painted in iridescent gold. Wispy clouds that streaked the pale sky were aglow with the same color. The quiet creak of the ship's timbers, the hum of the wind in the rigging, the whisper and gurgle of the waves surging alongside the hull—all seemed to combine into a hymn to the newborn sun.

"She's a brigantine."

The sound of Logan's deep voice jerked Kit's attention from the beauty of the morning. She was unpleasantly reminded that this glorious dawn heralded danger for the tiny speck of a ship that was just visible on the horizon. Logan was standing with a spyglass trained on the distant vessel. No doubt the villain was estimating the treasure he would soon plunder.

"Looks dead in the water. The one visible sail is tattered. I don't see any activity."

Logan passed the glass to the man beside him, a lean fellow with shoulder-length blond hair and the face of a hawk. Kit dimly recognized him as the man on the beach—Van Halen, they'd called him—who had stopped Michael Carmody from slitting her throat.

"What do you think, Peter?" Logan's brows were drawn together in a dark scowl.

"It bears the mark of the Jackal's work. You're right about that. There's a fire still burning aft. Couldn't have been attacked more than an hour ago. At first light I'd guess." The Dutchman passed the spyglass back to Logan.

The brigantine was rapidly becoming more than a tiny speck. Kit could now see the one tattered sail flapping listlessly in the morning breeze. Only one mast was still standing. Someone had apparently downed the prey before Logan had sighted her. No doubt that was why the rogue looked so unhappy.

Kit mounted the quarterdeck companionway and moved to the rail. "Why do you say it's the Jackal's deed?" she asked.

Logan and his first officer both turned in surprise at the sound of her voice.

"What are you doing here?" Logan demanded.

"That's what I've asked myself every hour of the past night."

Logan scowled. "I see you've awakened with a saucy tongue, Katarina."

Van Halen backed away from the two of them, trying to suppress an amused smile.

"Where are you going?" Logan shifted his glare to his first officer.

"I thought you two might like some privacy," the Dutchman answered with a grin.

"Think again." Logan closed the spyglass with an angry snap. "Have the helmsman come around to an intercept course. And reef down the main. Go in slowly. I want to give that ship a thorough looking over before we board."

"Aye, sir."

Logan turned his frown back to Kit.

"Don't try to frighten me with that fierce scowl," she

said archly. "You can't expect me to stay in that cramped cabin day and night. You didn't mind my being on deck last evening."

"I mind now."

"Why?"

He gestured to the dismasted vessel that was now only a few hundred yards off the bow.

Kit raised one brow. "It certainly doesn't appear that you're going into battle, Captain Steele. I've never seen a ship that looks less able to defend herself."

"There's always the possibility of a trap."

"Unlikely," she countered, ignoring the angry tightening of his jaw. "You didn't answer my question. Why do you say this is the work of the Jackal?"

"Have you been so sheltered on your rich plantation that you don't know who the Jackal is?"

"I know who he is," Kit assured him. "He's the masked fellow with the gray-painted ship. Colonel Modyford once told me the Jackal is the most villainous pirate alive—and the most successful." She slanted him a cynical smile. "Are you envious?"

"Envious!" Logan snorted with disgust. "Envious of a man who kills for the fun of it and entertains himself by putting brave men to the torture?"

"He's different from you, then, this Jackal."

Logan shook his head at Kit's sarcastic sneer. "Believe it or not, Katarina, I have little stomach for pirating, and little use for pirates. But it seemed a reasonable alternative when compared to slaving for you and your brother. I don't do well working for others, as you have seen."

"So this fellow is not a comrade of yours?"

"Hardly!" His lips twisted. "I'd sooner call your brother friend."

Kit searched the intent, chiseled features for a hint of sarcasm. She found none. The glittering blue eyes, the frowning dark brows, the tight narrow lips—all bespoke a genuine anger.

"You must really hate him, then, this Jackal."

Logan turned to regard her with an almost frightening intensity. "Aye, I do indeed. Only once have I met that gray ghost of a ship. We scarcely escaped with our lives and our ship still afloat. When next we meet, I may have a few surprises for that hyena."

"So that's it," Kit said knowingly. "The Jackal bested you."

"He did best me once," Logan admitted. "But he won't ever again."

He opened his spyglass once more and swept the decks of the brigantine with a suspicious eye. They were almost alongside. The stink of gunpowder and rotting corpses floated on the breeze.

"Grappling hooks!" he ordered in a terse voice, then snapped the glass shut. "And keep a sharp watch aloft. If the Jackal is cruising nearby, we want to see him before he sees us."

The two ships were only feet apart. Grappling hooks flew across the intervening space and crewmen set their backs to the task of pulling the hulls together.

Logan started for the main deck. Kit followed.

"I'm coming with you."

He turned abruptly. "Beg pardon, my lady, but the bloody hell you are! You may stay on deck if the sight of carnage entertains you, but I expect you would be happier below."

"I am not quite the delicate miss you believe me, sir. I may be able to help."

"I have never made the mistake of believing you delicate, Katarina," Logan shot back contemptuously. "And believe me, those people over there are beyond all help other than prayers for their souls. You are staying here. If you move a foot off this quarterdeck, it will be to go below."

Kit set her jaw at a stubborn angle and set both hands on her hips, a posture that had long been the despair of both her father and brother. "I am coming with you," she said in a measured voice.

Logan took two steps toward her, bringing him close enough for her to see the spasmodic jumping of the muscle in his jaw. "You are a spoiled and foolish bitch, little Katarina, without the sense God gave a stubborn mule. I'm beginning to think your brother will be getting just what he deserves when I return you to him."

Without giving her a chance to reply, he turned and stalked toward the companionway. She stared after him, for once in her life bereft of words.

"Come if you insist," he tossed over his shoulder. "I haven't the time to save you from your foolish notions. But don't whine to me about your bruised sensibilities if you see something you don't like."

The instant Kit set foot on the ravaged *Carrie Ann* she regretted her decision. She had insisted on coming aboard simply because it had seemed an excellent way to annoy that rascally ex-slave. She hadn't counted on the horror that greeted her.

The *Carrie Ann* was a three-masted brigantine. Only one mast remained standing. The two others had been shattered by cannon fire and had crashed to the deck in a confused morass of spars, rigging, and sails. Three men lay crushed under the remains of the mainmast, one other under the toppled mizzen.

Kit turned her face from the arms and legs that sprawled from under the heavy timbers and tangled rigging. But turning her face did little good. Death was everywhere. The crew had evidently put up a brave fight, and had been rewarded by wholesale carnage. The deck was black with dried blood.

One pathetic body in particular drew Kit's reluctant eyes. He had been a boy—younger, Kit guessed, than she was herself. Pale blond hair ruffled in the morning breeze. Staring blue eyes gazed sightlessly into the uncaring sky. He had died slowly. The skin was peeled away from his chest in gory strips. One hand was missing. The fingers of the other were bent at odd, unnatural angles. Kit recalled with horror what Logan had said about torture being the Jackal's favorite entertainment.

"You shouldn't be here, miss."

It was Doc. His lined face looked younger than Kit remembered it, and much fuller. The aging, emaciated body had filled out to the point of boasting a paunch. Worried eyes regarded her with fatherly concern.

Kit took his proffered arm, suddenly feeling a bit unsteady on her feet. "Yes, maybe you're right. I shouldn't be here."

Just then she caught Logan's eye upon her. He was smiling in grim satisfaction. Gloating, Kit thought angrily that he'd been right. She pressed her lips into a tight line, willing her queasy stomach to behave.

"I thought there might be someone still alive," she explained to the old man, "someone whom I might be able to help."

Doc shook his gray head. "There's no help for these poor souls. You should go back to the *Ice Maiden*."

"No." The single syllable was soft but carried a ring of determination.

The old doctor looked at Kit's pale, set face, then glanced to where Logan stood inspecting the one standing mast. He had seen the look his captain had given the girl, and he'd also noted Kit's response. He didn't know what was between the two of them, but whatever it was, it wasn't doing either of them any good. The captain had moved in to share his cabin when the girl was brought on board the *Ice Maiden*, and the old physician had been robbed of a whole night's sleep listening to Logan toss and curse in the hammock he'd slung between two timbers. Doc thanked the stars that he was old and no longer subject to the trials that plagued young hearts.

"Well, Miss St. John, if you insist on staying aboard this floating charnel house, at least come with me. I was about to see what's below. It should be better there." He patted her arm sympathetically.

Doc was wrong. It was not better below. A young freckled lad who must have been a cabin boy lay sprawled on the mess table. His face was splotched with purple and blue bruises, and blood still seeped sluggishly from a deep sword cut over his ribs.

Doc leaned close to the boy's mouth. "He's still breathing," he pronounced.

While Doc called for help to move this one pathetic survivor, Kit moved down the passageway that led to the passengers' cabins. The cabin doors were all flung open. One door was ripped from its hinges.

The first two cabins were empty. No doubt their occupants were among the unfortunates above. In a third cabin a sea chest was opened and its contents—women's underthings, nightgowns, stockings, a plain wooden comb, several severe, dark-colored gowns—were strewn about the small space. A narrow door led to an adjoining cabin. Kit waded through the mess and poked her head through the door.

She immediately regretted her inquisitiveness. A middle-aged woman and a young girl lay sprawled in positions that made their mistreatment obvious. The girl looked scarcely into her teens. Her limbs had stiffened in the obscene position in which the pirates had left her. Her face still wore the rictus grin of her agony. The older woman, apparently a servant or nanny, had died no more easily.

Kit felt the blood drain from her face. For a moment she could not tear her eyes away from the grisly scene, so hypnotic was the horror of it. Then her stomach rebelled. Kit's hand flew to her mouth as she fled the room. She brushed Doc aside in her headlong flight to gain the open air. Once topside, she rushed to the rail to let her stomach empty itself into the sea.

A gentle hand landed on her neck, another on her forehead.

"Welcome to the real world," Logan said.

At the moment Kit didn't care that the last shreds of her dignity had been coughed up with the bile from her stomach, or that the insufferable Logan Steele had every right to say "I told you so." The hard-callused hand supporting her head was a comfort. And she was sorely in need of comfort, no matter what the source.

Her heaving stopped. Without thinking, she allowed herself to lean weakly against the broad chest that was so convenient a prop. "Down there . . ." she began in a hoarse voice.

"I can imagine." He set her back from him. "Go across to the *Ice Maiden* with Doc. He could use your help in tending the boy. Try to forget what you saw."

"You knew?"

"No," Logan denied with a shake of his head. "Not until Doc came up a moment ago and told me. But would it have made any difference, Katarina? You would insist on having your own way."

"I..."

"Just do as I say. For once. Now go."

His face reflected none of the gloating victory Kit expected, just troubled sympathy. The blue eyes were dark, the mouth a tight, narrow line.

He gave her a gentle push in Doc's direction. "Go," he repeated.

Doc pursed his lips in concentration as he bent over the *Carrie Ann's* young survivor, laboring to clean the dirt and gore from the open cut creasing the boy's ribs. Kit stood by his side, handing him clean toweling when he asked for it and holding the heavy lantern at just the spot he demanded. Her clothing was smeared with blood, as was her face. It was fortunate that Doc had commandeered breeches and shirt from one of the more slender crewmen. He had demanded that she change into the masculine attire and tie her hair back from her face before she assumed the role of his assistant. It would not do, the doctor insisted, that she be put ashore in Barbados looking as if she had just stepped from a slaughterhouse.

"Fascinating," Doc mumbled as he worked. "In spite of all the blood, the blade missed anything vital. If we can keep the wound from putrefying, the boy should be up and about in no time."

Kit mumbled noncommittally. She was having trouble keeping her stomach down where it belonged. It took all her concentration to keep her queasiness at bay.

"Move the lantern," Doc ordered. "There. That's better."

A low moan was torn from the patient's throat.

"He's awakening," Kit warned the old physician.

Doc looked up from his task as the boy moaned again and jerked himself half off the table where they were tending him.

"Hold him, girl! Hang the lantern up there. Yes, that's

good enough. Now hold him while I finish. If he moves the wrong way, it'll be the end of him."

Kit took the boy by the shoulders and pushed him back flat on the table. He cried out and jerked again. For once in her life Kit was glad she was tall and strong, not petite and delicate like Mavis Edmond or Elizabeth Rogers.

The boy's eyes opened and he stared wildly into her face.

"Try to lie still," she encouraged quietly. "You're going to be fine."

At the sight of her the boy only struggled more. His moans turned to loud cries.

"God! Oh, God! Leave me alone!"

"Hold him still!" Doc ordered impatiently.

The boy's cries rose to screams. "Don't kill me, Cap'n Jackal. I ain't seen nuthin'!"

"You're with friends!" Kit explained in what she hoped was a soothing voice. "The pirates are gone. Friends! We're friends!"

Kit's calming words fell on deaf ears. The boy was in another world, it seemed, where the Jackal and his men beset him from all sides.

"Stay away!" It was a plea rather than a demand. "Cap'n Jackal! Please don't kill me. No! No!"

Peter Van Halen came to Kit's rescue. His hands replaced hers on the boy's shoulders. Kit backed away, and the boy calmed.

"Get out. Get out." Doc waved her back. "He mustn't see you again if he's going to react like a madman."

Kit tried to stop the trembling of her hands as she backed out of the little infirmary. Her heart pounded. Her mouth was dry. Imagine being mistaken for a bloody pirate. The Jackal, no less!

"It seems your appearance upset the lad."

Logan had just climbed down from above. His voice made Kit jump. She merely nodded and pressed her hands together to stop their shaking. She was too upset to meet the knave's mocking tone with the sharp retort it deserved.

"He thought I was . . . he thought I was a pirate."

Logan took in her appearance with thoughtful eyes. "I can't say that I blame him," he commented. "You do look thoroughly disreputable. I would certainly take you for a pirate."

She slapped his hand aside as he reached out and turned her face to examine it in profile.

"Don't touch me!" Her nerves were frayed beyond repair, and Logan was the closest target for her venom. "And don't call me a pirate!"

She had too recently seen the results of piratical blood lust, and it sickened her to think that the man standing before her had undoubtedly committed atrocities just as horrible as the brutality visited on the *Carrie Ann*.

"You may be proud of what you are," she said, her nostrils flaring in anger and disgust, "but I would die before sinking to such a level. Pirate, indeed!"

She turned and fled up the companionway.

The days that followed were a nightmare of waiting. Kit suspected that the pirate Steele wanted to be rid of her as much as she wanted to be off his ship, but his every attempt to set her ashore was foiled. For three days the *Ice Maiden* was forced to seek shelter in a hidden cove, like a fox crouching in its hole. The hounds, in the form of two British frigates, were sniffing around the Barbadian coast with far too much diligence. Even at night the coast patrol made it impossible to move without detection.

Kit paced the quarterdeck like a caged lioness. The stern cabin was not large enough to contain her restlessness. Tonight would be the night they would be successful, she thought. Since midmorning the sun had been hidden by clouds, and by sunset the heavy layers of gray had swept so low they seemed to touch the sullen sea. The moon that had shone so brightly and revealingly on the previous nights was hidden from sight. Not a single silvery ray pierced the blackness. A cool breeze was heavy with the threat of rain. It was a perfect night, Kit thought, for a pirate frigate to go skulking along the coast to Half Moon Bay and set an unwanted passenger safely ashore. Once she was home, the whole British Navy could descend on the pirates for all she cared. Logan Steele and his crew of cutthroats could sink to the bottom of the sea, and the human race would be better by far for his demise.

As if her thoughts had conjured him from the darkness, Logan materialized at her side, very much alive and showing no inclination to grant her silent wish by throwing himself over the rail. Kit turned her face away, trying to ignore the impact of his presence.

"We'll be weighing anchor shortly," he said.

"Good." The one syllable was frosted with icicles.

"You should get home tonight. Even if the British are patrolling, they'll never see us in this weather."

"I suppose you think I should thank you for setting me ashore in one piece."

"You might." There was the hint of a smile underlying Logan's voice. "After all, my men did pluck you out of a nasty situation."

"And deposited me right into another one."

"Indeed, Katarina, I think you've been well-treated, considering the circumstances."

"Well-treated?" she scoffed. "Carried off to sea and held on this ship for three wretched days while your crew glare at me—that's when they're not snickering in my face."

"Ah, well," Logan said with a smile, "piratical life seldom breeds good manners."

"So I've learned. And you! You're the worst of the lot."

Logan lifted a questioning brow.

"Don't think I haven't noticed the name of this loathsome vessel!" Kit told him in an acid voice.

Kit had heard the name that the young men of Barbados had dubbed her—Ice Maiden. Oliver had once thrown it in her face that even the slaves tittered about it in their huts.

"I suppose everyone aboard this villainous vessel has been laughing behind my back, thinking what a jolly good joke it is every time they see that name painted on the hull. And you've enjoyed it immensely, I have no doubt."

A slow smile spread across Logan's face. Even in the fast-fading light he could see the sparks shooting from those eyes of velvet brown.

"You, Captain Steele, are an ungentlemanly, ill-mannered

cur, an intolerable blackguard, and an inconsiderate lout! Well-treated, indeed!''

Logan chuckled and shook his head. "Do you think such a small bit of fun is mistreatment, Katarina? You still have a lot to learn."

Kit threw him a look of disgust, then turned away and lifted her nose a bit higher into the air.

"In truth, I think you owe me and my crew a debt for not venting our anger on you, seeing that you're helpless here in our midst. There are a few ex-slaves and indentureds on this ship who wouldn't mind seeing your head on a pike. They hold slave owners in low regard."

"And I suppose a simple thank-you won't do." Kit regarded him warily. She should have known better than to think this rogue would let her go with no profit to himself. "What do you want?" she asked. "Money?"

"I've no use for your money, Katarina."

That infuriating, mocking smile was back on his face. It seemed to Kit that the scoundrel was never without it.

"What, then? It's obvious you want something."

Logan shifted his gaze from Kit to the sea. "It seems I am in need of your help," he said, suddenly serious. "I need a way to meet your honored uncle."

Logan thought back to the hour before, when he had met in Van Halen's cabin with his four officers. For a week they had been trying to come up with a plan to free thirteen of his crewmen—a prize crew sailing a captured sloop back to Tortuga. The little ship had run afoul of the Spanish, and its crew was imprisoned in Santo Domingo. No one had been able to propose a scheme that wouldn't land the rescuers in prison with the unfortunates who were already there, until Logan had listened to Kit's proud recitation of her unusual family connections. Since then he had been hatching a wild scheme in his mind, and as little as he relished the company of Katarina St. John, he had finally admitted that her help was the only lifeline for his comrades.

Kit's eyes opened wide with amazement as she listened to Logan explain his needs. Then a soft chuckle bubbled up in her throat, growing within a few seconds to outright laughter.

"You're mad!" she chortled. "Absolutely mad! You think

I would deceive my own uncle to help you free a pack of murdering thieves? You've lost your mind!''

"Have I, now?" He sounded not in the least discouraged.

"You have! You can hold me on this wretched ship till Judgment Day. You can threaten me with anything you please. I won't betray my own flesh and blood, so do your worst!"

"A noble speech," he conceded. "But I'm not asking you to betray your uncle. He doesn't need the lives of my men, and whatever information he seeks he will have already gained from them. No man lasts overly long under torture, and Spanish jailers are the best I know at inflicting pain."

"Oh, no!" Kit denied. "You can't justify this with your facile words. You can talk and threaten all the night long, and I still won't be a party to this villainy. I should have known better than to trust your word."

"You mistake my intent." Logan's words were stiff, as though she had insulted him. "You will be set ashore this night. I promised you would come to no harm on this ship, and I meant it. I am a man who keeps my promises."

Kit arched a haughty brow. "Then there is no reason in the world why I should help you."

Even in the darkness she could see the contemptuous twist to his smile.

"I had hoped to appeal to your sense of fair play—to your honor. You owe me a debt, Katarina St. John. Can you think of a better way to repay it?"

She turned abruptly away, unable to face that knowing smile. "You're a fine one to prate of honor—a murderer, a mutineer, a thieving pirate. What do you know of honor?"

"I know enough to recognize its lack."

The night air seemed to shiver with the tension between them. Finally Kit turned back toward him. Her mouth was pressed into a tight line as she desperately tried to stop her lower lip from quivering.

"Damn you!" she said in a broken voice. "I'm not some hoyden to go sailing around the Caribbean with the likes of you and your villainous crew. I just want to go home."

Sensing her surrender, Logan allowed himself a gloating

smile. "So go home, Katarina. Go home and count your slaves and weep on your brother's shoulder. I'll send a message when and where I want to meet you. It will be several days hence. I need more actors before we can begin this play." Satisfied he had won, he turned to walk away.

Kit drew herself up to her full proud height and lifted her chin in determination. "Wait one minute, Captain Steele." His name rolled off her tongue like sour vinegar. "You think you've won, do you?"

"Haven't I?" He turned and gave her a devilish grin. His white teeth flashed in the night, and she itched to scatter them with her balled fist.

"This is a monstrous task you've set for me. More, I think, than my debt demands. I think I will demand something in return."

"Indeed?"

"I have a need of my own, Logan Steele, and I think you might fit the bill very well."

The saner part of Kit's mind screamed at her to stop. But she plunged on. It was the only way out. She would see just what price the scoundrel was willing to pay for her help.

"And what is your need, mistress?" he asked in an amused voice.

"How can I put this delicately?" Kit wondered aloud. "You see, Captain Steele, my brother, Oliver, thinks of nothing but marrying me off to an odious friend of his, and though he can't force me to the match, he plagues me constantly."

"I don't see how I can be of help."

"Oh, you can." A wicked gleam twinkled in Kit's eyes. "If another man should come to claim my hand, then Oliver would certainly have to cease his harping."

All amusement fled from Logan's voice. "You want me to marry you?"

Kit laughed, savoring his dismay. "Marriage? Don't flatter yourself, you loathsome pirate! I merely need a suitor— an acceptable gentleman to whom I will appear to give my affection, thus easing Oliver's concern about my spinsterhood."

"You're joking!" Logan accused hopefully.

"Not at all," Kit assured him. "You have some ill-gotten

wealth, I assume. And you at least have the appearance of a gentleman, if not the conscience. Sail into Bridgetown like a legitimate merchant. Buy a house and establish yourself as a man of rank and breeding. Then come courting. And be sure it's in full view of my brother." She cocked a brow in coy mischief. She hadn't felt so good since first setting foot aboard this wretched ship. "A man with your talent at chicanery ought to be able to pull it off."

"Ridiculous! I'd be recognized."

"I think not." Kit smiled wickedly. "No one would recognize you for the pitiful slave who escaped Greenhaven's stockade."

"You ask the impossible!"

"Tsk!" she sighed. "Think of those poor men languishing in my uncle's prison. How badly do you want them freed?"

Logan started to retort, but stopped and snapped his mouth shut. She could almost feel the heat of his helpless anger as he turned and stared into the night. Check and mate, she chortled to herself. It was all she could do to keep from laughing aloud.

When he turned back and spoke, his voice was calmer than Kit expected. Some of the amused lilt had returned.

"Faith, woman! You demand a great deal."

"Little enough, considering what you ask of me."

Logan sighed, and there was a quality to that sigh that sparked a hint of suspicion in Kit's mind.

"It's a bargain, then," he conceded. "You get what you want, and I get what I want. Fair enough?"

Kit hesitated. Was that a smirk on his face? Or was the darkness deceiving her. Why did she feel as though she had backed herself into a corner?

She summoned her steadiest voice. "A bargain. As you say."

Before she knew it, Logan was close in front of her, his big hands on her shoulders and his breath ruffling her hair.

"Let's seal it, then."

His lips came down on hers before Kit could object. His mouth was soft and sensuous, exploring, seeking. His tongue probed, and against her will Kit's lips opened to his quest. He smelled of the sea and fresh air. The prickly roughness of his face set her nerves atingle. The intimate invasion of his tongue should have been nauseating, but instead it was delicious. Everything he was doing to her felt right—so right. Kit felt her soul was beginning to melt when he pulled away.

For a moment she stood as though stunned. Then her senses returned. Her face flamed in humiliation. She raised her hand to strike a blow, but her wrist was caught in the steel trap of Logan's fingers before her palm reached his face.

"An ill-considered move, my lady."

He was laughing at her, damn the man! Kit could hear the mockery in his voice.

"The bargain is well sealed," he continued. He brought her captured hand down to her side and cautiously left it there, poised to defend himself again if need be. "I believe we are committed, little Katarina."

Before Kit could reply, Logan turned and disappeared into the darkness. Muffled by the fog that was closing the gap between clouds and sea, his voice commanded up anchor.

Kit turned and pounded furiously on the quarterdeck rail. If Logan Steele thought he'd bested her, he had a lot to learn. If he thought to scare her out of holding him to his task, he would have to think of something better than one stupid kiss!

She stopped her frustrated abuse of the rail and let her head sink into her hands. One stupid kiss and she had been ready to . . . what had she been ready to do? What happened to her whenever that scoundrel touched her?

Kit stared into the darkness and wondered what would come of the adventure before her. Stupid, silly fool. Why could she have not simply and sensibly said no?

Chapter 6

"Wake up, love!"

Mandy's painfully cheerful voice broke into Kit's dreams. One eyelid creaked open, then closed again, still heavy with sleep.

"Ye'll feel much better after a bath, me love. Come on now. Up with ye!"

Kit mumbled into her pillow, reluctant to move. The dreams that had moved through her slumber were fading before this rude intrusion of daylight. They had been quite pleasant, leaving her with a feeling of fulfillment that was almost wickedly carnal. Reluctant to let them fade into complete oblivion, Kit let her mind drift back toward sleep. An image swam into focus. Logan Steele.

Kit's eyes flew open with dismay. Logan Steele! The image wore a devilish grin and regarded her with a proprietary intimacy that jolted the last vestiges of sleep from her mind. How dare that blackguard invade her dreams! If he had to haunt her so, he might at least have the decency to appear in a nightmare, where pirates belonged.

"'Ere ye go, now!" Mandy threw back the bedclothes and held out a silk dressing robe for Kit to wrap around herself. "The bathing chamber's all warm and steamy. I'll be in t' 'elp ye wash yer 'air." The redhead clucked and tsked as her charge reluctantly crawled from bed and into the robe, then stumbled toward the bathing chamber.

Kit sank gratefully into the tub of warm water and let the heat drive the stiffness from her limbs. How long had she slept? she wondered. The sunlight spearing through the louvered window shutter was bright and hot. The day must be well along toward noon.

Sinking more deeply into the water, Kit let her heavy eyelids drop. Only twelve hours had she been home and already her little adventure seemed like a half-forgotten dream—as unreal as the image of Logan Steele conjured up in her sleep. Had she really been rowed ashore at the black midnight hour by pirates? Had she really spent these last few days balanced on the life-and-death fulcrum of a criminal's goodwill? It seemed impossible.

Just as Kit had about decided the whole escapade was a dream, Mandy bustled in from the bedroom. The maid stooped beside the tub and started to lather a lilac-scented shampoo into Kit's hair.

"It's so good t'ave ye back, miss. When those rascals jumped us on the road, I thought we were both doomed. That I did! And then when Mr. Oliver couldn't find no trace o' ye, I thought ye was dead for certain. Or worse," she whispered dramatically.

Apparently everyone else had thought the same thing. Kit's midnight return had roused a house full of servants who had looked at her as though she were a ghost. Mr. Raleigh had turned white as a sheet. Mrs. Calloway the housekeeper had swooned, and parlor maids Susan and Lucy had roused themselves from their beds and regarded her in wide-eyed disbelief. Oliver had not been there to greet her, having set sail to search for her within hours of the kidnapping.

"Do ye feel more alive now, me pet?"

"I feel like I could use another ten hours of sleep." Kit rose reluctantly from the tub and allowed Mandy to wrap her in a voluminous towel.

"It's no wonder, considerin' what ye've been through. But ye told me t' wake ye before noon. Ye said ye 'ad much to do."

Kit sighed. There was much to do. But she wished she had been a bit more generous with herself. Surely the plantation could have survived a few more hours while she slept. She crossed to the full-length wall mirror. Her face was stamped with weariness, with dull eyes framed in faint mauve shadows. "I'll wear a riding habit," Kit said finally. "The green one... no, the red one."

She discarded the damp towel and donned the chemise and petticoats Mandy had laid out on the bed. Her image in the mirror looked bonier than before. She'd lost weight while enjoying the pirates' hospitality. The image that stared at her out of the mirror looked like an overly tall twelve-year-old hoyden, Kit thought. She smiled, revealing small, even white teeth. To her critical eyes the smile didn't help. Her coloring was all wrong, her frame too thin and too tall, her hair too heavy and hopelessly unruly with its stubborn waves.

"Come over 'ere in the sun, miss, and let me brush yer 'air dry before ye put on yer gown."

Kit obeyed, only too happy to get away from her image in the mirror. She leaned back her head and closed her eyes, enjoying the rhythmic strokes of the brush.

"Mandy?" she ventured in a tentative voice.

"Yes, miss?"

"Just how plain am I?"

Mandy snorted. "What kind o' question is that?"

"One that requires an honest answer," Kit replied.

"Now I've never been aught but honest with ye, love. Ye know that."

"So answer my question."

Mandy thought a moment. "Ye're not plain at all, miss. The truth is, I've always thought ye were quite lovely in yer own way."

"I thought you were going to be honest," Kit reminded her.

"That were an honest answer, miss. Ye're not all peaches an' cream, like the fashionable gents moon over. But I'll tell ye true, love—an' I should know—there's not a man alive who would mind wakin' up t' yer face next t' 'is on the pillow. Gents' tastes don't always just stick t' fashion, ye know. There's a lot o' different shapes o' female, an' it seems t' me that fer every shape we come in, there's some gent that likes it. Why, I remember in a bawdy 'ouse where I worked years ago, there was this girl who... well..." Mandy lifted a brow at the memory and thought better of her story. "But that were a long time ago. Not that things 'ave changed much. You trust me, miss. If I'd 'ad yer face and figure in my former line o' work, I could've got some gent to set me up in a nice 'ouse wit' me own carriage an' servants t' fetch an' carry."

"Then why do men fall all over themselves paying homage to those simpering ladies who posture and flutter their lashes, but the fellows who come courting to Greenhaven treat me like their brother—then check with our accounts man to determine my worth? Tell me that!"

Mandy paused in her brushing and met Kit's troubled gaze in the small mirror that hung above the dressing table. "Perhaps, love, it's because ye treat the gents like they was yer brothers. That's when ye're not treatin' 'em like they was gutter trash. Even the tenderest bud don't get picked, me dear, if it's surrounded by thistles."

Kit looked thoughtful for a moment, then grimaced. "Oh, bother! It's really of no consequence. I haven't ever met a man who would be worth the trouble!"

Mandy smiled and resumed her brushing. "Aye. Perhaps not. There aren't many on this godforsaken island, I'll tell ye!" She smoothed back Kit's ebony mane and caught it at the nape of her neck.

Kit looked into the mirror critically. "Let's try something different today—something a little more... feminine."

Mandy raised a brow in wonder. The mistress had always shown nothing but impatience when Mandy tried to adorn her hair in a fashion more becoming than the plain twisted knot she habitually wore.

"Miss Kit?" Her voice was suspicious. "Have you got a gent on yer mind?"

"Certainly not!" Kit had the grace to blush.

"Where did you say you've been for the past four days?"

"With a shipload of filthy pirates, that's where. Hardly a place to find a gentleman friend."

"Aye, love. An' ye'd best remember that." Mandy scowled into the mirror at the image of Kit's rosily blushing face. Something was certainly going on with Kit St. John, and whatever or whoever it was, Mandy didn't approve.

Simon Brownlow was waiting to see her when Kit finally descended the stairs. Raleigh announced the overseer's presence in disparaging tones and suggested that miss might care to break her fast before admitting the man to her presence.

"Oh, that's all right, Raleigh." Kit ignored a disapproving twitch of the butler's lip. "Tell Mr. Brownlow I'll see him in my office."

Brownlow welcomed her safe return with polite phrases that rang with the man's insincerity. Kit suspected the overseer would pay to get rid of her if he thought he could get away with it. The idea ignited a spark of suspicion in her mind, but she immediately dismissed it. Brownlow couldn't have hired the ghouls that attacked her carriage on the road that night. He hadn't known she was spending the day in Bridgetown.

"We had a group of five blacks run last night," he told her when the preliminary courtesies were completed.

Kit was surprised. With the exception of Logan Steele and his fellow convicts, Greenhaven had never had a single slave try to escape. They knew they lived better at Greenhaven than they could anywhere else on the island.

"Did you get them back?" she asked.

Brownlow gave a snort of disgust. "No," he admitted. "They disappeared. I don't know where. The dogs got the trail, then lost it. It's as though they suddenly sprouted wings and flew away."

"Where did the trail lead?" An uncomfortable suspicion was growing in Kit's mind.

"That's the thing that doesn't make sense." Brownlow frowned and scratched his none-too-clean head. "The trail led toward the beach."

Kit sighed, remembering the black men and women who had climbed aboard Logan's ship that first night. She would be willing to wager that her five slaves had gone the same route. But what on earth was that blackguard pirate doing with escaped slaves? Was he luring them aboard his ship with promises of freedom and then reselling them? It seemed the only answer. And that villain had had the arrogance to chastise *her* for dealing in slaves!

"Keep looking for them," Kit instructed the overseer. "But if you find them, bring them here to me. I have a few questions to ask."

"Yes, miss."

"And, Mr. Brownlow, I don't want to see a mark on them. Understand?"

"Yes, miss," he growled, already starting for the door.

Two days later Oliver returned. He greeted Kit with a shout of joy and a hug that could have crushed a bear. Wrapped in her brother's fond embrace, Kit wondered how she had ever had so many uncharitable thoughts about him. Hadn't he ignored the pain of his still healing arm and set sail in hopes of finding her?

"Kit!" He pushed her back to arm's length and swept her, head to toe, with assessing eyes. "Kit, my love, I can't believe you're here! And all in one piece! You can't guess the things I've imagined, or how worried I've been!"

He did indeed look worried, Kit observed, and her heart melted toward him. It was good to have someone who cared about her, even if that someone did get a bit difficult at times.

"I'm fine, Oliver, as you can see."

"I do see, little sister. You look much better than I feel!" He shook his head. "You can't imagine the confusion here with that woman of yours screeching out the tale that you'd been attacked. And when we searched the road and beach, you were gone without a trace. All we found was one of the villains laid out with his head smashed up against a rock. God, Kit! I was frantic!"

He gave her another hug—gentler this time in deference to his injured arm. "I decided they'd taken you off the island, and that very night I set sail in pursuit. But I found nothing. I'm not sure I even knew what I was looking for."

"Well, I'm back now, Oliver, so you can stop your worrying." Kit took his arm and guided him toward the small family parlor, where they could talk in privacy.

"What happened?" he demanded. "Where have you been? Are you sure you're all right?"

Kit waved the servants from the room and sat down with her brother on the settee. "It's very confusing, Oliver. I'm not sure I myself understand what happened."

"Did you recognize anyone in this band that carted you off? If I ever catch up to them, heads will roll. You can be sure of that!"

"It was dark when the carriage was attacked," Kit explained. "I couldn't really see any faces. And as for the people I've been with since that night... they weren't really connected with the attack. In fact, I owe them my life."

She remembered silently that Logan Steele had conceived his own method of retrieving that debt, but as three days had passed without word from him, she was more sure than ever that he wasn't going to collect.

"Why do you say that?"

Kit smiled at Oliver's frown of confusion. "They rescued me from the original attackers and took me to safety on their ship."

"Ship?" Oliver frowned. "Damn! What ship was this?"

"I... I don't know what ship," Kit lied. "I didn't think to ask. Stupid of me, but after that attack, I was a bit confused. They were engaged in... in some urgent business that they couldn't delay, or I would have returned home sooner."

She couldn't very well tell him that her rescuers were rascally pirates. The truth would have disastrous consequences for her reputation, and Oliver's peace of mind.

"It was all rather humdrum, really, except..."

"Except what?"

"We came upon a most dreadful ship. It had been attacked by the Jackal."

Oliver's scowl got blacker by the second. "What made you think it was the Jackal who attacked this ship?"

"Only that the captain of the ship I was on told me so. He said no other pirate is quite so brutal."

Oliver looked thoughtful. Kit wondered if he had seen any trace of the infamous pirate. He would have been at sea looking for her the morning the *Carrie Ann* was attacked.

"It was truly awful, Oliver. I can't seem to get it out of my mind. It makes me almost wish you weren't out there sailing the same seas as that monster."

Oliver laughed humorlessly. "You don't need to worry about me, sister mine. I can take care of myself. And that bloody fool captain of yours shouldn't have let you anywhere near that ship." Oliver looked away, massaged his forehead with a hand, then breathed a morose sigh. "I hope this rescuer of yours doesn't come around demanding a reward from me. I suppose his intentions were good, but he certainly made a mess of things."

"Whatever do you mean?" Kit eyed him suspiciously. When Oliver got that look in his eye, she could be sure that he'd been up to trouble.

"I suppose the truth will out, so I'd best tell you." He sighed again. "You would have come to no harm from those fellows who stopped your carriage. In fact, very shortly you would have been gallantly saved by the one who was supposed to come to your aid."

"Indeed? I think you had better explain."

Oliver stood and started to pace uneasily. "You're going to be angry. I can hear it in your voice already. But really, Kit, I did it for your own good—for your future happiness."

"Just what did you do?"

"I . . . I hired those fellows to stop your carriage. Now, don't get that look on your face. It was all planned out very neatly. They were to scare you and cart you off to the beach. Then Nick was going to rescue you. Only, those other meddling fools got to you first."

"Of all the stupid . . . !" So it hadn't been her imagination! Nick Basey really had been on the beach that night, waving frantically as she was shoved aboard the *Ice Maiden's* longboat.

"I did it for your own good, dammit!" Oliver raised a hand as though to ward off his sister's anger. She stood and stalked toward him, looking as though she would dearly love to scratch the eyes from his face.

"My own good?" Kit exploded. "How is having me hauled from my carriage and carried upside down over some ape's shoulder supposed to be for my good, Oliver? Those fellows you hired weren't exactly gentlemen, you know. One nearly knocked my head off—twice! Mandy or I could have been hurt! Killed even! And what about poor Adam? He's still walking like a drunkard because of that blow to his head!"

"Now, Kit . . . !"

"Why in the name of God did you do such a thing?"

Oliver shrugged and backed up from her slow, threatening advance. "I thought you needed some romance—some excitement in your life. I thought if Nick rescued you, you might see what a fine, brave fellow he really is."

"Of all the . . . ! Oliver! You are such a nitwit! I don't

want to hear your excuses! I don't even want to look at you!" Kit clenched her fist, only with difficulty holding it back from flying into her brother's face. Oliver made haste to back up out of reach.

"Now, Kit!" he repeated.

Kit turned away and kicked at the settee to vent some of her anger. "If you say 'Now, Kit' one more time I'm going to . . . I'm going to . . . Lord! How could you presume? Oh!"

"Pardon me, Master St. John, Miss St. John. . . ." Raleigh stepped through the door and regarded them with a bland face. "There is a messenger at the door asking for Miss St. John."

Kit's dark eyes snapped with fury. "Not now, Raleigh!"

"Oh, yes!" Oliver grabbed at the chance to escape. "Show him in!"

The messenger was a youngster who looked to be still in his early teens. His sandy-colored hair was a curly, unruly mop and his face was covered with a mask of freckles and rapidly fading bruises. Kit recognized him at once. His name was Tom Trelawny, formerly of the *Carrie Ann*. Now that he was on the mend, he did double duty as assistant boatswain and Logan Steele's cabin boy.

The boy bowed with great dignity while handing Kit the missive. Then, glancing at Oliver, he abruptly froze. For a mere second he seemed to stagger, and behind the freckles his face went white.

Kit paid little heed to Tom. Her hand shook as she pulled the note from its envelope. The message was brief. Her bluff had been called. Praying that Oliver didn't notice her agitation, she stuffed the note back into its envelope and thought fast.

"Tell your . . . uh . . . your mistress that I gladly accept her invitation."

Keeping his eyes on Kit, Tom smiled and bowed again, then turned and walked out of the room.

"I say!" Oliver objected. "What an impudent-looking lad. Haven't I seen him around before?"

Kit improvised. "He's one of Mavis Edmond's footmen. The note was from her."

"And what does that twitterbrain want?"

"She and Lionel are giving a ball at the end of next week. Mavis has invited me to come and spend some time with her before the event." She crumpled the envelope. "I think I'll go, Oliver—just to get away from you before I'm tempted to push your face into that pile of manure outside the stable. I need to get away from you and cool off.'

Oliver's mouth tightened to a disapproving line at Kit's unladylike threat. But he sensed that now was not the time to bring such a lapse of manners to his sister's attention.

"And one more thing, Oliver."

"Yes?" the long-suffering brother replied.

"If your precious Nick Basey had rescued me that night, don't be too sure I would have fallen into his arms in gratitude. Knowing Nick, he would have tried one of his loathsome kisses and I would have been obliged to knock the stuffings from him and leave him for the beach scavengers. And don't think I wouldn't have!"

Oliver could think of no reply to that outrageous statement. He could only glare at his sister's back as she stalked from the room.

The whole scheme had been ridiculously easy to arrange, Kit mused as she peered out into the wet darkness. But she would certainly look like a complete fool if that blackguard pirate didn't appear.

"What time did 'e tell you to meet 'im?" Mandy's whisper was scarcely audible over the soft pattering of rain on the palmetto that sheltered them.

"Midnight," Kit replied just as softly.

"I don't think 'e's coming. Let's go back, love."

"He'll be here."

Kit didn't know why they were whispering. There was certainly no one on the beach to hear them. "You can go back if you wish," she said in a bolder voice. "You needn't have come in the first place."

Kit had taken Mandy into her confidence. She had been inexplicably excited after rereading Logan's note in the privacy of her bedchamber, and she needed to talk to someone who could understand her feelings. She hadn't really expected to hear from Logan Steele ever again, but now that she had, an unruly flock of butterflies had been set loose in her stomach.

Mandy had been prompt to quash the butterflies, though. She had been outraged at what her charge was planning to do. Kit could still hear the tongue-lashing she had received.

"Ye're goin' off with a filthy pirate?!" Mandy had asked, hands on her ample hips and eyes flashing indignant fire. "Ye've taken leave of yer senses, girl!"

Kit had tried to explain the bargain, the debt she owed. Mandy had brushed her explanations aside.

"Ye owe the scum nothin'," the plump redhead had countered. "Didn't ye just say yer brother set us up for the whole thing? Ye wouldn't 'ave been 'urt, so 'ow do ye figure ye owe this rascal pirate anything?"

"It makes no difference," Kit had insisted. "Besides, you're making something out of nothing. This fellow is a gentleman... of sorts."

"Ye don't know what ye're gettin' into, that's fer sure, miss." Mandy had shaken her head despairingly. "Ye're playing with fire, an' I don't care how much of a gent this fellow seems. Ye should listen to a body who's known every sort of man there is to know—pirates included, me love. Ye're gettin' in t' the water a ways over yer head, an' yer likely t' get swept out by the tide."

Mandy had delivered similar lectures all the way to the Edmond plantation, but Kit had ignored her. Mavis had greeted them with some surprise, but when Kit had confided the purpose of her visit, she was eager to help. Kit had known she would be. A petite, ethereal beauty with soft brown hair and quiet gray eyes, Mavis Carter Edmond had been Kit's best friend since they both were scarcely out of the cradle. Mischievous little Mavis had always been drawn by Kit's brashness, and over the long years of their friendship she had never balked at doing anything Kit wanted her to do. As a result, Mavis had endured a somewhat more adventurous childhood than she might have otherwise had.

The beach continued to be peaceful, the soft patter of rain the only sound other than the faraway thunder of surf pounding the offshore shoals. Where was the rogue? Kit wondered. Did he expect her to wait all night?

"Ye can still back out, love," Mandy reminded her. " 'E couldn't do a thing to ye."

"I will not back out," Kit answered firmly. "I'm a woman of my word. St. Johns always keep their promises."

"A promise to a thieving scoundrel of a pirate doesn't count as a promise."

"Stop worrying," Kit advised. "Nothing is going to go wrong."

At least, nothing *should* go wrong, Kit hoped. The story would be that she had taken sick while visiting Mavis and was confined to her room. Mandy and Mavis would both cover for her, and if all went well she would be back in time to make an appearance at the Edmonds' ball. Mavis had thought the whole scheme terribly romantic. Kit had assured her that Logan Steele was anything but romantic, but she had not been able to bring her friend down from her flights of fancy.

" 'E's not coming, love. It must be well past midnight."

Kit sighed. Mandy had insisted on coming to the rendezvous point with her—to see this villainous rogue for herself, she had said. Kit had seen no harm in bringing her. She had not fancied waiting alone on the beach for the pirate to come. But now she was regretting it. She was nervous enough without Mandy's voice echoing the doubts in her own head.

Kit was almost ready to agree with Mandy when she heard the quiet splash of an oar.

"He's coming," she whispered.

The rain-scented night suddenly took on a new vibrancy. Kit's heart pounded in her chest as she saw the *Ice Maiden*'s longboat become visible as a dark shadow against an even darker sea. The crew of four jumped out and steadied the little craft in the gentle surge of the water. Then a tall figure stepped apart from the other three. He walked up past the water's edge and stood for a moment looking around him. His long legs were spread apart, as if he were balanced to spring in any direction. One hand rested on the hilt of his rapier.

Kit could feel Logan's eyes searching the concealing vegetation, could almost imagine the icy-blue intensity of his gaze. Was he even bigger than she remembered? Or was it simply the darkness that made his figure loom so threateningly there at the water's edge.

Kit motioned Mandy to stay out of sight, then impulsively kissed the maid on the cheek. With her heart in her throat, she grabbed her small bundle of clothing and walked out to join the man who awaited her.

The maid watched her go, noting the stiff set of her shoulders and the proud tilt of her chin. The lass was scared out of her wits, Mandy thought, and well she might be. She was a lamb walking straight into a lion's den—a lamb who thought she was a lioness, no doubt. Mandy continued to watch as the big pirate picked Kit up in his arms and carried her through the water to the waiting boat. The crew turned the little craft until its prow pointed toward the open sea. She heard the splash of oars for only a brief moment after the longboat had disappeared into blackness, and then nothing.

Foolish little lass, Mandy thought. When next I see you, if ever again I see you, you'll not be the same girl who walked down this beach. Foolish, foolish little lass.

Chapter 7

The *Ice Maiden* sailed into Santo Domingo harbor as though she had every right to be there. At her masthead, the flag of Imperial Spain snapped in the morning breeze as the frigate calmly slipped within reach of the forbidding fortress that guarded the channel. The cannon mounted on the fortress battlements seemed to follow their progress like malevolent, unwinking black eyes. But the guns were mercifully silent. Logan wondered if they would be as silent when the *Ice Maiden* left. If she left.

Peter Van Halen snapped the spyglass closed. "That's the

first hurdle," he said. He offered the glass to his captain. "Want to take a look at that armament?"

"I know it's more than enough to send us to the bottom," Logan said with a wry smile. "That's all I need to know."

Van Halen shook his head. "This plan had better work, Logan. I feel like a rabbit poking its nose into a fox's den."

"It will work," Logan assured him. "All you have to do is stand there and look Spanish. And don't let anyone on the dock hear that Dutch accent of yours."

Both men were resplendent in uniforms of the Spanish Navy. The only others visible on deck and in the rigging were the renegade Spaniards in the *Ice Maiden*'s crew—a number which in recent days had climbed to ten. In the hold below were chained the fifteen members of the crew who were Englishmen. The remainder of the frigate's complement—two Dutchmen, one Portuguese, and one Frenchman—had all been ordered to stay in their quarters and not show their faces abovedecks unless there was a fight.

Logan turned to the girl who stood stiffly beside him. Her face was pale beneath its natural golden tint. The knuckles of the hand that grasped the rail were white.

"Are you all right?" he asked.

"I'm fine," she snapped. "But I think this is a lunatic scheme. I've thought so from the very beginning."

"It's the lunatic schemes that most often succeed."

Logan smiled wolfishly. He looked as if he enjoyed sailing into the jaws of death, Kit thought. She hadn't seen him look so alive since they had set sail for Hispaniola four days ago. He had been reserved, distant, and icily polite with her, snappish with his crew.

From the moment he had brought her aboard the ship and deposited her in the cabin that the first officer had vacated for her use, the *Ice Maiden*'s captain had almost completely ignored her. Kit might have convinced herself that Logan was almost unaware of her presence on board his ship except for the few occasions she had caught his gaze upon her. That gaze was intense, deeply contemplative, anything but unaware. The heat of it seared her. Kit remembered only too clearly Mandy's warnings, and at times it occurred to her that she was putting far too much faith in Logan Steele's scruples, even though she had ample evidence that he had none.

"I hope for your sake that the scheme does work, Captain Steele." Kit gave Logan a malicious smile. "After all, we made a bargain. I would hate to see you swinging at the end of a Spanish rope rather than dancing attendance on me in Barbados."

Logan laughed. "Just you remember that when you speak to your uncle, Katarina."

Less than fifteen minutes after she had passed safely under the cannon of the fortress, the *Ice Maiden* dropped her anchor two cable lengths from the busy wharf. Even before her sails were furled and secured, a boat crowded with Spanish uniforms and muskets departed the dock and headed in their direction.

"Here they come, little Katarina."

Logan squeezed Kit's arm in a gentle grip, and for a moment Kit's breath caught in her throat. It was the approaching danger, she told herself, not Logan's damnable touch, that made her so giddy.

"The part of an outraged Englishwoman should be a natural for you," he said, a hint of laughter in his voice. "Play it well, or we'll end up sharing a cell with the men we came to rescue."

Kit pulled her arm from his light grasp. "I'll see to my part," she assured him coldly. "You see to yours."

The Spanish colonel looked around arrogantly as he mounted the boarding nets and stepped into the waist of the frigate. He was black-haired and black-eyed, with fine features that bespoke generations of aristocratic breeding. With a distrustful sweep of the eyes, he surveyed the ship and her crew as his men clambered one by one over the side and ranged themselves behind him, muskets at the ready. The *Ice Maiden*'s crew stared back with the insolent contempt that veteran seamen feel for the landbound.

"I am Colonel Esteban del Vargas," the Spanish officer announced, "commandant of the King's forces in Santo Domingo." His eyes locked on to Logan. Two cold pools of glittering obsidian, they reminded Kit of the eyes of a snake.

Logan lifted a brow at the colonel's arrogance and met his sneer with a haughty gaze that would have done the most aristocratic Spaniard proud. Never taking his eyes from the commandant's face, he executed a courteous but perfunctory bow.

"Don Hernando Delgado, at your service, Colonel. I have the honor of being second officer aboard His Most Catholic Majesty's frigate *Santa Clara*." Logan prayed that the *Santa Clara* had not made port in Santo Domingo recently. If so, his story would be blown full of holes, and more than likely, so would he.

"Then what are you doing here, Lieutenant?" The Spaniard frowned suspiciously. "And on this ship which is so obviously English."

A smile played around Logan's narrow lips.

"This little vessel is one we took as a prize three days ago off the island of St. Kitts. The captain claimed to be a legitimate trader." He gave the colonel a knowing smile. "But of course we have all heard that story before, have we not?"

"Go on," the Spaniard demanded coldly.

"Captain Enriquez ordered me to Santo Domingo to take care of . . . uh . . . a rather delicate matter. Then I am to effect repairs—if your governor should be so generous—and sail to meet the *Santa Clara* at Vera Cruz in three weeks' time."

Colonel del Vargas was not going to settle for Logan's evasiveness. "And what is this . . . delicate business?" His suspicious eyes roamed the decks, rested on the Spanish seamen who moved unhurriedly about their business, passed with disinterest over Peter leaning casually upon the quarterdeck rail, then came to rest with frightening intensity on Kit. "Might it have something to do with this . . . woman?"

Logan's gaze joined that of the Spanish officer. He looked amazingly relaxed, Kit thought. Her knowledge of Spanish had faded since her mother had died, and she was able to catch only isolated words and phrases of the men's conversation. The Spanish officer sounded suspicious and hostile to her anxious ears, but Logan looked cool and unruffled and utterly confident. He was enjoying himself, Kit decided, and cursed him for a natural-born scoundrel.

"You are very discerning, Colonel."

"Is the woman someone of consequence?"

Kit didn't like the way the Spaniard was looking at her. His eyes seemed to crawl over her from head to foot.

"She claims to be the niece of your honored governor."

The colonel's brows lifted in amazement. He favored Kit with an even closer scrutiny, then gave a short laugh that sounded like a bark. "Ridiculous, Don Hernando. Any fool could see that she is an Englishwoman."

"Very astute of you," Logan acknowledged wryly. "Undoubtedly she is English. But still she claims to be the daughter of Don Juan de Mendez Arguello's youngest sister. Colonel, are you prepared to risk offending your governor by not bothering to confirm or disprove her claim?"

The Spaniard hesitated.

"Perhaps we should let the governor see her for himself," Logan suggested. "If you would be so kind as to convey my request for an audience, you may also tell his excellency that Captain Enriquez of the *Santa Clara* has sent him a small part of the plunder taken from this... pirate ship in recompense for any inconvenience this woman's audacious claim might cause him."

Two hours later Kit and Logan were escorted to the governor's *palacio* by a stiffly formal honor guard. The carriage in which they rode was well-sprung and richly appointed—one of the governor's own, the colonel had informed them. The cushions were crimson velvet, the woodwork dark mahogany—almost the exact color of Logan Steele's hair, Kit noted.

How could the damnable pirate be so calm in the midst of so many well-armed Spaniards? Didn't he realize the myriad of little slips that could betray him, including a slip of her own tongue? If her uncle found out Logan's true identity, the pirate certainly would not be exiting the *palacio* in the plush fashion that he was entering it. That was, if he left it at all.

Logan met Kit's uneasy gaze and gave her a reassuring smile. Kit had to give the scoundrel credit. He didn't lack raw courage, or sheer audaciousness. The spark of excitement in his crystalline-blue eyes sent a little thrill of anticipation coursing through her veins. God help her if she wasn't getting into the mood of this escapade herself!

"Where did you learn to speak such fluent Spanish?" she asked. "It seems that every time I turn around you surprise me with something new."

"My father demanded that all his sons learn French, Spanish, and Dutch." Logan chuckled. "The old fox contended that whether fighting a man or trading with him, it is wise to speak his language."

"Your father was a merchant, then?"

"Nothing so useful as that. He was a peer of the realm."

Kit's mouth fell open, but she had no time to indulge her curiosity, for the carriage had come to a halt and a guard was opening the door.

Kit's uncle, Don Juan Fernandino de Mendez Arguello, Count of Penalva, Presidente of the Audiencia at Santo Domingo, and Governor of Hispaniola, greeted his niece with surprise and affection. He left little doubt about the truth of her claim when he opened his arms and enfolded her in a fond embrace. Looking over her uncle's shoulder while being smothered by his welcome, Kit saw Logan smile. It appeared to be a smile of tolerant amusement at this unusual family reunion, but she could sense relief in that relaxed, arrogant curve of the mouth.

Don Juan finally released her and spouted a hearty welcome in Castilian. Kit smiled ruefully and shook her head.

"My little Katarina," he boomed in English. "Forgive me. I forget your Spanish is not what it should be. Welcome to my home. And you, Lieutenant—you have my gratitude for bringing her to me. You must tell me what happened. But first, come, sit down. We will have wine and then go in to dine. You have arrived just in time."

Don Juan was much shorter than his niece, but compensated in bulk for his lack of height. His double chins wobbled when he talked, and even the sturdiest corset was unable to restrain his ample belly. All in all, he looked like a short, corpulent clown in his gold-and-green-slashed breeches and his gold-embroidered padded doublet. But Kit knew that anyone mistaking her uncle for a foolish clown would be sadly mistaken. He often posed as a fool, but never thought like one.

It had been eight years since Kit had seen her mother's brother. Constantly strained relations between Spain and Britain had limited their contact with each other. But his short visits to Greenhaven, accomplished mostly in secret with the aid of Kit's father, had given the little man a permanent place in his niece's heart.

When the fiery Isabella had eloped with Roger St. John, she had been disowned by her father. Of all the children in the family, only the second oldest son, Juan, had maintained any contact with his young sister. A tentative friendship had formed between Roger and Juan, despite their natural differences. And Juan's fondness for his sister Isabella had carried down to Isabella's little daughter, Katarina. Despite the long separations, his affection for his niece had never faded.

Kit and Logan were invited to seat themselves with Don Juan and several Spanish officers in the huge formal parlor. While unobtrusive servants poured wine, Colonel del Vargas repeated the story that Logan had told him earlier. When the tale was finished, the governor smiled warmly at his niece.

"Unfortunate circumstances for a visit, my dear. But I trust you received every courtesy from our fine Spanish navy."

It wasn't difficult for Kit to pretend outrage. She had only to remember the way the loathsome colonel's eyes had crawled over her on the deck of the *Ice Maiden*.

"I would hardly call your navy courteous, Uncle. What were they doing attacking a peaceful British vessel going about legitimate business, murdering honest merchant seamen as if they were pirates! Spain is not at war with England!"

Don Juan sighed. "True, Katarina, we are not formally at war—yet. Though from the reports I have of the war fleet anchored at your lovely home island, I would think we might well be at war very soon. But it remains, my dear, that most English ships in these waters are pirates, whether or not they own the fact. England, unfortunately, is little better than a nation of pirates."

"This ship was not a pirate!" Kit insisted hotly. "I took passage on her to England! Would I willingly set foot on a cursed outlaw vessel?"

She threw Logan a look of haughty disdain. He returned a courteous, tolerant smile. Only she could see the secret amusement in his eyes.

"Of course you wouldn't, my dear. How could you be expected to know the true nature of the ship? But our experienced naval officers know a pirate when they see one. Do they not, Don...uh...Hernando?"

"Most certainly, your excellency, though I feel we must apologize to Doña Katarina for causing her distress."

"Ah, yes," Don Juan agreed. "It is most unfortunate you have had to endure this experience, Katarina. But you are unharmed, and here you are welcome and safe. I myself will arrange your passage back to your home. Captain Enriquez and Don Hernando here are to be commended in bringing you safely to my care." The governor's bland gaze moved to Logan. "Will you be staying at Santo Domingo long, Lieutenant? You are welcome to enjoy the hospitality of the *palacio* for as long as you need."

Logan smiled regretfully. "That is most generous of you, your excellency, but I must meet the *Santa Clara* in Vera Cruz as soon as possible. The English vessel requires minor repairs before I can set sail, but as soon as those are accomplished I must be on my way. As much as I would enjoy your hospitality...and the company of your lovely niece...."

"Yes," Don Juan said without interest. "Of course."

Logan continued, his voice casual, his manner nonchalant. "The surviving members of the English—of the pirate crew are chained in the hold of the frigate, your excellency. It makes me uneasy to have the rogues aboard while we are effecting repairs. I wonder if I could temporarily house them ashore. I hear the facilities in your fortress are very secure."

"By all means," the governor said. "I will have a detachment sent to your ship to transfer them."

Katarina tensed, then forced herself to relax. She smiled at one of the Spanish officers as if she found him much more interesting than the conversation between Logan and her uncle.

"There is no need to bother your men," Logan demurred. "My seamen are accustomed to handling this unruly lot. With your permission, I will go and see to the transfer now."

Kit thought the look her uncle gave Logan was unnaturally penetrating, his hesitation unreasonably drawn out. She hardly dared breathe. But then the governor's face resumed its bored disinterest.

"All that can wait awhile, Lieutenant. I insist you dine with us, and I see that the meal is ready. I do hate to keep good food waiting, don't you? There's time enough to attend to your duty after you've enjoyed the meal."

"You are too generous, your excellency." Logan's acceptance was gracious. But Kit sensed the strain underlying his smile.

Kit enjoyed the meal, in spite of realizing that the longer Logan was in her uncle's presence, the more likely he would say or do something that would unmask the charade. They were joined in the dining room by Don Juan's new young wife, Doña Anita. Kit had not realized that she had a new aunt. The last time she had seen her uncle he had been a widower who was thoroughly enjoying his solitary state. But she immediately liked the young Spanish noblewoman and could easily see how the redheaded, green-eyed beauty had charmed her uncle into making her his wife. Her youth and vitality were a sharp contrast to Don Juan's aging corpulence, but Kit was happy to note that the young woman did appear to have a genuine fondness for her husband.

"Tell me, Katarina," Don Juan said as the soup course was served. "Why were you making a journey to England at this miserable time of year? Why trade your lovely warm island for the dreariness of Kent? I assume that is where you were going. Is that not where your father's cousin lives?"

Kit wondered if it was suspicion that gleamed in her uncle's eyes, or merely interest.

"Yes, Cousin Alice is a widow in Kent. I was going to pay her a visit. To tell the truth, Uncle"—this was close enough to reality, Kit thought, for her uncle to recognize the ring of truth—"Oliver has been home these last few weeks, and he's been trying to marry me off to one of his worthless friends. He was being most irritating. I needed to get away from Greenhaven before I threw my dear brother in with the cane to be crushed. We had a bit of a row. That's why I booked passage on the *Ice Maiden* rather than go to England on one of our own ships. I was afraid Oliver might stop me."

Don Juan chuckled. "Ah, yes. Oliver. I can see why you might want to escape him." He had never liked Kit's older half brother, and now that worked to Kit's advantage.

Platters of a white fish broiled in herbed butter were placed on the table as the soup was removed.

"And how fares your lovely plantation?" Don Juan asked around mouthfuls of fish.

"Very well, thank you, Uncle." Kit relaxed as she found herself actually enjoying her role. Even the tingling sense of danger was becoming exhilarating. "Though my brother has seen fit lately to saddle us with a host of worthless gallows dregs that Lord Cromwell has shipped to the island as slaves." The mischievous malice in her eyes was aimed solely at Logan, even though her smile was directed at her uncle. "I can't imagine what the Lord Protector expects us to do with those troublemaking criminals. They're too puny to work the fields, and too lazy to be of use anywhere else."

Colonel del Vargas agreed heartily. "The English have always been too soft with their criminals." He chuckled. "Perhaps it is because they are a nation of thieves and miscreants, eh? Present company excepted, of course."

He raised his glass in silent toast to the governor's niece. Kit still didn't like the way his eyes clung to her. A chill ran down her spine, intensifying when she noted that Logan was watching the colonel as the Spanish commandant watched her. His eyes were blue shards of ice, his face a study in stone. Then he caught her anxious glance and smiled. That smile promised revenge for her saucy comments, but it also conveyed a sense of reassurance that quieted her sudden flutterings of fear.

The meal seemed to stretch on forever. The fish course

was followed by platters of roast fowl and beef, vegetables swimming in a heavy cream sauce, and then finally sweet pastries and fruit. Kit had tried to eat only enough of each dish to be polite, but by the end of the meal she felt as though the seams of her gown were about to split. If they had to escape now, Kit thought ruefully, she would be able to move about as fast as a cartload of bricks.

But there was no need for escape. All was going well. The dinner conversation continued in polite small talk, and no subject was broached that Logan could not address as well as any well-educated Spanish aristocrat. Kit was amazed at his knowledge of politics and naval tactics. He dropped names from the Spanish Admiralty as if he knew them personally. He could discuss military history with the Spanish officers without batting an eye, and moments later converse with Don Juan's pretty wife like a courtier born and bred. The scoundrel was a source of constant befuddlement to Kit, who began to wonder from moment to moment what new facet of his character would be revealed. The more Kit knew of the man, the less he fit in with her image of what a murderer, mutineer, and pirate should be.

When Logan finally begged leave to see to his duties—duties which Kit knew had nothing to do with putting prisoners into the fortress, but rather with taking them out—his absence snuffed the exhilaration she was beginning to feel and left her with a hollow place inside that was quickly filled with cold fear.

The town of Santo Domingo was the center of government and commerce on the island of Hispaniola. It was also the hub of the wheel of Spanish rule in the eastern Caribbean. The streets were bustling as Logan, Peter, and ten Spanish crewman from the *Ice Maiden* marched their sorry lot of English prisoners toward the fortress that guarded the harbor. The governor had dispatched four of his own *palacio* guards to make the transfer easier. Logan had tried to demur politely, but had not argued when the governor insisted. His lads could handle four more Spaniards, Logan decided. If they couldn't, then they had no right to call themselves buccaneers.

The sun was hot as the group trudged up the steep climb to the fortress gates. Logan was sweating from more than the heat, however. They were so close to succeeding—so close. But if anything were to go wrong now.... He could almost feel the noose closing around his neck.

Beside him, Peter stiffened as one of the governor's *palacio* guards began to throw insults at the English prisoners. To make the charade look more real, his own renegade Spaniards followed suit. Michael Carmody bore the brunt of their gibes, and as always, he was more than ready to rise to the bait. Even under these circumstances the little Irishman couldn't resist a fight.

"Look at that little scrawny chicken!" a *palacio* guard chortled in Spanish. "You'd think even pirates would have higher standards than to sign on something like that. Suppose it can fight?"

"Naw," another Spaniard replied—this time one of Logan's own, who welcomed a chance to stab at the hot-tempered Irishman. "It's probably just a mascot. Like one of those trained monkeys you hear about."

The first guard snickered. "It does sort of look like a damned monkey."

Unfortunately, Carmody understood Spanish. He lunged at the *palacio* guard. Surprised at the prisoner's audacity, the man was caught off balance and unprepared. Carmody knocked the musket from the Spaniard's hand and before anyone could grab him, he wrapped the chains linking his wrists around the startled man's throat and started to squeeze.

Logan was on the struggling pair before the action was well begun. He pulled Carmody off the gasping Spaniard and struck the Irishman across the face with a backhanded blow that was not half as vicious as it looked. The blow was hard enough to land the little man flat in the dusty street, however.

"Irish dog!" Logan spat. "The only thing worse than an Englishman is an Irishman."

Carmody lunged from the street like a tightly wound spring, only to find himself flat on his back again with

Logan's booted foot squarely on his chest. A light of maniacal hatred shone in his eyes until Logan's ice-blue crystalline gaze brought him back to the reality of the time and place. Logan removed his foot as two of the guards hauled the Irishman to his feet and shoved him back in line. The warning in Logan's face was plain for Carmody to read.

The most secure cells in Santo Domingo's fortress were those below ground. A dank corridor wound through the bowels of the fortress and finally opened onto a torch-lit guardroom. Here a contingent of ten guards threw dice, swapped stories, slept, or otherwise entertained themselves while their prisoners languished in vermin-infested cells. It was boring duty. No one could escape from the fortress. No one ever had. No one ever would. Even if a prisoner managed to break out of his cell—an impossible feat—he would have ten guards to elude before passing through the guardroom door to freedom. And if by some miracle that intrepid prisoner managed to subdue the guards and unbolt the door, then he still must negotiate the maze of corridors that riddled the lower levels like wormholes in a rotten apple.

So the guards welcomed the diversion when a hail from the barred door told of the arrival of new prisoners. New prisoners meant that some would be put to the question, and that process always provided lively entertainment for a day or two, or sometimes longer if one or two of the prisoners were exceptionally strong.

One of the governor's *palacio* guards pounded on the guardroom door. "Open up, Diego! We don't have all day to stand here at the door."

"These English dogs are anxious to see their new quarters," another taunted.

"All right. All right." Diego lifted a ring of keys from his belt and strolled toward the door. "Do you think all we have to do all day is come running when you call?"

"Yes!" the governor's guard laughed. "That is why you are so round, my friend. Come on duty in the *palacio*, and I'll show you what real work is."

The door squeaked open. Diego stuck his untidily bearded face into the gap. "Who are these you bring?" he challenged in an officious voice. "We had no notice of new prisoners."

"More pirates for you. Temporary guests, you might say."

The door swung the rest of the way open. Diego moved his considerable bulk aside and motioned the newcomers to enter. The guards lounging at the guardroom tables looked up in interest as the fifteen prisoners were herded in.

"Temporary, eh?" Diego chuckled. "You might say the others are temporary, too. They'll swing now that Don Esteban is through with them. And good riddance to them, I say. The place here is beginning to smell like Englishmen."

"This lot won't be here long," the *palacio* guard told his friend. He turned back toward Logan. "How long will you be here, Lieutenant? One week? Two?"

"No more than two."

Logan stepped through the door and swept the guardroom with assessing eyes. Ten prison guards and four *palacio* guards against his ten Spanish renegades and fifteen good English buccaneers. He almost pitied the Spaniards. Almost, but not quite. He closed and barred the door behind him.

"No need to be so cautious, Lieutenant." Diego chuckled. "We will not let your pirates escape."

They were a sorry-looking lot, Diego thought to himself. A more broken-down, cringing group he'd never seen. They looked as if all fifteen of them couldn't fight their way out of a whorehouse, much less a well-guarded prison. Then he noted with wonder that one of the English wretches was grinning at him. And the whoreson's manacles were loose. It was the last thing Diego saw before someone clubbed him from behind.

The guards stood like stunned statues as Diego toppled. The tables shook when his bulk hit the stone floor. Behind the fallen man a prisoner held up his hands and let his loose manacles clatter to the paving stones.

"Surprise!" he called in English.

Fourteen pairs of manacles followed the first. The clanging of steel on stone reverberated around the room.

Guards and prisoners stood regarding each other for a

moment, the prisoners grinning wickedly and the guards wide-eyed with surprise. Then the Spaniards lurched from their benches and reached for their weapons. They put on a brave show of ferocity, confident that the tough-looking prize crew from the *Ice Maiden* would shortly have their prisoners back in order. After all, the scoundrels were weaponless, and there were more than twenty good Spaniards against fifteen rascally buccaneers. Those were the kind of odds the guards liked.

Swords to the fore, they advanced on the Englishmen, who retreated in cowardly fashion across the room. Logan's Spanish renegades headed for the weapons locker. If the Spanish guardsmen thought it strange that these fighting seamen needed extra weapons, they were even more confused when rapiers and daggers were lofted through the air to the English pirates cowering against the wall. The guards turned to see insolent grins stretching the faces of their presumed comrades, and then the English pirates were cowering no more. The Spaniards were suddenly, unexpectedly surrounded by sharp, hostile steel. Choosing wisdom as the better part of valor, they laid down their weapons.

"A wise move, friends." Logan stepped out from the crowd, a half-smile twisting his narrow lips. He motioned Peter to remove the discarded weapons beyond tempting reach. "And now, gentlemen, if you would kindly remove your clothing."

A wail of protest arose from the guards.

"Don't worry, gents," Logan assured them. "We're not interested in your manly charms. Just your uniforms." To hurry along the disrobing, he prodded a *palacio* guard with the tip of his rapier. "You too, friend. And don't dawdle. That's right," he commended as doublets, breeches, and boots began to litter the floor. "You'll survive quite well in your underwear, I think."

While the erstwhile English prisoners were donning Spanish uniforms, Logan moved to the still peacefully unconscious Diego and brought him rudely awake with a cold splash of water from a pitcher on the table. The corpulent guard sputtered, rose to his elbows to look around, and then lay flat again when the first thing to meet his eye was the sharp tip of Logan's rapier.

"Good afternoon," Logan said in a conversational tone. "Have a nice nap?"

Eyes focused on the deadly steel that hovered two inches from his nose, Diego could only soundlessly open and close his mouth. His multiple chins flapped in rhythm.

Logan knelt down and held a ring of keys in front of the man's face. "Now, my good sergeant, you will tell me which key opens the cell where the pirates are held." He smiled in a deceptively friendly manner. "Of course, I could try them all. But I might get angry at such a waste of time, and I just might vent my anger on you." The rapier moved a hair closer. "Understand?"

Without a second's hesitation Diego carefully lifted his hand and pointed to a key. Logan handed it to Peter.

"See if it works," he ordered. He turned ice-blue eyes back to his victim. "It had better, my friend."

Diego whimpered and nodded his head. Beads of sweat popped out on his furrowed brow and trickled down through his scraggly beard into the folds of fat on his neck. When the Dutchman finally came back into the guardroom followed by eight tattered and broken men, the good sergeant released his pent-up breath in a sigh of relief.

"We're missing five," Logan noted.

"Dead," Peter said. "Three killed when the sloop was taken—Harrison, Miller, and Daughtery. Dugan and Lovell broke under torture."

Logan's chiseled features sharpened into a mask of anger. "No!" Diego gasped as the point of the rapier wavered.

The sword lifted. Logan looked down contemptuously. "Don't cower so, my fat friend. I doubt that taking your miserable life would bring theirs back."

The English "prisoners" had by now donned ill-fitting Spanish doublets, breeches, and boots and were standing around the room looking at each other with amused smiles on their faces. Logan motioned to Carmody, directing him toward the eight who stood by the Dutchman.

"See if you can find some more uniforms for these eight

here, and the rest of you escort our hosts to a cell. And don't forget to manacle their hands."

Peter sheathed his sword and looked around in satisfaction as everyone jumped to his task. "We did it!" he said with a slow smile. "I didn't think it was possible, but we did it!"

Logan was more cautious. "We did it so far. All that's left is to get back to the ship." His mouth twisted sardonically. "And to rescue our lovely little ally from the clutches of her uncle."

Chapter 8

"My dear Katarina, this has been a very special occasion for me." Don Juan raised his snifter of brandy in salute. The others in the parlor did the same. "To my beautiful niece, whom fate has delivered for a brief but welcome visit before politics tears us apart once again."

Kit smiled uneasily. This occasion might well turn out to be much more special than her uncle guessed. For the hundredth time her eyes darted to the doorway. Logan had been gone for over two hours. Surely something must have gone awry. Or perhaps, just perhaps, the rogue was planning to leave her here to face the aftermath of his escapade. His plans for getting into the *palacio* and from there into the fortress had been discussed at great length. His plans for getting Kit out of the hotbed into which he had dumped her had hardly been discussed at all.

The heavy meal she had consumed was churning in Kit's stomach as she continued to make small talk. She found that innocuous conversation was almost impossible under the circumstances. Her uncle was loud in his complaints about Cromwell's Caribbean policies and dominated the discourse with dire predictions of what would happen to the British fleet if it dared to violate Spanish territory. The others in the room listened to his monologue as though they had heard it many times before. They nodded their heads and made noises of agreement in the appropriate places. Only the arrogant Colonel del Vargas paid no heed to his governor's comments. His gaze was riveted on Kit, and the weight of his unwavering attention was making Kit's stomach churn all the harder. Something in his eyes made her suspect the colonel was not completely taken in by Logan's facile story.

Doña Anita finally interrupted her husband's harangue. "You are tiring poor Katarina, my love, with all this talk of war and politics. She has nothing to do with Lord Cromwell's sins."

Don Juan shook his head. "No, no. Of course not. You do look a bit weary, Katarina. No surprise after what you've been through. Perhaps you would like to retire for a bit and take a nap?"

"No, thank you, Uncle. It would be a waste to sleep. I see you so seldom, and once I leave, who knows when circumstances will allow us to meet again." Especially after you discover my part in this deception, she continued silently. Dash it all, where was Logan? What was happening? The afternoon was almost fled.

"Ah!" the governor said. "Here is Don Hernando back from the fortress."

Kit's breath caught as she turned her head to see Logan standing in the entrance archway, looking as unruffled as if he had just come from a sedate walk in the garden.

"Did the transfer go well, Lieutenant?"

"Extremely well, your excellency. Your fortress guards are every bit as efficient as I expected them to be."

Kit wondered if anyone else could detect the piratical glitter in those crystalline-blue eyes. Her heart skipped a beat. Now that Logan was back, fear was dissolving and the afternoon was once again glowing with excitement.

"Excellent. Excellent." The governor signaled a servant to pour Logan a snifter of brandy. "You can be confident that your prisoners will be secure for however long you must linger here, Don Hernando. No one has ever escaped our fortress cells. Colonel del Vargas prides himself that passing through that prison gate is more final than passing through the gates of hell."

Logan gave the colonel an icy smile. "You personally command the fortress, Colonel?"

The colonel gave a brief nod. "I have that honor."

"I must congratulate you for your efficiency." He took a snifter proffered by a servant, rotated the glass between the palms of his hands, and looked contemplatively into the brandy's amber depths. "Are you the one who devised the questioning techniques that were used on those wretches I saw down there, Colonel del Vargas?"

Kit tensed. The sharp edge of steel in Logan's voice scraped across her raw nerves. The reckless villain was going to get himself killed yet!

"I attended to that personally," the colonel admitted with pride. "There's not a man alive who can't be persuaded to babble everything he knows. It just takes the right touch."

"I can imagine." Logan smiled blandly, but his eyes glittered like newly honed knives. "Obviously you have the right touch."

The colonel chuckled. "There's many a buccaneer who'll find his safe little nest not so safe after all, thanks to my effort." He caught Logan's eyes with his own. "You see, Don Hernando, I have a particular hatred for pirates. And in my estimation all English seamen are pirates at heart."

"Oh, my!" Doña Anita interrupted the tension that was growing between the two men. "Such talk in front of ladies! If you gentlemen wish to discuss such things as pirates and torture and prison, Katarina and I will retire to another room. I'm sure Katarina wishes to hear such things no more than I do. See how pale she has become. Shame on you heedless gentlemen!"

Logan smiled an apology. "I imagine Doña Katarina has had her fill of English pirates in the last few days."

Kit glared a warning at him, then turned to her uncle. "I certainly have had my fill of pirates of all nationalities! One is just as bad as another! The thought of all those pirates in your prison fills me with"—her eyes flashed a private message to Logan—"with a most terrible apprehension."

"You need not bother yourself about those scoundrels, my dear," her uncle assured her. "They'll soon be going to the fate that they deserve."

"They certainly will." Logan's eyes twinkled, and Kit felt some measure of relief. He wouldn't be standing there looking so arrogantly self-satisfied if his errand hadn't gone well.

Just then a servant appeared in the parlor entranceway. "Pardon, your excellency, but the escort you ordered is waiting without."

The governor frowned. "Escort?"

In an unhurried movement, Logan rose from the settee where he was sitting and strolled to a position behind Kit's chair. Kit tried to still the hammering of her heart, certain that all the others in the room could hear it.

"I ordered no escort!" Don Juan said impatiently.

"Of course you did, your excellency," Logan said with unruffled calm. "You ordered an escort to convey me and Doña Katarina back to my ship."

"Back to your ship?" The governor looked at him in blank befuddlement.

Kit felt Logan's hand come to rest on her shoulder. The heat of it burned through the thin muslin of her gown and sent peculiar shivers down her spine.

"I'm afraid I have a little confession to make." Logan's tone was not at all repentant. "I am not Don Hernando Delgado, second officer on the *Santa Clara*. I am Captain Logan Steele, commander of the poor wretches who've endured your prison hospitality these last weeks. I'm afraid your perfect record has been destroyed, Colonel del Vargas. You now have eight men who have escaped your foul fortress."

For a moment Logan's announcement was met with stunned silence. Don Juan looked at Logan in amazement, and Doña Anita looked ready to topple over in a swoon.

Del Vargas stood abruptly and reached for his sword. "Dog! You won't get away with this!" The two other military officers in the room started to follow his lead.

"I wouldn't." Logan advised, a lazy smile curving his lips. One hand fingered the hilt of his rapier. The other rested lightly against Kit's neck. She could feel her pulse bump erratically against his fingers as a new fear took hold of her heart.

"Doña Katarina's neck is much too lovely to be broken," Logan continued in a conversational tone. "Do you doubt I could do the deed with just one hand, your excellency, while dispatching your henchmen with the other?" His rapier came scraping out of its scabbard.

The governor did not hesitate to meet the flinty hardness of Logan's eyes. "I am only too familiar with the ferocity of buccaneers. If you lead such rogues, then I concede that you must be counted a formidable foe. I don't doubt your ability to accomplish any villainous feat." He waved the officers to back off.

Logan's hand didn't move. Kit felt her blood hammer in her head. Surely Logan was bluffing. He wouldn't really hurt her. They had become comrades during this escapade—even friends of a sort. Hadn't they?

"Stand up, Katarina."

Logan's voice held no hint of reassurance. Kit rose stiffly and followed the guiding pressure of his hand. They backed away from the chair. Out of the corner of her eye she saw his rapier wave in the direction of del Vargas.

"You may think, gentlemen, that four against one is very good odds, indeed. But I assure you the governor's niece will not be alive to share in your victory celebration."

"Katarina," the governor began, "I don't understand what . . ."

"Don't be too put out with her," Logan interrupted. "You see, your excellency, I kidnapped your niece from her island for the sole purpose of gaining entrance to your fair city. She is a very good actress when she's acting to preserve her life, is she not?"

"Uncle . . . !"

"No need to draw out the performance, my dear."

A gentle pressure on her throat urged Kit to stop. She had half a notion to blurt out the truth—that she wasn't really in any danger. The fear on Doña Anita's face was almost too much to bear. But now was not the time for confessions. Nor was she sure anymore of just what was the truth.

"Dispatch a man to the fortess, your excellency." Logan's voice was cold as death. "Make sure no one pursues me on the way to the wharf, and give orders that my ship is to be allowed out of the harbor. Then summon a carriage suitable for a lady of Katarina's rank. And make sure all your men behave themselves." One of his long fingers caressed Kit's windpipe with a featherlike touch. "A woman's life is such a fragile thing."

It was all an act, Kit told herself. Lies, just like the lie he had told about kidnapping her. Still, the pressure of his fingers did not relent. Was he really strong enough to break her neck with just one hand? Kit didn't want to find out.

"It will be done as you say," the governor said fearfully. With a hurried gesture he summoned the servant and gave him terse instructions. The man gave Logan a look of wide-eyed fear and ran from the room.

"A carriage will be here momentarily," Don Juan assured him. "No one will interfere. Just leave my niece with me. I will allow you out of the harbor unharmed. You have my word of honor."

Logan chuckled and shook his head. "Sorry, your excellency. I've been a fool at times in my life, but never that much of a fool. Your niece is safe enough with me, unless you or one of your men do something rash."

"Please!" Doña Anita added her pleading to her husband's request. "Have mercy."

"I am sorry, my lady. Mercy is a virtue that a pirate cannot afford."

For a few tense minutes they all stood looking at each other in silence. Del Vargas and the other officers were stiff with anger. Their hands rested on the hilts of their weapons. Their eyes never left the pirate who dared to defy this bastion of Spanish power. The governor wrung his hands in impotent frustration, while his wife wept silently into the bowl of her hands. After what seemed an eternity, the servant returned and announced breathlessly that the carriage was waiting.

Kit felt Logan release a quiet sigh of relief. She wished she could look into his eyes and determine how much of this vicious charade was real.

"Then it is time for us to take our leave. Your excellency, it has been a pleasure." Logan pointed his rapier at Colonel del Vargas, who looked ready to spring in spite of the governor's orders. "You, Colonel!" he ordered. "You are coming with us for a bit."

Del Vargas freed his sword. "I'll see you in hell!"

"Perhaps you will someday," Logan agreed calmly. His hand tightened on Kit's neck. "Are you sure you want it to be today?"

"Do as he says!" the governor shouted. "Do as he says, man, or I'll have you up on charges. I swear I will! This is not the time for heroics!"

The colonel eyed both Logan and Kit malevolently.

Logan motioned with his sword. "Come along, Colonel. Sheath the sword. And smile. We wouldn't want anyone to think that something is wrong in here, would we?"

Kit gave her uncle a quivery smile as they backed out the parlor archway. The helpless agony in his eyes made her want to shout that he shouldn't worry, that the whole thing was an elaborate piece of mummery. Except she wasn't really sure that it was.

Kit recognized the escort that awaited them as the Englishmen who had posed as prisoners. Their uniforms were ill-fitting, and their eyes danced with a gleeful mischief that was very unmilitary. She didn't think anyone could mistake them for honest Spanish soldiers, uniformed or not.

The ride to the wharf proceeded in tense silence, with Logan and del Vargas eyeing each other like wolves circling before a battle. No one on the dusty streets took notice of the governor's carriage escorted by fifteen rather sloppily dressed troopers. The governor's carriage and the governor's troops were sights to be avoided, not to be remarked upon by the peasants and merchants who thronged the plazas and alleyways.

Peter and Logan's Spanish renegades awaited them on the wharf. With them were eight of the sorriest-looking wretches that Kit had ever seen. They, too, were uniformed as Spanish infantrymen, but they were less convincing even than the carriage escort. Even in the open air Kit could smell the filth that matted their hair and coated their skin. More than one had to lean on a comrade for support.

"This couldn't be my uncle's doing!" she choked.

"Most prisons are the same," Logan commented. "No doubt your uncle leaves the details of fortress hospitality to our friend the colonel."

Kit flung a shocked glance at del Vargas, who returned her look with one of sharp hostility.

"My Captain!" One of Logan's Spaniards had been dickering with a peasant boatman. Now he turned with an angry frown. "This dog turd is reluctant to give us passage." He fingered his dagger hopefully. "Shall I slit his throat?"

"No need for such measures, Ricardo." Logan gave del Vargas a wolfish smile. "We will need two boats, Colonel. Arrange it."

Del Vargas stood in hostile silence. The Spanish boatman looked at him curiously.

"You can make it difficult for us, Colonel, but you won't live to enjoy the moment." Logan spoke in English so the boatman would not understand. His eyes were hard as fine-tempered steel.

Kit backed away. Suddenly Logan seemed almost as frightening as the Spaniard. She jumped when Peter took her arm.

"*Buenos días, señorita*," he said in the only Spanish he knew. His smiling eyes conveyed a message of silent reassurance. "Don't look so fearful, Miss St. John. Logan will get us out of this cursed town in one piece. If any man can, he can."

Del Vargas gave in after a tense moment of hesitation. A single word from him prompted the boatman's hasty capitulation. Prodded by the threat in Logan's eyes, the colonel reluctantly stepped into one of the two boats he had commandeered for the pirates' use. As they rowed toward the *Ice Maiden*, the Spaniard stared up at the fortress with hate-filled eyes. Kit believed the grim colonel would have gladly been blown apart with the rest of them if he could have ordered those silent cannon to open fire.

The fortress crouched above the harbor in mute helplessness

as the *Ice Maiden* sailed regally through the narrow channel that led to the open sea. Bound by his governor's orders, the duty officer could only watch from the ramparts and curse as the English ship reached for the wind and blithely slipped out of range of his guns.

Two hours later a sodden and exhausted Colonel Esteban del Vargas dragged himself up onto the rocky beach below his unassailable fortress. He was a sorry picture, indeed. His boots had been left behind with the pirates who had so ignominiously flung him into the sea. His shirt and skin were equally tattered from being dragged along the rocky bottom by the surf. He sat gasping for air and looking out toward the blue horizon, his eyes riveted on the frigate whose sails were spread on the wind like gleaming white wings. No sooner had he regained his breath than he spent it uselessly cursing the villains whose ship so gracefully skimmed through the swells, bound for the open sea and freedom.

A raucous celebration hailed the success of the rescue. Rum and ale flowed freely. Stories of other adventures were bandied back and forth, and new songs extolling the crew of the *Ice Maiden* were composed on the spot. Little was said about the two comrades who had not survived the fortress prison, or the three others who had been killed when the sloop was taken. Buccaneers lived for the moment, reveling in the present, giving no thought to the future. Death was always close enough at hand without giving its presence undue notice.

Kit was amazed to find that the pirate crew who had once regarded her with such hostility was now ready to accept her as a comrade-in-arms. In fact, they not only accepted her, they treated her like a heroine. The moment she took a sip from her cup someone was refilling it to the brim with ale, rum, wine, or all three. Several drunken crewmen together composed a boisterous song in her honor, then sang it loudly and repeatedly. The words made Kit blush, and as subsequent versions got bawdier and bawdier, Logan finally waved them to silence. But he laughed as hard as everyone else.

A strange euphoria settled over Kit as she enjoyed all the unaccustomed attention. These rough-cut men actually seemed to like her. She was admired, lauded, included in their jokes, regaled with their ridiculously exaggerated stories. Never in her life had she felt so much in harmony with a group of people. She had always been the different one, the one who was ignored when other girls were dancing, the one the young men laughed about and dubbed with hurtful names, the one whose worth suitors assessed by sizing up her fortune. She was not accustomed to the rowdy good-humored glee with which she had suddenly been accepted by these hard-bitten, dangerous wolves of the sea. The feeling of sudden comradeship was overwhelming.

Also overwhelming was the amount of liquor that Kit consumed. But she did not care one whit that the pleasant buzz that numbed her usually sharp sense of reason owed much to the volume of alcohol in her blood. She was having a marvelous time, and she didn't want it to end. The euphoric cloud on which she floated was so delightful, in fact, that she almost didn't notice when the noise in the stern cabin faded to a few laughing voices. And when someone gently covered her with a quilt and snuffed the lantern flame, she simply allowed herself to float away to peaceful, happy oblivion.

When Kit's eyes slitted open again, the stern windows were squares of black. The cabin was dim. Only a single small lantern cast a wavering light on the desk where Logan Steele sat making an entry in his log.

Her eyes creaked the rest of the way open. She was lying on the bed, she discovered, fully clothed and feeling as though someone had taken a hammer to her entire body. She felt sticky all over. Her mouth was coated with an evil-tasting slime, and her head felt as if the cane crushers had been working inside her skull.

She groaned. Logan's eyes immediately swiveled to the bed. He regarded her with an expression Kit found most odd. Then he smiled.

"I see you're still alive." One brow arched in gentle mockery.

Kit grimaced. "I don't feel alive."

"Never try to outdrink a buccaneer, Katarina. The task is impossible."

She groaned again. "Is that what I did?"

"Very nearly." He nodded toward a pitcher and basin that sat on the washstand. "There's some water there to wash, if you like—one of the luxuries of the captain's quarters. I'll fetch you a change of clothes."

Kit wrinkled her nose. "Is that me I smell?"

"It's not a flower garden." Logan laughed at the mortified expression on her face, then got up and headed for the door. "I'll give you some privacy. But make it fast. I could use some sleep myself."

Kit felt much better after a thorough sponge bath. The tension of the day had fled, and the giddiness of the party had not completely deserted her. She felt as if she had opened a new door in her life and stepped through. She was a new person, a different Kit St. John—one who did not balk at adventure, one who could drink and laugh with pirates without batting an eyelash. Feeling greatly daring, she rummaged through the neatly arranged masculine garments in the wardrobe. One of Logan's linen shirts managed to cover her from neck to knees, though she did wish that the V of the neckline did not plunge quite so low.

She was making good use of Logan's hairbrush when the cabin door swung open. Kit stopped her brushing in midstroke as Logan walked in. She dropped the brush and hastily pulled the neck of the shirt together. Bare calves and ankles suddenly seemed the height of indecency.

"Uh . . . hello." Hot scarlet crawled slowly up her neck and face. Why hadn't she had the sense to put on her gown, soiled or not!

Logan was clearly distracted. His eyes traveled up Kit's length from her bare toes to her reddened face. She burned from the heat of his gaze. The sudden, white-knuckled clenching of his fists made her long to back away.

"I hope you don't mind." She pulled the collar more

tightly closed and backed up a step. "I could hardly put my gown back on."

"Mind?" he croaked. "No. Of course not. Why should I mind?"

Logan closed the door with unnecessary vigor. Kit jumped. She had halfway expected him to turn around and leave. But he didn't! He moved to the cabinet and poured himself a full tankard of wine.

"You were quite magnificent today," he said, not looking at her. "Most women would have been scared silly and given the whole charade away. Not you."

Kit was warmed by his praise. At the moment it was difficult to remember this man was a scoundrel of the lowest sort. But she did desperately wish she had at least a decent dressing robe.

"You gave a very fine performance yourself," she offered with a tentative smile.

"Thank you."

His eyes swung back to hers as if drawn against his will. What Kit read there made her heart beat faster. She had seen men's eyes light with greed when they looked at her, and sometimes with what she thought must be lust. But never had she seen the kind of look that burned in Logan's eyes. Desire, wonder, and longing all flowed from one fountain of fire. It terrified her and made her feel warm and quivery all at the same time. But mostly it terrified her.

"It was a performance, wasn't it?" she asked shakily.

"What do you mean?"

His intense gaze wouldn't let her go. Only half of her heard what they were saying. The other half was careening between fear and wonder at the sensations bombarding her. All from the simple caress of those impossibly blue eyes. She labored to bring her mind back to the halting conversation.

"Would you really have . . . broken my neck?"

Logan laughed, then downed a hefty draught of the wine. "Did you think I would?"

"I . . . maybe. I don't know. It seems I never quite know what you will do next."

He set the tankard on the desk and moved toward her, looking like a wolf stalking its prey. She sensed that some sort of decision had been made. There was no longer any uncertainty in those burning blue eyes—only a fire that seemed to flow from his very soul. He reached out a hand and placed it on her shoulder. His fingers rested lightly against her neck, burning her skin with their heat.

"Little Katarina. Silly girl." His voice was a caress. "I couldn't break your neck with one hand, even if I tried. And I wouldn't have tried. It was all a bluff. Surely you knew that."

"I knew that," she said, feeling more than a little silly.

"I didn't mean to frighten you."

He smiled and gently unclasped the hands that clung so desperately to the neckline of the overlarge shirt. Kit offered no resistance. She felt herself galloping toward a precipice. Soon she would fly over the edge, but the exhilaration of the day's adventure, the giddiness of the celebration, and the burning invitation in Logan's eyes were combining to make her helpless. She couldn't stop. She didn't want to.

"I would never hurt you," Logan promised. His mouth was a soft line of desire.

He placed Kit's hands on his shoulders, and gently grasping her by the waist, pulled her body closer to his. For a moment they just stood there looking at each other in the dim lanternlight.

"You're quite a woman, Katarina St. John."

Kit's heart stopped. The whole world was suspended as his mouth slowly lowered to hers. She was aware dimly that the precipice had been reached. Now was the time to spread her wings and fly.

Logan's kiss was gentle, almost cautious. His lips brushed hers like the fleeting touch of warm silk, then grew more insistent in their caress. Strong hands slipped from her waist to her buttocks and pressed her tightly against his hips. The hard evidence of his desire terrified her, and at the same time sent a lightninglike jolt of sensation quivering through her body. Kit's lips parted willingly and her arms wound around Logan's neck. She was melting inside. Forgotten was his past. Forgotten was her future. Her whole world became focused on the two of them at that very moment in time. Nothing else mattered.

"Katarina," Logan said quietly.

Kit answered him with a radiant smile. How had she ever thought she hated him—this complex, unpredictable, extraordinary man? The way he was looking at her made her feel beautiful and achingly female. She wanted to stretch in sensuous abandon, purr in kittenish delight. She was a bird learning how to fly, wings spread, soaring through the sky with a song in her throat. She wanted . . . she wanted . . . She wasn't quite sure what she wanted.

"Katarina, you should return to your room."

The wings crumpled. The bird plunged to earth with a frightful splat.

"Return to my room?" Kit said in a small voice. "Why?"

Logan set her back from him, separating her from the delicious warmth of his body. The room suddenly felt cold.

"Because if you don't leave now, Katarina—" His voice was low and husky, his eyes a steely blue, as though he were girding himself for an impossible task. "If you don't leave now—right now—I'm going to carry you to that bed and take what perhaps you are not ready to give."

Kit thought she could hear his heart pounding as loudly as her own in the silence that followed. He was giving her a choice she didn't want, opening the door for an escape back to the world of propriety and reason.

"I should leave," she agreed, drawing away from his magnetism, reminding herself that Logan Steele was a pirate, a traitorous mutineer, a criminal of the lowest sort.

"That would be best." Logan's face was carved in granite. The level, dark brows knitted together in a slash of tension.

Kit dropped her eyes, not able to bear the weight of his gaze. The choice was hers, but the advantage was his. How could any woman stand before the battering ram of Logan's masculine appeal? Tentatively she returned her hands to his shoulders.

"I want to stay." Her voice was so low she could scarcely hear it herself.

Logan lifted her chin and forced her to look into his eyes, to see the passion burning there. One dark masculine brow lifted in doubt. "Are you sure?"

Kit's smile was tantalizing. "No. But I'll stay anyway."

"So be it, then."

His voice had the sound of surrender, but Kit had no time to analyze just why, for in the space of a heartbeat she was lifted in his arms and carried toward the bed, which suddenly seemed huge and ominous in the dim light.

"No backing out now," Logan warned her with a devilish smile.

"St. Johns never back out. I'm a woman of my word. I keep my promises."

"And I keep mine." He gently laid her on the bed and sank down beside her. "So chase that fear from your eyes, my lady. I would never hurt you."

Kit wasn't really afraid. The sight of Logan's face so close above hers, the feel of his hand stroking her cheek, the pressure of his hip against her thigh—all these delicious sensations made her quiver, but not with fear. The linen shirt proved a flimsy barrier against his attentions. It was unbuttoned and removed before Kit could object. She made a halfhearted attempt to cover her breasts with her arms, but at a shake of Logan's head, she let her arms fall back onto the bed. For a moment she felt awkward and exposed, and the rosy flush that heated her face crept down to the rest of her body.

"At least . . . at least douse the lantern."

"No," Logan said softly. "I want to see you. All of you."

His eyes swept over the perfectly molded contours of small breasts, the slender indentation of the waist, the gentle flare of smoothly rounded hips, and the long, graceful lines of shapely legs. Slowly he reached out a hand and cupped a breast, his thumb gently rubbing the dusky nipple.

Kit jumped.

"Easy," he crooned. "I said I would never hurt you. Trust me."

Logan stretched out full length beside her while his hand seared a molten trail from her breast, over her abdomen, finally coming to rest on her hip. Kit closed her eyes and let sensation carry her away. She could feel his warm breath in her hair, then the fire of his lips moving across her cheek and down her neck. Her heart hammered in impossible frenzy. Something was melting inside her. Her whole body was becoming liquid and warm and delightfully languid.

"You're beautiful," he murmured. "So damned beautiful."

"Rubbish!" Kit cuffed him on the shoulder, half playfully, half angrily. Surely now the scoundrel was making fun of her.

Logan laughed, regarding her in amused reproof. "A lady does not deny the compliments a gentleman gives her when she's about to be . . . to be . . ."

Kit stared at him, then matched his laughter. "Well, sir! If you must give me compliments, then tell me something I can believe. Tell me I'm brave, witty, clever. . . ."

"All true," Logan admitted. "But you're also beautiful. You're an exotic orchid"—he cocked a brow—"surrounded by thorns, it's true, but an orchid nonetheless."

"Liar." She smiled, almost believing him.

"Never. I never lie to women. They have too many ways of getting even."

Logan's gaze traveled the length of her once again, and Kit's shyness melted before the heat of his gaze. She liked the reflection of her that she saw in his eyes. She liked the way his hands made her feel as they acquainted themselves with the curves and angles, the hills and valleys and secret recesses of her body. She reveled in the touch of his mouth, his tongue, in the feel of his slightly roughened beard scratching across her silky skin. If this was the essence of being a woman, then Kit heartily approved.

When Logan's weight lifted from the bed, Kit's hand reached after him in impatient need. She reluctantly opened her eyes.

"Don't leave," she whispered.

He was silhouetted against the dim lanternlight, hastily peeling clothes from his body. "Leave?" He chuckled, a low, throaty male sound that strummed Kit's nerves in delicious vibration. "Hardly, my love."

Kit had never seen a man completely naked before, and her eyes widened at the sight of him. Logan seemed even taller and broader without garments. There was nothing left of the scarecrow who had slaved in her cane fields. Sun-bronzed and superbly muscled, he exuded an animallike power that rekindled a remnant of Kit's apprehension. His arms and chest were corded with sinew, as were his straight, well-shaped legs. The broadness of his naked chest tapered to a flat, muscle-ridged belly and narrow hips. A thin line of coarse dark hair pointed the way from a taut navel to the proof of his rampant masculinity.

At the sight of what was standing at attention in her honor, Kit unconsciously inched toward the far side of the bed. Her pleasant languor fled. Suddenly she wasn't so sure this was such a good idea after all.

Logan reached over to douse the lantern. The bed sagged once again under his weight. Warm hands grasped Kit by the waist and pulled her against naked male flesh.

"Katarina," he murmured, his lips against her throat. "Don't run, my love."

This time Kit had no saucy comment. She stiffened as his thigh slipped between her legs and gently brushed against the soft down of her most private of places. His knee urged her thighs apart as he slipped a finger gently inside her. She jumped and gave a cry of alarm.

"Don't." His voice was low and hoarse with urgency. "I'm not going to hurt you, love—but Lord, I can't wait any longer!"

He was true to his word. Slowly, expertly Logan buried his swollen, throbbing flesh within the tender sheath that seemed made just for him. There was no pain, only a delicious feeling of wholeness. His lips moved across Kit's hair and her brow, then finally came to rest on her lips in a gentle kiss.

"Did I hurt you?"

"No." Her voice was breathless, trembling.

Gently, carefully, Logan began to move. Kit arched toward him, wanting him closer still, wanting him inside her forever. With innocent abandon she wrapped her long legs around his hips, pulling him more deeply inside of her with every thrust and wrenching an ecstatic moan from his lips. The tempo of Logan's rhythm increased, and Kit matched it with her own. She sprouted wings and soared into a new world where they clung together, melted together, floated together on currents of sensation that vibrated every nerve. Passion swelled and crested, then swelled and crested again, until the world exploded in a reeling, dizzy dance of ecstasy that left sated exhaustion in its wake. Kit clung to Logan in desperation, feeling that he had opened her soul as well as her body. He was her only anchor in a universe that was suddenly full of violent joy and uncontrolled desire. Finally, slowly, she and her lover floated once again toward earth. Breathing slowed. Hearts regained an even rhythm. The world came back into focus.

Logan moved slightly, reluctantly withdrawing himself from the warm cocoon of Kit's body. "Are you all right?"

At his whispered query Kit opened her eyes. The cabin was dark. The shadow of her lover loomed above her. Nothing had changed. And yet everything had changed.

"I'm fine," she answered. "I'm... wonderful."

She could feel his smile rather than see it.

"You certainly are. I think I should rename this ship the *Siren*. It would be more fitting."

Kit snuggled closer to his broad, naked form. Their legs intertwined. She didn't want to talk. She just wanted to lie still and feel him near her for as long as possible. With the dawn would come reality, and reason, and conscience. Logan would be once again a rogue and a scoundrel, and she would revert to a plain brown mouse well on her way to spinsterhood. But for the rest of this night she was a brazen adventuress, and he her bold pirate lover. She was a fool indeed, Kit acknowledged to herself as she drifted off to sleep. But tomorrow would be time enough to pay the price for her foolishness.

Logan watched as Kit surrendered to exhaustion. Wakeful and restless, he continued to watch as she slept, marveling at the innocence of her slumber, the quiet peacefulness of her face.

What a fool he was—like a schoolboy who couldn't resist dipping his hand in a bin of sweets, and damn the consequences. How hard he had tried to resist the silken web of Kit's innocent allure—tried and failed miserably. She was the first good thing that had crossed his path in so many years. How could he ignore the spell of her innocence, her courage, her unpretentious charm, her unpracticed but irresistible seductiveness? Even had Logan been made of stone, one touch from her hand, one smile from that mouth, and he would have crumbled to dust.

And yet what had he done to himself, to her? Given the task he had been sent to do, Logan Steele loving Katarina St. John could only bring disaster to them both.

Logan lay back on the pillow and stared morosely into the darkness. He had always been a fool, unable to accept what could not be changed, always reaching for things beyond his grasp. He was still a fool, Logan admitted. Never more so than now. For right at this moment all the reason and good sense in the world could not drive Katarina St. John from the spot she had carved in his heart.

Chapter 9

Each year, Mavis Edmond and her husband, Lionel, gave one of the finest balls on Barbados, and they saw no reason to break the tradition simply because Lord Cromwell and his Puritans disapproved of dancing. The music at the Edmonds' party was always superb, the feast sumptuous, and the company lively. Even Kit, who hated the socializing obligatory for her rank and position, always had a good time at Mavis's balls. If she didn't dance, or worse, was forced out of courtesy to dance with some oaf who counted the assets of her fortune more diligently than he counted time to the music, there was always Mavis to talk to. And Lionel Edmond wasn't a bad sort, either. His rather bland face and pudgy figure were offset by a sharp wit and lively sense of humor. Being with Mavis and Lionel usually compensated Kit for the fuss and bother of squeezing herself into a tightly laced corset, dressing in stifling satins, brocades, lace, and ruffles, and putting up with sweaty-palmed fortune hunters who insisted on showering her with compliments she didn't believe, wine and sweets she didn't want, and advances she promptly repulsed.

But on this balmy night in March Kit did not feel like talking, not even to Mavis or Lionel. She stood alone on the shadowed balcony that overlooked the garden. Music drifted out through the French doors, along with hints of laughter and conversation. But the merriment of the ball held no attraction for Kit. She preferred the hyacinth-perfumed breezes of Mavis's garden and the sight of the full moon drifting regally over the distant, glittering sea.

Somewhere out on that sea, Kit thought, Logan might be looking at the same bright moon. He might even be thinking of her, but it wasn't likely. Three days had passed since he had set her ashore on the same stretch of beach where he had met her eleven days ago, and that was doubtless enough time for his mind to turn to other, more important concerns. She wished her mind could turn as easily.

The trip back from Hispaniola had been much too short. Kit had allowed herself that brief interval of fantasy and had shut out reason and conscience and anything else that distracted her from her newfound passion. Much of the time she had spent in Logan's arms, either making love or talking of the myriad things that lovers find to talk about. Nothing was ever said about his past, his future, her future. They concentrated on the moment at hand, laughing, teasing, exploring each other's mind, bodies, and souls.

When they had emerged from the private sanctuary of the stern cabin, Logan had let her explore the ship at will. In the eyes of the *Ice Maiden*'s crew she could do no wrong. They were happy to teach her about the ship and spin her stories of the sea. She thoroughly enjoyed the company of Doc, Gabriel Potter, Jud Smythe, and young Tom Trelawny, who followed her around like an adoring puppy. Even the hardened buccaneers who hailed from Tortuga softened in Kit's presence. And not once did she have to make use of Doc's bitter draught for seasickness. For the first time in her life Kit was completely carefree, ecstatically happy.

The days had passed in sunshine and soft breezes only

occasionally punctuated by periods of warm rain. Dolphins danced upon their bow wave, and schools of tiny flying fish skimmed the waves like swarms of seagoing insects. The sea was a kaleidoscope of changing moods, now glittering sapphire dotted with frothy tufts of windblown foam, at other times green and smooth with satin surface unruffled by a breath of air. The ship became in Kit's mind a living being, graceful, swift, plunging and bucking with ceaseless energy beneath white canvas wings. Together the sea and the ship seemed like lovers, often playing, sometimes fighting, always belonging together.

Logan sensed Kit's new love and let her take a turn at the helm. That had been one of the most precious moments of all. With the plunging ship a slave to her will, she stood with hands firmly on the huge wheel. The sea was her kingdom and she was its queen, with Logan's hard-muscled body pressing against her back, the fresh sea wind blowing through her hair, the smell of salt and seawater and warm wood and canvas all mingling with the masculine scent of the man who stood so close behind her. Kit had felt free and bold and beautiful, one with the sea, the ship, and the man who was her lover. If the moment could have gone on forever, she would have asked for nothing more.

But of course it had not gone on forever. It had ended, and the trip home had ended. If only the memories had ended as well.

The time with Logan had added a whole new dimension to Kit's life. He made her feel as though a bright and shining new Kit St. John had emerged from the cocoon of the old. No more was she the solitary woman who was doomed to live out a lonely life watching her cane grow and her slaves toil and her wealth accumulate. She was just as solitary, and just as doomed. But now she knew what she was missing.

Kit had thought that when she once again set foot on dry land she could effortlessly step back over the line that divided dreams from reality. Hispaniola and Logan Steele would be an exciting memory, and her life would take up where it had left off. It turned out not to be so easy. Logan was gone, but his memory wouldn't let her be. His image haunted her days and tortured her dreams. She heard his voice in the breeze that swept in from the sea, saw his form in every tall, dark-haired man she encountered.

Time was what she needed, Kit told herself. Time would surely dull the longings and still the rovings of her imagination. Weeks from this night, all would be as it had been, and she would once again be the Kit St. John who was content to nurture her plantation with only the company of her servants and slaves.

"What are you doing moping out here on the balcony?" Mavis's voice brought Kit back from her ramblings. "Are you thinking about your handsome pirate?"

"Certainly not!" Kit fibbed. "I just came out for some fresh air."

"Is that why you're gazing into the night like a moonstruck swan?" Mavis's gray eyes sparkled, and a knowing smile curved her generous lips. "He is handsome, is he not—this pirate of yours? If he weren't, then this scandalous adventure would not be nearly so delicious."

"He is not *my* pirate," Kit corrected in a firm voice. "And I suppose he is handsome, in a roguish way. If you like that sort of vulgar display of muscle."

Kit had given Mavis a bare-bones version of the escapade in Hispaniola. She had certainly not even hinted at the flame that had ignited between her and Logan. Was she so transparent that her foolish heart was in everyone's view? What a horrible thought.

"Well, if you aren't out here sighing about your lost love," Mavis pouted prettily, "it seems you ought to be. It's twisted fortune that sees me married with two babies while you get to run off on such an exciting adventure. I would know how to appreciate the romance of being carried off into the night by a bold pirate captain and spirited off to sea aboard his outlaw ship. You, Kit St. John, have far too practical a mind to see the excitement of such a thing."

Kit laughed. "And you, Mavis Edmond, are too imaginative by far. You should appreciate your Lionel and your two precious babies. Pirates are not nearly as romantic as they sound, believe me."

"Just the same, you have been mysteriously pensive these

past few days. I worry about you, you know. Why don't you come in and be social. Eat, drink, snub a few of the younger sons who are always panting after your money. Be yourself again." Mavis shot Kit a wicked grin. "Your brother, Oliver, has been wanting to talk to you all night—all week, as a matter of fact. I don't think he quite believes that story about your being sick in your room."

"Maybe he wants to apologize for being such a jackass," Kit speculated hopefully.

"Not likely, dear. But his scowls are ruining my party, so do go in and placate him. But be fast about it." She lowered her voice and raised her brows meaningfully. "There's a gentleman I want you to meet. Absolutely devastating, I vow. He came with Colonel Modyford. Why, if I weren't married, I'd be after him in a minute!"

As Mavis had predicted, Oliver did not want to apologize. He frostily inquired if Kit was ready to be reasonable and come back to Greenhaven where she belonged. Kit assured him that she was indeed ready to return home, but if he ever again brought Nicholas Basey into her presence and expected her to be polite, he could expect to see reason fly out the window, along with Master Basey. And if he ever dared to concoct another scheme like the one that had gotten her carried off to sea, she would have him up on charges before the governor himself.

Oliver accused her of indulging in childish histrionics, but Kit was pleased to note that he couldn't look her directly in the eyes. She was even more pleased to observe that Nick Basey, whom she spotted on the edge of the dance floor, was taking great pains to be wherever Kit was not.

Mavis found her again before she even had a chance to cool her temper with a glass of cold punch.

"Come on, Kit," she insisted, "I want to introduce you to this toothome fellow before the poor man is completely mobbed by matrons hunting husbands for their silly daughters. This is one man you absolutely must meet."

Mavis pulled Kit through the crowd that hemmed in the dance floor. Colonel Modyford and his friend did look as if they were under siege. They were surrounded by a troop of eager middle-aged women whose daughters waited on the sidelines eyeing each other with all the civility of starved dogs coveting the same bone. When the object of all this attention turned to acknowledge Mavis's greeting, Kit's feet froze to the floor, her mouth dropped open, and it seemed that every bit of blood in her body rushed to her face. Logan Steele's crystalline-blue eyes twinkled at her discomfiture.

"Mr. Pettijohn," Mavis said, "I would like you to meet a very dear friend of mine, Miss Katarina St. John of Greenhaven Plantation."

Mavis's words scarcely penetrated the fog that enveloped Kit's brain. The ballroom and its occupants faded into a hazy blur. All she could see was the bold sculpture of Logan's face, the warm sea-blue of his eyes, the sardonic smile that lifted one corner of his mouth.

"It's my very great pleasure, Miss St. John." Logan lifted her limp hand in his and brushed it with his lips. The light touch of his mouth seemed to sear her fingers with a permanent imprint.

"Kit, this is Mr. Edward Pettijohn. He's bringing a new shipping line into Bridgetown. Since your family is also in the shipping business, you should have much in common."

Kit looked dumbly at Mavis, then back at Logan.

Modyford grinned. "Congratulations, my man. You appear to have made a conquest. I've never before known this young lady to be at a loss for words."

Kit's blush burned even hotter.

"Perhaps she's afraid you'll give her ships a run for their money, eh?" Modyford continued with a chuckle.

"I . . . not at all." Kit managed to regain her equilibrium. "I'm pleased to make your acquaintance, Mr. . . . Pettijohn."

Mavis was delighted with Kit's reaction. She had never seen her friend so dumbstruck. If she was indeed pining away for her pirate captain, this was surely the man to take her mind off the scoundrel. She tapped Sir Thomas lightly on the arm with her fan.

"Colonel, there is someone in the music salon who has been asking to meet you." She gave Kit a subtle but meaningful wink and completely ignored her friend's look of panic. "Why don't we leave these two to become better acquainted while you come with me to meet him. I know you'll find him most interesting.''

Sir Thomas graciously allowed himself to be dragged away, leaving Kit and Logan staring at each other over their cups of fruit punch.

"What in the world are you doing here?" Kit asked without preamble.

Logan managed to look offended. "Is that the way a gracious lady addresses a new gentleman friend? No 'How nice to meet you. How long are you staying on the island?' Or even, 'How are you enjoying the ball?' "

"Rubbish!" she replied. "You are hardly a gentleman, and a doubtful friend at best. I want to know what a pirate, scoundrel, and blackguard is doing among the respected company gathered in this house."

"Are we back to that now?" Logan's smile was pure wickedness. "I thought we had gone beyond this sort of sniping."

Kit took his arm and guided him toward the privacy of the garden, ignoring the indignant stares of several matrons at her high-handed appropriation of the man they had decided was the prize catch of the season.

"Quit hedging and answer my question!" The relative quiet of Mavis's garden closed about them. "Are you here to launch some sort of mayhem on these people? I'll have you know that they are my friends, and I'll not let you play your pirate games to their detriment."

"How soon you forget." Logan arched a teasing brow. "We had a bargain, did we not? You fulfilled your part quite admirably. Did you expect me to do less?"

The bargain! Kit had all but forgotten her folly of that night aboard the *Ice Maiden*.

"No... that is... I didn't expect to see you this soon. You work fast."

Logan smiled. "I always have." He executed a graceful bow. With his elegantly tailored, eminently fashionable gold-embroidered doublet and matching wide breeches, no one would guess him to be other than a gentleman of considerable wealth and breeding. Even Kit had to admit he cut a most splendid figure. "Consider yourself to have a most ardent suitor, my lady. One who will certainly put your brother's matrimonial ambitions for you to rest."

"You really took me seriously?" Kit asked with amazement.

"Of course." His smile broadened to the infuriating grin she knew so well. "You seemed most definite in your demands. Dance, my lady?"

Before Kit could protest, Logan took her by the arm and guided her through the figures of a courante in time to the music drifting out from the ballroom. When the figure brought them close together, she could feel the familiar liquid warmth begin to seep through her veins.

"You needn't show off so!" She jerked her hand from his and flounced out of his reach. "How on earth did you get Sir Thomas Modyford to sponsor you?"

"He seemed the logical choice."

"Of all the audacious, reckless pranks! Do you enjoy putting your own neck in the hangman's noose?"

Logan retrieved her arm and guided her toward one of the benches that bordered a pleasant, splashing fountain. "Don't worry so. As you noted earlier," he said with a chuckle, "I have a talent for chicanery."

"You certainly do," Kit agreed. "I'm beginning to think you're a more dangerous man than you appear."

"Only to my enemies. Not to you, love."

They sat down on the bench and she snapped open the fan she carried at her wrist. Kit had always considered such things a ridiculous affectation, but right now she was grateful to be able to cool her face. Logan's proximity was wreaking havoc with her senses. She tried to slow her frantic heartbeat by concentrating on the moon-silvered ripples of water that spread out from the fountain. Her fantasy lover had stepped into her everyday humdrum life. Now how was she ever to regain that sensible woman of cold reason who was her former self?

Kit jumped at the feathery touch of Logan's lips at her temple.

"What are you doing?"

The lips trailed down over her ear to her neck, leaving a tingling path of fire in their wake. "I'm wooing you in sight of your brother," Logan whispered against her throat. "Is that not what you wanted?"

"Dash it! Is Oliver watching?" Kit tried to pull back, but Logan's arms held her fast.

"Probably not." His lips grazed her cheek, and she felt his mouth curve into a wicked smile. "But the practice is pleasant, don't you think?"

"Don't..." Kit's objection was smothered as Logan's mouth moved to plunder hers. His hand was warm on her breast. She remembered the wonders of ecstasy it could work there—there and other places that no other man would ever invade. She felt the need building, the need for him to engulf her, enfold her, possess her until she became entwined in his very being—the way he had done so often and so well in their private sanctuary of the *Ice Maiden*'s stern cabin.

This wouldn't do! This wouldn't do at all! She pushed Logan away, fighting her own longing as well as his strength. Hastily she tried to pull herself together.

He looked at her quizzically. "What is this change of tune, Katarina?"

Kit willed her breathing to slow and her heart to resume a steady beat. "Logan..."

He raised an admonishing brow.

"Edward... whoever you wish to be." Eyes filled with conflict lifted and met his. "I have no regrets about our time on your ship."

"Good. Neither do I." He smiled a smile that should have set Kit's heart afire, but instead made her feel as though he were ripping that tender organ from her chest.

"You don't understand."

"What don't I understand?"

"To you our time together may have been just a pleasant way to while away the time. To me it was... you were... my whole world. I am not some sophisticated woman who can dismiss such things as... as a passing fancy. Part of you will be with me for the rest of my life."

"Katarina..."

Kit silenced him with her fingers on his lips. Did she hear an edge of panic to his voice? Did he think she was about to declare undying love and try to bind him forever?

"Logan..." She steeled herself, remembering what he was, what she was, and the yawning crevice that separated them. "You taught me how to fly, but my feet are back on the ground now. I have my life to deal with, and you will never be a part of it after this silly charade is over. You are a pirate, an ex-slave, and God knows what else. Whatever I feel for you I have to forget. And I can't do that if I allow... this."

Logan was deathly silent. She wished he would speak, laugh, curse, do anything but look at her with that bland expression that told her nothing of what he was thinking.

"Your part of the bargain was to convince my brother of your passion," Kit continued in a shaky voice, "not me."

"It seems I have already convinced you of my passion," Logan replied in an even voice, "and frightened you by it. I did not think you were a woman who gives herself only halfway, or a coward who runs from life. Was I wrong, Katarina?"

Kit stood so abruptly she almost overbalanced herself. "I do not run from life!"

Blue eyes seemed to pierce her very soul, leaving her vulnerable to Logan's merciless contempt.

"You are not my life," she denied hotly. "You are just... just a week's worth of foolishness. Whatever was between us is in the past. I've already forgotten it. So if you want to play out your part of the bargain, you can just behave like a gentleman. If you know how!"

She tore her eyes away from his and fled, leaving only the faint scent of her perfume to keep Logan company as he broodingly watched the moonlight play on the fountain.

"How dare he accuse me of running away from life! The mannerless cur!"

Kit flounced onto the bed, took off her shoes, and threw them across the room. One followed the other like lethal missiles. Ricocheting off the wall, they both landed in the pile of her shipboard breeches and shirt that she had intended to discard.

"Dancing shoes!" Kit scoffed aloud. "Bah! That's where they belong! In with the trash."

And she belonged at Greenhaven, not in Mavis Edmond's fancy ballroom, and certainly not in a moonlit garden making love with a sneaky pirate. She would go home this minute if it wouldn't hurt Mavis's feelings. Who was she trying to fool, wearing this fancy ball gown and those ridiculous dainty slippers? She didn't want to dance or socialize or be witty and charming and flutter her lashes as ladies were expected to do. She just wanted to be herself— the Kit St. John who was independent and self-assured and competent, and who didn't need a man.

What a fool she had been to allow herself even that brief interval of forgetting who and what she was. She was exactly what the young roosters of Barbados called her—Ice Maiden. She was a maiden no longer, thanks to her own giddiness and that wickedly seductive, unscrupulous scoundrel, but she was still made of ice, and she liked it that way. Logan Steele could just take his blue eyes and devilish smile and fly off to light upon some other hapless flower. In fact, he could go straight to hell and she wouldn't care one whit. She would tell him to forget the cursed bargain and get out of her life, but doubtless that would be playing right into his hands. The unprincipled rogue!

A knock on the door brought Kit abruptly off the bed. Had Logan had the temerity to follow her?

"Who is it?"

She ignored the twinge of disappointment when Mandy Carpenter's voice answered.

"And just 'oo was ye expectin', love?" Mandy gave her a curious look as she came into the room. "I saw ye fly up the stairs like a bee was in yer petticoats. Is somethin' amiss?"

"No . . . yes. No. Not really."

Mandy pursed her lips. "Now that's a nice an' definite answer, I'd say."

Kit crossed to the wardrobe and started to pull out her clothes.

" 'Ere now. I'll do that, dear. Are we goin' somewhere?"

"We're going back to Greenhaven tomorrow. Early."

"Time enough to pack in the mornin', don't ye think?"

"I'd rather pack now."

Mandy sighed. "Why don't ye tell me what's wrong?"

"Nothing's wrong."

"I saw ye talkin' with that 'andsome devil 'oo was with Colonel Modyford. We're 'aving a bit of a party ourselves belowstairs, but I been keeping an eye on ye, me love, as I always do. 'E seems right popular, that gent. Did 'e snub ye fer another lady? Is that what 'as ye in such a dither?"

"Snub me for another woman? That's ridiculous. Besides, why should I care . . . ?"

" 'E was dancing with that tart Elizabeth Rogers when I was climbin' up the stairs."

"Elizabeth Rogers! Why the . . . the . . . !"

Kit could think of no name vile enough to describe the man who had once called her an exotic orchid and who was now blithely enjoying the charms of that overblown English rose—and not minutes after he had tried to make love to her in the garden.

"He's supposed to be courting me—that weasel!—not that gaudy blond china doll."

Kit retrieved her delicate dancing slippers and jammed them back on her feet. A moment before, a team of horses could not have dragged her back into the ballroom. Now the same team could not have held her back.

Elizabeth Rogers was a pretty thing, Logan mused. She was exactly the type of woman he had always preferred. Pale blue eyes were fringed with long golden lashes, and honey-blond hair framed a face of porcelain perfection. Her coy glances teased, and her smiles were shy and inviting at the same time. A low-cut gown artfully displayed the lush bounty with which nature had endowed her, and Logan could imagine the firm white flesh that was hidden under the layers of silk and lace.

As they postured through the figures of the courante, Elizabeth gave him a smile that could have heated any man to the inner core. Doubtless it would be easy enough to maneuver Miss Rogers into bed. Most likely he would not be the first to enjoy her more private charms, for there was nothing in those pale blue eyes that bespoke innocence or inexperience.

A month ago Logan would have hastened to answer the challenge in those inviting eyes. He liked his women flirtatious, experienced, pliant, and willing—all of which attributes Miss Rogers displayed to perfection. But tonight the spark was missing. Her smiling lips and bright eyes could have more easily warmed a pillar of granite.

"You are so quiet," Elizabeth pouted prettily as the dance ended.

"You must forgive me," Logan replied. "I have business matters on my mind."

She took his arm as he led the way from the dance floor. "La! Mr. Pettijohn. A ball is no place for worries of that sort. A ball is a place to...enjoy yourself." The subtle brush of her breast on his elbow confirmed that she would be most happy to contribute to his enjoyment.

She was a fetching piece, Logan acknowledged. But it seemed of late his tastes had turned from bland to spicy.

"Good evening, Elizabeth," Kit's voice purred.

They turned. Elizabeth frowned in annoyance. Logan smiled. The spice was making an unexpected appearance. And considering the icy setdown the little witch had given him earlier, he was surprised to see the fire that was burning in her eyes.

Elizabeth's delicate brows drew together in a frown which she promptly replaced with a bland mask of boredom. "Good evening, Kit. Have you met Mr. Pettijohn?"

"Indeed I have." Kit flashed him an innocent smile. "Mr. Pettijohn and I had quite a conversation earlier—about his outstanding debts."

"Then you were the one who turned his thoughts to gloomy business. Poor Edward!" The smile that spread slowly across her perfect face was an invitation to feminine battle. "I have just now managed to cheer him."

"So I see," Kit replied in an acid voice. "How like you to be so generous in your efforts."

Logan cleared his throat uneasily as Elizabeth's eyes narrowed to pale blue slits.

"I believe you promised me this dance, Mr. Pettijohn." Kit's voice dripped with honeyed vinegar.

"Did I?"

Now it was Kit's eyes that narrowed dangerously. "You did indeed," she insisted.

"Then by all means, let us dance." Logan's eyes were dancing already. "I always keep my promises, particularly to lovely ladies." He took her hand in his. "Excuse us, Miss Rogers. It was certainly a pleasure to make your acquaintance."

"A great pleasure," Elizabeth said with sugary sweetness, her eyes shooting knives at Kit's back as the couple turned and joined the other dancers.

"You should watch out for Elizabeth," Kit warned when they were safely on the dance floor. "She's interested only in money and influence. Her interest in you is strictly ... strictly ..."

"Carnal?" Logan supplied.

"Yes." Her voice was cold, but her face heated rapidly under his regard.

"Do you fear for my virtue?" he asked with a crooked smile.

"Hardly!" she snapped. "But you do me no good if your reputation is in tatters, as it will be if your name is linked with hers. Besides, she has claws, that one."

Logan laughed softly. "Believe me, Katarina, hers are a kitten's claws compared to yours. You are a veritable tigress. You, my sweet lady, have claws that I wouldn't like to tangle with ... again."

She glared at him. "Just you remember that."

"Smile," he said, and swept her closer to him than the dance called for. "Your illustrious brother is watching."

Kit smiled and managed to look doe-eyed, though the look of amusement on Logan's face made her want to kick his shins, or any other convenient and sensitive part of his anatomy. She hoped Oliver was buying this farce. For the price she was having to pay, she deserved a little peace at home.

"You're not being very convincing," she complained.

Logan gave her a wicked smile. "I'm willing to be more

convincing, but if I swept you into my arms and made love to you here on the floor, some of these tiresome people might take offense."

It was all Kit could do to maintain her expression of a smitten maid. "You are an animal!" she gritted out from between painfully smiling lips.

"It's one of the more charming sides of my character."

Would the dance never end? Kit thought desperately. Was there no safe subject of innocent conversation that did not lead directly to memories of nights—and days—spent together in the stern cabin of the *Ice Maiden*?

"Are you staying with Sir Thomas?" she asked with a hint of desperation.

"No. I've taken a house just north of town. It's quite nice, really. You'll like it."

"I don't plan to see it."

He sighed. "What a dull courtship this is going to be."

"You sound as though you're setting yourself up here quite permanently. Oliver will only be here for another month at most. There's no sense in your taking risks."

"Are you concerned for me?" Logan asked, one brow cocked doubtfully. "I wouldn't have guessed it."

She frowned. "I wouldn't want to be responsible for your hanging."

"Put your mind at ease, my lady. Did you think I would walk into the lion's den for you alone? You and your little bargain?" He smiled enigmatically. "I have other matters of business on this island that need my attention."

Kit felt properly rebuffed, and oddly miffed. "Do you indeed?" She raised a skeptical brow. "And what might they be?"

"Matters that don't concern you. So you see, if my neck is stretched on Execution Dock, you need weep no tears of guilty remorse. I am not fool enough to risk my life for a woman's sake. Especially for the sake of a child who isn't wise enough to know her own heart."

The dance ended then, fortunately for Logan, for the tigress looked ready to spring with claws unsheathed.

"Your brother is watching," Logan warned with an innocent smile.

"The devil take my brother!"

"My sentiments exactly."

Kit saw that Oliver was indeed watching them with interest. She reminded herself, with some difficulty, that she had an investment in this charade. Logan was trying to get out of their bargain by being totally hateful, but she was certainly not going to oblige him. She smiled up at him sweetly and raised her voice enough for it to carry to the people surrounding them, one of whom was Elizabeth Rogers, who was practicing her charms on an attentive Colonel Modyford.

"Of course you may call on me, Mr. Pettijohn. How sweet of you to ask." She snapped open her fan in a flirtatious gesture that she had seen Elizabeth use to good effect, then lowered her lashes in coy modesty. "Tomorrow at one o'clock would be splendid."

Kit turned to make her exit and threw him a sweet smile over her shoulder. Only Logan could see the daggers shooting from her eyes. He watched her go, admiring the performance and wondering how he had ever been fool enough to let that daughter of the devil get her claws into his heart. Fire and ice she was, and he was being burned by them both.

Chapter 10

Life was a deadly bore, Kit decided. If the rest of her days on this earth were going to be no more interesting than the last week had been, then she might as well just skip the next few decades and go straight to her grave. It couldn't be any duller than what she was enduring now.

She leaned on the railing of her bedchamber balcony and stared out into the moonless night. The world was as dark as her mood. The warm rain that had earlier washed the island had stopped, but still no starlight sparkled on the distant bay, and clouds and mist still hugged the mountains that rose inland from the plantation. The air smelled steamy and dank, and everything—clothing, bed sheets, skin, hair, even the carved wood railing beneath her hand—felt damp to the touch.

The sound of distant singing carried through the heavy night air. The tones were mellow, the melody haunting. Kit had always loved to listen to the slaves singing in their village. From the time she was a child she had often watched their songfests as a quiet, unobtrusive visitor. The blacks would be sitting around a fire, Kit knew, even though the night was warm. Between songs the old men and women would tell stories—tales from their homelands, or sometimes tales from their new land. Oona had been one of the best storytellers in the village. She had made the land of her girlhood come alive with vibrant color as she filled her listeners' ears with strange gods and goddesses, spirits and demons, wars and heroes and villains and lovers. Then the communal singing would take up the theme. The slaves' songs had always moved Kit's heart. She wondered why she had never before this night noticed how like they were to a dirge.

Logan Steele had ruined her enjoyment of the slave songfests, Kit thought resentfully, with his prating of human misery and the evils of slavery—just as he had ruined her enjoyment of almost everything else in life. Her brief taste of adventure and passion had made the simple pleasures of Greenhaven pale in comparison. Overseeing the smooth operation of the plantation no longer seemed such a challenge. Riding through the fields, touring the mill, coordinating the sale and shipping of the raw sugar—all these tasks that she used to perform with love and pride had become a chore.

A voice from her bedchamber interrupted Kit's sulk.

"Are ye still up, love? I noticed yer lamp still shinin'. Do ye need anything?"

"No, Mandy," Kit answered. "I'm just restless. You can go on to bed."

Mandy stepped out onto the balcony. A voluminous

dressing gown swathed her ample frame, and errant wisps of faded red hair poked out from under a ruffled nightcap. "It's no wonder ye can't sleep, what with those blackies caterwaulin' up at the village. Like to drive a body mad. Why don't they settle down t' sleep like decent folk?"

Kit wondered how Mandy could fail to hear the beauty in the singing. If she ever left Barbados, the ghostly sound of the slaves' songs rising into the night sky would be the clearest memory she would carry from her home.

"It's just their way," Kit tried to explain. "They may keep it up until dawn, so you might as well go to bed and cover your ears with a pillow."

Mandy scowled and stumped back into the bedchamber. "'Eathen spells is what they're making, if ye ask me! 'Eathen spells!" She turned and threw Kit an admonishing look. "Don't ye be off and riding so early in the morn, miss. Ye promised to take a ride in that Mr. Pettijohn's new carriage—just in case ye forgot. An' ye also promised t' let me pin up yer hair in a way that's more becomin' to a lady."

Kit sighed. "I won't forget."

When Mandy had closed the door behind her, Kit snuffed the lamp and reluctantly climbed into bed. A carriage ride tomorrow, and two days before there had been a private little picnic, and before that several formal calls from her attentive new "suitor." Logan was certainly diligent about this pretend courtship. Almost too diligent for Kit's peace of mind.

But the ruse did seem to be working. Not once in the week since the Edmonds' ball had Oliver bothered to push forward Nicholas Basey or any other favorite for her consideration. He was watching Kit and Logan with great interest. In fact, he had been a deal more circumspect in his comments than was his wont. Even when Logan had called at the house, Oliver had not taken offense at the biting wit and annoying impudence of his sister's suitor. He seemed to be very carefully taking Logan's measure and proceeding cautiously until he was sure of his man. Kit had been grateful for his restraint, and had rounded on Logan with a sharp scolding for his deliberately provoking behavior. Logan had simply grinned and commented that when a woman must pay to be courted, she must take what she could get. He had bargained to court her, not her brother.

The damp breeze that fluttered through the open balcony doors did nothing to cool the stifling bedroom. Kit tossed for a few moments, irritated by the damp, the heat, the tangled mosquito netting, and her own frame of mind. Finally, her restlessness drove her from the bed. She stripped off her limp night rail and donned a loose muslin shirt and coarse cotton breeches—the same highly improper attire that Doc had obtained for her during that first harrowing trip aboard the *Ice Maiden*. She had intended to discard the clothing but somehow just couldn't bring herself to do it.

What she needed, Kit decided, was a nice long walk to clear the musty cobwebs from her head. She would hike up to the village and listen to the songs she had loved since childhood. Perhaps they would bring back the peace of mind she seemed to have lost.

Twisting her heavy black hair into a loose knot, Kit completed her costume with a serviceable scarf wound around her head to keep back the loose ebony tendrils that insisted on curling around her face. Then she climbed over the balcony railing, swung out to a limb of the tamarisk tree that had served as her escape route since her tomboy childhood, and lithely shinnied down the trunk. Oliver would certainly take her to task if he caught her heading for the village at this time of night. Since her brother frequently sat in the library reading until the small hours of the morning, she wouldn't chance descending the front stairs and meeting him.

Kit was halfway along the trail to the village when she thought better of her plan. She remembered how restless the slaves had become. And wasn't there a haunting, mournful quality to their songs on this night that had not been there before? Perhaps going to the village right now was not such a good idea after all.

She turned off the trail and headed for the beach, thinking to watch the waves come in off the bay, and dabble her stockingless feet in the water as it ran up the sand. That would be just as good as watching the songfest. Better, in fact, for there would be no sharp pricks from the guilt Logan had so maliciously planted in her mind.

The beach was quiet, for the slaves' songs could not travel so far through the heavy night air. Even the little waves breaking on the sand seemed hushed and stealthy. An occasional glow of greenish luminescence lit up the incoming waves and flooded the night with an eerie glow.

Kit sat down on a driftwood log and enjoyed the cooling breeze that ruffled her shirt and played with loose wisps of her hair. She could sleep here, she thought, with the quiet whisper of the waves to still her thoughts and pleasant breaths of air to cool her skin. But of course she dared not. If she wasn't in her bed when Mandy arose in the morning, there would be a stiff price to pay. But it was so very pleasant....

Kit was just slipping into a drowse when a sound brought her senses flooding back. Her head came up with a jerk and her eyes flew open. Had that been the snap of a twig? She thought she heard a soft masculine voice whisper somewhere in the tangle of trees, vines, and brush that buried the back beach. Then there was naught but silence.

Mind stuttering with indecision, Kit froze. Should she stay still, hoping that whoever was in the brush would not notice her silhouette against the black sea, or should she quietly run for cover?

The ghostly green light from the sea flashed again. Kit could imagine her own clear outline etched against the glow. She sidled in a low crouch toward the concealing vegetation, hoping that the miscreants trespassing on her beach hadn't been looking toward the bay. She had no doubt that whoever they were, they were up to no good. A witness to their nocturnal activities would probably be welcomed with a pistol ball or the business end of a knife.

When the leaves and vines closed around her, Kit stopped and listened. There was no sound other than the quiet rumble of the waves. Minutes passed. Still nothing. With a puzzled frown she advanced, carefully stalking through the vines and creepers, meticulously moving branches from her path without a sound. But no more clues came to give away the trespassers' location. The brush was deathly quiet. Too quiet.

Then with heart-stopping suddenness a tree reached out and grabbed her. Or at least it seemed to be a tree coming alive like a monster in a child's nightmare. But the hand that clamped firmly over Kit's mouth was warm and human, and the hard body that pressed against her back was pliant muscle and sinew, not rigid wood.

"What am I going to do with you, Katarina?" came Logan's whisper. "You have a most unwise habit of sticking your nose in where it isn't wanted."

Kit breathed a sigh of relief, but the viselike grip did not slacken.

"Can I trust you to keep quiet?"

She promptly nodded her head. The hand over her mouth was removed, but the steel band of Logan's arm around her waist remained. Kit turned in the circle of his arm. His face was shadowed, but she could imagine those blue eyes burning down at her. The feel of his hard body against hers conjured up memories that sent her blood racing. She tried to twist out of his grasp, but he held her fast.

"Wh–What are you doing here?"

"Quiet." Logan's hand came up once again to cover her mouth. "Unless you want to see me swing, keep your voice down!"

She pushed his hand away. "What are you doing here?" she repeated in a whispered hiss. "Stealing slaves, no doubt! And probably mine! What else would you be doing here? Lord! Have you no scruples at all?"

"None, my love."

A soft hail made her stiffen in his grip. She recognized the Irish lilt of Michael Carmody's voice. "Is everything fine, Captain?"

"Everything is fine," Logan confirmed in a low voice. "Get our guests back to where we left the longboat. Tell Peter to take over. I'm going to be detained."

Carmody's disapproving gaze seemed to burn a hole in Kit's back. Then he was gone.

"Your guests!" she hissed. "You lying villain, bleating of human dignity and freedom while you make yourself wealthy by bartering slaves! Why don't you make your fortune like an honest pirate—by pillaging the Spaniards' gold? At least they can afford it!"

Logan laughed softly. "I've plucked enough feathers from the Spanish plumage to keep me well set up for a long time. Noble deeds are very satisfying to the soul, but they make for a poor living, I've found."

"Noble deeds! God but you have a twisted mind if you think . . . !"

"Relax, Katarina." Logan's voice was a calm, cold counterpoint to her own frenzied anger. "And quit being so damned indignant. I'm not quite the villain that you think me. I am stealing your slaves, and any other slaves who can manage to escape their masters. But not to barter them. I'm setting them free."

"Rubbish!" Kit tried to wrench herself out of his grip, but his arms were like a steel trap. "How can you set them free? They've no place to go."

"They do now." With wary caution he released her. "Come along. I'll explain on the way."

"On the way where?"

"Back to the house, of course. You shouldn't be wandering around alone out here, you know. Never can tell what sort of rogues you might run into on a night like this."

"Like filthy pirate slave traders?"

Perfect white teeth flashed in a sardonic grin. "Among other unsavory characters. I wouldn't want you to meet with a mishap and miss our appointment for a carriage ride tomorrow."

"I don't need your protection on my own property. I can take care of myself, thank you!"

"Faith, can you now? Seems to me you were headed into a bit of trouble when I waylaid you. My crew has a certain fondness for you, I'll admit, but some of them still might not like your snooping into our business."

Logan ignored her sulky petulance and steered her firmly up the slope from the beach. "We're taking the blacks to a small island about one day's good sail from here. It's large enough to support vegetation and some small game, but small enough to escape most people's notice."

Kit's eyes narrowed in suspicion. "And have I perhaps been dragged along on one of these trips?"

Logan grinned. "Perhaps."

One mystery solved, Kit thought. What she had seen that first dark night aboard the *Ice Maiden* was a transfer of escaped slaves—if Logan's story was true. She suspected he could be a convincing liar if he chose.

"The island is just a temporary refuge. From there several other buccaneers who've been slaves like myself convey the blacks back to their homes, if they know where their homes are. Some of the blacks don't want to leave the island, and they're forming quite a society on their own."

Kit was silent for a moment as Logan urged her through the dripping jungle. "That's a hard tale to believe," she finally commented.

"Is it?"

"If you're bent on revenge, you could surely think of a more telling scheme. The number of slaves you help to escape is a mere pinprick to the planters here."

His laugh was cynical. "Perhaps I am willing to only prick, for now."

Logan took hold of her arm and stopped. They had reached the trail to the village. The slaves were still singing. Kit wondered if the songfest was the village's way of bidding farewell to those who had run for freedom.

"Beautiful sound, isn't it?" he commented quietly.

Strange that Logan should appreciate the sound of those eerie songs drifting through the air. Kit had never credited him with such sensitivity. She suddenly found herself wanting to believe his story, even though her good sense told her not to credit a word of it.

"I don't believe for one minute that you're not making some kind of profit from all this," Kit insisted, defying her urge to soften toward him.

"Believe what you like, my lady." Suddenly impatient, Logan started down the trail toward the house, pulling Kit with him. "It makes little difference."

"What makes you think I won't run to the governor and tell him of this little scheme of yours?"

"You wouldn't be so foolish."

"Wouldn't I?" Her voice was breathless from the effort to match his long-legged pace.

"You wouldn't," he repeated with confidence. "Where would your little bargain be with me a corpse strung up on Execution Dock? I wouldn't be a very pretty suitor then, would I?"

"Perhaps I'm beginning to think that my little bargain was a bad piece of work best forgotten. Oliver is more easily borne than you are."

"Is that so?" Logan asked innocently.

"Yes! That's so. Suppose I release you from this ill-conceived scheme of mine?"

Logan merely grinned in a manner calculated to infuriate. "Not possible, my lady. I always pay my debts."

"Is that a threat?"

"Take it however you like."

Kit marched on in silence. It was hard to believe that they had once been lovers, she and Logan. Here she was pricking at him like a vicious little bitch, threatening to betray him, and here he was promising some nebulous revenge. How had she ever woven such a tangled web?

"I'm sorry," she said, suddenly finding the game tiresome. "I'm acting like a witch. Just forget you saw me here tonight, and I'll forget I saw you."

"It's not quite that easy, Katarina." Even in the darkness Kit could sense the intensity of his speculative regard. "What I had in mind was that you join me in my... uh ... business of liberation."

"What do you mean?" she demanded warily.

"The slaves have quite a communication system. All I need is one person—someone above suspicion—to convey notice of the time and place of our rendezvous. It wouldn't be difficult."

Wouldn't be difficult! The man was not only arrogant, he was mad.

"What in heaven's name makes you believe I would do a thing like that? You're the one who's a thief and a scoundrel, not me!"

It was starting to rain again. Warm rivulets ran down Kit's scarf and down the collar of her shirt. Getting soaked was an appropriate way to top off this night, she thought. Why hadn't she had the sense to stay in bed?

"I thought you might want to make up for past sins," Logan ventured.

"Past sins! I have no sins to atone for! My slaves are well treated and happy."

"Are they now?"

"Yes!" Kit stopped in her tracks, pulled the scarf from her head, and wrung it out. "I'm getting soaked. And I don't want to talk about this anymore."

"Of course you don't." Logan smiled condescendingly.

"Don't look at me like that. I don't have to justify myself to you—a thief, pirate, destroyer of innocence!"

"Destroyer of illusions, more likely."

Kit stomped angrily onward, her feet slapping wetly on the muddy path. "You're the one misled by illusions!"

"Perhaps," Logan conceded. "But think about it, Katarina. And if you just happen to visit the Elliot plantation, and just happen to talk to their cook Clarissa, tell her to have her people on the beach at Kendal's Point on the night of the twenty-fifth."

"She won't hear it from me!" Kit said stubbornly.

"Perhaps you don't know yourself as well as I do." He smiled gently.

Kit had a wild urge to hit him and wipe the smile from his face, but she knew the consequences would not be to her liking. Logan might put on the airs of a gentleman when it suited his fancy, but under that polished veneer lay the heart of a ruffian who would not hesitate to pay her back in kind.

"You needn't accompany me any farther." She came to a stiff-backed halt. "The house is just around the corner. If Oliver found us together at this time of night, you might find this false courtship swiftly becoming a very real marriage ceremony. I don't think that would suit either of us!"

"A disaster indeed!" Logan chuckled. "I will leave you to make your own way from here. Remember—Clarissa at the Elliots'."

He disappeared into the brush before Kit could throw a scathing retort. She certainly didn't like the lightness of his tone. Didn't the man take anything seriously?

* * *

The dapper merchant Edward Pettijohn called at Greenhaven promptly at eleven o'clock the next morning, just as he had promised. Kit watched him from the library window as he proudly showed Oliver his brand-new carriage and matched team of blood bays. By the time she walked out onto the veranda to greet him he was waxing eloquent about the design of his new rig, like any other well-to-do gentleman with a new toy, and had managed to inspire Oliver to yawns of boredom.

Edward's smile of greeting to her was bright and cheerful, with just the right amount of deference. His attire was eminently fashionable without being overdone or gaudy—tastefully subdued, as befitted a gentleman merchant. He looked harmless and hopelessly dull. There was no sign of the pirate who had only the night before filled her ears with threats and outrageous propositions. Logan Steele, Kit decided, should be on the stage in London. Mummery was where his true talent lay.

"Ah, my dear Katarina. You look absolutely ravishing this morning. Are you ready for our spin in my new equipage?"

"Of course." Kit gave him an icy smile. She wouldn't have him think that he was fooling her with this gentleman act. "I'm looking forward to it."

Oliver watched as Logan handed Kit politely into the carriage. Kit tossed back the curls that Mandy had laboriously wrought with the curling iron, adjusted the angle of her broad-brimmed plumed hat, then settled her voluminous silk skirts around her legs as Logan climbed up beside her. Oliver looked suspicious, as though he didn't quite believe the serene picture of his sister with her handsome, rich, and eminently suitable caller. He was still staring at them with a frown on his face as the new carriage rolled down the drive behind the lively stepping bays.

Hard as she tried, Kit could not lure Logan into a resumption of the last night's squabble. As they drove along the peaceful coast road to Bridgetown, he insisted on making pleasant conversation about the shipping business, the price of sugar, the latest Cromwellian politics, and the news that the Venables and Penn expedition was expected to sail for Hispaniola at the beginning of April. With anyone else Kit would have been delighted to converse in this vein, but with Logan there were matters closer to home that needed settling.

"Living rather high, aren't you?" she asked during a lull in the one-sided chatter. "This rig must have cost you a pretty penny."

"Indeed it did. But the Spaniards have been generous of late."

Kit arched one brow. "I wonder what the good residents of Barbados would say if they knew how you came by your wealth? It seems you have fooled them all with your charming disguise. It's a shame they don't know what you are—as I do."

"Are you so certain you know what I am?"

The look in those crystalline-blue eyes was unnerving, and Kit found that she couldn't hold her gaze level with his. "I know well enough," she replied softly. But suddenly she wasn't at all certain of that.

They stopped for tea at Bridgetown's fanciest hotel. The dining room was quite crowded, and Kit recognized several members of the governor's inner circle with their wives.

A prominent member of the Barbados militia detained them as they made their way to a table.

"Ah! Mr. Pettijohn. Miss St. John. Have you heard the good news?"

Kit nodded to the colonel's dowdy, gray-haired wife. She nodded back and eyed Logan speculatively.

"What good news is that, Colonel?" Logan asked.

"Rumors, really," the colonel admitted. "But damned—pardon me, ladies—dashed welcome good news if it's true. It's being said that the bloody Jackal has been taken and hanged by the Spaniards. I can credit that it might be true. Nobody's seen hide nor hair of that devil in months. Cause for celebration for you, Mr. Pettijohn. Your brother, Oliver, too, Miss St. John. Welcome news to anyone who sails these waters of ours, eh?"

"Welcome indeed," Logan said thoughtfully. "If it's true."

"Must be true. Else where is the fellow?"

Logan shook his head. "Never can tell what those devil pirates are up to."

"That's true enough!" Kit gave Logan a malicious smile as they excused themselves and made their way to a table. "You never can tell what those devil pirates are up to!"

"Indeed!" The grin he shot back was entirely unrepentant.

Kit sobered abruptly, thinking that in a week or so the *Carrie Ann* would be overdue in England, and speculation about her fate would begin. Only the crew of the *Ice Maiden* knew for certain that her demise had been at the Jackal's hands. But it was curious that no one else had sighted the infamous pirate in the last few months.

"Do you know anything about this?" she demanded in an urgent whisper. "You've been sailing the same seas, and on the same business. Have you seen any trace of that scoundrel's gray brigantine?"

"No trace at all."

"Do you think he's dead?"

"No," Logan said quietly.

"Why?"

"I'll tell you sometime later," he evaded. "Now tell me—that young gentleman there, and that other one over there, are they two of the host of suitors that your brother has shoved down your throat? They certainly pricked up their ears when you walked in."

For the first time Kit noticed George Porter sitting with Sherman Preston's giggly daughter. And two tables away Shelton Wheeler sat with an older man she didn't know. Both had pursued her favor, and her fortune, over the last few years. They were eyeing Logan with unfriendly interest.

"They're not Oliver's favorites," she told Logan. "They're younger sons of planters who thought to make a fortune by overwhelming me with their charm." She returned each of their glares with a devastating smile of the sort she had seen Mavis Edmond use on rejected suitors in her courting days. Logan watched Kit with amusement.

"You're a heartless female, do you know?" He politely held a chair for her to be seated.

"None of your business what I am," she replied in an equally soft voice. "What about all those winsome smiles that have been coming your way from every woman under fifty on the streets of Bridgetown, not to mention in this very room? Elizabeth Rogers is sitting over there against the wall, positively drooling in her plate of scones. What have you been doing since you got here—flirting with every woman in town?"

Logan gave her a bright smile. "Nay, Miss Jealousy. There is only one woman I've wanted since escaping my bonds. I'm afraid a delightful taste of her charms has quite spoiled me for more bland fare."

Kit labored to keep a polite smile on her face. She willed the hot flush that burned her skin to subside. Other people seated in the room were watching them with interest. She couldn't afford to make a slip here.

"I am not jealous." Every word was a soft hiss that belied the tender smile she gave him for the benefit of their audience. "Your reputation here in Bridgetown affects our bargain. That is my only concern."

He took her hand in a fond but most proper gesture of affection. Several matrons who were peeking out of the corners of their eyes smiled in approval. It appeared that the unconventional St. John chit was about to succumb to the matrimonial trap. And about time, too.

"Is that the same bargain you attempted to put aside last night?"

"As long as you insist on carrying on with your obligations," Kit said, withdrawing her hand in what appeared to be modest bemusement, "you might as well do it right."

"I'm glad you agree, my lady." Logan's tone was suddenly hearty, making interested onlookers wonder just what Kit had agreed to. "Drink up your tea and finish your scones. We've an errand to run."

The errand that Logan had in mind was not exactly to Kit's liking.

"This is most improper!" Kit frowned as Logan halted his new carriage in front of Bridgetown's most prominent dressmaker. "People will definitely get the wrong idea about our relationship!"

"Isn't that what you want?" Logan asked in an innocent voice. "Besides, no one is going to believe you're in love if you continue to be seen in such frumpish attire. A woman in love dresses to please her man."

"This is my best day gown!"

"Then you need more help than I thought."

Kit's frown was thunderous. "I fail to see how *you* could be a connoisseur of ladies' fashion."

"Smile, my dear." He handed her down from the carriage, eyes twinkling with mischief. "This is a busy part of town. People are watching. We wouldn't want word of your displeasure getting back to dear Oliver."

Kit pasted a smile on her face and felt her cheek muscles strain with the effort. "Dash Oliver!" she whispered as she accepted his proffered arm. "I don't know whose badgering is worse, his or yours! You're both cut from the same odious cloth, I'm thinking!"

Logan laughed softly, with an undercurrent of cynical amusement that Kit didn't like. "You may be closer to the truth than you know."

The seamstress called herself Madame Roget, and though her "French" accent sounded more like Cornwall than Paris, the creations that were displayed around her workshop bore witness to her talent. Her tongue clucked approvingly as she took Kit's measurements.

"Ah! *Bon! Magnifique, mademoiselle!* Eet ees so good to see a mademoiselle who does not look like she weel blow away in ze next poof of wind, *oui*?"

Kit suspected the lady had a different line of enthusiastic approval for every customer who walked through her door, but she smiled anyway.

"I 'ave designs that will make you look like a queen, no? As eef they were made just for you! I will fetch them for you to see."

When the little dressmaker bustled out of the room, Kit turned to Logan and regarded him with a baleful stare. "This is ridiculous, and most improper."

"How so, my love? I owe you at least one gown, for the

one you wore into Hispaniola was soiled past redemption at our little victory party, if I remember correctly. And it would be a shame to disappoint sweet Madame Roget by purchasing only one."

"Well, I don't like this one bit."

Logan shook his head. "You're the most unnatural female I've ever known. Most ladies are constantly thinking of the gowns and hats and fripperies they're going to buy. A herd of woman racing to be first in some new fashion is harder to withstand than a hurricane."

"Well, sir, I am not one of the herd!"

"No," Logan agreed with a smile. "I never thought you were."

Over Kit's strenuous objections, Logan ended up purchasing four gowns, two hats, and a lacy shawl before Kit could manage to drag him out of the shop.

"You must admit that they become you very well," he insisted, setting the two bays into a brisk trot and heading the carriage out of town.

"What I already have in my wardrobe becomes me just fine!" Kit replied, chin set at a determined angle.

"But you will wear them." His eyes swept her present attire in an impudent assessment. "They are much more flattering, and more fashionable, than the plain, colorless gowns in which you usually hide yourself."

Kit tilted her chin higher. "I wear what is appropriate for my frame, and that does not always fit the dictates of fashion."

Logan laughed, ignoring her pique. "I've quite an intimate acquaintance with your frame, Katarina. And I can assure you that these gowns will show it off to perfection! You sell yourself short, my sweet. You are really quite a stunning female, you know."

"Rubbish! I do not sell myself short. I do not sell myself at all! Perhaps that is something you should remember!"

"Don't worry," he replied with a grin. "There's very little about you that I could forget!"

Katarina doubted very much that his last words were meant as a compliment. The rest of the ride to Greenhaven was spent in silence.

Hours later Kit stared at her image in the full-length beveled glass mirror beside her wardrobe. Mandy's painstakingly wrought curls had been defeated by the weight of her hair. The broad-brimmed hat that had looked so perky that morning was limp from the damp air. The plume sagged over the brim and bounced in front of her eyes. And the gown... Maybe Logan was right. Dove-gray just wasn't her color. She had to admit that the fabrics Logan had selected, the reds, bright yellows, robin's-egg blue, and stunning lilac, had made her look alive and vital.

Alive and vital—certainly not how she had felt these past days. She remembered how glorious it had been to be alive and young that blessed week sailing home from Hispaniola. She had felt beautiful then, even dressed in a crewman's cast-off shirt and breeches. Every time Logan's eyes had fallen upon her she had come more alive, and every night when he took her in his arms and wooed her with that splendid body of his, she had felt her very soul burst with joy.

How sad that one must waste life on reality, when fantasy and dreams were so much more vibrant. For reality's sake she had destroyed the tenderness that lay between her and her private lover. That night in Mavis's garden she had spurned his advances with acid vehemence. He was a villainous criminal and not good enough for the pure and lofty Kit St. John. It was not what she had meant to say, but that was the way it had come out of her foolish mouth. In only a few moments she had managed to change their carefree dance of passion into a wary, bitter duel. She had stood up to temptation and spit in its eye, but in doing so she had spit in the eye of her own happiness as well.

Kit turned away from the mirror, not liking the image that stared back at her. She liked much better the temptress who had spent one magic week riding the sea in her lover's arms. Logan Steele was in her blood. There was something in the rogue that she couldn't stand against, no matter how aloof and indifferent she pretended to be. What she would give for one more night in his arms. Or better still, a lifetime in his arms.

Foolish girl, Kit thought. At heart you're no different

from any other witless ninnyhammer who melts at the sight of a handsome man. Frowning, she peeled off her limp gown, unpinned her hat, and shook out her hair until it fell in an ebony cascade about her shoulders. Then she turned once again to the mirror.

She did have her good points, Kit decided. While her face was not the pale heart-shaped vision favored by fashion, the slant of her dark sable eyes did give her a look of mystery, and her skin, olive tinted though it was, was very fine and had not a single blemish. Her breasts were small, but they were beautifully formed. Her figure was a bit boyish, perhaps, but there wasn't a single ounce of fat to mar the flowing, sinuous curves. She struck several poses, blushingly recalled several rather lewd comments Logan had made in the days of their intimacy, and decided that Kit St. John wasn't half bad after all. If a man like Logan could find her attractive...

Of course, even in their moments of greatest intimacy, Logan had never said that he loved her. Did she want him to love her? Did she love him? Kit wondered. The answer eluded her, but she couldn't let the man go until she found out.

Perhaps she would wear those bright new gowns Logan had bought for her. Kit smiled and imagined her transformed image. The rogue had outfoxed himself this time. He himself had handed her the weapons she would use to bring him to heel.

Chapter 11

"Is tonight's dinner not to your liking, miss?"

Kit idly pushed at the roast pork that she had scarcely touched. The heavy gravy on her plate was grooved with the paths that her toying had created. Her meal had been rearranged, but little had been consumed.

"The dinner is splendid, as always, Raleigh. You can give Mrs. Simpson my compliments."

"Of course, miss."

Raleigh gave her plate a disapproving look out of the corner of his eye and left the room.

"What's wrong, Kit?" Oliver took up the butler's theme. "You've hardly eaten a thing. Are you ill?"

"Of course I'm not ill," Kit denied halfheartedly. "I'm just tired, that's all. I think I'll go up to bed early tonight, if you'll excuse me."

"You do look a bit peaked. A bit of extra sleep will no doubt do you good."

One advantage of being female, Kit mused as she climbed the stairs to her room, was that gentlemen very rarely pressed the matter when a woman complained of an indisposition. There were too many mysterious female functions that were stricly taboo for male conversation, and the simple declaration that a woman was feeling slightly off-color was sufficient to send most men groping for a change of subject.

Not that Kit was in the least bit ill. She was healthy as an ox, and had been all of her life. The days when she had not been absolutely in the pink could be counted on one hand, and today wasn't one of them. It was just that she was restless, or perhaps one might go so far as to say she was nervous, Kit admitted to herself. Today was the twenty-fifth of March—the day when four of the Elliots' slaves were supposed to meet Logan at Kendal's Point. She had delivered the message two days before on a call to Mrs. Elliot and her bevy of daughters. Getting a private moment with the old black cook Clarissa had taken some doing, but Kit had managed. She had felt quite proud of her ingenuity, in fact. But there had been no chance to brag to Logan about her cleverness, for she hadn't seen him since their trip into Bridgetown. She hated to think of the trouble in store for those poor slaves if Logan didn't show up at the appointed time.

Logan's continued absence irked Kit in more ways than one. How was she to settle the confusion of her feelings for the insolent rogue if he stopped keeping her company? And worse still, she missed him—missed the quiet smile that could so suddenly turn into a wicked grin, missed the roguish sparkle in those clear blue eyes, and yes, even missed his damned irreverent impudence. Could it be that she truly loved him? Was it possible that the practical, realistic, down-to-earth Kit St. John could fall for a charming, unprincipled, disreputable, unreliable rogue like Logan Steele? Of course not! Highly unlikely. Well, perhaps....

This bothersome line of thought always came down to the same uncertainties. It seemed impossible to Kit that she could be truly enamored of a scoundrel whose past was littered with violence and rebellion. She was for the most part a moral and upstanding woman. How could she possibly love a man with a character so dark? It wasn't right. It didn't fit with her idea of what was possible and logical. Unless, of course, Logan Steele was not what he seemed.

Kit's imagination had leapt on the idea as soon as it had flashed across her mind. In the days since their visit to Bridgetown she had reflected on a hundred possibilities, casting Logan as everything from a military officer on a secret mission to a nobleman beset and betrayed by scheming relatives. Logan was much too educated, too cultured in speech and manners, Kit decided, to be a common criminal. The solution to the puzzle should have occurred to her before, but she was too blinded by prejudice, and then by passion, to see what was right in front of her face. Kit had spent long hours imagining how she could worm the truth from Logan next time he came to call. But the days had passed one by one, and he hadn't come to call. And here it was the twenty-fifth of March.

Kit paced back and forth, stopping now and then to look out the panes of the French doors, as if the answer to her problem might be found in the dark night sky. The thin crescent moon had dropped below the horizon. The hour was getting on toward midnight. If Logan didn't show up, those poor slaves would surely be caught. By the time they gave up waiting for their savior, it would be too late for them to sneak back to the Elliot slave village. They would be brutally punished, and it would all be Kit's fault. She had done too good a job of convincing Logan that she wouldn't do as he asked, too stubborn and nearsighted to recognize that there was more at stake in this game than her own precious pride. Kit fumed, paced, stared into the night, then made her decision.

"Dash it!" she muttered to herself. "I'll probably regret this before morning!"

Five minutes later she was once again sliding down the tamarisk tree in breeches and shirt. She ran to the stables in silent haste and, careful not to wake Adam, who slept in the tack room, she saddled Windwalker, swung lithely to the mare's back, and headed down the drive.

Kendal's Point was a good thirty-minute ride from Greenhaven. Kit and Windy traveled the distance in twenty. With every passing minute Kit became more convinced that Logan would not be there as promised. He would have believed her curt refusal to set up the rendezvous. After all, she had said nothing the following day to indicate she might relent. How could he know she would have a change of heart? She had been so sure that Logan would call at Greenhaven before the week was out and she would be able to tell him that the rendezvous was set. Damn his rotten hide! Why did he have to be so unpredictable?

A bank of clouds was rolling in from the sea, bringing a fine mist of rain that made the going soggy. If Kit had not ridden this way a hundred times before, she would have missed the sandy point of land that jutted out into the bay. Visibility was poor, but from what little Kit could discern, the sand appeared empty of everything but several sharp outcroppings of coral and the dark tangle of seaweed that marked the high tide. It had to be midnight, or maybe just after. Had the slaves come and gone? Or perhaps Logan had picked them up and they were safely on their way to the *Ice Maiden*.

Kit tethered her mare and crept silently along the edge of the vegetation. She was beginning to think she was on a fool's errand. Her clothes were soaked through. Her hair had escaped the coil at her neck and hung in dripping strands down her back. And worst of all, the night air had begun to take on a chill. She had about decided that no one except she was at Kendal's Point this night when a muffled sound of voices reached her ears.

She veered slightly inland to follow the sound, and in a very few moments came upon a scene that halted her in her tracks. Ducking behind a tree at the edge of the little clearing, she counted three men standing in the dim light of a torch. One of them she recognized as Logan, for no other man she knew could boast his height or those impossibly broad shoulders. His arms were crossed and his legs spread in an impatient pose that Kit knew only too well. Other men—slaves, by the look of their thin bodies—knelt or squatted on the ground. She couldn't quite make out the number. There were six, maybe seven. Certainly a larger number than she had expected. From the middle of their crude circle rose a soft moan. Apparently someone was hurt.

Kit sensed that not all was as it should be, but that wasn't her problem. Logan had come after all. Somehow he had known she would relent and deliver his message. Perhaps he did know her better than she knew herself—a rather frightening thought. Now that he was here, she could slip silently away and return home with an easy conscience. And there she could serenely await the praise and gratitude that would surely be forthcoming. If Logan was vexed with her, certainly now he would forgive her arrogant standoffishness. This would be a good start in pinning down that elusive heart of his.

Kit faded back the way she came. She was careful, but not careful enough. The sharp snap of a twig under her foot sounded like a gunshot echoing through the night. The figures in the clearing froze. Logan drew a pistol from the sash at his waist. The distinct cock of the hammer was every bit as loud as the ill-timed snap of the twig.

"Wait here!"

Pistol held at the ready, Logan advanced directly toward Kit's hiding place. She didn't know whether to flee or stay. If she ran and was caught, she would look hopelessly foolish, and Logan might well suspect her sneakiness stemmed from less than straightforward intentions. On the other hand, to stay would mean getting more deeply involved in this criminal escape plot, and would certainly involve a humiliating dressing-down from the very man she was determined to impress.

Split-second decisions were not one of Kit's talents. She hesitated for an agonized moment of vacillation. Then she ran. It was a mistake.

The way out of the jungle seemed much farther than the way in. Wet palmetto fronds slapped at her face, and vines entangled her feet. The darkness seemed like a cold blanket that muffled her in a wet, blinding embrace. If only she could make it to the edge of the jungle and Windwalker! If only she hadn't let her foolish conscience prod her into leaving her safe bed in the first place!

Then Kit remembered with horror that Logan had a pistol. Her steps faltered. She could almost feel a lead ball plowing into her back. Facing Logan's anger would have been better than being mowed down in her tracks. She stopped abruptly and started to turn when Logan's flying tackle sent her sprawling to the ground.

"Ooomph!"

Kit landed with a thud, Logan's body on top of hers. Together they slid on the wet and rotting vegetation and finally came to rest against the bole of a tree.

"Ouch! Dash it all, Logan! Let me up!"

There was a moment of stunned silence. Kit couldn't see Logan's face, but she was willing to wager that the all-too-familiar, infuriating grin was spreading across his features.

"What the devil?"

Kit made a hasty reassessment of his mood, for that tone never came out of a smiling mouth.

"Christ, woman! Don't you ever learn?" Logan made no move to release her, and she could feel his heart beating fast and heavily above her own. "Don't you ever use the brain God gave you?"

"You don't understand. . . ." Kit attempted to explain.

"You could have been shot! Damnation! If I had more skill with a pistol, you would have been shot! What in hell are you doing here?"

"If you'd just let me explain. . . ."

"Dammit! I don't have time to listen to your excuses."

But in spite of the declared shortness of time, Logan made no attempt to get up. They were neatly entangled in their damp bed of decaying leaves and vines. Kit looked up into the hollow of Logan's throat and could imagine the pulse beating there in time with her own. His broad chest flattened her breasts, and one of his legs was wedged between hers. She could feel the hard evidence of his passion rising as surely and steadily as the tide.

"Just what I need," Logan whispered, dropping his head and letting his brow rest against the wet ground. But there was a touch of wry humor in his voice. "You are fortunate, Katarina, that duty calls. Else we would finish this matter with you still on your back."

For a moment it seemed that desire might win out over duty, as Logan made no attempt to ease the intimacy of their position. Kit's body was awakening beneath the relentless pressure of his. She felt a sharp stab of disappointment when he finally heaved a sigh and rolled off her.

"You can explain later what foolishness brought you out here, but as long as you're already here, I suppose I could use your help." Logan grasped Kit's hand and pulled her to her feet.

"Oh, no," she objected, pulling her hand from his. "I was just going to go on home now."

His steellike fingers promptly closed upon her upper arm. "You're not going anywhere, except with me."

The matter in which Logan needed help became apparent when they reached the clearing. Three extra slaves had joined the original party of four, and one of those slaves was a young woman very obviously in the last stages of pregnancy. They were her moans that had risen from inside the circle of squatting blacks. Mother Nature had decided to intrude in a very untimely fashion.

Doc was kneeling above the girl when Logan and Kit stepped into the clearing. He looked up and recognized Kit, but didn't ask the obvious question. Instead, he raised a questioning brow at Logan.

"She know how to deliver a baby?"

"If she doesn't," Logan replied, "then she's about to learn."

"Now wait a minute!" Kit tried to back away, but Logan only gripped her arm more tightly and pulled her forward. She turned to Doc. "You're a doctor! You know how to deliver babies!"

"Girl starts screaming her fool head off if I so much as touch her. Doesn't want a man in on what she thinks is a female function."

"Well, don't look at me! Father didn't even let me watch our mares foal!"

"I suppose I can't force you to help." Logan released his hold on her and folded his arms across his chest, waiting. His face, lit dimly by the flickering light of Doc's torch, was a study in contempt for her cowardice. The eyes of the slaves, wide and white against their ebony faces, were filled with an expectancy that sat like a lead weight on Kit's conscience.

"Oh, all right! Dash it all!"

Kit stepped into the circle and knelt above the girl. She was quite a pretty thing, Kit thought, pushing damp crinkly hair back from a face that was ashy gray with fear. But she looked entirely too young to be giving birth to a child. Kit recognized her as one of the Elliots' household slaves, a kitchen maid or some such.

When the girl opened her eyes and saw Kit's face above hers, her face relaxed into a tentative smile. The smile ended in a contorted grimace as another pain bore down upon her.

"Is her husband here?" Kit surveyed the black faces that circled the girl.

"Ain't got no man, Becky doesn't," one of them supplied.

Kit glared at them in accusation. "Well, she's obviously got some man!"

"She's got a man," Logan agreed, "but I doubt he's black. The girl has been abused. Slaves don't do that to their women. They know they'll be whipped for damaging their master's property."

"You can't mean . . . !"

"Mr. Elliot or one of the overseers, no doubt. Good reason for her to run. When Mrs. Elliot sees the color of the babe's skin, she'll put the girl out of the house and into the fields. She's a tiny thing. I doubt she would last long cutting cane."

"That's nonsense!" Kit declared hotly. "I know Mr. Elliot, and he would never do such a thing."

Logan shook his head. "For having lived your entire life on a sugar plantation, Katarina, you've grown up remarkably innocent."

Kit didn't wish to discuss her innocence, or the matter of the baby's paternity.

"Well, she's obviously about to deliver. You can't be taking her to your ship in this condition."

"We don't have any choice," Logan said. "We've got to get these people out of here. Now that you're tending the girl, she at least will stop screaming at Doc."

"You can't move her! Dash it all, Logan, have some mercy! The girl is in labor! She'll die!"

Logan sighed impatiently as the blacks murmured among themselves. "What would you have us do, Katarina? Leave her here for the hounds to find when the escape is discovered in the morning? She will die in any case."

He gestured to the six black men who squatted around the girl. "Pick her up. Gently. Like this." He showed them how to make a cradle with interlocking arms. "We will take her to the boat. Katarina, walk with them and comfort her as best you can."

"But I can't go with you! My horse ... !"

"Will still be here when I row you ashore. Grow up, Katarina. This girl needs you."

The long, wave-tossed pull to the *Ice Maiden* was one of the most extraordinary experiences of Kit's life. The men grunted and heaved at the oars, while poor Becky grunted and heaved in the bottom of the boat. Her head in Kit's lap, her feet braced against the gunwales, she strained to eject the babe that Kit prayed would not make an appearance until long after they were safely aboard the ship.

Kit's prayers were answered. It wasn't until the small hours of the morning that the babe finally made his way into the world. When the slippery little morsel of new humanity slipped squalling from his mother's womb, Kit felt as proud, and as exhausted, as Becky herself. Logan had been right. The babe's skin was the dusky color of creamed coffee, and the wet little tufts of curly hair that plastered his head were medium brown instead of coal black. Kit wondered how the little mulatto would fare where he was going. Better, no doubt, than he would have fared on the Elliot plantation. This was a side of plantation life that Kit's father had never shown her. She suddenly felt older and sadder than she had just a few hours past.

The sky to the east was showing the first pale streaks of dawn when Logan set Kit back on the beach at Kendal's Point. The pull from the ship had been a silent one, and from the set of Logan's jaw Kit could tell that he was still angry over her intrusion into the night's adventure.

Kit was too numb to care if he was mad or not. She felt as though she had left the last of her energy, and the last of her illusions, on the *Ice Maiden* with Becky and her new baby boy. And Logan was no help. She had helped him out of a very awkward fix, and he couldn't spare one word of gratitude or comfort. Instead, he sat there glowering at her as if she were some misbehaving child. At the moment Kit wouldn't give tuppence for any man—Oliver, seducer of planters' daughters; George Elliot, abuser of young female slaves; or Logan Steele, exploiter of naive simpletons like herself. Did she really love this man? Did she want to love any man?

Logan kissed her before she mounted her mare, a kiss chaste enough to give a sister. Kit sensed that now was not the time to discuss her confused feelings about their relationship. He would no doubt laugh in her face, and that would be too much to bear. Life had become a tangle of uncertainties—about Logan, about herself, about the very foundations of right and wrong. Would she ever be able to sort them out?

Kit woke long after the sun had reached its zenith. Her head felt as if someone had stuffed it with cotton, her throat ached and rasped at every swallow, and her body seemed weighted down with lead.

Mandy was not sympathetic.

"Ye was up t' no good, last night, I know, miss. I was up late, I was, an' when I peeked in t' check on my lady, she wasn't here. An' it were well after midnight."

Kit saw no reason to dissemble. "I was with Capted Steele last dnight. He . . . he dneeded by help." Her voice was so nasal and raspy she could scarcely understand herself.

"I c'n imagine what kind o' help he needed!"

"Oh, Bandy! For heaved's sake. I was delivering a baby, dnot baking one."

"Well, you just watch yerself, love. I've seen that look in yer eye these past weeks. That rascal pirate has gotten under yer skin, an' ye mind my words, 'e's goin' t' lead ye in t' trouble! Ye should be settin' yer cap fer that nice Mr. Pettijohn who keeps callin'. Now there's a gent who 'as manners, an' 'andsome as well. Ye could do a lot worse, miss."

Kit would have laughed, but she was too miserable. "Just brig be some hot tea, Bandy. Leave the lectures until I feel better."

"Serves ye right! Runnin' about with pirates in the middle of a rainy night." Mandy was still muttering as she walked out the door.

Kit spent the rest of the day in bed, feeling sorry for herself and cursing Logan Steele for dragging her through the cold rain and causing her to catch this dreadful cold. And the scoundrel hadn't even had the decency to thank her for her help, or for carrying his cursed message to the Elliot plantation. As the day progressed, her cold got worse, and Kit got angrier. By the time the sun set, she had mentally rehearsed the vitriolic scolding she planned for Logan at least a dozen times.

Oliver knocked on her door right after she had finished the bowl of soup and soft bread that Mrs. Simpson had sent up to her room. When she called for him to enter—actually, it was more of a croak than a call—he pulled a chair up beside her bed and sat down with a properly sympathetic expression on his face.

"My Lord, Kit! Your woman Mandy said you were

feeling poorly, but I had no idea you were this sick." He grimaced and turned his face away as Kit endured a fit of sneezing. "Do you want me to send for a doctor?"

"Dno."

"How on earth did you get yourself in this condition?"

"Just luck, I guess," Kit wheezed.

"Well, this will cheer you up. I know how my being here has driven you mad. But my arm is healing very nicely, and I'm setting sail tomorrow for Portsmouth. It's time I started making us some money again." He grinned. "St. John Shipping just isn't the same without me at the helm. You'll be happy to get me out of your hair, eh?"

Kit nodded and attempted to smile.

"But there's one thing I'd like to talk to you about."

"What?"

"I wish you wouldn't see quite so much of that chap Pettijohn while I'm gone. Now, now!" He raised a hand as though to wipe away the frown that was gathering on Kit's face. "I know I've no right to tell you who you can or cannot associate with. I've learned my lesson there."

Kit wasn't sure that he had, but she let him continue. It was too much effort to interrupt.

"It's just that I've done some checking up on the fellow and I can't find a single soul who knows of his family in Sussex, from where he claims to hail. Even old Thomas Hathaway, who only came from Sussex five years ago, has never heard of any merchant family named Pettijohn. Modyford's the only proof of character the fellow has, and I don't trust Sir Thomas by half."

Kit sniffed. "I thought you'd be happy dthat I'b seeig subone."

"I'm delighted that you're coming out of your shell, dear. Just please come out of it with someone else—someone more reputable."

Kit sighed and let herself fall wearily back on the pillows. Now why would Oliver consider a thieving pirate and former slave disreputable? She permitted herself a smile. If he only knew.

"Dno promises," she replied.

Oliver shook his head and pursed his mouth. "That's

what I thought you would say. But don't you even consider marrying the fellow. If he's wooing you to get half control of our holdings, he's going to have a fight on his hands."

"Dno." Kit managed a little laugh. Not much chance of her marrying Logan Steele. He had been alternately treating her like an ignorant half-wit and a naughty child. And right now, she wasn't even sure she was on speaking terms with the scoundrel. "Dno. I do't thigk so."

Logan came calling at Greenhaven two days later. He walked through the archway into the stuffy parlor, bringing an eddy of fresh air with him, and an equally fresh grin.

"I hear you've been ill," he said as he crossed to the daybed where she lay. "Serves you right."

Kit grimaced. Not only no gratitude, no sympathy either. Didn't he care at all? "I see you're still mad," she sighed.

"Damn right I'm mad." He lowered his voice to an intense hiss. "What did you think you were doing, barging in on an operation like that? I could have shot you, dammit!"

Kit pouted, then glanced around to make sure none of the servants were within hearing distance. "You said you wanted my help, didn't you? I distinctly remember your asking me to join you in this scheme of yours!"

"I asked you to deliver messages, you little idiot. You had no right to endanger yourself!"

"What do you care if I endanger myself?" All the uncertainties that had teased Kit's mind suddenly rose and aimed themselves at Logan. If he cared about her, he wouldn't scoff at her illness. If he cared, he would acknowledge that she had endangered herself to help him. "Seems to me the biggest danger around here is you. First you threaten me, then you bully me into indulging in criminal behavior, then you drag me through the cold rain until I nearly catch pneumonia"—she coughed to emphasize her point—"and now you walk in here and call me an idiot when you should be thanking me for delivering your bloody message and helping you save Becky and . . . and not delivering up your rotten hide to Governor Searle and the militia! All that sweet talk you fed me aboard your ship, and in Mavis's garden—all that was a load of predictable masculine lies."

Kit paused for breath. She saw Logan's eyes congeal to brittle ice, saw his hand curl into an angry fist at his side. The smidgen of good sense that she still retained warned her she was going too far. But now she was on a roll, and she couldn't stop the bitterness from spewing forth.

"You've been using me all along. First to get your precious crew out of Santo Domingo, and now to get your precious slaves away from Barbados. You never cared one whit, did you? I was just a convenient bedmate, a gullible little mouse-brain who was foolish enough to believe that she could be loved, if only for a precious week. You must have laughed all the way back from Hispaniola!"

"Quiet, you little witch!" Logan ended her tirade by pulling her up and holding her inches from his forbidding face. "Do you honestly think I don't care about you?" He grasped her stubbornly set jaw in his long fingers. "Answer me, dammit!"

She opened her mouth to answer, suddenly frightened by his intensity. What her answer would have been promptly became irrelevant, for before a word could escape her mouth, his lips were on hers in a plundering, searing, angry kiss. This was not the gentle lover who had wooed her so tenderly in that wonderful week of dreams come true; this was the pirate, fiercely angry, brutally possessive, achingly passionate.

"I care," he rasped, releasing her mouth but holding her chin fast in his hand. "Don't you doubt it. And don't you forget it! And there might be some question as to who has been using whom these past few weeks!"

Kit ignored the accusation in his voice. As quickly as it had come, her anger dissipated. All the questions in her mind seemed no longer important. Logan cared! He really cared! All Kit's doubts exploded in a frenzy of joy as his mouth came down in another fierce kiss. Her arms went around him, savoring the breadth of his shoulders, reveling in the hard ridges of muscle that rippled in his back. She was melting, turning liquid and warm like molasses on a hot summer day. When his mouth left hers and he looked down at her, she could see reflected in those impossibly blue eyes the passion that was glowing in her own. Logan Steele loved her. She loved him. The world was set right again.

"Oh, Logan! I love you. It's taken me awhile to admit that there's more to you than meets the eye—or the ear—but I think I've always known, really, that you weren't truly the scoundrel everybody said you were."

Now, Kit thought, he would confide in her about who he really was, and why he was letting everyone think he was the scum of the earth. Then they would make sweet love. He would close and bolt the parlor door so no one would disturb them. Then he would come to her, push her gently down upon the couch, and brand her forever with the heat of his passion, the completeness of his love. Now was the moment. She waited hopefully.

"Faith!" He laughed. "I'm afraid there's not much more to me at that, darling girl." Logan caressed her cheek with the back of one hand, and Kit thought she saw a flash of regret darken his eyes.

She shook her head. "You don't need to pretend with me. I know you, Logan. You're not what Brownlow and Oliver said you were. You're not a mutineer. And I don't for a moment believe you're really a pirate. I love you. You're good and kind and gentle . . . willing to endanger yourself for the sake of a poor pregnant slave girl, and willing to risk your life to deliver your comrades from torture and death. You can tell me, Logan. I'll keep mum as a mute."

Logan sighed and gently set her from him. "I think you have the wrong man."

Kit's brows drew together in confusion. "What do you mean?"

"I mean you concocted some fantasy man of your dreams and poured me into his mold."

"That's not . . ."

"It is true! You really haven't grown up at all, have you?"

"What do you . . . ?"

"I'll tell you what I mean. I am not a fantasy. I am a man. And maybe I am a villain, a scoundrel, a rogue—as you've so often insisted."

"But . . ."

Logan advanced toward her again, forcing her back until her knees connected with the settee and she toppled backward onto the cushions.

"You listen, Katarina. Listen, and remember. I love you—God help me—in spite of your being a spoiled, hardheaded, childish female who doesn't know her own mind and usually doesn't have the sense God gave a mouse. But you love—heaven alone knows who or what you love. As for me, I'm not some hero running in a shoddy disguise. I'm every bit as shoddy as I appear."

"No," Kit said stubbornly. "I don't believe you."

"Believe me." Logan poked an angry finger at her face. "I was eight years a naval officer, and then I committed the worst crime a seaman can. I tried to wrest command of my ship from its duly appointed captain. The British Navy is a bit unforgiving about mutiny, no matter that my captain was more a madman than a commander." He turned away, his face tightening with pain. "I would rise against that bastard again if I had it to do over, even knowing the consequences. Maybe that makes me a scoundrel. In my eyes it makes me a man who does what he has to do to survive. If you can't love that, then you don't love me."

Kit looked at him in stunned amazement. Where was the Logan Steele she loved? Surely he wasn't this angry man who looked at her with such bitterness in his eyes.

"I don't believe you. You won't trust me with the truth. You're saying this just to test my love. And you're being totally unfair!"

"And you are acting like some ignorant maidenly schoolgirl. You expect everything to be painted in black and white. Everyone's either a saint or sinner. The real world doesn't work that way, Katarina."

His condescending tone made her even angrier.

"You of all people should know better than to call me maidenly, or a saint!" Kit's voice was sharp and bitter. Her dreams were shattering before her eyes.

"That's right," he replied calmly, one arrogant brow angled toward the ceiling. "You do occasionally slip off your virginal pedestal in a thoroughly delicious manner. Don't think I've forgotten."

Kit's fists curled into tight balls at her side. How could he? How could he take her trusting surrender to him and throw it back in her face? He was truly a villain of the lowest order!

"Climbing in bed with a man doesn't make you a woman, Katarina."

She jumped up from the settee, anger crowding good sense and caution out of her mind. Her hand came up and landed a stinging blow to that infuriating, sardonic face. Logan didn't budge, didn't flinch, only regarded her with cynical detachment. But a spark of raw anger ignited in the depths of his eyes.

"I'll show you who's a grown woman, you unprincipled oaf! I'm woman enough to toss you out on your ear, woman enough to do without the dubious pleasure of your rotten company for the rest of my days. Go find someone else to play games with, you vicious scum. Just leave me be!"

Before Kit had finished her tantrum Logan had left, and strangely enough, without his presence the room seemed bereft of life.

Chapter 12

Tom Trelawny shook his head dubiously. "You'll have to talk fast to get out of this one. Cap'n Steele's not going to like it. And he's been in a devil of a mood these last few days."

Kit pretended unconcern. "Don't worry. I'll take care of the captain. And I promise he'll never know you're involved." She peered into the dark little cubbyhole and grimaced. "Are you sure no one will find me in here?"

Tom shrugged. "Ship's all loaded and ready to sail. There's no reason for anyone to be nosin' around down here."

Kit sighed, squared her shoulders, and started to step into the little-used closet of the *Ice Maiden*'s main cargo hold. Then on second thought she turned and gave Tom a brief hug.

"Thank you, Tom. You're a real friend."

Tom blushed, then ducked his head to hide his face. "S'nothin'. Just hope Cap'n Steele don't have my hide fer this."

"I won't breathe a word."

Kit smiled a reassurance as the boy shut the closet door. As the sound of his steps faded, so did her smile. Trying to ignore a sudden feeling of claustrophobia, she settled herself as comfortably as she could.

It had been three long days since she had ordered Logan out of her life. Thinking back on that afternoon, Kit shook her head at her own stupidity. Her impulsive burst of temper had lasted only brief minutes after Logan had made his exit. And the time since then had been spent in regret and self-recrimination.

How far did she have to go to apologize? She had sent a note around to his house. Logan had ignored it. She had ridden into town specifically to see him. Logan hadn't been at home. But she had learned from his doorman, a brute from the *Ice Maiden*'s crew by the name of John Bonny, that Captain Steele, alias Edward Pettijohn, had offered his ship and crew to Admiral Penn and was to sail with the fleet the first of April.

It had not taken long for Kit to think of the perfect way to get Logan's attention, an idea inspired by Lady Searle's casual mention that there were some women sailing with the fleet. Many of the officers and a few of the soldiers and volunteers had brought their wives. If those females could go, Kit figured, then so could she. Mandy had thrown a fit, and the new overseer had looked worried when she announced her plans. But Kit was not about to let Logan sail away without so much as a fare-thee-well. Not with their relationship in such turmoil.

At the time it had not seemed like such an outrageous idea. Now that the deed was done, Kit was tempted to reconsider.

The closet was one pace wide and two paces deep, and after only a few moments crouching within its narrow confines, Kit was convinced that her little cubbyhole was a little slice of hell delivered up especially for her benefit. The air was stiflingly hot and reeked of tar, turpentine, and hemp. No ray of light penetrated the gloom—not even a sliver of the outer world to let her distinguish night from day. Time was marked only by the slow progression of dips, lurches, and plunges as the ship plowed through the Caribbean swells, the movement greatly exaggerated in the dark, stifling hole that had become Kit's world.

The hours marched slowly by, each one more miserable than the last, and each one bringing more and more doubt into Kit's mind. The motion of the ship had summoned up the old enemy—seasickness. Kit knew if she tossed up the contents of her stomach, the confined little prison would become unbearable indeed. So she spent the slow minutes and hours concentrating all her will toward keeping the queasiness at bay, forcing herself to breathe slowly and deeply of the fetid air, imagining the cool breezes and open skies on the deck above, and trying to convince herself that she had good reasons for being here. In this miserable closet, with the ship heaving under her and a rebellious stomach heaving inside of her, the need to follow and confront Logan did not seem nearly as pressing as when she had concocted her scheme. Perhaps she had once more demonstrated that, as Logan had once succinctly phrased it, she hadn't the common sense that God gave a mouse.

Kit's stomach was about to stage its final rebellion when Tom finally came to fetch her.

"You look green," Tom noted as he helped Kit pry her stiff body from the closet.

"I feel green." Kit swayed slightly as her stomach gave a demanding lurch. "Seems like I've been in there for hours."

"You have." The boy shrugged. "It took a bit longer than I thought for us to get this far out. The wind has been playing coy little games, and the most we've been able to make is two knots. I had to wait until we were too far out to turn back." Tom grinned sympathetically at Kit's doubtful look. "Don't look so glum. It won't be so bad. The worst he can do is keelhaul you."

Somehow, that assurance was not a comfort.

Logan did not keelhaul Kit. But the idea did occur to him, along with a number of other unpleasant and unsavory punishments. When Tom presented the stowaway, claiming in an innocent voice to have found her hiding in a closet in the hold, it was all he could do to keep from reaching out and shaking Kit until her sorry excuse for a brain rattled in her head. But he satisfied himself by simply glaring at the foolish twit standing so impudently before him. He hoped that the murder in his eyes would give her something to think about while he tried to think of something to do with her—or to her.

Kit nervously clutched her hands behind her and tried to look humble and contrite—something in which she had very little practice. She was glad there were other people on the quarterdeck, for she had never seen Logan look so darkly angry, glowering at her out of eyes that could have sliced through steel. Who knew what he might have done had they been alone? He looked as though he were mentally cutting her up and throwing her to the sharks.

Kit opened her mouth to make the excuses she had so carefully rehearsed. "I . . ."

"Don't say a word." Logan's curt order cut her off before she began. He looked big and thoroughly frightening, and to Kit's uncertain eyes, his every pore seemed to ooze menace. She was more than ready to admit that this little caper certainly wasn't one of her better ideas.

"You're damned lucky I'm a gentleman," he continued softly, bringing his face close to hers. "I've half a mind to turn you across my knee and pound your little backside until it's black and blue. With one and all here to watch."

"You wouldn't dare."

"Don't tempt me."

He took her ungently by the arm and hustled her down to the main deck and thence to the companionway leading belowdecks. She caught a glimpse of Peter sending Tom a mischievous and knowing smile, and Doc shaking his head in mock despair. The crew eyed her sympathetically. They were glad not to be in her shoes, Kit realized. At the moment she would be glad not to be in her shoes.

Logan deposited her in the stern cabin and left without so much as a word. When he closed the door behind him, Kit heard the snick of the lock sliding home. That was that, she thought. Not an auspicious beginning for the grand reconciliation she had planned.

She sighed and sat down on the bed, looking around her. So many blissful hours she had spent in this cabin. The memories came back in a flood—the slow awakening of her passion at Logan's expert hands, the dark hours of love play and discovery and laughter. How had she been fool enough to give all that up?

The cabin had changed considerably since she had last seen it. The unfortunate Spaniards had indeed been generous. A fine walnut table now stood by the door, and the old ratty wardrobe was gone. In its place was an ornately carved, double-doored wardrobe of fine oak. It was a piece of furniture fit for a prince. One of the heavy doors even displayed a gold-etched beveled mirror. The cabinet beside the desk, whose shelves were formerly lined only with dust and an occasional bottle of wine, now boasted at least a dozen leather-bound volumes. The wine was still there, but it was of decidedly higher quality. A rich wool carpet of Oriental design covered the bare wooden planks of the deck. Kit doubted that the little frigate had ever before seen such grandeur. Logan Steele was certainly making a profit from piracy.

Kit got up from the bed and went to the cabinet to examine the titles of Logan's new library. It was then that her eye was caught by the pencil drawing above the desk. The drawing that had hung there before had shown a many-gabled stone house surrounded by enormous trees. The name Somerset was penciled in one corner. She remembered the drawing well, for it was a striking piece of work. Logan had admitted to her one night, when they were both mellow from well-sated passion, that he himself was the artist. He refused to reveal how he came to know the house or what it meant to him, but Kit had guessed from the skilled and loving detail of the drawing that it represented something important in his life.

But the drawing of the house was no longer above the desk. In its place hung a lovingly drawn portrait of a young woman, a head and shoulders study that was so beautiful Kit scarcely recognized herself. Was that how Logan saw her? That exotic face, half angel, half imp; those dark mysterious eyes, from one angle dancing with mischief and from another burning with sensuous fire; those delicate lips, curved in a smile that was at once an invitation and a challenge. Was that how Kit St. John really looked? Or was the woman in the picture as much a figment of Logan's imagination as the mysterious hero Logan Steele had been of hers?

The hours crawled slowly by. Logan did not come. Kit paced restlessly from the bed to the wardrobe and back again. Evening came, and she paused in her pacing to light the lanterns and watch the sea grow dark. Tom Trelawny brought her a meal of biscuits and hearty beef soup, then came again to clear away the remains. And still Logan didn't come.

Kit's apprehension grew as the night grew slowly older. Logan must be truly angry to stay away this long. Most likely he was sifting through his catalogue of pirate tortures in search of a punishment suited to her crime. Or perhaps her presence meant so little to him that she was not worth the bother of a confrontation.

Kit resumed her pacing, rehearsing in her mind the words she would say, words that would convince Logan that everything between them could be so right if he would only show a willingness to be reasonable. Of course he hadn't looked a bit reasonable when he had stalked out of the cabin and slammed the door behind him, and he certainly hadn't looked reasonable when she had faced him on the quarter-deck. He had looked like a man ready to do murder.

She stopped in front of the beveled, gold-etched mirror and frowned at herself. Perhaps this time she had bitten off more than she could chew. She had given Logan quite a set-down, Kit admitted, and perhaps he shouldn't have to make excuses to a woman who claimed to love him. But at least he could have declared that her love had made him a new man who would walk the straight and narrow path from that day on. At least he could have done that. Any man with an ounce of decency would have done that. Not that she had really given him a chance. Her show of temper had left no room for rebuttals. But then, if Logan expected her to forgive his little faults, why couldn't he forgive hers?

Kit was still frowning into the mirror when Logan strode in and slammed the door behind him. He did not look to be in a mood either to forgive or be forgiven.

Silence stretched between them like the breathless quiet before a hurricane. Logan stood in the middle of the cabin, legs spread apart in an arrogant stance, arms crossed over his chest. Through narrowed eyes he regarded Kit with the same affection he might bestow upon a slug trailing slime across his newly holystoned deck. Finally he spoke.

"Tell me, Katarina. To what imp of misfortune do I owe the dubious pleasure of your presence aboard my vessel?"

"I . . ."

"Let me guess. Thinking you were too gentle at our last parting, you've thought of additional insults to hurl my way. You followed me out to sea just to deliver them."

Kit bristled. "We had a bargain, if you recall. Did you think I would let you sail off without so much as a by-your-leave? I have an investment in you, sir!"

"The bargain is over." He smiled wickedly. "Your brother sailed five days ago for parts unknown. I believe the debt is paid in full."

"Portsmouth," Kit corrected, meeting his smile with one just as wicked. "Not parts unknown. I thought you were the one who knows everything, Captain Steele."

"Portsmouth, then. No matter. He's gone. You and I, Miss St. John, are finished with each other. I believe you have been paid in full for services rendered."

"Is that what you think?" The nerve of the scoundrel! Services rendered indeed! "Our bargain did not include your leaving so abruptly and jilting me under the eyes of all Barbados!"

"It was you who demanded I get out of your life."

Kit lifted a haughty brow. "I changed my mind."

"Faith! Did you now?" For a moment Logan looked as though he would dearly love to strangle her. Then he laughed and shook his head. "Trust a woman to change her mind. Is that why you came running after me?"

Nose in the air, jaw set at a determined angle, Kit gave Logan her most withering glare. "I am not running after you."

"What would you call it?"

Kit groped for an explanation. The real reason for her behavior would only give a boost to Logan's already insufferable ego. "I . . . I am . . ."

"You are the biggest fool I've ever had the displeasure to meet. That's what you are. Especially if you think that silly bargain of yours is the only thing between us now."

His voice was clipped and merciless. His gaze caught and held hers, seeming to pierce to her very soul. What was the use of dissembling? Kit thought. He saw through her every ploy. He always had, it seemed, since the first moment they had laid eyes on each other.

She threw up her hands in a gesture of despair. "All right, I did run after you. I couldn't let you sail out of my life thinking that I . . ."

"That you don't love me?" Logan's gaze was relentless, refusing to spare even an inch of her pride.

"I might have said some things. . . ." Kit grimaced painfully. Surrender was not easy, especially to someone already gloating with victory. "Everything I said that day . . . it was my temper speaking."

"I never would have guessed." A tiny smile pulled at one corner of Logan's mouth, cracking the granite of his face.

For a moment they simply looked at one another, Kit's eyes full of doubt, Logan's full of triumph. Then he moved, coming toward her like a hungry tiger stalking his prey. Kit's breath caught in her throat. She backed up one step, then two. Then the bulkhead was behind her and she was caged by his arms, one on either side of her shoulders. Her body stiffened, half with fright, half with wayward longing.

"You are an unspeakable little idiot," Logan growled. "Did you really believe I would sail out of your life? I wouldn't make it that easy for you, Katarina. I would have come back to plague you. Never doubt it.''

Kit opened her mouth to answer, but whatever words were on her tongue remained unspoken, for her lips were swiftly appropriated by Logan's. His mouth was the only part of him that touched her, and it promptly became the focus of her existence. She felt herself melt inside, turning warm and liquid like sweet syrup on a hot summer day. His tongue thrust and plundered, exploring the sweet hidden caverns of her mouth, slipping over the pearly gems of her teeth, and playfully twisting and warring with her own. When he finally drew back, it seemed as though Kit's soul went with him.

"God help me!" Logan groaned. "I'm out of my mind with love for you."

Kit closed her eyes and reveled in the sound. "Say it again," she pleaded.

"I'm out of my mind."

"No! You villain!" She laughed and shoved him back.

"I love you." He relented with a smile.

"And I love you, Logan Steele." She raised one hand and traced with a wondering finger the firm line of his jaw. "I've loved you since I first saw you, I think, skinny as a stalk of cane and insolent as a braying jackass."

"I know you have," he said with a modest grin. "It's just taken you this long to come to your senses. Tell me, Katarina, love. Are you ready to stop being so spoiled and childish?"

"Probably not," she said with an impish smile. "Are you ready to stop being insolent and stubborn and unreasonable?"

"Certainly not." He pulled her gently forward and cradled her against his chest. His heart drummed pleasantly against her ear. "God only knows what will become of the two of us. I think we're both out of our minds." He sighed at the visions of disaster that flashed across his mind. "This isn't going to be easy."

He was right. It wasn't going to be easy at all.

* * *

Kit sat cross-legged on the deck, a rope coiled in her lap like a tame snake. For all the cooperation she was getting from the length of limp hemp, it might as well have been a snake.

"No!" Tom admonished for the fifth time. "Through the loop, over, around, and through again. Like this!" He took the rope from Kit's hands and demonstrated once again the proper procedure.

Kit sighed. For two days now she had been studying the science of nautical knots. The knots seemed simple enough when Tom explained them, but when the rope was put into her hands, Kit promptly grew five thumbs on each finger.

"Let's give up for today," Kit suggested hopefully.

"Good idea." Tom was trying to be a patient teacher, but his limits were stretched so far they were about to snap. "I have work to do anyway."

Kit strolled over to the rail and looked out at the endless expanse of blue. She seemed a world away from the green fields and lush jungles of Greenhaven, and yet only three days had passed since Tom had stuffed her into that loathsome closet in the hold below, two days since she had emerged to face Logan's wrath.

Her days had been well occupied doing light chores on deck or helping Jud Smythe in the galley. Logan insisted that everyone on the ship pull his own weight, so he had put her to work. Time between chores was filled with instruction on subjects Logan deemed necessary to her welfare—swordplay, knife-fighting, wrestling, rudiments of sailing, and young Tom's particular favorite—dirty-trick dueling.

Tom had puffed up with pride when his captain had asked him to teach Kit the rudiments of fencing. But Kit's lack of talent had quickly convinced him of the hopelessness of his task. So he taught her the unconventional tricks and unchivalrous cheats that might give a more skilled attacker a nasty surprise or two. Kit might as well learn to defend herself in the most efficient manner possible, Tom insisted, even if it meant cheating. One never could tell when a lady might be called on to defend herself. The boy had cast a glance in the direction of the forecastle, where fifty of Venables's troops took their exercise. His meaning had been

clear, for the men that Cromwell had sent to conquer the
Spanish colonies made Logan's buccaneers look like gentlemen.

If Kit's days were busy, her nights were less than restful.
It had seemed only natural that she share Logan's cabin.
And it had seemed equally natural when Logan wanted her
to share more than the cabin. But Kit had promptly squelched
any ideas about resuming their physical intimacy.

"You don't understand!" she had attempted to explain
her feelings that first night, facing Logan across the big bed.

"You're right," he had thundered. "I don't understand!
You want me to sleep alone while the woman I love sleeps
three feet away on the damned window seat? Lady, you have
an indecent flair for torture that puts the Spanish Inquisition
to shame!"

"Must be my Spanish blood," she had quipped, attempting
to chase away the dark clouds that were gathering on
Logan's face. But he was in no mood for humor.

"Damn fickle-hearted female!"

"I am not fickle!" She had been desperate enough to
plead. "Promise me that when you get back from this fool
expedition you'll not resume your pirate life. Say you'll go
to one of the Dutch or French colonies and earn your fortune
honestly. Promise me that and I'll be yours, however you
want me, whenever you want me."

Logan's eyes had narrowed. "You're the one who doesn't
understand. You are already mine. You have been since that
first night out from Santo Domingo. This night is no
different from the others when we lay together."

"It is!" she insisted. "Then I was a fool. I didn't realize
that making love was more than just a . . . a physical act—
that it spins a web of need and dependence that makes two
people belong to each other."

"It is only so when you truly love, Katarina." His voice
had been quietly intense as he reached out for her across the
bed. Kit's body had strained toward Logan of its own will,
and drawing back from his touch was the hardest thing she
had ever forced herself to do.

"No." Her voice was quietly determined. "I will not
give myself to a man I can't have for my own. And I'll not
have an unrepentant renegade."

At that Logan had laughed bitterly. The sound had tripped warning bells in Kit's brain, for there was a hurricane gathering in his eyes.

"Unrepentant renegade, am I? Perhaps I shouldn't bother to argue. Perhaps I should just push you down on the bed and make love to you until you're too exhausted to protest."

"You wouldn't!"

"Wouldn't I? An unrepentant renegade would hardly balk at rape." He had smiled wickedly at the expression on her face. "Don't look so frightened, Katarina. I would make sure you enjoyed it."

Kit's heart had pounded in her chest. Half of her had wanted him to do it, and she was ashamed of her weakness. She had stared at him across the little distance that separated them, eyes wide with horror both at the leashed violence she sensed in him and the undisciplined passion in herself.

The tension had snapped abruptly as Logan turned away in disgust. "Take your half of the bed," he had said gruffly. "The sun hasn't yet risen on the day when I have to resort to rape to get what I want."

He had left the statement hanging in the air between them, implying that he had ammunition yet unfired. And now, standing and staring at the empty blue sea, Kit shivered, remembering the confident sensuality of his voice.

It wasn't until they anchored off Point Nizao on the island of Hispaniola that Logan brought out the big guns for his final attack. The night was perfect for a battle of the sexes. The air was balmy, the sea still. The whole ship was dark and quiet. Venables's troops crouched together in the forward hold, honing their weapons and gathering their courage. Elsewhere in the quiet fleet men prayed for victory. Others dreamed of the riches waiting for them in a crushed and beaten Santo Domingo.

But Logan thought of none of these things. The victory he prayed for would soon be at hand, and all the riches he wanted lay sleeping on the big bed in the stern cabin.

Kit stirred sleepily as Logan lowered his weight onto the

bed. For two nights he had reined in his desires and acted the gentleman. No more. He wasn't a gentleman. He was an unrepentant renegade, just as Kit had named him. He always had been, and always would be. He was also a man in love. And though he might be above rape, he was certainly not above seduction.

"Katarina." His voice was a whisper of promise in the night.

Kit murmured in protest.

"What is this?" His breath was warm against her neck. "Will you send me off without even a good-bye kiss?"

One eye slitted opened. "Where are you going?"

"Where do you think I'm going?" Logan's perfect white teeth flashed in the dark. "To oust your fat uncle from Santo Domingo."

The other eye opened. Kit turned toward him with a frown. "You said none of the *Ice Maiden*'s crew had to fight."

"But I wish to fight."

His arm circled her waist. She could feel the warmth of his flesh through the thin muslin shirt that she wore as a sleeping garment.

"Why?"

He chuckled. "Perhaps I lust for the Spanish riches like everyone else."

"Rubbish! You've riches enough of your own." With both hands she firmly set his arm away from her. "I know what you lust after, Logan Steele, and you're not going to get it. Not unless you've decided to become a decent and upstanding man." She turned over and gave him her back.

"I'm a very upstanding man." He pressed against her, demonstrating just how very upstanding he was. His breath tickled her ear. "What's more, I love you."

Kit could feel the warmth of his body as Logan stretched out beside her. His nearness played havoc with her senses. On the nights before, she had forced herself to ignore the masculine temptation lying next to her. But tonight it was impossible. There was a sense of waiting, a coiled-spring tightness of his presence that set the very air aquiver.

"You shouldn't go," she finally said, keeping her back to

him. "If you're captured, my uncle will have you roasted for dinner."

"I have to go."

There was enough regret in his tone to make Kit believe him. Dark visions crept into her brain—Logan lying shattered and bloody on a Spanish hillside, or broken and screaming on a Spanish torture rack, his spirit and body buckling under Esteban del Vargas's unrelenting cruelty. Try as she would, Kit couldn't push the images away. She turned back to face him.

"You're not going to tell me why, are you?"

"No."

They looked at each other for a moment that seemed suspended in time. Her eyes roamed over the familiar rugged contours of his face. How could she let him go without a single word of kindness from her?

"I am sorry to be such a witch, Logan. I do still love you. Believe that."

"I believe it."

He loomed above her, so overpoweringly masculine that Kit's breath caught in her throat.

"Maybe one little good-bye kiss," she said in a soft voice.

It was surrender. Kit knew as well as Logan that one little kiss wasn't possible between them. His mouth came down on hers in a gentle exploration that soon became a savage demand. She yielded, opening her mouth to his thrusting tongue and arching against his hard body with a silent plea of her own.

"Katarina, my love. God, how I've missed you!"

Kit herself unbuttoned the front of her shirt to give his mouth access to her aching breasts. His hands circled her waist, holding her captive while his tongue teased her nipples into rigid delight. When she managed to wriggle completely out of her shirt, they lay flesh to warm flesh, craving closeness as a dying man might crave life.

"Don't go tomorrow." There was pleading in her voice. She hated it, but it was there just the same.

"There is no tomorrow, Katarina." The low, husky voice was laced with passion. It vibrated through Kit's body and set every nerve aquiver. "There is only tonight," he whispered. "And when you remember tonight, remember that you are mine, completely, and I am yours."

He proceeded to demonstrate what it meant to be his. Hard, callused hands drifted across the hills and plains and hollows of Kit's body, firing a blaze of sweet fire wherever they touched. Lips grazed on the satin of skin, recognizing no boundaries and no limits to their wandering caress, devouring the heat of her desire and feeding it back again tenfold.

Kit willingly gave herself over to Logan's tender attentions. She drifted on a warm sea of passion, floated above the tawdry world of conventions and proper behavior. Her own hands went brazenly exploring. Smooth muscles bunched and flowed beneath her touch. Male nipples, flat and hard, puckered at the merest brush of her tongue. Never before had she felt so flushed with seductive power. It exhilarated her beyond all reason. Greatly daring as she never had been before, she trailed her hand down Logan's muscle-ridged belly, and lower still, following the line of coarse springy hair that arrowed down to his groin. Holding her breath, she circled the instrument of his desire with her fingers.

"God, woman! You don't know what you're doing." Logan breathed a muffled groan as he buried his face in her aching and swollen breasts. His hair brushed her chin, silky soft and smelling of sea wind and sunlight.

Kit did know what she was doing. Her fingers traced the hot, throbbing length of him, teasing, caressing, playfully stroking. His response was immediate.

With gentle insistence he pulled her beneath him. His knee wedged between her legs, and his hand worked wicked magic of unspeakable intimacy. She felt his manhood poised against her thigh, hard, hot, and straining toward her softness.

"Please," she whispered. "Now, Logan. Now."

He eagerly complied. It was as if they were made to fit together, two halves of a whole. Kit wrapped her legs around him and urged him deeper, faster. He answered her urgency with a surge of raw power that sent her soaring up to the crest of fulfillment. Then he held her there for long, tortured, ecstatic moments, until she could bear no more.

She pleaded. He responded. They broke through the limits of sight and sound and feeling, spiraling into a flight that even angels might envy, locked together, one mind, one soul, one heart. In a distant corner of her brain, Kit wondered why it had taken so long for her to realize how completely she belonged to Logan Steele.

Chapter 13

When Kit's eyes finally opened the next morning, sunlight washed the stern windows and painted bright waves and ripples on the deck above her head. The bright patterns swayed in unrhythmic drunkenness as the *Ice Maiden* wallowed in a moderate swell. Kit was warm and drowsy and utterly content, even though her sleep the night before had been limited to brief naps between sessions of energetic loving. She had never felt so rested, and so completely at peace with herself and the world.

Then her seeking hand encountered the empty space on the bed beside her. Logan was gone. Even his warmth was gone. The only thing left of him was the indentation of his head on the pillow and the faint masculine scent of him that intermingled with the musky fragrance of their passion.

Kit muttered an unladylike epithet and shut her eyes against the morning. How could she have slept through Logan's leavetaking? How could he have let her? She hadn't had a chance to tell him that reality and common sense no longer mattered. Promises for the future didn't matter. She was his even if he wanted to be a pirate and scoundrel for the rest of his days. Just so he was her pirate and scoundrel. He was her reality, and nothing else was worth the breath to blow it away.

The joy of the morning dimmed. Logan was not there to

say good-bye, or to share a farewell kiss, or to reassure her of his love. He had declared imperiously that there was no tomorrow. But he had been wrong. Tomorrow had come, bringing with it renewed visions of Logan surrounded by the smoke of battle, spilling out his life on the hills above Santo Domingo.

Kit opened her eyes again. With determined energy she swung her legs out of bed. Why was she filling the morning with gloom? Of course Logan would return. He was too alive, too strong, too clever, to be cut down in a silly battle such as this one. Hastily she donned stockings, breeches, and shirt, splashed cool water on her face, and moved to the mirror to brush her hair and fashion it into her usual sedate bun.

A breeze from the stern windows played around the cabin as she smoothed back her ebony mane. From the corner of her eye she caught the fluttering of a piece of vellum. It was a note, pinned to—she dropped the twisted length of her hair in surprise. The note was pinned to the pencil sketch of her that hung above the desk. Half afraid, she moved near to read it.

"Katarina," the note began. "I can make only one promise for the future—that I will love you for all my days, and cherish you as a drowning man cherishes his last breath. You are the best part of my life. Guard yourself, and don't forget that you are mine. And I am yours."

Carefully Kit unpinned the note, holding it in her hand as though it were a delicate jewel of great value. Then she folded it and put it into the pocket that lay over her heart. Logan loved her! She was not just a moment's passion. He would love her for all of his days. He had promised. Kit wanted to break into song right then and there, to give voice to the joyous melody that echoed in her heart. The crew would think her daft, but what did she care. Logan Steele loved her. He had taken a drab little mouse and made her feel like a princess. He loved her!

She twirled around the cabin, stopping only when dizziness sent her sprawling onto the bed. Bouncing back up, she headed gleefully for the door, anxious to shout her joy to the open sky. With her hand on the door latch she found herself facing another note in Logan's hasty scrawl.

"I can also promise this—if you try to follow with the second load of troops, you will not be able to sit for a month. Behave yourself, Katarina. I should return within a week."

Now, how did he know that in the small hours of the night her mind had dwelled upon just such a plan? But even she had more sense than to follow Venables's misbegotten troops on the trail to battle. Did Logan think her a fool? A smile touched Kit's lips. No doubt he did. He had named her one often enough. And not without reason, she had to admit.

Up on deck the sun was bright, even though the air held a hint of coolness. The masts and yards of the frigate swayed starkly against the intense blue of the sky. Kit paused at the rail to survey the exceptional view of thirty-nine ships crowded together in one small, semiprotected anchorage. The stripped poles and spars looked like a forest of naked trees.

"Hi," Tom said, slipping up beside her.

"Hello." Kit sighed, looking like a cat that has just lapped up an entire bowl of cream. "It's a wonderful day, isn't it?"

"Yeah, I guess." The boy looked longingly toward the shore.

Kit came down from her cloud long enough to notice her young friend's mood.

"You don't look happy."

"Yeah. Well, I wish I was with the troops. I wanted to go, but the cap'n wouldn't let me. Everybody treats me like a kid."

Kit's voice assumed a motherly tone. "Captain Steele is just thinking of your welfare. There's going to be fighting in Santo Domingo. People are going to get hurt."

The thought knocked Kit off her cloud. There was going to be fighting, and if Logan should happen to be taken prisoner... Kit jerked her mind away from the possibility. She had written her uncle, telling him of her safe return to Barbados, and he had replied with a missive so angry it might have burned the paper where it was written. He wasn't angry at her. He was all sympathy where his niece was concerned. But he swore that the "wretched pirate" would live to rue the day he had trifled with Don Juan Fernandino de Mendez Arguello.

"I'm not scared to fight," Tom asserted, breaking in on Kit's sober thoughts. "Besides, no one can beat Cap'n Steele. Our fellows will win."

"Yes. I suppose they will."

The doubting tone of her voice belied her words. She remembered Logan's bitter complaints against Admiral Penn and General Venables. Kit had learned some new descriptive language as Logan had cursed the fool who concocted the idea of giving Penn and Venables divided but equal command of this misguided sortie against Spain's colonial might. The expedition was poorly equipped, morale was low, and Penn and Venables did nothing but squabble. Logan had been talking treason, of course, criticizing Lord Cromwell that way. But added to the list of his other crimes, treason seemed a minor thing. And Kit agreed with him. Perhaps she was prejudiced because it was her uncle that was being targeted as the enemy.

"Not many of the crew went with the troops," Kit noted.

"They're pirates, not soldiers." Tom screwed up his freckled face in a grimace. "Pirating is one thing. Mucking through the forest to fight a pack of bloody Spaniards on their own territory is something else again. At least it is for these fellows."

"You seem anxious enough to go."

"I'm not going to be a pirate all my life. I want to be a military man."

"Oh." Kit glanced around the deck. "I don't see Peter around. Did he go?"

"Yeah. He went. Said the captain shouldn't be the only one from the *Ice Maiden* to fight." Tom snorted. "They should've taken me with them. I'm not a kid anymore."

Kit put her arm around the boy's shoulder, bringing a faint blush to his face. "I don't think you're a child, Tom. But all the same, I'm glad you're here with me."

Ten days passed in a slow, plodding succession of sunrises

and sunsets. There was nothing for Kit to do except stare at the hazy green hills that had swallowed her love—stare in hopes that those same hills would cough him up again whole and healthy and victorious. On the eleventh day, part of her wish was granted.

It was a sorry lot who finally returned from Santo Domingo, tails between their legs and heads bowed with exhaustion. The troops poured out of the longboats and up the sides in a bloody, tattered mass. Some hobbled aboard under their own power. Others had to be tied into slings and hoisted over the side. Of the five thousand men who had set out eleven days before, one thousand did not return at all. The captain and first officer of the *Ice Maiden* were among the fortunate few who came back with most of their parts intact.

Kit waited impatiently on the quarterdeck and scanned the face of each man who climbed aboard. Peter climbed through the gangway and gave her a smile, then gestured her toward him. Kit obeyed, the knot of apprehension in her stomach drawing tighter by the second. She stopped in her tracks as Logan stepped over the side, then, ignoring the knowing smirks of the crew, rushed forward to fling herself into his arms.

"Oh, sweet Lord!" she cried, wide eyes taking in the crimson stain on his shirt. "You're hurt."

"A scratch. Nothing more." He touched her face, looking like a man who had just found water in the desert. His face was haggard and gray.

Kit hastened to pull Logan toward the hatchway and into their cabin, where she could clean his wound. Peter followed behind.

"I don't know why I worried about you," she scolded. Her throat threatened to close with the swell of relief she felt. "You're too damned obnoxious to die. God wouldn't want you, and neither would the devil. At least not until you've mellowed some."

Logan managed a smile. "For that, I'm grateful."

Peter stood and watched as Kit helped Logan out of his bloodstained doublet and shirt. "You ducked too fast, my friend, or that musket ball wouldn't have come near you. Those bloody dons can't hit anything they aim at."

"Hell!" Logan grimaced as Kit cleaned the grime from the bloody crease in his shoulder. "I shouldn't have ducked at all. I should have run, as every man with sense was doing. God, what a rout!"

"What happened?" Kit asked. She almost didn't want to hear.

Peter shook his head ruefully. "They hit us while we were still strung out along the trail. Goddamn but they kicked our . . . pardon me, Kit—they gave us quite a pounding."

"And then?"

"We continued the march to Santo Domingo, like the fools we were. At least those of us marched that weren't shot up or sick. Most of those poor troops can't walk for three minutes without diving into the bushes to squat. What a fiasco!"

"So the Spaniards beat you in Santo Domingo."

"Beat us? Lord, they trounced us!"

"And my uncle?" Kit asked in a tentative voice.

"Safe in his *palacio* the whole time." Logan joined the conversation in a hoarse voice. "You didn't expect him to come out and fight, did you?"

She laughed shakily. "He certainly would had he known you were among the invaders."

Logan's only answer was a grunt as Kit cleaned the last bits of grime from his shoulder wound.

"Should we have Doc look at this?" Kit asked.

"He's needed in the infirmary more than here. There are a number of wounded that are going to turn into corpses without his attention. Besides, your touch is improving." Logan laughed shakily. "I remember the last time you doctored me the healing hurt worse than the whipping."

Kit's brow shot up. "That was because you were being an insolent toad. I happen to be quite good at doctoring."

"Among other things." He gave her a private smile.

Peter cleared his throat awkwardly. "Do you know what those damned fools are planning next?" he asked Logan.

"Aye."

"And us, Logan? What do we do?"

"We follow," Logan said with regret. "I gave my word, my promise."

Peter snorted in disgust. "When I lost my own privateer command, I signed on with you because I thought you were smarter than a lot of those wild buccaneers. But now..."

"You were right." Logan grinned modestly. "I am smarter."

"That was a stupid promise to give, Logan."

"You're right again. And you don't know the half of it."

"The crew won't like it."

Logan chuckled cynically. "I've made them all enough money to retire on. They can humor me for a while longer."

Peter shook his head in disgust. "Logan Steele, for an intelligent man, you certainly can be a fool."

"A promise is a promise."

Logan shot a look at Kit. Her heart suddenly grew wings, for his eyes told her that his promise about the ship—whatever that promise was—was not the only promise he intended to keep.

"Where the fleet goes, we go. For a while."

And so it was that the *Ice Maiden* unfurled her sails to the wind and, with thirty-eight British ships of war, pointed her bow toward the Spanish colony of Jamaica.

"What do you mean, I can't go?" Kit huffed indignantly and gave Logan her back. The soft green coastline of Jamaica was visible out the stern windows.

"Just what I said." Logan faced Kit's burst of temper without wavering in his determination. "You can't go. You're not up to it."

"That's not true!"

"It is true." He put a hand on her shoulder and turned her toward him. A hint of a smile played about his finely sculpted lips.

"You are a woman of many talents, my love, but holding your own in battle is not one of them. And I'll not have time to worry about keeping you in one piece."

Kit pouted. "That's not fair!" I've been drilling every

day with Tom. I'm getting to be good. Really, I am. Yesterday I scored a touch that would have gone right through Tom's heart."

"Aye," Logan chuckled. "And the day before you almost spitted yourself on your own blade. You handle a knife as if it's going to turn and bite you. Your swordplay might be adequate to defend you against a two-year-old child. And if you carried a pistol you'd doubtless shoot one of our own men, or yourself. With a weapon in your hand, Katarina, my love, you would be the enemy's greatest asset."

The argument continued in periodic skirmishes while final preparations were made to land Venables's decimated army on an uninhabited stretch of beach in Jamaica. Kit was determined not to be left behind to wait and wonder while Logan went off once again into battle. She used every argument she could devise.

Logan still needed her nursing skills, Kit insisted. After all, it had only been four short days since he had returned to the ship. Logan laughed and flexed his rapidly healing shoulder. She had not thought him an invalid these past few nights while she lay beneath him and purred like a kitten, he reminded her with a lecherous grin. She blushed bright scarlet, but refused to give up, quoting him his own words about how easily Jamaica would fall to the British forces. What possible danger could there be if she stayed in the rear guard and away from most of the action?

Logan refused to listen to all of Kit's reasoning and pleading. He was of half a mind not to go on this miserable expedition himself. Penn and Venables were fighting like cocks, each blaming the other for the rout at Santo Domingo. The remains of the army were weak, demoralized, and disgruntled. Logan confided to Peter that the troops following them on this foray would probably be more danger to themselves than to the poor inhabitants of Jamaica. It was fortunate indeed that the island had so few residents—a couple of thousand Indians and a few hundred Spanish. If Jamaica were anything other than a poorly defended and little regarded outpost of colonial Spain, Venables's miserable excuse for an army would be cut to pieces. And considering the luck of the expedition so far, something still might go wrong.

The night before the landing, Logan attempted to explain his reasoning to Kit as they lay together in the big four-poster bed. But Kit was in no mood to listen.

"You are being totally unreasonable!" she insisted. "Hardheaded, stubborn, selfish, and completely hateful!"

"*I* am being unreasonable? *I* am being selfish?" His voice shook. Logan was a patient man, but at times he could swear that Katarina St. John was enough to try the patience of God Himself. "*I* am the only one in this cabin with a head on my shoulders! What *you* are proposing is pure folly, woman!"

"It would be worse folly for me to stay on this perishing ship and worry myself to death! Logan, please." Kit's voice softened in a sudden shift of strategy. "Don't leave me behind. You have no idea how hard it is to wait while someone you love goes into danger." A fat tear dropped from her eye. "I love you so much. I can't bear to let you out of my sight for fear that I'll lose this happiness you've brought me."

Logan's flare of temper faded as his eyes gleamed in amusement. He had far more practice defending himself against feminine wiles than Kit had in using them. Of course, with this particular woman, the wiles didn't have to be refined to be effective. There was no harm in playing along with her game for a time.

Logan wiped the tear from Kit's cheek and brushed her lips with his own. "I have every intention of coming back to you in one piece, Katarina. There is no sense in worrying. The island will probably surrender without so much as a shot being fired."

Kit's lips pursed into a fair imitation of Mavis Edmond's pretty pout. "Then why can't I come?"

"I'd as soon take along a loaded pistol set to backfire."

The pretty pout fled. Kit's lips returned to their former tight, stubborn line. "Dash it all, Logan! You are a vile, stubborn scoundrel!"

"What? Willing to give up so easily?"

She started to roll away from him, but it was too late for

retreat. In one supple movement Logan rolled on top of her. His knee played suggestive games between her trapped legs.

"Isn't there something else you would care to offer as bait?"

Kit sighed in resignation. Already she could feel her pique dissolving. She couldn't stay mad at Logan more than a few moments. Especially not when he was distracting her with such a tantalizing invitation. She readily gave up her mouth when he captured it in a kiss.

"I'll follow you, you know," she told him in a last grasp at her fading purpose. "There's not a man aboard this ship I can't twist around my little fnger. I'll get someone to row me ashore."

"Do and I'll pound your backside until it's black and blue," he murmured against the soft pillow of her breasts.

"It would be worth it." She grinned up at him as he paused in his attentions and propped himself above her. "I would be far safer with the troops than on my own."

Logan closed his eyes and sighed. With a resigned groan he let his head sink forward onto the pillows, where he was assaulted by the fragrance of Kit's hair, the sweetness of her warm breath against his shoulder, the silky smooth feel of her slender body stretched beneath his.

"Faith but you're a spoiled little witch."

Her arms wound around him, and his loins urgently reminded him that putting up with this spoiled little witch was worth every bit of trouble that it caused.

Kit smiled as Logan's mouth came down on hers. She had won.

Jamaica was nothing like Kit had imagined. The sultry, unspoiled jungle made the tamed forests of her beautiful Barbados look like a landscaped garden in comparison. The heat bore down like a wet, stifling blanket. Sweat poured from her body in an irritating flood, even though she was expending very little effort dawdling along in the rear guard with the men who were the most wasted with disease and diarrhea. Fronds and leaves and vines slapped at her face, and creepers laid in wait for her feet. And worst of all, insects seemed to crawl over every inch of greenery in their path—tiny buzzing flying insects, big fat leaf munchers, sithery wormlike fuzzies with endless pairs of legs. As Kit pushed doggedly through the vegetation, one of the fuzzies—an especially large one—was knocked off a palmetto frond and plopped down firmly on her shoulder. Her shriek earned a withering glare from the troops around her.

"Quiet!" a gray-faced soldier ordered. "Do you want the whole world to know we're here?"

Kit did a little dance and gingerly brushed the insect off her shirt. "Lord!" she mumbled irritably. "Who cares! Why do we want this miserable island in the first place?"

Kit grimaced and swept back the loose, damp tendrils of hair that brushed against her cheeks. Anything that touched her skin was a torture in this steamy heat. She was sure that she would soon be parboiled. Sweat trickling down her overheated skin was a minor torture, making her feel like insects were crawling in armies beneath her soaked clothing. The rest of the rear guard looked just as miserable as she felt. More miserable even, for most of them were plagued by frequent needs to duck into the brush. Every few hours a runner from the vanguard would check on their progress and urge them to greater speed. But it was not she who was holding up the rear, Kit thought with some satisfaction. It was Cromwell's precious soldiers, who had stupidly stuffed themselves with exotic fruits while waiting in Barbados and were now paying the miserable price.

The nighttime was the worst part of this miserable march, Kit decided that evening as she settled wearily on the damp blanket that served as her bed. She had thought that during the hours of dark she and Logan could slip away to some secluded area for a time of privacy. Making love in a moonlit tropical glade would be so pleasant. The soft cushion of leaves and fronds would serve as their bed. A cool, quiet pool would serve to wash away the sweat of their passion. The night birds would trill in accompaniment to their whispers of love. A nice idea, Kit decided. Unrealistic in the extreme, it turned out, but still very nice.

Reality was somewhat less than nice. Logan had checked

on the rear guard briefly while they ate their unappetizing dinner of salt pork and hard biscuits. A casual kiss was all Kit had gotten before he was off again to see to some military problem. It had been the same the night before. Even though Logan kept a diligent eye on her safety, she hardly ever saw him. So much for romancing her way to Spanish Jamaica!

Romance was not tossing and turning on a damp blanket, stewing in her own sweat, disgusted by the stench of her own unwashed body, and listening to the unholy rattling of the giant crabs clicking their claws together in the night. Romance was not listening to the frightened whispers of her companions or overhearing their periodic visits into the surrounding brush and the sounds of their misery there. The whole world seemed miserable, and Kit was in the most miserable part of it. Where had she gone wrong? The idea of being Logan's camp follower had seemed so exciting back on the clean, comfortable *Ice Maiden*.

The next morning, bad got worse. Kit woke to the pelting of warm rain on her face. Everything was wet. Her bed was a morass of mud, her clothes clung to her with soggy, miserable tenacity, and her boots squished with every step. Rain dribbled down her face and into her eyes. Droplets clung to her eyelashes and turned the world into a watery blur at every blink.

The rear guard breakfasted on soggy biscuits, rolled their blankets into a sodden mass, and pushed slowly ahead. If possible, Kit thought, her companions looked even paler and weaker than the day before. It was a good thing that their group would arrive at their destination long after the serious fighting was over. They were in no condition to whip a lame dog, much less win a battle.

In the next moments Kit's musings proved painfully true as the brush suddenly seemed to give birth to a troop of Spaniards, bristling with weapons and grinning in bloodthirsty anticipation of an easy victory. The loud pounding of the rain masked the scrape of the Spaniards' weapons as they rasped from their scabbards, just as it had masked the sound of the troops' approach.

It seemed to Kit that for a moment the world stood still.

Surrounded by the threat of slaughter, the little group of British was suspended in collective dismay, their expressions ranging from terror to disbelief to frightened resignation. Then one brave soul drew his sword and ventured forward. He was cut down before he'd gone five steps. The world exploded into chaos.

Kit aged at least ten years in the next ten minutes. All around her men poured their life's blood into the soupy Jamaica mud. Death screams battered her ears and images of violence assaulted her eyes. Her mind and senses overflowed with the sights and sounds and smells of carnage until life itself seemed no longer to matter.

But Kit continued to live. Dark Spanish faces leered at her. Bloodied hands pushed her this way and that, sometimes sending her to her knees in the mud. But none ventured to cut her down. And when finally all the other Bristish had fallen to Spanish steel, Kit still stood, gasping for breath and numb with shock. She was the only victim left for the Spanish wolves to devour.

Kit choked back sobs of fear and raised the heavy sword that she'd taken from a bloody corpse. She vowed these Spanish dogs would get a surprise or two before Kit St. John's blood poured out onto the mud.

It was then that Kit spotted a familiar face. Esteban del Vargas recognized her at the same time. He shoved through the crowd of soldiers that surrounded her, pushing them aside with curses, kicks, and the point of his sword.

"Stand back! This British bitch is mine!"

The crowd faded reluctantly into the background and hushed into an expectant silence.

"Señorita St. John, what a pleasure to see you again."

The Spaniard's obsidian eyes still reminded Kit of a snake. Surely this was some evil nightmare. Esteban del Vargas belonged on Hispaniola, not Jamaica.

"What are you doing here?" she choked out, warily keeping her sword between them, as Tom had taught her.

"What am I doing here? A good question, indeed." The snake seemed in no hurry to strike. He enjoyed letting his victim dangle on a thread of fear. "A question I have frequently asked myself over the last weeks."

He paused and regarded Kit with mock sympathy. "Are you not getting weary of holding that heavy sword, señorita? I can assure you that your fate will be the same whether you fight or surrender."

"Go to hell!"

"I am already there, thanks to you and your pirate friend. How disappointing that he is not here to defend you."

"He is far away," Kit lied. "Safe from you."

"How sad. Your uncle took vengeance on me, you see, for your Captain Steele's escapade in Santo Domingo. He relieved me of my post and sent me to this godforsaken pesthole of unenlightened provincialism." The Spaniard bared his teeth in an ugly grin. "But God is kind, is He not? He has most generously delivered you into my hands. Vengeance is going to afford me a great deal of pleasure, Señorita St. John, though I doubt it will do the same for you."

"You'll have to take me first, you braying jackass!"

"I doubt that will be a problem."

Del Vargas lunged. Kit managed to parry. Her awkward movement inspired a gale of laughter from their audience. They were even more amused when she stumbled over a body in trying to avoid the Spaniard's next attack. She splashed into the mud, and recalling Tom Trelawny's first law of defending yourself—never play fair—she grasped a handful of black slime and flung it into del Vargas's face.

The Spaniard sputtered and tried to wipe the mud from his eyes. Kit saw her chance and knew it would be her last. She scrambled to her feet and ran, waving her sword in front of her. The onlookers were too surprised to do anything other than avoid her wildly swinging weapon. Kit flung the heavy sword aside as she plunged into the jungle. She ran perhaps twenty feet before a bolt of fire and pain sent her spiraling down into a black void.

Kit clawed her way up through the sticky black morass of unconsciousness. Time and again she reached the surface, only to sink once again into the void. Sounds came and went in a tide of confusion. A persistent voice urged her upward, finally bringing her fully and painfully awake.

"I am glad my bullet did not kill you, Señorita St.

John," del Vargas gloated down at her, his eyes burning with hatred. "You and I have much to do before I will give you up to death."

Kit attempted to rise. A lightning bolt of pain was her reward. Her horrified eyes were drawn to her shoulder, which was crusted with dried blood. Bright scarlet rivulets flowered briefly, then trickled down her shoulder.

"Do not worry, señorita. It is a little thing only. Nothing compared to what is to come." Del Vargas gave her an obscene smile. "I'm going to make you regret you were born a woman, Miss St. John, and when I have had my fill, I will show you how artful I can be with a knife. I will start here." He knelt beside her and pressed his hand to the juncture of her thighs. "And then I will carve a design on your golden skin that will be a connoisseur's delight." His finger lazily traced convoluted spirals and sworls on her abdomen and breasts. "Crimson against gold. Too bad you will not be in a position to appreciate it."

Kit's mind reeled. Too much horror was flooding over her in too short a time. Desperately she wondered if she could make del Vargas angry enough to kill her before he carried out his plan of rape and torture. But she had no time to try. The Spaniard had stood and was reaching for the fastenings of his breeches. Already his weapon of flesh was straining against the confining cloth. His eyes never left Kit's bloodless face as he slowly allowed the breeches to drop.

Del Vargas's waistband was around his knees when Logan's troop attacked, pouring out of the brush in a screaming horde, pistols belching fire and sharp steel flashing in the sun. The Spaniard instinctively reached for his sword and found only bare flesh where honed steel should have been. With a curse he jerked up his breeches and bellowed for his weapon to be brought to him. His men swarmed in confusion, more than one of them caught with minds on matters more entertaining than warfare. They were rapidly mowed under by the scythe of Logan's attack. Only a few were left standing by the time del Vargas had pulled himself together and joined in the fighting, and those few pleaded for mercy with hands raised over their heads and swords thrown in the scarlet-stained mud.

"You!"

Del Vargas and Logan both spoke at the same time. The Spaniard grinned, heedless of the slaughter of his men. The Englishman he most hated was within reach of his blade. Without warning he lunged.

Logan dodged, almost caught off guard. Esteban del Vargas was the last man he had expected to meet in the jungles of Jamaica. The sight of that aristocratic Castilian face sent a surge of fierce joy through Logan's veins. He also had a score to settle. Two men who had trusted him were dead by torture, and countless others had met the same fate at the hands of this Spanish devil.

"I will kill you by inches, pirate dog. You will feel every drop of blood ooze from your body, I promise." To demonstrate his point, Vargas flicked his blade and a spot of crimson appeared and slowly spread on Logan's sleeve.

Logan ignored the nick. "You Spaniards always were sorry braggarts. Wasn't it you who claimed that no man could escape your pestilential fortress?"

"You will not escape my blade, English scum. I will cut you to pieces. Then I will continue my sport with your woman."

Logan threw a hasty glance at Kit gathering the tatters of her bloody clothing around naked flesh. He seemed to relax. The fighting anger that had flung him into the clearing became a quiet, coiled tension. His narrow lips curled in a smile that would have sent Satan's own imps running for cover.

The duel that followed held Kit spellbound with horror. She had never seen the Logan Steele who fought in the clearing that day. Del Vargas was an accomplished swordsman, but he was not up to defending himself against the cool ferocity of Logan's attack. The Englishman drove him back again and again, breaking through his defense as though it didn't exist, parrying his desperate attacks with impossible ease. Like a wolf choosing to run his prey to exhaustion rather than to down it with a clean swipe of his fangs, Logan drew out the contest, enjoying the Spaniard's slowly dawning realization of his doom.

It was del Vargas who chose the place of the duel's

finish, staggering back against the bole of a tree and refusing to run any farther. He read his own death in the chips of ice that were Logan Steele's eyes, and in the cruel curl of a smile that curved his mouth.

"Should I give you a taste of your own methods, Esteban?" Logan asked with deceptive gentleness. "There's many a soul fled from this world who would rest easier for hearing your screams."

Del Vargas's obsidian eyes were rimmed with white.

Logan's sword flashed. A streak of scarlet spread obliquely across the Spaniard's chest. Another flash of steel, another slash of crimson.

Del Vargas whimpered as Logan's cold gaze came to rest on the swell of the manly weapon he had so proudly flaunted just moments before.

"I should cut if off, Esteban. That would no doubt please many poor women who've had to bear your abuse."

"No." The Spaniard's voice quivered.

Logan let him roast in his own fear for a long moment; then he lunged. Del Vargas managed one last parry. Logan's blade slipped down the length of the other and caught on the guard. For a moment, strength seemed to return to the Spaniard. His left hand reached for the poniard at his belt.

Del Vargas thrust the wicked blade toward Logan's ribs, but the movement was arrested by Logan's hand on his wrist. Cords of tendons stood out in the necks of both men as they fought for control of the deadly blade, but the cold smile that was not a smile never left Logan's face. Slowly the blade turned. Del Vargas's teeth bared in a grimace of death as his own hand, guided by Logan's arm, plunged the blade into his heart. The Spaniard crumpled at Logan's feet.

"Be grateful, you stinking vermin, that I'm an even-tempered man, or I would have cut out your liver and made you eat it. It was what you deserved."

Kit couldn't help but draw back when Logan came to stand before her, his eyes still aglow with anger and his arms and chest covered with the blood of the man he had just killed.

"This is war, Katarina," he said, noting her cringe. "Is

this what you wanted to see when you begged so to come along?"

Kit had no answer for him. She could only stare back into his cold blue eyes, fascinated and horrified at how her gentle lover had been suddenly transformed into a monster of deadly power.

Then Logan noted the bloodied flesh of her shoulder. The fire of anger in his eyes flickered and died as he knelt at her side.

"You're hurt."

She flinched at his touch, having nearly forgotten her pain in the horror of the last few moments.

"Here, let me...."

"No. Don't touch me." She cringed away, then buried her face in her hands. "I'm sorry, I didn't mean that. I...I'm..."

"It's all right," Logan said softly.

"All I want to do is wash," she choked. "I've got to wash."

Kit stumbled off toward the sound of a small stream, Logan following. She plunged into the shallow water, clothes and all, and let the sluggish current wash the mud and grime from her body. Good as the water felt, however, it could not wash the pain from her soul.

"Let me see to that shoulder now." Logan waded out beside her. He ripped a piece of his own shirt and bound it tightly around her wounded shoulder. "Just a flesh wound. You'll be as good as new in a couple of days."

It wasn't true, Kit thought bitterly. Never again would she be as good as new. Lying with a man did not rob a girl of her innocence, she thought bitterly. But seeing the cruelty and viciousness of the world did.

Logan gently touched her face. Kit longed to lose herself in his arms. But she couldn't bring herself to turn to him. Just then, his blatantly masculine presence repelled her. With a bitterness new to her soul, Kit wondered if love could survive in this vicious and bloodstained world.

Chapter 14

Edward Pettijohn's plush carriage bounced along the coast road toward Greenhaven. Two weary figures were perched on the fine leather seats—Logan with the reins in his hands and Kit beside him.

Kit thought that the quiet forests of Barbados were the most welcome sight that had ever greeted her eyes. The thought of a cool bath and the softness of her own beautiful clean bed was a dream of luxury. After Jamaica, even one of the huts in the slave village would seem a luxury.

"We're almost there," Kit said with a smile. "Soon we'll be sipping cool drinks, and Mandy will be fussing over us like a mother hen."

Kit sighed and closed her eyes, trying to chase unwelcome memories from her mind. She felt as though she had aged ten years since setting foot on that deserted Jamaican beach.

Jamaica had been a victory for the English forces, regardless of its being a nightmare for one English woman. The largest Jamaican town, Villa la Vega, had been easily taken by Venables's rabble of an army, and the island had surrendered on May 17, only seven days after the English forces had first landed. But it had been a Pyrrhic victory for the troops who had won it. Disease was rampant, food was scarce, clean water was all but nonexistent. Spanish soldiers who had fled to the mountains before the English advance continued to harry the conquerors at every opportunity. English morale was a shambles.

The first days after the Spanish attack, Kit had kept to herself, silent and withdrawn, talking to no one, constantly frowning at her own thoughts. Her world was washed in dreary gray. There was a new bitterness in her soul that all of Logan's tender concern and gentle loving could not wash away. She had been robbed of the last shreds of her innocence in that blood-spattered clearing, and she wept for the loss. It seemed that nothing would ever again be as bright or clean or beautiful as it had been before.

But the world did look brighter now that Jamaica and its memories had been left behind. The warm Barbados sun seemed to drive away dingy cobwebs of pessimism and depression. Under Greenhaven's dazzling blue sky, beside its sparkling beaches and warm aquamarine sea, surely Jamaica would fade into the background like a nightmare fleeing before the bright morning sun. Kit's heart ached with the desire to push aside the dark memories and start building the future.

Logan pulled the flashy blood bays to a halt at the crest of a hill overlooking Greenhaven. The coral-stone house, the landscaped lawns and serene little lake, the neat stable, quiet slave village, busy mill, and carefully cultivated fields were all a soothing balm to Kit's eyes. No other sight had ever been as welcome. A slow smile curved her lips and lit her face.

"I haven't seen that smile in days," Logan said.

"I haven't felt like smiling in days."

"Now you do?" he asked gently.

The smile grew wider. "Now I do."

Logan reached out and touched Kit's cheek with one finger. His eyes communicated a silent message of love. "God help me if I ever let anyone hurt you again."

The words hung between them like a vow, until Kit chuckled ruefully. "Will you save me from myself as well?"

Logan laughed. "I'll try."

He clucked to the horses, urging them down the short descent to the plantation house.

Kit's relief at finally being home became mixed with apprehension when the carriage finally came to a halt below the front veranda, for awaiting them at the top of the stairs, arms folded stiffly across his chest and one foot tapping an angry cadence on the porch, was a dour-faced and tight-lipped Oliver.

"You're supposed to be in Portsmouth!" Kit blurted out

as Oliver descended the stairs, eyeing them with cold disapproval. "What are you doing home?"

"I changed my mind and made a short run to the colonies up north," Oliver explained in a chilly voice. "Obviously you were expecting me to be away much longer." He offered his hand to assist Kit from the carriage. "May I ask, sister mine, just where you have been these last weeks? The servants could tell me nothing, only that you fired Brownlow, hired a new overseer—a man not especially to my liking, I might add—and left Greenhaven in his charge with no explanation of where you were going or when you would return."

It didn't occur to Kit that she might be better off with a lie. "I've been off to Hispaniola and Jamaica with General Venables and Admiral Penn. Well, actually, with Mr. . . . uh . . . Pettijohn."

Oliver's face was getting darker with her every word. "You what?" His voice was a hiss of anger. His eyes came to rest on the neat bandage that wrapped her shoulder. "And may I take it that this is a souvenir of your journey?"

"Well . . ." Kit had expected Oliver to understand. Was he not fond of adventure himself?

Logan looked on in seeming amusement as Kit got taken to task.

"I don't believe that even you would do something so foolish and . . . and inappropriate!"

"Now, Oliver, I'm not a child you can scold for misbehaving! I'm my own woman, and—"

"You're an imbecile, that's what you are!" Oliver's dark gaze fastened on Logan, who looked very much as if he agreed with Oliver's assessment of his sister's behavior. "You, sir! How dare your lure my sister on such a vile adventure! What kind of an irresponsible scoundrel would endanger the life and ruin the reputation of an innocent girl!"

"Oliver, stop! It was all my idea!"

He ignored her plea. "I call on you to defend whatever shreds of honor you have, Mr. Pettijohn. Name the time, the place, and the weapon of your choice!"

"No!" Kit shouted and grabbed her brother's arm. "Oliver, I forbid this!"

Logan gave Oliver a look of cool speculation. The smile

that flitted across his mouth reminded Kit uncomfortably of the deadly smile she had seen once before in a bloody clearing on Jamaica. She shot him a look of desperate pleading, only too aware of his capacity for savagery.

"What a pity that I'm not a fighting man," Logan finally answered, one brow raised in arrogant disdain. "I'm afraid I must decline."

Oliver's features contorted into a mask of fury. At least three different shades of crimson colored his face in rapid succession, until a mottled scarlet came to stay. His eyes burned like two hot coals set deep within the dark sockets. Kit had never seen him so dreadfully angry.

"You are both a fool and a coward." Oliver's voice was choked with rage. "Do not think you can escape so lightly. No one slights the honor of a St. John and gets away with it."

"I assure you that your sister is quite capable of defending her own honor."

Oliver lunged, but was stopped by Logan's booted foot thrust abruptly against his chest.

"Tsk!" Logan admonished with a mocking smile. "You wouldn't attack an unarmed man now, would you, friend?"

Kit tugged on her brother's arm to pull him back. She sent Logan a cautioning glare.

Oliver brushed ineffectively at the bootprint that marred his whiteshirt. His eyes shot shards of glittering hatred at the calmly smiling Logan. "Next time I see you, Pettijohn, you had best have a weapon about you. This isn't settled yet!"

"I think you had better go," Kit said to Logan in a despairing voice.

A knot of servants crowded in the front entranceway, watching the exchange with avid curiosity but staying out of range of the master's temper. Kit signaled the burly footman Harry to help with the small amount of baggage that she had brought from the *Ice Maiden*. Then, ignoring Oliver's angry glare, she smiled up at Logan.

"Don't mind Oliver," she whispered. "His bark is mighty, but I've never seen him bite. He'll cool off. I'll explain things to him."

Logan gave her a look that bordered on pity. "Have a care for yourself," he said softly. "Soon, very soon, we need to talk."

"Yes," she agreed readily.

Kit stood in the drive and watched while the blood bays pulled the carriage back toward the coast road. Oliver's dark scowl didn't dim the happy glow that warmed her heart. They would talk, Logan had said. And soon. The sooner the better, Kit thought. Humdrum reality was engulfing her once again, but this time she was determined that there would be a place in her reality for Logan Steele.

Three days passed and there was no appreciable softening in Oliver's mood. He raged at Kit for her waywardness and filled the air with threats of what he would do to Edward Pettijohn if the cowardly scoundrel could scrape up sufficient courage to answer his challenge. Then he continued to lambaste Kit for firing Brownlow and replacing him with a man who was too lily-livered to use a whip as it should be used. The plantation was going to hell, Oliver complained, and Kit was going to hell with it. And for certain Edward Pettijohn was going to hell, for Oliver was going to send him there himself.

Kit explained and cajoled until she felt blue in the face. She claimed all the blame for herself and stubbornly insisted that whatever she did was none of Oliver's affair. She was a grown woman, and if she wanted to go off adventuring, she would. If she wanted to let Edward Pettijohn court her, she would. If she wanted to marry him, she would. Her life was her own, and she ran it as she saw fit—just as she ran Greenhaven. And she would thank Oliver to keep his nose out of both the plantation and her life.

The argument raged continually from morning to night. Whenever brother and sister met, hot words flew like sparks from a furnace. The household servants ducked out of any room where Oliver and Kit came together, and they avoided Oliver completely. Blasts of his volcanic temper had seared more than one unfortunate soul since the mistress had returned.

"The man treats me like I'm a ten-year-old child!" Kit complained to Mandy one afternoon. She stood before the mirror in her bedchamber, watching her reflection as Mandy fitted a new day gown to her slender figure.

"Well, miss!" Mandy mumbled around a mouthful of pins. "You must admit that sailing off to war with a shipload of rough seamen is hardly the thing a proper lady would do."

"Rubbish! There were other women aboard."

"Wives." The plump redhead jabbed a pin into the gown with unnecessary vigor, and Kit gave a little squeak of pain. "All the other women were proper wives, not 'oyden lasses who 'ave nothing better to do than run around gettin' into trouble."

"Well, maybe soon I'll be a wife, too."

Mandy's brows lifted in surprise. "Are ye goin' to marry that Mr. Pettijohn?"

Kit smiled, her eyes glazing dreamily. "Maybe I will."

"Best thing you could do, seein' as ye been rovin' about with 'im like no lady should." She gave her mistress a shrewd look. "Though right now I can't say that gent is much better than that pirate scoundrel you skipped off with." The maid turned Kit around to see if the pinned hem was hanging properly. "You mark my words, love; that brother o' yours'll 'ave none of it. 'E's in an evil temper over that Mr. Pettijohn." Mandy shook her head pessimistically. "'As the gent asked you?"

"Not exactly."

The question caused Kit only minor uneasiness. It was true that during all the times Logan had held her close, all the times he had branded her with his need and the fire of his passion, not once had he mentioned marriage. The only promise he had made for the future was to love her, not to marry her.

"But I'm sure he wants to marry me."

"Humph!" Mandy's grunt was one of disbelief. "Many an innocent lass 'as been taken in by thinkin' the same thing."

Of course Logan wanted to marry her. He loved her. She was the very best part of his life. He had said so himself. He could not expect her to continue to run the gauntlet of risks engendered by their unblessed union.

"He'll marry me," she said with more confidence than she felt. "And if Oliver is still worked up about Lo . . . about Mr. Pettijohn abusing my reputation, a wedding should satisfy his notions of honor."

Mandy just shook her head. "'Ave it all worked out, do ye?" She stabbed with another pin, ignoring Kit's squeal, then stepped back to admire her handiwork.

Kit sniffed in annoyance at her maid's tone. "I thought you were in favor of my finding a gentleman to marry."

"Oh, aye, if ye think that Mr. Pettijohn is a proper gent. Just don't ye underestimate that brother of yours, miss. 'E's a fearsome man when 'e gets riled. An' that temper of 'is don't cool off quite as quick as yours. When ye get yer dander up, ye're like a summer storm full o' lightnin' and thunder. All the noise an' blowin' are over before they're 'alf begun. But Master Oliver, now, 'e's a different sort. 'E simmer's under the suface, like one o'them mountains that blows its top."

Kit laughed. "Oliver will get over his pique. Everything will work out. You'll see."

At least, Oliver had better get over his pique. Logan was a man who could be pushed just so far, and if Oliver didn't quit pushing, who knew what could happen? If either one of them hurt the other. . . Kit grimaced. It didn't bear thinking about. Logan was her love, her very life. He was the most important thing in her world. But Oliver was her brother. He might be an exasperating, infuriating pest, but he was the only family she had. It was well indeed that Logan's hand was stayed by his love for her. Heaven knew that he had reason enough to hate Oliver. And her brother wouldn't stand a chance against a man to whom violence had long been a way of life.

Kit squirmed. "Aren't you finished yet? Do you think I have nothing better to do than to stand here and be turned into a pincushion?"

"Don't take yer ill temper out on me, miss!" Mandy huffed. "I'm not the one who got ye into this mess."

Midmorning the next day Logan trotted up to the house mounted on a dapple gray stallion Kit had never seen before. She hurried out onto the veranda, trying to quiet the stomach butterflies that were all aflutter at the sight of him. Smoothing the cool silk of her gown—one of the four that Logan had purchased for her—and patting the ebony curls that Mandy had so laboriously tamed and arranged, Kit told herself that today they would have their talk, and she would let nothing interfere. Nothing.

"Like him?" Logan asked Kit as he dismounted and handed the reins to the groom. "I bought him from Sir Thomas Modyford. Keeps a good stable, that man."

"He's beautiful," Kit acknowledged as they walked toward the house. "You seem to be settling yourself quite permanently in our midst. First the fancy house—bought, mind you, not rented. Then the carriage and those bays, and now you add this fancy stallion to your stable. If I didn't know better, I would think you were planning to stay."

He grinned. "Did you expect me to leave?"

"I don't know what to expect anymore," she admitted, all teasing gone from her voice. They paused at the top of the veranda steps. "You don't need to continue this charade any longer, not for my sake. The bargain is off, even though Oliver has returned."

"Do you still have that silly bargain on your mind?" Logan took her chin in his hand and turned her face toward his. Clear blue eyes crinkled in amusement, coaxing a smile from Kit in return. "Do you think it was for that useless bargain that I've been following you around these past months like a puppy on a leash, letting you get away with the most god-awful pranks every time you bat your lashes at me? Do you think that was all a charade?"

She answered him with a question. "Do you really love me, Logan? In spite of my being spoiled, and childish, and selfish."

"Do you still doubt it?"

"Should I?"

"I intend to make sure you don't."

Kit allowed herself a moment of wild hope. "Then you will be staying?"

"I'll be around for a while yet." Logan leaned back against the veranda rail, and for a moment his eyes turned dark. "The word in Bridgetown is that the Jackal has been sighted again just east of Barbados. I imagine most of the Spanish merchants will wait and sail with the armada, putting them beyond his reach, and mine."

He gave Kit a speculative look, seeming to gage her reaction. She frowned, confused by the sudden hard glitter that came into his eyes.

"Then the Jackal isn't dead after all?"

"No. He's not dead."

Seemingly satisfied by what he saw in Kit's face, Logan continued with a smile, "We'll be cruising close to the coast for a while, so I should have plenty of time to convince you that being loved by a scoundrel isn't really that bad."

Kit lowered her voice. "Cruising close to the coast, indeed! If you're back to your old tricks, you pirate, just stay away from my slaves. I need every one that I have this season."

Logan returned her mock glare with an unrepentant grin.

"What have we here?" Oliver's voice took them both by surprise. He had materialized by the corner of the house as if conjured out of thin air, sitting tensely aboard his chestnut gelding, a riding quirt slapping in rhythmic unease against his booted calf. "Am I mistaken, sir, or did I instruct you to be armed the next time we met? Do I dare presume you've come ready to defend whatever passes as your honor?"

Kit stiffened. "Leave off, Oliver! Mr. Pettijohn is here as my guest. I'll not have you insult him."

"I'll do more than insult him if he doesn't get off my property."

Kit wasn't sure whether the property referred to was Greenhaven or herself.

Logan rose from his seat on the veranda rail. Even though they weren't touching, Kit could feel the tension coil in his body and ripple through his lithe movement. Kit laid her hand on his arm, as though her touch would cool his rising temper.

"Mr. Pettijohn can visit Greenhaven as often as I will have him," she told her brother in clipped, cool words. "You aren't my guardian, Oliver, and you have no say as to whom I choose to have as guests. I'll thank you to remember that."

"Can't Mr. Pettijohn speak for himself?"

Oliver pronounced the name as if he didn't quite believe it, sending a pulse of fear racing through Kit's veins. Could he suspect? No. Impossible.

"If I spoke for myself," Logan said in a dangerous voice, "you wouldn't like what I said, friend." Logan gave Oliver a look he might have given a poisonous snake, or a spider that was due for extermination under the heel of his boot.

"We were just going riding," Kit said hastily. Anything to break up the explosive combination of her brother and her lover. "Come, Edward." She tugged at his arm, ignoring Oliver's glare. "You were going to put that new horse of yours through his paces."

"Coward!" Oliver flung as Logan allowed Kit to drag him off toward the stables. "My sister won't always be around for you to hide behind."

"Why does he hate you so?" Kit wondered aloud, hugging her knees to her chest. "He can't recognize you as the man who was once a slave here. No one could."

Logan didn't answer. He simply sat and stared out at the quiet green glade that had been the site of the first violent confrontation between them. He remembered very clearly how Kit had looked on that day, willful, proud, and cool as the very depths of the sea. The kiss he had forced from her had lit a spark. The spark had grown to a conflagration somewhere along the way, and now that wildfire ruled both of their lives.

Fool that he was, Logan had known from the very start

that loving Katarina St. John was tempting disaster. He had been right. They had had their dance. Soon, very soon, they would have to pay the piper.

"I've explained to the dolt time and time again that it was my fault that I went on that benighted expedition. And he believes me. He knows how stupidly impulsive I can be, but still he hates you. I don't understand it." Kit dropped her chin to her drawn-up knees with a weary sigh.

"Don't worry about it," Logan advised her.

"Promise you won't fight him."

Logan's face was carved from stone.

"I know Oliver's being a beast, calling you a coward and harping on honor and all that. But he's my brother, Logan. If he were to be hurt... He's my only family."

"Family is important, I guess," Logan answered in a noncommittal voice.

"He won't be here long. He's always at sea. I have no idea why he's hanging around making a pest of himself. He'll be gone soon. And then..." She paused and looked down at the damp ground on which they sat. For a moment she was silent and tense. Then she lifted her face and caught his eyes with hers. "Logan, do you love me enough to marry me?"

The dark brooding left Logan's eyes. A wry grin curled his lips. "Is that a proposal, Miss St. John?"

Kit's face flooded with scarlet. "I..."

Her reply was cut off by the finger Logan placed across her lips. The finger was quickly replaced by his mouth. Their lips moved softly together in a gentle prelude to passion.

"Let me show you how much I love you." His words were a whisper against her cheek as he pushed her down onto the soft, fragrant soil.

"Here?"

"Why not here?" The lazy smile he gave her made a warm tendril of desire uncoil slowly, deliciously in Kit's belly. "The horses over there might watch, but I doubt they would be shocked." Logan's finger traced her lips, then trailed a path down her throat and, flicking aside the satin lapel of her riding jacket, dove teasingly into the shadowed cleavage of her breasts. "If you remember, the first time I touched you, right here beside this pond, we left the deed unfinished."

Kit smiled a siren's smile and reached up to coil a strand of his mahoghany hair around her fingers. "You could have had me that day, you know, had Oliver not come."

"Yes, I know." Something dark joined with the desire in his eyes. "Had Oliver not come..."

There was no more talk. It seemed that the mention of that long-ago incident infused Logan with the same desperate passion that he had known that day, a passion that had been cut short in pain and degradation. But this day the fire building within him would not meet such a fate. It grew into an inferno of need, feeding on itself and on the willing and eager response of the woman who molded herself to him in matching passion.

Kit was a little frightened of the dark shadow in Logan's eyes. But she was not so frightened that she could resist the lure of his desire, and of her own. As he undressed her, she performed the same service for him, and they managed somehow to divest themselves of clothing without once being completely separated from each other's touch.

Her caressing hands, traveling over the hard ridges of muscle and the familiar patterns of scars on his back, felt a tension quivering inside him that had never been there before. It was as though he wanted to sear her with the heat of his need, brand her with the fire of his male possession. A frenzied urgency took hold of them both, squeezing them in its grip until they had no thought but to yield to its demands. Scarcely had they pushed their clothing aside than Logan was demanding entrance between her thighs. Willingly Kit opened herself to receive him, eager as he to slake the pulsing waves of need that were flooding through her body.

It was a short and almost violent mating, and it left them both quivering in the aftermath, slick with their own sweat and the offerings of their passion. They clung to one another in wonder, a little frightened by the desperation that had overcome them both.

Logan heaved a shaky sigh as his heart returned to its normal pace. "I think we need a bath."

Kit laughed uncertainly as he picked her up in his arms and carried her toward the pond. "What are you doing, you oaf?"

"Going for a swim. With you. I've always wanted to do that, ever since I first saw this pond. You do swim, don't you?"

"Of course I swim! But...!"

Her objections were too late. He gave her a mighty toss, and she landed, rump first, with a squeal and an ungainly flailing of arms and legs. She came up sputtering, her ebony hair plastered across her shoulders and breasts, and was promptly doused again by the splash of Logan's big body crashing into the water beside her.

"Ooooh! You!"

She got revenge by fountaining a stream of water into his lazily smiling, smugly satisfied face as he glided up beside her. He promptly dove beneath the roiled green surface that up until a few short moments ago had been so glassily calm.

"Where did you go, you... oh!"

Kit's legs were pulled out from beneath her. Cool green water enveloped her. Strong arms encircled her. Through the bubbles of her breath she could see the white flash of Logan's wicked grin. They rolled together into the shadowed depths, wrapped in the silken strands of Kit's hair like two bodies bound forever into one.

Finally, with two strong scissors kicks Logan propelled them toward the sandy bank. Kit gasped for air when they finally broke the surface.

"Now look what you've done!" She laughed, treading water. "My hair will be wet for hours. How am I supposed to explain this to my dolt of a brother?"

"To hell with Oliver. Tell him you went swimming. Tell him you were cavorting like a lusty sea-nymph on the banks of the millpond."

"With you?"

"Certainly." His voice was husky. "Never with anyone else."

"Do you know"—she glided toward him with smooth, easy strokes—"you truly are a rogue."

"And you truly are a siren."

He caught her by the waist and lifted her partly out of the water. The rough texture of his cheek sent a thrill racing along her nerves as he nuzzled a wet breast.

"Love me again?" she invited tentatively.

He smiled. "I thought you would never ask."

She started to swim toward the bank, but he pulled her back into his arms. Lifting her up so that her long legs wrapped around his waist, he brought her to rest against his hips. Kit gasped with surprise as the hot, hard length of him slid gently into her welcoming sheath.

"I don't know how to do this," she whispered hesitantly into the ear that was so close to her lips.

"Wait," he said softly against her neck. "You will."

With a knowledge as primitive as Eve herself, Kit began to move her hips against his, delighted with the unique feeling of controlling his movement inside her. She tightened her legs around his waist and closed her eyes, matching the rhythm of water as it rose and fell against their entwined bodies.

Logan's hand tightened spasmodically on her buttocks, and a low male groan rasped in her ear. In one long stride they were on the bank and he was laying her gently on the sand, carefully sustaining the joyous link between them. With deep, slow thrusts he took control of their mating, worshipping her body with his hands and mouth while caressing her velvet depths with his hard, hungry flesh. When her body shuddered beneath him, he took her cry of ecstasy into his own mouth and allowed his own body the release it craved.

Minutes later Kit was asleep with Logan stretched out beside her. All the vibrant energy of her body had been transformed into quiet softness. Pond water beaded on her dark lashes. Her lips were pink and slightly swollen from Logan's kisses, her olive-tinted skin golden and dappled with the sunlight streaming through the roof of leaves. Logan brushed a finger lightly across her cheek. She stirred, curling against him in her sleep like a kitten seeking warmth.

Logan sighed quietly, content even knowing the battle that lay ahead. When he had first come to Greenhaven, there had been no future. There was nothing left for him in life but to complete the task he had undertaken and then... And then nothing. He hadn't even thought about the aftermath of what he had promised to do.

But now he had his Katarina. How could he have guessed when he first saw her standing so coolly arrogant at that slave auction that in a few short months she would be lying beside him, sated with his loving, and wanting a future with him—demanding a future with him, in fact. He had won an unlikely prize, one that changed the tenor of his life. Now the trick was to keep it.

Logan sighed again and lay back on the cool sand. There was a great deal to be done before he could count his victory and enjoy the spoils. Oliver had always been a problem, but now he was an even greater obstacle. He must decide what to do about Kit's half brother, and quickly. Soon it might be too late.

Kit stirred again, and he turned his face toward hers. Fingering a strand of ebony hair, he searched her features with brooding eyes. God, but he didn't want to lose her!

Logan rose on one elbow and whispered a promise unheard by the sleeping girl. "I love you, Katarina St. John, you wonderful tempest of a woman. And nothing and no one is going to stand in the way of my having you. Nothing. No one."

Logan's mouth curled in a cynical smile at his own naiveté. He would be a more clever man than most if he managed to keep that vow.

Chapter 15

It wasn't until many hours later, as Kit lay in her bed, drifting quietly toward slumber, that she remembered that

Logan had never answered her question about marriage. A cloud of euphoria had enveloped her ever since she had dreamily bid him good-bye. Now her mind snapped joltingly back into focus. The thought that she had been deliberately distracted by the powerful lure of Logan's loving brought her fully awake in a fit of irritation.

"Dash it all!"

Her fist punched at her pillow, punishing it for Logan's transgressions.

"How can he be so slippery, the scoundrel! He loves me! I know he does!"

He did love her. Not only had he said it, but she saw it in his eyes, felt it in his touch. Why would he shy away from the idea of marriage? A man with Logan's wry twist of humor should appreciate the irony of being master where he had once been an ill-treated slave.

Of course there were a few problems, Kit acknowledged, letting herself fall back onto the abused pillows. A proud man like Logan wouldn't want to live under an assumed name the rest of his life. But then—she smiled impishly at a mischievous thought—he had only ten years of servitude to pay off his crimes. She wondered how the courts would feel about his serving his term of slavery as her husband. After all, convict slaves could be put to any task for which their owner felt they were suited. And Logan Steele was certainly best suited to making her happy. Kit sighed contentedly, remembering their day together.

If one wanted to be strict about the facts, of course, the situation did get sticky. Logan had not escaped from her. He had escaped from Oliver. And if Oliver ever discovered who Edward Pettijohn really was, he would raise one devil of a stink.

Kit turned over and restlessly rearranged the pillows and mosquito netting. Life had become so complex. A few months ago the only worries nagging at her were the yield of the cane fields and Oliver's annoying matchmaking. Now she had involved herself in a morass of deception and lies, and instinct told her that even now she didn't know all the factors involved in this mess. Love could certainly lead a girl into an amazing pile of trouble!

The next two weeks saw no opportunities for Kit to question Logan about their future. The wet season, which generally stretched from June until December, blew in with a vengeance. The coast road between Greenhaven and Bridgetown was dangerous mire that gave even the hardiest souls pause.

The cutting season was over for the year, and fields could be neither cleared nor planted while the rain beat down with such punishing fury. So the slaves huddled in their huts, swapped stories, sang songs, and occasionally disappeared into the night with no trace.

In the big house, activities were not so much different from those in the slave village. The servants and slaves moved slowly about their chores, spirits dampened by the gray sullenness outside the windows. Oliver was gone more often than not, first on a short trip to St. Kitts, then a longer trip to the North American colonies. But he was never gone long enough to let Kit get over her irritation with him. A truce held between brother and sister, but both knew that it would break the moment that a blue-eyed, mahogany-haired troublemaker came calling again.

Kit sat and read, or reviewed the accounts, or mapped out plans for the planting season with Reginald Bartlett, her new overseer. But she was not busy enough to keep from thinking about Logan, and her nights were full of longing for the closeness of his body and the sound of his voice. Her dreams were beset by blue eyes that could melt to a dark pool of desire, by narrow lips that could curl in wry humor or soften in tender passion. Her life felt empty without his presence, and she swore that no matter what it took, Logan Steele would be a permanent part of her life. Even if she had to leave Greenhaven and become a pirate's mistress for the rest of her days.

The first day that the sun broke through the clouds, Kit stood at the library window and watched a lone horseman trot up the drive. Horse, tack, and man were spattered with mud, and the steam that swirled up from the water-laden gravel made the figure unrecognizable. Kit's heart beat with hope as she hastened to the front entrance, not waiting for Raleigh to open the door and announce the visitor.

It was not Logan that greeted her at the front door, however. It was Peter.

"Why, Peter!" Kit greeted him in a surprised voice. "How nice to see you. Do come in."

"Uh... you'll have to pardon my appearance, Kit. It's a sea of mud out there. Reminds me of..." He almost said Jamaica before remembering her sensitivity to that subject.

"Yes," Kit said graciously. "It is a mess, isn't it? What brings you out this way?"

"I... uh..."

She watched Peter look around uneasily as they entered the parlor and sat down. The cool-eyed Dutchman was very obviously out of his element.

"Will you have some tea or some rum punch? Mrs. Simpson has a delicious recipe for rum punch."

Peter accepted with alacrity. "The rum part of the punch sounds good."

Smiling, Kit motioned to one of the parlor maids.

"I imagine our mutual friend has been keeping you busy," Kit commented as a servant handed Peter a tall glass of cool punch and then left the room. "Three of my slaves disappeared two nights ago, so I assume Logan's up to his old tricks. I'm surprised he dares to set sail in the weather we've been having."

"Aye. We've been busy enough. Logan's not a man to let a little wind and rain stand in his way. We have a rendezvous tonight, in fact." Peter scowled, then concentrated on the floor for a long moment. "The subject of slave escapes is what I came to talk to you about."

At these words, Kit felt a chill of foreboding gallop down her spine.

"Your escaped slaves," Peter continued.

Kit lifted a brow. "It's a little late for Logan to apologize for taking my slaves."

Peter continued as though she hadn't spoken. "One of them is a girl."

"That would be Lottie," Kit supplied, remembering the overseer's report.

"She's been badly battered. Doc's afraid she won't make

it to the island. He thinks it best if she comes back here. If you're willing to care for her—and protect her."

"Protect her against what?" Kit's voice was sharpening to a brittle edge. "And what do you mean, she's been battered?"

"I guess Oliver raped her and beat her until running seemed like the safer option, from what she says. Doc is afraid that one of her ribs has punctured a lung."

Kit's sable-brown eyes turned black with anger. "That's impossible. Lottie is only fourteen years old. Besides, Oliver never goes near the field hands—or any other of my people, for that matter—without my permission."

"He went near this one. We had it from the girl's own mouth."

"Then she lied."

"Not many people tell lies when they're staring death in the face, Kit. Lottie thinks she's on death's doorstep. She could well be right."

Kit rose abruptly and began to pace back and forth. "Why didn't Logan come himself to tell me about this?"

"I wouldn't expect him to be out while your brother is still around. Logan's boiling and I don't think he trusts himself not to throttle Oliver with his own hands."

Kit's mouth tightened. "Of course Logan would be ready to believe that Oliver did this thing."

Peter grimaced, wishing that he had not taken on this chore. "That man loves you, Kit, if you'll pardon my boldness in speaking of it. He doesn't want to come against your brother any more than you want him to. Logan is a patient man with a temper that's slow to spark. But he's not a man to be trifled with. He can only be pushed so far."

Kit stared at him in angry amazement. "You think I'm trifling with Logan?"

"No, Kit," Peter replied deliberately. "I think your brother is." He hesitated. "Will you take her back?"

"Yes. Of course," Kit said sharply.

Peter rose and started for the door. "I'm sorry I've upset you."

"You haven't upset me," Kit denied sourly. "Whatever the problem is, I will take care of it. I won't have my people abused. I know it's not Oliver doing it, but I shall find out who is."

For a long time after Peter left, Kit stood and stared out the window with unseeing eyes. Then, her decision made, she left the house with determined strides and headed for the stable.

The warm, earthy odor of horses, hay, and well-oiled leather greeted Kit as she slipped through the stable door. Dusky golden light filtered through tiny motes of alfalfa that hung in the air, and the quiet somnolence was only emphasized by the occasional whickers and rustling of the horses in their stalls.

Kit shooed a barn cat from under her feet and walked toward the tack room.

"Oh, Miss St. John. I thought I 'eard someone out 'ere." Greenhaven's new assistant stableman greeted Kit at the tack room door. He was tall with tousled black hair, dark eyes, and a boyish leanness that belied the lines of middle age gathering around his mouth and eyes. He displayed a perfect set of teeth in a friendly grin. "Is there somethin' I can 'elp you with?"

"Where's Adam?" Kit asked. "I want him to drive me into town."

"'E's out workin' that new stallion o' yer brother's, miss." The stableman shook his head. "Demon's a good name fer that devil. 'E thinks 'e's king o' the 'ill, 'e does! Adam 'as 'is 'ands full with that 'un."

"Get him," Kit ordered, impatiently cutting off the man's loquacious rambling. "I want to get to town and back before dark."

"Yes, miss."

Kit frowned as the stableman trotted out the door, her mind still very much on Peter's accusations. She knew that Oliver wouldn't abuse a woman, even a slave woman. Not her brother. She was sure he wouldn't. Just the same, she wanted to get to the bottom of this. She had some questions to put to Captain Logan Steele.

* * *

At the same time Kit's carriage headed down the drive, Logan sat his mount atop the hill behind the big house, watching with hooded eyes. That was one problem he wouldn't have to deal with, he thought with relief. It would have been damnably awkward confronting Oliver St. John with Katarina in the house.

He headed his horse down the muddy trail, his mind still gnawing on his course of action. What he was about to do was a dangerous move in an even more dangerous game. But any other course led to a checkmate, or at least a stalemate. In that case Oliver St. John lost, and Logan lost as well. But if that bastard Oliver would listen to reason, both of them might win. Logan could take Kit and sail beyond the reach of those who would seek revenge for broken promises, and Oliver, while he might feel the loss of a rich plantation and a prosperous shipping line, would still have his life. That was better than the villain deserved.

The man who came up to take Logan's horse was unfamiliar.

"Where is Adam?" Logan asked.

The stableman's appreciative eye assessed Logan's long-legged dapple gray. "Adam drove Miss St. John into Bridgetown, sir. I'm George Marshall, Miss St. John's new indenture. I'll take right good care o' yer horse."

"I'm sure you will. Is Master St. John in?"

"I 'aven't seen 'im leave, sir," George replied. "Will ye be staying long? Should I give 'im a good rubdown?"

"I won't be here that long." Logan looked toward the house and felt a tense muscle twitch in his jaw. "I may be in a hurry when I leave. Just cool the horse down, but keep him saddled."

"Yes, sir."

George watched the visitor walk in bold strides toward the house, then turned and gave the gray a pat. Fine figure of a horse this was, he thought. Fine figure of a man, too. But the fellow had an irked look in his eye that the groom wouldn't like to be directed against him. In a sudden flash of intuition, he was glad that Miss Kit was not in the house.

Logan turned down Raleigh's offer to announce his presence to the master. "I'll announce myself," he insisted.

"But Mr. Pettijohn! I don't think that is wise, sir! Master

St. John is not in the best of humors!" Of course, the master was never in the best of humors when it came to dealing with his sister's latest suitor.

Raleigh followed Logan down the corridor toward Oliver's study, bleating his indignation to an uncaring back. There would be hell to pay for this breach of protocol, and he, Raleigh, would have to pay it. He fluttered his hands helplessly as Logan opened the study door, stepped in to the master's private sanctuary, and then closed it firmly in Raleigh's face.

Oliver looked up with an angry frown as the study door slammed. But his face grew truly thunderous when he saw who it was standing before him.

"You!"

"None other." Logan grinned cockily.

"How dare you! What do you think you're doing?"

"Faith, what a greeting! And to a man who has come to make you a very valuable proposition—one that might be very beneficial to your health, Oliver, old friend."

Oliver gasped with outrage. "Get out! Get out right now! Just who do you think you are, you outrageous . . . !"

Logan abruptly cut him off. "I think you know exactly who I am. And you've known for some time. Just as I know who you are."

Oliver stared at him open-mouthed. "You're not only insolent, you're mad! Just what was that ridiculous statement supposed to mean?"

Logan produced a smile that sent chills racing down Oliver's spine. "Going to play ignorant, are you? Then let me tell you just exactly what I mean."

Raleigh cocked an inquisitive ear as closely as he dared to the study door. Miss Kit's gentleman friend had certainly not been his usual considerate self today. And the sounds emanating from the master's study were most distressing. There was sure to be trouble over this.

Indeed, Raleigh had known the minute that he opened the door—with the unfailing instinct that should be possessed by every head of household staff—that Mr. Pettijohn brought nothing but trouble with him today. One look at the gentleman's face had sufficed to trip the warning bells in the butler's mind. And now this!

Raleigh pressed his ear even more closely to the door. Master Oliver was laughing, and it certainly wasn't a pleasant-sounding laugh. If only Miss Kit were here! She was the only one who could handle the two of them when they got into a tussle. And sometimes even she was hard put to break them apart. Like two fighting cocks they were, the master and Mr. Pettijohn. And it sounded as if they were going at it beak and talon! The words that were leaking through the door, though for the most part indistinguishable as words, were most heated in tone.

"Why, Mr. Raleigh! Whatever are you doing, sir?"

The housekeeper's querulous voice broke through Raleigh's concentration and momentarily rattled his usual aplomb. He falteringly tried to recover his dignity.

"Mrs. Calloway. I was simply . . . simply . . ."

"Eavesdropping! That's what you were doing! I'm ashamed of you, sir! I never thought a gentleman of your caliber would stoop so low!"

"Master St. John has a visitor who is giving him a great deal of trouble. I was merely listening discreetly to determine if my assistance is required." He arched the housekeeper a look of disdain.

"Pish and tush!" she answered. "The master is a strapping young man. Why should he need assistance from a pudgy old plowhorse like you, Mr. Raleigh?"

"I'll have you know, Mrs. Calloway, that . . . !"

"Hush!" By now the sounds coming from the study had caught the housekeeper's attention as well. "They are having a row, aren't they?"

"As I said . . ." Raleigh began, only to be shushed again with an imperious hiss.

"What do ye suppose the two o' them are arguing about?"

"I haven't the slightest idea. As I was saying . . ."

"If only Miss Kit were here. She would set them both on their ears. That she would!"

"My thought exactly."

The voices inside suddenly rose in volume, and both

butler and housekeeper pressed their ears unashamedly to the door.

"You're a bigger fool than I thought you were," Oliver sneered. "You have no proof. Only guesses, hunches, wild inferences."

"Until I came here today that was all I had," Logan admitted. "Perhaps there was even the slightest hint of a doubt in my own mind. But now I know, once and for all."

"And how is that?"

Logan smiled wolfishly. "How could you possibly know of those piratical exploits that you so obligingly throw in my face had you not met me at sea, Oliver, old friend? From where else could you have recognized me besides our one unfriendly engagement?"

"Rubbish!"

"Is it? You were the one wearing the mask, Master Jackal, not I. You have known from the moment Modyford introduced us that I was a buccaneer masquerading as a merchant. That is why you have tried to set your sister against me."

Oliver scowled.

"And then there's the matter of your being recognized by a certain young man whom I plucked off one of your sinking victims. You lost your mask that day and failed to kill the boy who saw your face. Most careless of you, Oliver. He recognized your sister, who looks enough like you to be a twin. And then he recognized you. Do you remember the messenger lad who called at Greenhaven a few days after your sister's return?"

Oliver scoffed. "That would never stand up in court."

"You think not? When I bring the boy forward to identify you, I'm sure he'll be glad to tell the story of what you did to him and his shipmates."

There was silence for a few moments as their eyes met—cold blue clashing with angry brown. Oliver curled a lip like a jackal baring his fangs. "I don't think so," he said. "I don't think you'll bring the boy to court. Think about it, Captain . . . Steele, is it? You offer those particular items as proof and you will hang alongside me. An escaped slave turned pirate will get no more mercy than a gentleman turned pirate."

Logan's smile was as cold and hard as the triumphant gleam in his eye. "I'm not a slave, friend, nor a pirate. I'm a man who has already been condemned to the noose, and the price of my freedom is your life. You have managed to offend some very powerful men in London, St. John."

Oliver stared at him, tense as a coiled snake prepared to strike. But Logan forestalled him.

"However, I am prepared to make a deal."

The Jackal laughed mirthlessly. "I thought it would come to this. It always does, doesn't it? What is it you want, Captain Steele? Money? Or has my little sister truly caught your fancy?"

"Personally," Logan told Oliver in a flat tone, "it would please me to see you roast in hell. But as you say, your sister has caught my fancy."

"I knew she would come in handy someday, nuisance though she is at times."

Logan put a damper on his temper. Let him say any vile thing he wanted. Soon Kit would be out of his reach.

"These are the terms, St. John. You quit the sea. Take your blood money and set yourself up someplace far from Greenhaven, far from your sister, and far from any English ship. And if I ever hear of you returning to your vicious ways I'll see you hanged. Or I'll kill you myself. That I can promise you."

"See me hanged? And see my poor sister suffer the consequences of disgrace?"

"I can take care of your poor sister. She won't stand in my way more than this once." Logan's words were weighted with threat. His temper was approaching a frayed edge. "Believe me, St. John, I can take care of you also."

Oliver pondered for a moment, watching Logan out of dark brown eyes that so resembled his sister's. How could the two of them look so much alike, Logan wondered despairingly, when one was like a breath of fresh air and the other like a stale sewer?

"I think," Oliver began softly, rising slowly from the

chair behind the desk, "that it would be much easier for me simply to take care of you, Captain Fool."

He brought his hand up from where it rested behind the desk. In it he held a pistol aimed at Logan's heart.

"Not as smart as you thought you were, now, are you?"

The muzzle of the pistol never wavered. Logan did not deign to look at it. Instead, he looked into Oliver's eyes.

"I'm going to kill you, Captain Steele. I only regret that I must permit you to die so cleanly. I would dearly love to have you aboard my ship, where I could take full pleasure in dispatching you from this world."

"I'm not that easy to kill, Jackal." Logan didn't flinch as Oliver's finger tightened on the trigger. The confidence in his gaze made Oliver hesitate for a fraction of a second. It was all that Logan needed. Ignoring the pistol, he launched himself across the desk, a battering ram of muscle and unleashed anger. At the same moment, Oliver fired.

Kit sat in stunned silence, feeling her world crash in upon her. The parlor seemed to tilt, and her senses began to whirl. She hoped desperately that this was a nasty dream from which she would soon wake to find the world just as it was when she left on her futile trip to Bridgetown six hours ago. But the nightmare continued on.

"There's no doubt about it, miss." Raleigh continued with officious relish. "Mrs. Calloway and I heard the whole affair, seeing as our duties had us both in the hallway at that particular time."

Mavis Edmond patted Kit's hand, and across the parlor her husband, Lionel, scowled grimly at the floor.

"There were harsh words between the gentleman and your brother, miss. We were beginning to wonder if the master needed assistance when a shot was fired." The butler ducked his head in a gesture of shame. "But when I finally gathered my courage to open the study door to investigate, there was nothing to be found."

"What?" Kit choked.

"No one was there, miss. The master's good Turkish

carpet was stained with blood, but no one was in the room. I sent straightaway for Master Edmond, since I didn't know how long you would be in town."

"So you don't know who shot whom?"

Lionel Edmond broke in. "We are assuming, Kit, that if Oliver had shot Pettijohn, he would have had no reason to run. After all, this is his home, and Pettijohn was an intruder of sorts. I'm afraid we must assume the worst."

"Oh, Lord!" Kit dropped her face into her trembling hands. Assume the worst. . . . Which was truly worse, Oliver shooting Logan or Logan shooting Oliver? Either way her world was ended. How could this have happened?

"Perhaps Pettijohn took the body away to hide it," Lionel speculated, "or perhaps Oliver was still alive and Pettijohn dragged him off for some purpose of his own. These two militia chaps have been searching the grounds looking for the body, if such is to be found. They were just about to go out again, weren't you, gents? And there are more militia on the way from Bridgetown."

"I want to see the study," Kit said, rising abruptly to her feet.

"Now Kit," Mavis chimed in sympathetically. "Do you think that's wise? Poor Mrs. Calloway went in there and fainted dead away, and the sight of all that blood sent your poor parlor maids to hysteria." Her eyes shifted to Mandy and begged for support.

Mandy hastily complied. "Why don't you just sit there, me love, and I'll have Mrs. Simpson send in some chamomile tea."

"Don't coddle me, Mavis! Or you either, Mandy. I want to see the study where all of this supposedly happened."

Kit searched the study as though it held some secret that would prove this whole tragedy a figment of Raleigh's imagination. But all was as the butler had said. The luxurious Turkish carpet that Oliver had so prized was splotched with dark and partially clotted blood that seemed to lead in a trail toward the window. A larger puddle soaked the carpet by the desk. The desk chair was overturned, and the paneling beside the door was shattered by the impact of the one lead ball that had been fired. Kit took it all in with wide, desperate eyes. Finally, numb with shock, she allowed herself to be led back to the parlor.

The next two hours were an eternity of waiting, pacing, and more waiting. Kit drove both Mavis and Mandy to distraction with her fretting. They begged her to retire to her room with a dose of sedative tea, but she refused. They could dose her with enough tea to drug a horse, she insisted, and it would not help. The only thing that could give her relief was to magically turn the world back several hours and somehow prevent this disaster from taking place.

After an hour or so of frantic conjecture, it occurred to Kit to send a message to Logan. In spite of what Raleigh said, she couldn't accept that he had done this thing. He would not squander what they had together in an act of senseless violence, no matter how much he hated Oliver. She would send him a message, and he would come and prove somehow that he was innocent. And perhaps his explanation would even lead them to a healthy and very much alive Oliver.

With hope born of desperation, Kit sat down at her desk, took a piece of vellum, and began to write. She had just dispatched Adam with the message when word came that a body had been found.

Chapter 16

The body had been found at the base of the southward-jutting point of land that curved around the east side of Half Moon Bay. It was a spot Kit knew well. As children, she and Oliver had been forbidden by their father to so much as dangle their feet in the water along that particular beach. The longshore currents were treacherous, and sharks preferred that part of the bay to any other. Kit remembered back to a day when she was only ten. She and Oliver, on a rare holiday from lessons, had been entertaining themselves on that beach below the point. She had been chasing the crabs as Oliver tossed a fishing line into the surf. Suddenly, not a hundred yards from where Kit stood, a black man burst from the forest. Right behind him had come baying hounds and mounted hunters. Too frightened to run, Kit had watched the escaped slave risk the sea rather than give himself up to slavery once again. His choice had been a poor one. Kit had watched as, screaming, the poor man had turned, trying to get back onto the land. She had seen what remained of the slave when, a few moments later, the waves had tossed him up onto the sand. It was not a pretty sight.

Neither was Oliver a pretty sight, if the grisly thing that the militiaman deposited on the manicured Greenhaven lawn was indeed Oliver.

"It's Oliver, all right," Lionel Edmonds confirmed as the blanket was pulled away.

"Aye," the sergeant said, "that's what we figured, sir. Can't see much detail, eaten away as it is, but it's got black hair, brown eyes, good teeth, and the general build is right. Couldn't be anybody else, now, could it?"

Kit finally gathered the courage to look at the body, despite Mavis's objections. She was immediately sorry. The thing was a nightmarish caricature of a man that had once lived and breathed and walked the earth as a whole and vital human being. She clamped her hand over her mouth in sick horror. The world started to reel. The ground tilted and started up to meet her.

Comforting, supporting arms reached out and circled Kit with their warmth. "Come now. Enough o' that. Come away." Mandy's voice seemed far away. The touch of her hands was Kit's only anchor in a spinning world. For once in her life bereft of both words and will, she allowed herself to be shepherded back to the house and up to her own chamber.

The bed was cold comfort. Only Mandy's hand grasping hers kept Kit from floating off to hysteria.

"That was my brother," she choked. "That...thing...was my brother! Oh, Lord! How could Logan do this?" Kit rocked back and forth in a misery too deep for words. "I thought he loved me. He said he loved me. How could he do this?"

"Men be strange beasts at times," Mandy said. "It's not fer us women to understand 'em."

"I should have known this would happen," Kit cried. "Logan hated Oliver ever since Oliver bought him off the block. He hated him for buying him, hated him for whipping him, hated him for beating that slave girl. And now he's killed him!" she sobbed in a tearful fury. "Oliver didn't hurt that girl. He couldn't have done anything like that. But Logan killed him anyway. He killed him... he killed him."

The tirade ended in a wail of lament as Mandy drew Kit into her arms. But the maid had no words of comfort to offer.

Finally Kit pulled out of her embrace and drew away. "I want to be alone," she said in a hoarse voice.

With a concerned frown, Mandy damped the single lantern that was burning and quietly left the room, murmuring a soft encouragement to try to sleep.

Outside the French doors and beyond the balcony, insects were making night noises. Songs from the village filtered softly through the forest. The slaves were singing again, and on this night their songs hinted at a celebration rather than a dirge.

Kit heard none of it. She stared at the canopy over her bed, seeing in her mind all the sweet memories that she had stored up over twenty-one years of living with Oliver St. John. His death had wiped away all the irritability and irascibility of his nature. It masked his egotism, his stubbornness, his sullen moods, and the host of spats and more serious disagreements that had so often come between them. All that was left were the good times—the picnics on the beach with their father, their rides around the plantation, swims in the pond above the mill. It was Oliver who had escorted her to the neighboring balls when no young swain could be found to be her partner, and Oliver who had once beaten a young man within an inch of his life for calling her plain. But, no, that was not a good memory. Oliver violent and vengeful was not what she wanted to remember.

Kit gave up trying to find refuge in sleep. She brushed the mosquito netting aside and laboriously pushed herself off the bed. Her every muscle ached as though she had done hard labor in the fields along with her slaves. Her eyes burned, and her head throbbed with an agony that reached from the back of her eyeballs to the top of her skull. But no physical discomfort could match the grief that was twisting her heart and tying her stomach into knots.

Life had been so beautiful for a while. So damned beautiful. But it had all been a sham, a fantasy that only a naive child would mistake for the truth. How could she have thought that such an improbable dream of love was anything but a deception? How could she—practical, down-to-earth, sensible Kit St. John—have been so fatally stupid?

Kit began to pace, her hands clenched into knots at her sides. Back and forth across the room she marched, her feet moving in cadence to the fury of her thoughts. She was a fool, her conscience told her. It was her own fault that Oliver was dead. The deed might have been perpetrated by her own hand, so much at fault was she. She had insisted on loving Logan even after she had it from his own lips that he was a scoundrel and a villain, even after she had seen with her own eyes the savagery of his anger. She had given herself to him like a wanton, chased after him like a strumpet, and all the time he had been using her to get at the man he hated.

That was most certainly the way it was. She was a plain brown moth who had been fatally attracted by the warmth of Logan's fire. Well, the moth had flirted too closely with the tempting flame, and had ended up singed. But while she had been singed, her poor innocent brother had been burned. Burned to ashes and blown away, his life squandered because his ignorant sister had been an easy mark for a set of strong arms and a pair of seductive blue eyes. Because his sister had acted the slut and laid herself down for a murdering villain who had used her to get at the last family she had in this world.

Kit stopped pacing and turned her face to the wall, eyes

closed in pain and fists pounding in helpless frustration against the wallpaper. Lord, if she could only turn back time! If she could only undo the mistakes that had led to Oliver's murder!

Drained by the intensity of her pain, Kit sank onto the floor in a miserable heap. Her mind was spinning downward toward a black pit of despair. She had to talk to Logan. She had to hear the truth from his own lips. No one really knew what had gone on in that study except Logan himself. She would force the truth from him, so help her God. And if he had murdered her brother in cold blood and then thrown him to the sharks, as it appeared, then she would make sure he regretted it the rest of his life.

Quickly, Kit crossed the room and pulled the bell cord that hung beside the bed. By the time Raleigh knocked on the chamber door, she had dabbed her face with cool water and gathered herself into a semblance of dignity.

"Yes, miss?" Raleigh asked as she opened the door.

"Tell George Marshall to saddle Windwalker. I'm riding into town."

The only surprise on the butler's face was an almost imperceptible lift of one brow. "If you don't mind my saying so, miss, it would be most unwise to be on the road at this hour."

Kit glanced at the window. It had grown dark without her noticing.

"What time is it?"

"Almost ten o'clock, miss."

"You're right, Raleigh. It's much too late to be on the road. Thank you." But come tomorrow, Logan Steele beware! "Have any messages arrived from Bridgetown?" she asked, still hoping against all reason that Logan would answer her message and somehow excuse himself from this mess.

"No, miss. But Adam asked me to tell you that the new man, George Marshall, has disappeared."

"Disappeared?"

"Yes, miss. He hasn't been seen by anyone since early this afternoon."

Kit sighed. So Logan had made off with another indentured servant. What did she care? What did she care if the whole damned plantation ran off to sea with the scoundrel? Oliver was dead. What good was the plantation without her brother to pester her about it?

"Very well, Raleigh. That will be all."

"Miss Carpenter asked if you would care for some soup, miss. She's very concerned."

"No, I don't want any soup. And tell her not to be concerned. I'm fine." Or at least she would be fine when she had Logan Steele called to account for his villainy.

"Raleigh?"

"Yes, miss."

"Bring me some brandy."

"Brandy, miss?"

"Yes, brandy. Open your ears, Raleigh."

"Yes, miss."

Raleigh's voice was sharp with disapproval. Kit didn't care. To hell with soup and sedative tea. She needed the real thing.

Kit woke to the sound of a soft tapping on her bedchamber door and a hesitant inquiry in Mavis's voice.

"Wha... What?" she croaked.

She allowed her eyes to creak open, then promptly squinted them shut to stave off an assault of bright daylight. Her head felt as though it were in the cane crusher. Her mouth was foul with bitter slime, and every movement sent of spasm of nausea surging up from her stomach.

"How do you feel?" Mavis peeked around the door, then ventured in.

"Like I'm going to die," Kit rasped. "What time is it?"

"Almost three o'clock. Governor and Lady Searle have come to call. They're in the parlor. Shall I tell them you're feeling too poorly to receive?"

"No," Kit sighed. "Why did Mandy let me sleep so long? Have any messages arrived today?"

"No, dear. No messages. Most of the island doesn't

know about... about yesterday. The governor and his lady know because of the militia, I suppose."

One man knew, Kit thought, and he hadn't responded to her urgent demand for an explanation. The only conclusion possible was that he was guilty as charged, and he didn't even care enough to plead his innocence. How he must have laughed at her declarations of love! What an easy target she had been!

Kit found that she didn't want to get out of bed—ever. What was the use of picking up the pieces?

"Are you getting up?" Mavis inquired gently. She eyed the empty brandy bottle on Kit's dresser with an uneasy frown.

"Yes," Kit sighed. "Send Mandy up. And tell the governor I will be down presently."

Mandy helped her dress in a plain gown of dove gray— the darkest that she owned. Kit supposed that she should tell the maid to make up some black garments. She would roast in black, but a little discomfort was certainly less punishment than she deserved for her part in Oliver's death.

"Serves ye right," Mandy said as Kit swayed on her feet, her face a pale shade of green. The maid sniffed disapprovingly at the faint scent of brandy that still lingered in the room. "Strong spirits won't solve yer problems, love. They only eats at yer gut. Believe me, I know."

Only once before had Kit felt this miserable—when she had awakened after that wild celebration aboard the *Ice Maiden*. But then she had forgotten her discomfort in the passion Logan had brought to her bed. He had been so tender a lover.

Kit closed her eyes in pain. It had all been a lie. Every bit of it. Even sweet memories were denied to her. Damn him, damn him, damn him!

Governor Searle and his lady were the picture of concern as they greeted her in the front parlor.

"My dear Miss St. John," Lady Searle crooned as she gave her a delicate embrace. "I simply cannot express how very sorry we are for your loss. And look at you. Oh, my dear, you look positively green. You must sit down." The lady summoned Lucy the parlormaid, with an imperious wave of her hand. "Fetch your mistress some hot tea, right now."

"Aye, and you'd best put some rum in it, from the looks of the lass!" the governor added.

"Daniel! Behave yourself. The poor girl doesn't need rum!"

On the contrary, Kit thought, she would love some rum. Anything to drive away the pain!

"We apologize for calling so promptly on the heels of your tragedy, my dear, but my husband needs a few details cleared up, and I thought it would be much easier on you for us to call than for him to summon you to Government House."

Governor Searle cleared his throat awkwardly. "Uh... yes. This is a very serious matter, Miss St. John. The militia report this morning was most disturbing. To think that one of the finest men on the island can be murdered in his own home, his own study, by God! It's appalling! And that daft militia sergeant reports that all the evidence points to Edward Pettijohn as the culprit."

He paused, as though waiting for Kit to deny it. At her quiet nod of agreement, his face puckered in a frown.

"Unbelievable," the governor sighed. "Mr. Pettijohn is very close to Sir Thomas Modyford, you know, and seems a very worthy gentleman. Venables and Penn both praised him highly for his action in Santo Domingo and Jamaica, and I understand from Sir Thomas that the fellow is closely connected to the Earl of Wallingham in Kent. Very powerful family. It doesn't do to fling wild accusations at such a man, you see. So I thought I'd come out and do a bit of investigating on my own."

"Yes, of course." Kit understood now what had brought the governor out to Greenhaven in such a rush. He was afraid of insulting the powerful Modyford by accusing his friend Pettijohn. What a web of deceit she had helped to weave. And now she herself was caught in its sticky strands. "Perhaps you had best talk to Mr. Raleigh, my butler. I was not here, you see, and it was Raleigh who talked to Mr. Pettijohn before he went into my brother's study."

Lucy brought the tea, unlaced, Kit noted regretfully, with any rum. Raleigh was summoned and retired to the scene of the crime with the governor, and Lady Searle attempted to banish the inevitable awkwardness with a monologue of chatter interspersed with comments of sympathy.

The governor returned to the parlor with a grim look on his face. "I must say," he admitted reluctantly, "the circumstances certainly do seem to point to Mr. Pettijohn. Though of course we don't know what happened exactly. Your Mr. Raleigh tells me that Oliver did not like Mr. Pettijohn any better than Mr. Pettijohn liked Oliver. Conceivably, your brother may have been the first to attack, and perhaps what we have here is self-defense. Of course, if that were the case, there would have been no reason for Mr. Pettijohn to try to dispose of the body."

"Daniel, my love," Lady Searle interrupted, "do you think that we should speak of this here? I think Miss St. John has had to bear quite enough as it is."

The governor harumphed with embarrassment. "Quite right, my dear. Quite right. No sense in subjecting the poor girl to all this unpleasant conjecture. But of course we cannot accuse Mr. Pettijohn without absolute proof, you understand."

The governor did not want Mr. Pettijohn accused at all, Kit realized. The rogue was going to get away with it. He was going to live the comfortable life of a well-connected merchant gentleman while the ravaged corpse of her brother lay rotting in a cold grave. How he must be laughing at the way he had used her.

"And of course we cannot consider the word of a mere servant in such a grave accusation," the governor explained. "We will need corroboration from another source."

Used. Used. The word echoed through Kit's mind like a curse. The blackguard was going to get away with it. Men lived to batter women, physically and emotionally, and the world didn't care. Had George Elliot been punished for poor Becky? No. And Lottie, poor girl. Had anyone suffered for her pain?

"Of course we will conduct a full investigation into the matter, my dear. But sometimes these mysteries simply cannot be unraveled. It's best that you don't set your expectations too high."

The nightmarish memory of Jamaica rose out of the darkest corner of Kit's mind, completing her bitterness. Logan had killed those Spaniards because they were the enemy, not because they had abused her. What did he care if she was abused? In his own way, he had battered her just as surely as Oliver had supposedly battered poor little Lottie, and discarded her with equal callousness. But Logan was one man who would not get away without paying. If that rogue thought Kit St. John was insipid enough to bow down and let him continue his vicious game, then he was sorely mistaken.

"Governor Searle," Kit said in a voice sharp and cold as a dagger, "sit down for a moment. I have a tale that I think may change your mind about the influential Mr. Pettijohn."

Kit stood on the veranda and watched the governor's carriage disappear around the bend. She felt as though she had been split down the middle and divided into two separate women—one cringing in horror at what she had just done, and the other enjoying vengeful satisfaction.

The governor at first had not believed her when she told him that the merchant gentleman Edward Pettijohn was Logan Steele, a convict slave who had escaped Greenhaven's stockade at the beginning of the year. Then he had demanded why she hadn't reported this fact earlier. Kit had replied with innocent calm that the merchant was so much changed from the slave that she had not been certain of his identity. And when she had become certain, she had delayed out of pity for the poor man. She had been sucked into his web of charm just as everyone else on Barbados had, Kit admitted, subtly reminding the governor that he also had been played for a fool.

The governor had abruptly ended his interrogation, looking both chagrined and angry. He collected the astounded Lady Searle and made his good-byes, promising to do everything possible to bring the scoundrel to justice.

How easily she lied these days, Kit thought, closing the door against the gathering dusk and wearily leaning her head on its warm oak panels. Would she ever again be the simple, straightforward person she had been before Logan Steele had come into her life? She thought not. Right now she could not even be honest with herself.

Kit had intended to tell all, then to laugh when they hauled Logan in by the heels and strung him up on Execution Dock. But in the end she had left the villain an avenue of escape. She had betrayed his slavery, but not his piracy. The scoundrel had no doubt already made his escape, taking his crew of cutthroats with him. Good riddance to them all, Kit thought. The only ones she would miss were Peter and Doc and young Tom Trelawny. The world would be better off with the rest of them at the bottom of the sea.

It gave Kit a rare glow of satisfaction to know that for all his cleverness, Logan could never again set foot on Barbados. Now his only refuge was Tortuga, a poisonous nest of vipers and rogues like himself. It would serve the villain right, Kit thought, to finally live in reality the life he had been living in secret. She hoped he had the devil's own time with it.

The house was dark, and had been for some time. On the hill that rose inland behind Greenhaven's kitchen buildings, Logan squatted in the brush. If he was going to move, now was the time to do it. He shook his head, trying to drive the weariness from his brain. Two days and nights without sleep were dragging him down. But this was a task he couldn't afford to delay.

Just this evening he had returned from the previous night's slave rendezvous. The crew that had remained in his house greeted him with the news that Oliver St. John was dead, supposedly by Edward Pettijohn's hand. The thought of Kit—the hurt she must be enduring, the doubts that must plague her mind—had prompted him to ride immediately for Greenhaven, but Peter's advice had held him back. Such haste had killed better men than he, the Dutchman had warned. If Logan didn't want to swing on Execution Dock, he would wait until the night was well progressed and Greenhaven was asleep.

So Logan had waited. And now, in the dark, dying hours of the night, he hid like a fox pursued by hounds. Peter had been right. One militia guard was posted in the barn, and three others ranged around the house. It wasn't a surprise, but the sight brought a sharp stab of pain just the same. Kit believed the worst, of course. Hadn't she always? No doubt he would have to get her in an arm lock before she would listen to what he had to say.

Logan moved stealthily down the hill, then stopped where the brush came within fifty feet of the house. For long minutes he waited until the nearest guard turned his back. Then he dashed across the moonlit yard to the tamarisk tree beneath Kit's window. It was then that his luck ran out. A cry from the militiaman at the barn door broke the stillness of the night.

"Hold there!" Moonlight glinted off the steel of the guard's sword as he ran from the barn. Before he reached the house he was joined by his three companions.

Backed against the house, Logan had no place to run. He drew his rapier and ignored the hounds of doom that bayed in his mind.

"Surrender!" a young voice ordered. "We outnumber you, sir! Lay down your weapon."

"Like hell!"

Logan leapt forward. The element of surprise was on his side, and his first stroke connected with flesh and bone. The guard from the barn screamed and clutched at his side. Warily, the others pressed forward.

Logan centered his mind on the task at hand, refusing to think of Kit, not allowing the image of a hangman's noose to cloud his vision. There were still three opponents between him and freedom, and survival depended on the strength of his arm and the concentration of his mind.

But his reflexes were dulled by weariness. One more guard went down before his sword, and then a flash of an opponent's steel turned into a searing stroke of pain. Logan felt his sword arm drop limply to his side before a thousand cannon exploded in his brain. The ground came up to meet him, and then all was black.

Kit opened her eyes with a start. Still groggy from sleep, she frowned at the moonlight pouring in through the French doors. No hint of dawn lightened the star-studded sky she could see beyond her balcony. What had awakened her?

There it was again. The clamor of shouts and ringing steel seemed right below her window, bringing her fully awake. She launched herself from the bed, grabbed a robe, and peered out into the milky-white yard. She could see nothing, but the ruckus continued.

Clutching the robe around her, Kit flew out of her chamber and down the stairs. A rumpled Raleigh in dressing gown and nightcap met her at the bottom of the stairs. Ranged behind him were Lionel and Mavis Edmond, and an alarmed-looking Mrs. Calloway.

"What is going on?" Kit demanded.

"I don't know, miss." Raleigh's voice was commendably calm, as though he were becoming accustomed to unexplained upheavals breaking Greenhaven's peace.

A knock sounded on the door. Raleigh, dignified despite his disheveled state, opened the door and regarded with chilling disdain the tall lieutenant of militia who was just raising his fist for another knock.

"I beg your pardon," the lieutenant said, peering around the butler's imposing bulk. "Miss St. John? You can rest easy now, miss. We've caught that villain who murdered your brother."

"What?" Kit rushed out onto the veranda to confront the officer. She was brought up short by the sight of Logan held firmly between two burly militiamen. Blood matted his hair, streamed down his face, and covered his right side in a flood of crimson. His head lolled drunkenly, and when his bleary gaze fastened upon Kit's face, not a spark of recognition lit his eyes.

"The governor thought the scoundrel might return here, miss, seeing as how he's...uh...paid court to you these past months. So he dispatched me with three men to stand a guard. We caught the villain trying to sneak into the house." The lieutenant swelled with pride, thinking he'd done a very nearly heroic job of saving the young lady from harm. "In fact, it looked as though the rogue was about to sneak into one of the bedroom windows," he continued. "Lucky for you the governor sent us here, miss."

For a moment Kit was speechless. "This is an outrage!" she finally choked out.

"I agree." The lieutenant grinned, completely mistaking her meaning. "It's getting so that a body can't sleep safely in his bed at night. But at least you don't have to worry about this scum anymore."

"Why didn't you ask before you . . . before you . . . ?"

"The governor didn't wish to upset you, miss. And he couldn't trust that one of your servants wouldn't run off and warn Mr. Pettijohn that we were here. But we do thank you for all your help. If it weren't for you, this rogue would still be running free. Now you can be sure he'll meet his just end."

Kit looked back to Logan, her eyes wide with horror. Awareness had come back into his gaze, along with a cold fire of hatred that set every nerve in her body aquiver with fear. Then he smiled the deadly smile that had been the last thing Esteban del Vargas had seen before he met his death. That smile stayed before Kit's horrified eyes long after they dragged Logan away.

Chapter 17

"Sweet heaven, what have I done? Can't I touch anything without creating a royal mess?"

Kit paced back and forth, seemingly intent on wearing a

path in the parlor carpet. In spite of the room's warmth, her body trembled. She clutched her dressing robe about her with white-knuckled fists.

"You've done what you had to do." Mavis, in similar dishabille, sat on the velvet settee and observed Kit's white countenance with a frown. Her own shock at the night's events was pushed aside in her concern for her friend. "Please don't distress yourself this way, Kit. I vow I've never seen you quite so agitated."

"You don't understand," Kit moaned. "The governor never would have arrested him if I hadn't told him.... Oh, never mind. I never dreamed he would be taken. I thought he was too clever. The fool! Why did he have to come back here?"

Mavis sighed. "Kit, dear, I agree that this all has been rather a shock, but Mr. Pettijohn committed a beastly crime, and against your own brother. You should be delighted to see him arrested and punished."

"You don't understand," Kit told her again.

Kit didn't understand, either. She shouldn't care one whit what happened to Logan Steele. He was a murdering, lying, conniving, utterly ruthless scoundrel. She should be happy to see the beast hanged. Oliver would be revenged. She would be revenged. And one more murdering pirate would be in hell, where he belonged. But Kit was not happy. She was devastated.

"No! No! No!" Kit pounded her fist on the wall. "I will not let this happen!"

Mavis blinked at the unladylike display of temper. "Kit, dear, I know you were sweet on this Mr. Pettijohn fellow, but surely you can't maintain an affection after what has happened."

"Affection! Hah!" What Kit felt for Logan Steele—love, hate, passion, contempt, need—all those could hardly be described by such a bland word.

"Truthfully," Mavis insisted on continuing, "aside from his good looks and rather awesome size, the fellow always impressed me as being rather dull. I'll admit I was rather taken with him that night at our ball, but since then he's seemed such a quiet, uninteresting man. Not at all the sort I had imagined for you."

"Oh, Mavis, stop!" Kit sighed in resignation and sank down on the settee next to her friend. "I might as well tell you. Mr. Pettijohn is not Mr. Pettijohn. The scoundrel's name is Logan Steele, and he's an escaped convict slave."

Mavis gazed at her in blank confusion.

"You remember that pirate who took me to Hispaniola—the time you told Oliver I was sick in bed at your place? You thought it was so romantic."

"Yes?" Mavis said cautiously.

"That pirate was Logan Steele. He came to Barbados because I—like a witless ninnyhammer—I demanded that he pretend to court me in return for my helping him free his men." Kit sighed. "I just wanted to keep Oliver from being such a pest, but look at the mess I created. I ended up falling in love with the scoundrel. And I thought he loved me. He made me feel so... Oh, Lord! Now I don't know what to think! All I know is that in spite of anything he's done, I still have this feeling for him. The feeling won't die. It's a part of me. Dash it all, he is a part of me."

"Oh, my!" Mavis exclaimed, patting Kit's hand in comfort. "I certainly had the fellow wrong, didn't I?"

"Why did he come back tonight?" Kit asked, rising from the settee and resuming her pacing. "Maybe he didn't kill Oliver. Maybe he was coming back to explain. But why didn't he come sooner? Lord, what am I going to do?"

"Of course he killed your brother, Kit. Who else could have done it? Now you tell me the man is an escaped convict and a pirate. How can you doubt that he killed Oliver?"

"Even if he killed Oliver... oh, Mavis! You don't know how Oliver taunted him, and the cruel way he treated him when he was a slave here at Greenhaven. I should never have told the governor who he is. But I was so upset, and I was so wretchedly sick from all that brandy. What a stupid idiot I am. What am I going to do?"

"You're going to bed and get some sleep," Mavis said in a feeble attempt to take charge. "I'm sure that in the morning you can think on these matters more sensibly."

"No." Kit paused in midstride, a thoughtful frown upon her face. "No. You go on, Mavis. No need to sit up with me. I'll be fine."

"Are you sure?" Mavis yawned, then shot Kit a suspicious look.

"Yes, I'm sure. Just don't tell anyone what I told you—about Logan Steele being a pirate. I told Governor Searle that he's an escaped slave. Nothing else."

"Kit, you're plotting something. I can tell."

"Oh, go to bed, silly." Kit tried her best to look blandly innocent.

Mavis scowled fiercely for a moment, then relented. "All right, then. But remember," she warned, shaking an admonitory finger in Kit's direction, "Governor Searle is no fool. Try one of your pranks on him and you'll likely get your wings clipped."

When Mavis had disappeared up the stairs, Kit went to her writing desk and took out a piece of vellum. She thought for a long moment, then penned a message to Governor Searle. She had to get Logan out of the militia's grasp before someone put two and two together and came up with piracy. Even now the militia might be dragging a full confession out of their hapless prisoner. Sweet merciful heaven! Did English jailers torture their prisoners the way the Spanish did? Oh, Logan! What a mess we cooked up, both of us adding our own particular poison.

Kit crumpled the vellum in her hand. To hell with sending a message. She would go herself. The governor had a soft heart for the ladies, and she was going to spin him a tale that would do Shakespeare proud. The devil take law and honor and honesty. Logan would not go to Execution Dock, if Kit had anything to say about it!

The mantel clock in the governor's office chimed two o'clock when Kit was finally admitted to his presence. It had taken her half a day to find an appropriate ready-made mourning gown, and another hour had been spent refining the details of her strategy. Kit hoped she looked appropriately mournful, and innocently truthful, when the governor took her hand in greeting.

"My dear Miss St. John! What an unexpected pleasure." Searle bowed politely over Kit's hand and led her to the baroque love seat that sat below the official portrait of Cromwell. "I didn't expect to see you out and about so soon after... after your tragic loss." He sat down beside her, shunning the imposing official chair behind the carved oak desk. "It must set your mind somewhat at ease that we have that murdering scoundrel Steele well in hand."

Kit managed to look embarrassed. "That is just what I've come to see you about, your excellency. I must tell you that I've made a dreadful mistake."

The governor looked politely concerned. "A mistake, my dear?"

"A most awful one, I fear. It appears that Logan Steele did not murder my brother." Kit braced herself for the blatant falsehood and silently begged George Marshall for forgiveness. But George was beyond danger's reach, probably safe aboard the *Ice Maiden*, and Logan was within a hairbreadth of death. "I believe that my brother was killed by an indentured man whose papers I bought several weeks ago, your excellency—a groom by the name of George Marshall. Late last night one of my young household slaves came forward to tell me quite an incredible story."

"Indeed?"

"Yes... well... the slave boy had been sent out to the garden by Mrs. Simpson—my cook, you know." Kit fingered her skirt nervously. She had never been good at lying, and this was surely the granddaddy of all lies. "The boy was dawdling by the side of the house, you see, and he heard the shot fired in Oliver's study. Then he saw Mr. Pettijohn—Mr. Steele, rather—thrown from the open window." Kit lowered her eyes in embarrassment. "My brother had a terrible temper, your excellency, and I can believe if he was sufficiently provoked he might resort to such violence." At least the part about the temper was true.

"Go on," the governor urged.

"Yes, well... the slave also saw this groom—Mr. Marshall—help Mr. Steele up from where he had fallen. He helped Mr.

Steele into the stable and then started toward the window to my brother's office. The slave claims he didn't see any more, but the implications are clear. Especially since George Marshall has not been seen since my brother disappeared. Don't you agree?''

The governor did not look as though he agreed at all. "Interesting," was his only comment. Kit's already knotted stomach tightened painfully. Horns should sprout from her head at such a bald-faced lie.

"I don't know why the thought didn't occur to me before," she continued, knowing she was rambling, but not knowing what else to do. "The groom and my brother had hot words the day before. I'm afraid my brother never dealt too kindly with servants."

The governor gave her a bemused look. "A slave's word is not generally taken as evidence, Miss St. John."

"No. Of course not, your excellency. But even so, I knew you would want to see justice done."

"Of course. Of course."

"Surely the most appropriate punishment for Mr. Steele would be for him to return to Greenhaven and serve out his sentence." At least the governor hadn't thrown her out of his office and called her a liar into the bargain. Not yet, at least.

Searle lifted a doubting brow. "You wish that audacious scoundrel returned to you?"

Kit shrugged, trying to look nonchalant. "The man was my brother's property, and Oliver did pay Lord Cromwell's ridiculous price out of Greenhaven profits. I do hate to lose an investment."

The governor cleared his throat uncomfortably. "This is a bit awkward, my dear."

"I know, your excellency." Kit rushed on, pulling out her last weapon. "But we needn't embarrass the good people of Barbados with the story of how they were fooled. Edward Pettijohn can simply disappear, perhaps summoned back to England by his relative the Earl of Wallingham."

"Yes, well. . . . My dear Miss St. John"—Searle patted her hand in fatherly concern—"this is a most illuminating story. Of course it was right for you to come to me with this new bit of . . . evidence. And we will certainly keep an eye out for that rascally groom."

He believed her. Incredible.

"And what you suggest would be all very well and good. I don't mind my saying it would spare me a bit of embarrassment, and no doubt spare Sir Thomas as well. The thing of it is, my dear, that we now have evidence that this Steele fellow has been using that ship of his in high crimes upon the sea."

"No!" Kit's distress was not at all feigned. The worst had happened.

"Shocking, isn't it? The fellow has added piracy to the list of his other crimes." The governor shrugged apologetically. "But I'm afraid there's no doubt about it. The rigging has been altered and the hull repainted—sufficient to deceive a casual observer—but it appears that this *Ice Maiden* is a ship stolen from none other than Sir Thomas himself at the beginning of the year. It appears that your Mr. Steele and his little band of convicts made off with it when they escaped from your plantation. That alone is enough to hang the lot of them, my dear."

"Yes. I see." Kit managed to keep her face calm, but her heart was pounding in a frantic tattoo of panic. Not only was Logan doomed, but Tom, Peter, Doc, and the whole crew as well. Searle would order the *Ice Maiden* seized, if he hadn't already. What damning evidence would the militia find aboard the frigate? How many runaway indentureds would they find among the crew? They might even find poor George Marshall, who now would be condemned by the monstrous lie that had come from her own lips. Kit had made a fine mess of things again, and there wasn't a blessed thing she could do about it.

The doctor poked and prodded with ungentle hands. At Logan's every wince the physician looked happier, and the patient made a vow to be more stoic when the man visited again. Not that he would have long to endure the pain of his wounds. He was surprised they hadn't already tied the noose around his neck.

"Now then," the doctor noted, "that doesn't look too bad, considering you wouldn't let me leech you the last time. You'll be fit in no time."

"Fit for what?" Logan asked with a wry smile, flexing stiff muscles. It was truly amazing how fast a man could heal—only to be hanged by the neck and left to rot, a meal for the sea gulls and a warning to other adventurous souls who might be tempted to stray beyond the bounds of the law.

The doctor gathered up his bandages and powders and called for the guard to let him out. Left to his own thoughts, Logan peered through the tiny barred window slit that looked out over Carlisle Bay.

The quarters could be worse, he mused. They could also be better. The cell was damp and stiflingly hot. The thin straw pad that served as a sleeping mattress was infested with so many vermin that it would have crawled away under its own power, if there had been anyplace to crawl. Twice a day the barred wooden door was opened and a pan of what passed for food was pushed through. It was swill fit only for pigs, and the water was warm and tasted of things that Logan did not care to contemplate.

Still, as prisons went, this was a palace of luxury compared to some that Logan had seen. A doctor had been called to tend his injuries, and no one had yet threatened him with hot pincers or the rack. While his jailers had scowled and glowered on occasion, no one since the vengeful militiamen had tried to beat him to a bloody pulp. And one couldn't really blame those fellows for being overenthusiatic in their duty. Logan had downed two—or was it three—of them before a blade had pierced his side and drained the fight from him, along with a goodly amount of blood.

Yes, indeed, Logan was being treated like a prince. Doubtless his neck would be stretched by a clean new rope as well. And he might even be cut down from the gallows before the seabirds had their fill of his cold flesh. Fine treatment. Better than any criminal could expect. And he owed it all to one man, Logan had no doubt. Modyford had a unique way of keeping his promises. Damn the man!

As if summoned by Logan's thought, Sir Thomas Modyford's face appeared in the barred opening of the heavy door. Seconds later the door swung inward on its iron hinges and Sir Thomas, lace handkerchief protecting his nose and mouth, stepped into the cell. He turned as the guard followed him in.

"You can run along, Corporal. I assure you that Mr. Steele poses no threat that I cannot handle myself."

Logan wasn't sure that Modyford was right. It would have been wickedly satisfying to have his hands around someone's throat just then, and Sir Thomas seemed a likely candidate.

The guard backed reluctantly out of the cell, glowering at Logan all the way. "You watch 'im, yer lordship," he cautioned. "'E's a mean beggar, that 'un is."

"You can be sure that I shall." Modyford waited for a moment until the guard was out of earshot, then turned to Logan and gingerly lowered the handkerchief from his nose. "My, my," he admonished with an offended grimace, "quite a predicament you've gotten yourself into, my boy. I, for one, did not expect you to be so clumsy."

Logan stared at him in silent contempt.

"I don't mind your killing the man out of hand that way"—his eyes narrowed to shrewd slits—"providing, of course, that you have sufficient evidence that Oliver St. John was the man we sought. But you could have been a bit more subtle about it, or at least come to me after the deed was accomplished. I could have shipped you off the island to a Dutch or French colony."

When Logan answered only with hostile silence, Sir Thomas shook his head morosely. "Returning to Greenhaven like that—I suppose that had something to do with St. John's fetching little sister, eh? But whatever, going back was a very foolish thing to do, Lieutenant Steele. I might have influenced the governor in your favor when the evidence against you was merely a servant's word, but after St. John's sister told him you were an escaped slave... Well, that capped it, old boy. The lady is quite put out with you,

you know. I'm surprised she didn't tell Searle about your pirating activities as well."

"She left that for you to do," Logan said caustically.

Modyford shrugged. "The ship was bound to be confiscated and identified. I didn't want to be implicated by holding back evidence. Did you expect me to tell the governor why I made that sleek little frigate so easy a target for you and your little band of convicts?"

"You might have," Logan suggested bitterly. "You said this scheme of yours was sanctioned by Cromwell himself."

"Indeed it was, my lad. But it would not do to have all this become widely known, would it? And I don't quite trust Searle to be as discreet as I would like."

"You would rather see me hang." It was a statement rather than a question.

"Not at all. Not at all." Modyford smiled. "After all, you did accomplish our purpose, no matter how clumsily. We can't very well let you hang or languish in prison. A promise is a promise."

"Yes indeed, Sir Thomas," Logan said, his voice almost a threat. "A promise is a promise. If you want me to keep my part of our bargain, then you get me out of here. And get me back my ship and crew as well. For if the Jackal is truly dead, it wasn't I who killed him. And until you're sure he's dead, you had best have me between that scoundrel pirate and your precious Barbados. I don't think your Cromwell is going to give you a frigate to fight him."

For a moment Sir Thomas regarded Logan with a canny look. Then he shrugged. "Oliver St. John is dead, Steele, whether it was you who killed him or someone else. His own sister identified the body. If the Jackal still sails, it seems that your investigative work was not terribly thorough."

Logan returned Modyford's regard in contemptuous silence.

"But be that as it may," Sir Thomas continued, "it appears I still have need of you. If I am forced to go to the governor and explain our little arrangement, then I shall. So keep your wits about you, lad. I'll have you out of here before they knot the noose around your neck."

Long after Modyford had left the cell, Logan stood and stared out at the little slit of Carlisle Bay that was his only view of the outside world. He didn't trust Sir Thomas. If he truly believed the Jackal dead, it would no doubt please the slippery politician to leave him in this cell to rot, and eventually to hang. As he had said, he would not be pleased to have his methods in this matter come into the public eye, or, more importantly, into the eye of the British Navy, who might think that their prerogatives had been usurped. On the other hand, if Sir Thomas did not get him out of this cell, Logan didn't know who would.

His answer came in the form of an unexpected visitor. He heard Kit's voice before he saw her face appear at the barred door. At the sound of those clear, mellow tones that he had once thought the sweetest music in the world, Logan's body stiffened almost as if with pain.

Kit followed the guard somewhat hesitantly. The governor had been reluctant to permit this visit, and she herself had grave misgivings about coming here. Her own faltering anger was a frail thing to stand up to Logan's hatred. And he must surely hate her with a white-hot fury, thinking as he did that she had deliberately lured him into a trap.

Now, walking down the narrow, dirty corridor that led to Logan's cell, her courage deserted her, leaving her to feel vulnerable in the parts of her soul that only Logan could reach. She stopped for a moment, drawing an impatient look from the guard.

"Come on, miss. I 'aven't all day."

"I'm coming."

Kit reminded herself that she had more than enough reason for hatred herself. Despite her protestations to the governor, in her own mind Kit was certain that Logan's hand had ended her brother's life—almost certain, that is. She could not go through the rest of her life not knowing for sure, and she had to have a confession from Logan's own lips before she would totally believe it.

With her face a mask of dogged determination, Kit nodded to the guard and stepped up to the cell door.

"Ye have a visitor, Steele," the guard grumbled.

"So I see." The voice was a sneer, and the face that appeared at the small barred window was an expressionless mask that might have belonged to a stranger. The eyes were hooded, making Kit wish she could see something in their ice-blue depths—hatred, anger, anything but the cold lifeless nothingness that greeted her from across the bars. "To what do I owe this honor... Miss St. John?"

Kit chewed her lip uneasily as she turned to the guard. "Leave us alone, please."

"Pardon, miss, but I couldn't think of leavin' ye alone wit' the likes o' that 'un. 'E c'n be an unruly beast at times."

"I'm grateful for your concern—Corporal, is it? But I don't think the beast can do me harm from across that heavy door."

The guard scratched the none-too-clean thatch on his head. "I don't think..."

"Governor Searle said I may speak alone with this man. What I have to say to him is quite personal."

"But..."

Kit arched a haughty brow.

"All right, miss. But if 'e gives ye trouble, I'll be right in the next room."

"That will be a great comfort," Kit assured him in a bland tone.

When the guard had gone, she found the courage to turn her face back to Logan's.

"Personal?" Logan asked in an acid voice. "Now what could we have to discuss that is personal?"

Kit didn't answer. She merely stared at him, feeling her heart grow sick at the sight of his swollen, yellowish-green right temple and cheek.

"Has a doctor been sent to tend you?" she asked softly, suddenly forgetting the urgent questions that had sent her here.

"How touching that you want me healthy for my hanging."

At the bitter rejection in his voice, the coals of Kit's anger began to warm to life. She stared at him for a long moment, trying to fan the anger to a heat that would burn away her pain.

"I shouldn't care what they do to you," she finally replied. "And if there is a just God in heaven, someday I won't."

"Did you come here to gloat? You must be quite pleased with what you've done."

"Why shouldn't I be pleased to see my brother's murderer imprisoned and waiting to hang?" she retorted caustically.

They exchanged hostile glares for a long moment. Kit was the first to lower her eyes.

"I came here to hear it from your own lips, Logan," she said in a milder voice. "What happened in the study? Why did you kill Oliver?"

Logan snorted contemptuously. "Did I kill Oliver? Would you believe the truth if you heard it? It seems you've already made up your mind."

"What do you expect me to think?" Kit asked, her voice growing jagged with pain. "Oliver is dead—shot through the head and then thrown to the sharks like . . . like a piece of offal. And everyone in the house saw you barge into his study in a high temper, and then heard a shot. What am I supposed to think?"

"So you call out the militia and arrange for my hanging, without even hearing what I had to say. Your faith in me is certainly touching, love."

"I did not call out the militia," Kit cried in frustration. "The governor did. Dammit, Logan! Tell me what happened! I need to know! Did you kill him because of what he did to you? Or because of me?"

"Do you think that all I ever have on my mind is you?" Derisive blue eyes roamed over her face and figure. The barb struck home, and Kit flinched.

Logan smiled bitterly. That was one thing about loving someone, he mused. You know so well how to hurt them. He hated himself for stooping to such petty revenge, and hated Kit for bringing him to it. The bitterness of her betrayal was eating at him, curdling his love to rancid bile. In the dark, vindictive depths of his soul, something stirred with satisfaction at the sight of her pain.

Kit gathered the tattered remnants of her pride about her like a protective cloak. It had been a mistake to come here. She should have known better than to expect anything approaching reasonable behavior from this rogue. How many times did she have to be burned before she knew to stay away from the fire? She had one more thing to do, and then Logan Steele could go to hell, for all she cared.

"I don't want to see you hang, Logan. No matter what you think or what you've done."

"That makes two of us," Logan quipped cynically.

"I did betray you to the governor, but I didn't think you would be stupid enough to walk into the militia's arms."

"Is that why you set your neat little trap, Katarina?" Logan's eyes glittered with malice. "If you were smart, my love, you would be grateful to see me hang. If I am scoundrel enough to kill your brother in cold blood, just think what I might do to the faithless bitch who betrayed me. You would be far safer with me dead, Katarina."

Logan saw the sable eyes grow dark with fear, and once again he found cause to hate himself. But a dark, bitter part of his soul seemed beyond the control of his better instincts.

"In that case," Kit replied in a frozen voice, "I'm a bigger fool than you are." With a quick, furtive motion she reached into her bodice and drew out a slim, tempered-steel dagger that she pushed toward him through the bars. "This is the only weapon I could manage to smuggle in."

Logan eyed the blade doubtfully. "Just what am I supposed to do with this?"

"If I weren't a lady, Mr. Steele, I would tell you just where you might stick it. But as it is, I suggest you use your head and employ it however you damn well please."

Without pausing to appreciate the look on his face, Kit turned and walked away, her skirts swishing in rhythm with her long stride.

At the end of three hours, the gleaming knife that Kit had handed to Logan was no longer polished and no longer sharp. Its blade was chipped and scratched from continuously picking at the grout around the door's window bars.

Not that there was any sense in what he was doing, Logan thought with disgust. He needed to remove at least three of the iron bars to make a space wide enough for his shoulders to pass through. And even should he succeed in removing the bars, the chances of squeezing himself out of his cell without being detected were about as great as his chances of flying out the window slit and gliding over Carlisle Bay to the *Ice Maiden*. Still, it was something to do, something to take his mind off the noose that was waiting on Execution Dock.

At the sound of voices in the guardroom, Logan quickly concealed the knife and brushed traces of loose grout from where he had been digging. He moved to the window slit to check the length of the shadows on the bay. It was time for the guard to change, and soon someone from the new shift would be ambling in to check on his status.

Logan moved back to the door and checked the half-loosened bar. He stared at it, his brows puckered in thought. With a cautious glance toward the guardroom, he took out the knife and resumed his digging, brushing away most of the grout dust but leaving a faint powder remaining around the bar.

The guard who finally came was one Logan knew well. A tall, thin, good-natured lad with a lantern jaw and a ready smile, Timothy Hawkins was not loath to pass the long hours of duty in amiable chatter with his prisoners. Since he'd been thrown into his cell, Logan had hardly been in the mood for friendly conversation, but he liked the lad all the same. He was sorry it was Timothy who had come for this afternoon's routine check, but not sorry enough to abandon his plan.

"See yer still survivin' the food." Timothy grinned at Logan through the bars of the window. "Hear tell ye 'ad yerself a right fetchin' visitor, too. From what ol' Alan says, she's a piece worth 'angin' fer."

Logan grasped the bars of the door with both hands. His lip curled in a snarl. "There isn't a woman in this world worth hanging for, boy. You might do well to remember that."

Timothy grinned crookedly. "I guess ye're the one t'know. I 'ear that new 'angman down at the Dock is right good. The last few 'as gone down there, why, they've 'ardly even twitched. Thought I'd pass that on, just in case ye was worried."

"There are better ways to go," Logan said darkly.

"Aye," the boy agreed. "An' worse, too. 'Ere now. What's this?"

Timothy had noticed the trace of powdered grout still clinging to one window bar. He came closer to examine his discovery, and bent closer still to the window when he noticed fresh scratches on the iron bar.

Logan's hands came through the bars in a flash and grabbed the boy by the hair. He pounded his head against the bars once—twice—three times, until the lad sagged unresistingly against the door. Then, with poor half-stunned Timothy secured with one hand, Logan wrapped his arm around the boy's neck. His free hand groped for the knife. Chipped and dull as it now was, it was still sharp enough to saw open a man's neck—a feat that Logan hoped he would not have to perform.

The young guard struggled feebly, clawing at Logan's arm with frantic hands. His face was rapidly growing red as the arm tightened slowly. Only a croak came out of his mouth when he opened it to scream. Then he changed his tactics and groped for the rapier that hung at his hip.

"Reach for that blade and you're a dead man," Logan warned. "Don't be a fool, lad. I can slit your neck before you have that sword out of the scabbard."

The boy croaked and lurched, but could neither escape nor call for help.

"Now, boy, reach down on your belt and unfasten those keys. And don't even think of being a hero and throwing them away, because if you do, this knife is going to make short work of your throat. I might as well hang for two killings as one. Understand?"

The guard managed to nod.

"That's right," Logan said as the boy fumbled at the keys. "Now, just feel around the latch until the key fits in the lock."

Timothy lurched in objection, and Logan's knife drew a ragged line of blood across his throat.

"Don't even think of it, boy," Logan warned. "Think of how sad your poor old mum will be if you don't come home tonight. That's the thing." He heard the key rasp in the lock. "Now turn it. Good."

Logan swung the door in, dragging the hapless Timothy with it. The lad didn't resist as he was pulled into the cell and bound and gagged with strips of his own uniform.

"Sorry, Hawkins." Logan gave the boy's bonds a final tug. "But you understand how it is. I've taken a fancy to this life of mine, humble though it is. I'm not ready to dangle from the end of a rope."

The two men in the guardroom were older but no wiser than Timothy Hawkins, and they ended up bound the same as he. They rolled their eyes in terror as Logan went to the weapons rack and selected a heavy cutlass and a brace of pistols, but the escaped renegade spared them not so much as a glance as he thrust the pistols into the waistband of his tattered breeches and, holding the cutlass ready before him, slipped silently out the guardroom door.

Chapter 18

Kit toyed absently with the coddled egg on her breakfast plate. Her muffin was cold from neglect, and generous slices of ham lay untouched.

There was no one at the table to scold her for not eating. Mavis and Lionel had departed the day before, and the servants were diligently trying to stay out of the way of her hair-trigger temper. The big house seemed unbearably empty. Her life seemed just as empty, and her future stretched away in countless days of aching loneliness.

Kit sighed and pushed her plate away. Her appetite had fled, along with the will to do anything but gaze forlornly out the window and mope about what a fool she was, and what a mess she made of everything she touched.

"I see ye're wastin' good food again, miss." Mandy's voice was sharp as she bustled into the room and eyed the untouched helpings. "Those mournin' gowns you ordered just arrived. At least two o' them did. Madame Roget sent a note that the others require one more fitting, an' she be askin' when ye're plannin' t' be in town."

Kit grimaced. Bridgetown was the last place she wanted to be in the next few days. As long as Logan was sitting in that stinking cell waiting to be hanged, she did not want to be anywhere nearby.

"I won't be in town for a while. Send a boy around to Madame Roget with a note for her to hold the gowns."

"I thought ye was in such an 'urry t' 'ave em, miss. If ye was content to wait, ye should've 'ad me stitch 'em up. That fraud of a Frenchwoman doesn't do 'alf..."

"Just send the note," Kit interrupted in a sharp voice.

"Ye know very well I can't write, miss."

"Then for heaven's sake bring me pen and paper and I shall write it."

Mandy left and returned a moment later with the necessary materials.

"Sit down and have a cup of tea while I compose a message," Kit told the maid.

Mandy sniffed. "It's not proper for servants to be sittin' at table with gentlefolk." She crossed her arms over her ample bosom and managed to look superior and humble at the same time.

"Rubbish!" Kit knew why Mandy was sulking. Kit had finally told her the truth about Edward Pettijohn. The maid was miffed by her mistress's foolish behavior, and even more put out because she hadn't been a part of it. "Quit being such a snob and sit down. You're the only servant in this whole house who doesn't run like a frightened hare every time I open my mouth."

"Well, ye 'ave been a bit touchy of late," Mandy said archly.

"You would be touchy too if you had been betrayed by someone you loved—and who supposedly loved you in return."

The double edge of that statement cut deeply as soon as

the words were out of Kit's mouth. Logan had been betrayed also—bitterly betrayed. But he had not the added bitterness of loving his betrayer. If he had felt anything akin to what she felt for him, he never would have raised his hand against Oliver.

"Ye should 'ave known better than to give yer 'eart to a scoundrel an' pirate," Mandy admonished unsympathetically. "Didn't I warn ye in the beginning o' all o' this? Didn't I, now?"

"You were right," Kit acknowledged dismally. "But you needn't rub it in. You've a heart of stone, Mandy."

"Aye. An' it got that way through dealin' with rogues the likes o' that pirate o' yours. Trust my word, miss. Ye'll be better off when that gentleman is dead and gone."

Raleigh stepped into the room and cast a scornful eye on Mandy, who despite her protestations had fetched herself a cup of tea and was now taking her leisure at the table.

"What is it, Raleigh?" Kit asked sharply. She had no patience right now to deal with the staid butler's irritation.

"A missive has just arrived from the governor, miss. The boy said it was quite urgent and is waiting for a reply."

Kit took the letter and stared at it. A long moment passed before she gathered the courage to break the seal. Her heart froze at the thought that Logan had already met his bitter fate, or perhaps... She scanned the first lines of spidery writing, and her mouth slanted upward in a wry smile.

"Logan Steele has escaped," she announced.

Raleigh's brows flew up in alarm. Mandy let loose a contemptuous snort.

"Gents like that fellow always do manage t' dodge what's rightfully comin' to 'em."

Kit summarized as she continued to read. "The governor has offered a troop of militia for our protection, though he says that he's confident the prisoner will be recaptured at any hour. The *Ice Maiden* has been confiscated and returned to Sir Thomas, who has placed it under guard. So Logan can't get off the island—supposedly."

Kit wondered if the governor knew that the servants employed in Logan's house were part of the pirate crew.

There were at least ten of them at the house—maybe more. Enough to take back the *Ice Maiden* if they were lucky.

"What reply shall I send with the boy, miss?" Raleigh asked.

Kit's winged brows puckered in thought. What were the words that Logan had thrown at her from his cell? She would be far safer with him dead. That was it. Had he merely been trying to frighten her, or did he really intend revenge? She remembered the grim promise of his cold smile, and a frightening image flashed across her mind— Logan reaching for his dagger, pressing it against her breast, smiling that frightening, deadly smile. Her heart jumped in distress as she shook the ghastly vision from her mind.

"Tell him that I thank the governor for his concern, but the militia will not be necessary. We will take precautions of our own." Kit had betrayed Logan to the militia once before. She would not do it again.

Raleigh's face was stony. Mandy's was incredulous. "What're ye thinkin' of, miss? I've never seen a fellow look so fierce as that pirate when they carted him off from 'ere. Just supposin' he comes t' pay a call?"

"There are enough men on this plantation that one man shouldn't be a threat to any of us," Kit said. "Besides, with the governor's men looking for him, I doubt that Logan Steele will have time to think of petty revenge. He'll be doing well to think of a way to keep his own skin intact."

Mandy snorted. "Fer all our sakes, miss, I do 'ope ye're right!"

"Of course I'm right. I don't think we have to worry about Mr. Steele anymore." Kit looked down at the eggs and ham congealed in gobbets of cold grease. "Mandy, be a love and tell Mrs. Simpson that my breakfast is cold. I'd like another couple of eggs and some fresh sliced ham."

For the first time in three days, Kit felt like eating.

Windwalker crow-hopped rebelliously as Kit pulled her to a halt a few feet from where Reginald Bartlett stood talking to one of his slave drivers. The new overseer looked up in amusement and tipped his hat respectfully.

"A bit saucy, is she?"

Kit laughed. It was good to laugh again. Just this morning she had thought she never would.

"Windy hasn't been out for a long while. She would dearly love to stretch her legs—not just stand around while I look at the fields. I must say, though, the work appears to be going quite well." She swept her arm in a gesture that took in the rows of burned cane stubble that were being meticulously cleared by slow-moving lines of stolid slaves. They would be followed by other slaves who would plant the cane in long shallow trenches. Soon green shoots would be pushing through the fertile ground.

The overseer laughed and gave the mare a pat on her impatiently arched neck. "You needn't take up your time here if you don't wish to, Miss St. John. I'd surely send for you if we had any problems."

"I know you would, Mr. Bartlett," Kit said with a smile. She trusted this overseer as she had never been able to trust Simon Brownlow. "But I've always liked to watch the clearing and planting. Somehow it's an assurance that there will always be another year, another harvest down the road."

The truth was that Kit found the planting much less interesting this year than she had before. The sight of sweating blacks bent over in backbreaking work made her feel vaguely uncomfortable. Riding out into the fields this afternoon had merely been an excuse to escape the house, where Mandy and Raleigh were both going about their duties with faces full of doom. The parlor maids and kitchen slaves had likewise heard the news of Oliver's murderer being loose on the island, and from their wide eyes and frantic whispers, Kit guessed that the version they had heard was liberally spiced with imagined danger to both Greenhaven and its mistress.

"Also, Mr. Bartlett, I need to talk to you. I've an extra chore for you."

"Yes, miss?"

"I'd like you to organize a troop of drivers to stand guard around the house and stable area, for a few days at least."

The overseer grinned knowingly. "Yes, miss. I heard about that scoundrel Steele getting loose from the prison in Bridgetown."

"I don't think he poses any real danger to anyone here," Kit said confidently, "but I'd rather take some extra precautions than be..."

Be what? she asked herself. Be dead? Beaten? Raped? What form would revenge take if Logan Steele were given a chance at her?

"...than be sorry," she finished lamely.

"Very wise of you," Bartlett agreed. He pushed his hat back on his head and wiped his brow with his arm, then gave Kit a cautious look. "If I'm not being too bold, Miss St. John, I might point out that things have been going very well since that last storm. Planting and clearing always makes for a dull season. If you wanted to take a vacation for a few months—get off the island, for instance—I think we could handle things here in your absence."

What he left unsaid, Kit thought, was that everyone at Greenhaven might be safer without her around for a time. And she might be safer also.

"It's an idea I might consider," Kit said thoughtfully.

Consider it she did for the rest of the afternoon. Everywhere she rode seemed to remind her of Logan Steele, until she could no longer force the vision of him from her mind. Here in the fields was where he had first confronted her with his impudence, gaunt and bedraggled and looking like an oversized, hairy scarecrow. And there in the stockade was where she had tended his lacerated back, and there in the village was where he had imprisoned her, and kissed her—that scorching mockery of a kiss—during his escape. And here at the pond above the mill...

There were too many bittersweet memories at the pond. Kit knew she should not have stopped there, though it lured her as a hot flame might draw a moth. When she halted Windy at the edge of the glade and looked upon the shadowed green water, images of Logan and herself seemed to dance on the mirrorlike surface. The air still seemed to quiver with the passion they had shared—though on Logan's part it had all been a sham.

The nightmarish vision of revenge that had earlier tortured Kit's mind sprang to life once again, mocking the memories of joy that still clung to the glade. Her face crumpled, along with the control that had held the conflicting emotions of fear and joy in check all this long day. She leaned forward and buried her face in Windy's mane, giving way to tears that had been dammed within for too long. All of Barbados had become her own personal hell. Kit sobbed and clung to the horse's neck, feeling the last remnant of her courage dissolve in the flood of tears.

Bartlett was right, bless him! Her father's cousin Alice lived in Kent. She could stay with her until Logan Steele was far away, and memories of him had faded into the back of her mind. Then she could take control of her life once again. Then she would prove to herself that Greenhaven was enough. She didn't need Oliver. She didn't need Logan Steele. The world would see that Kit St. John didn't need anybody but herself.

The hum of insects vibrated through the warm night. In the western sky, the moon was about to sink below the low hills that rose from the waters of Half Moon Bay. Its waning light outlined the silhouette of Greenhaven's coral-stone mansion, poured milky radiance into the silent stable yard, and shimmered in silver ripples on the peaceful lake. Apart from the occasional slam of a door from the house or restless equine nicker from the barn, all was quiet. The three figures crouching in the shadowed foliage appeared to be part of the uncleared brush, their low whispers blending with light stirrings of the breeze.

"I don't like this, Logan," Peter whispered. "Why can't you leave her alone—call the whole thing over and done?"

Logan's teeth flashed in a wolfish grin. "It's not over and done until I say it's over and done. And I have a few matters to take up with Miss Katarina St. John."

"This isn't like you," Peter insisted in a quiet voice. "The girl doesn't deserve this."

"Van Halen's right, m'lord," Carmody chimed in. "Never

been much taken with the English bitch myself. But gettin' back at a damned doxy ain't worth shovin' all our necks in a noose. And we'll all hang for sure if one o' them drivers gets the breeze in his sails and finds us out here."

"You're welcome to join the rest of the crew if you're nervous, Carmody," Logan replied curtly.

"Now don't be gettin' yer hackles up, m'lord. I ain't nervous, just cautious. Seems t'me that we're in a tight enough spot without worryin' about a worthless bit o' female fluff. Besides"—Carmody frowned, uncomfortable with the role of advocate—"the bitch did try to undo the knot she tied ye in. I heard about the dandy bit of a lie she told the governor—rot his hide. Fer a woman, an' English to boot, she ain't a bad sort."

"From you, Carmody, that's a recommendation of the highest order. I see the little witch has won you over as well, eh?"

"No woman's ever won me over," Carmody mumbled.

"Relax, you two." Logan smiled wickedly. "I'm not in a bloodthirsty mood tonight. If she's lucky, our little Katarina may even survive my visit." He glanced toward the house. The bustle of the servants in the detached kitchen building had died away, and most of the slaves had headed for their quarters in the village. "I think it's time for me to pay a call to the mistress of the manor. You two be quiet and wait for me here. Keep your ears open in case I run into trouble."

Carmody shook his head as Logan stole toward the house. "Bleedin' fool makes everythin' so hard. If he wants to pay the slut fer what she did, he oughta just slit the bitch's throat. Why cart her off in the middle o' the night?"

"Quiet," Peter ordered tersely. "It's brutes like you who give piracy a bad name."

Logan slipped through the servants' entrance and made his way through the pantries at the back of the house. He passed the closed doors to the seldom-used ballroom, skulked past the darkened dining room, and stole silently past the empty front parlor. Voices came from the small back parlor that Kit had converted into an office for the plantation accounts. The door to the office was open, and as Logan pressed himself into the shadows next to the door frame, he could see Kit and her redheaded indentured woman conversing in unhappy tones.

"Well, miss," Mandy said with pursed lips, "I wish ye would think on takin' a manservant with us. Like 'Arry. 'E's a strapping lad, and Lord knows 'e wouldn't be missed a bit. Mr. Raleigh's always complainin' that 'e don't do much besides chase after the parlor maids."

"There's no reason to have a man along," Kit said, looking as though the mention right now of a man—even the inoffensive footman Harry—had set her to fuming. "We can get along very well on our own, Mandy. I have never depended on man since Father died. I don't intend to start now."

The sight of Kit almost took Logan's breath away. How many times had he seen that sharp glimmer of irritation directed at him? How familiar was the stubborn set of that chin, the puckered V of the dark, winged brows. She paced back and forth across the room in the long, graceful strides that were so alluringly unlike the mincing gait favored by ladies of fashion. The softly draped skirts of her simple muslin gown swayed rhythmically as she moved, accentuating the slenderness of her waist and the supple length of her legs.

"It's not right fer two females to cross the ocean on their own," Mandy insisted, not at all intimidated by the vexed look on her mistress's face. "The way the seas are now, miss, why anythin' could 'appen. What would we do if we were to be boarded by pirates, now, tell me?"

Kit gave a short, bitter laugh. "The pirate I'm worried about is right here on Barbados, not lurking somewhere out at sea."

"An' 'ow about that Jackal fellow?" Mandy reminded her. "'E's supposed to be a real villain, is that one!"

Kit's sable eyes darkened almost to black as memories of the *Carrie Ann* flashed across her mind. "If we are unfortunate enough to be boarded by the Jackal, then having Harry along—'strapping lad' though he is—would be no help to us. In that case, Mandy, all that would be left for us would be to drop to our knees and pray for a merciful death."

Mandy snorted, unmoved by the picture Kit presented. "I'd still feel better with that good lad's protection."

"Aye, and his companionship, no doubt, on those long nights at sea." Kit bedeviled the servant with a knowing grin. "Harry will still be here when we get back, Mandy."

"That 'e will, miss," Mandy said with a resigned sigh. "An' so will those damned pert little maids. One o' them will 'ave 'im wrapped around 'er little finger by then. An' there goes me chance fer a man o' me own."

Kit shook her head and smiled. "I thought you had given up men."

"Only in a professional way," Mandy replied with a wink. "Once ye've got the appetite, men is 'ard t' give up."

How true, Kit thought ruefully. At least one man she knew was impossible to give up. Hastily she changed the subject.

"We won't have much time to pack. I want to be ready to leave in two days' time. I sent a note around to our agent in Bridgetown and told him to have the *Isabella* ready to sail as soon as possible."

"The *Isabella*?" Mandy raised a contemptuous brow. "That little scow?"

"Don't be pettish. The *Isabella* is perhaps not as large as the *Elizabeth*, but it is quite capable of carrying us to England in comfort. The larger ship sailed for the North American colonies the day... Oliver died, just as it was scheduled. So I'm afraid we haven't much choice. There is no scheduled passenger ship for two weeks."

"Aye," Mandy grumbled. "If they 'ad 'anged that fellow like they was supposed to, we wouldn't 'ave this problem."

"Mandy!" Kit said with an ill-tempered glare. "I don't want to hear any more muttering."

"Hmmph! Well, pardon me, miss, but I can't 'elp thinkin' it. An' if ye'll excuse me now, I think I'll go see what Mr. Bartlett 'as done about preventin' our bein' murdered in our sleep this night."

As the plump little woman passed through the door, Logan sank back deeper into shadow. He permitted himself a smile at the thought that Kit was planning to run from him like a frightened rabbit. She had evidently believed those bitter threats he had made. He had half believed them himself. Logan conceded that he might run, too, if he were in her position.

Alone now, Kit turned to gaze out the window. Her face was pensive, her eyes as dark and gloomy as the blackness beyond the windowpanes. Logan thought she looked lonely and sad, and so lovely that his heart contracted in pain. He almost felt sorry for her, remembering that as strong and self-possessed as she sounded, underneath that well-schooled exterior was a vulnerable woman who was hurt, and perhaps frightened—a woman he had once loved.

Still loved. Still loved, dammit! The realization brought a derisive curl to Logan's lip. How in the name of all that was holy could he still love a woman who had betrayed him, lied to him, and done her damnedest to see him strung up on the end of a rope? The treacherous bitch had declared her love for him, then lured him onto the swords of his enemies. So eager to believe the worst, she had never given him a chance. The twit was fortunate that he was a mild-tempered fellow, or her punishment would be much harder than the one he intended.

His lips pressed into a grim line of determination, Logan moved to step into the room. But Mandy's reappearance brought him to an abrupt halt. He squeezed himself farther back into the shadowed hallway where he couldn't be seen.

"That Mr. Bartlett 'as things well under control, love. 'E's got them drivers standing all around the grounds—loyal men, every one, 'e says. 'E says to tell ye that no one and nothin' can get past 'em tonight."

"Good." Kit sighed and turned away from the window. "It seems we can both rest easy then, doesn't it?"

"I'll rest easy, to be sure!" Mandy agreed. She held up the vicious-looking butcher knife she had brought from the kitchen. "Anyone does get past those drivers, 'e'll meet up with the likes o' this!"

Kit quelled the sudden urge to get a similar weapon for herself. Mandy was being silly. Logan Steele was far away, trying to save his own skin, and certainly not thinking of an insignificant girl whom he had tempted into love and then betrayed. And even should the snake show up at her door, Kit knew she would never be able to use the knife.

"Mandy, I think I'll retire. And you probably should as well," Kit advised as Mandy's eyes drifted in the direction of the back pantries and Harry's quarters. "But first find Mr. Bartlett again and tell him that if by some chance his men do apprehend Mr. Steele, the villain is to be brought to me, and no word is to be sent to the governor or the militia until I order it."

"Yes, miss," Mandy said, one brow raised in disapproval.

"I just want to talk to him," Kit said defensively. "Now go do as I tell you."

Kit followed Mandy out of the office, not noticing the glittering blue eyes that tracked her from the hidden recesses of the hallway.

Logan stood unmoving long after Kit had passed, a deceptively gentle smile curving his lips. So she wanted to talk to him, did she? He would make certain that she got her chance.

It was not long before the house was still. Logan was patient. He crouched in the dark hallway until the last servant's voice had faded into silence and the last pair of feet had ambled their way toward bed. Time moved along slowly, measured by the faint chimes of the mantel clock in Oliver's study.

When the chimes struck midnight, Logan finally moved. He crept up the staircase without a sound and moved unerringly toward Kit's chamber. The door was closed, and a faint light streamed out from beneath it. Laying his ear to the door, Logan heard only silence within. Kit was asleep, he hoped. But not for long.

Kit lay in her rumpled bed, staring into the recesses of her imagination. The dim glow of the lamp cast mysterious shadows into every corner of the room, shadows that her uneasy mind peopled with lurkers who were just waiting for her to fall asleep. The house was well guarded. Kit was well guarded. But just the same, her imagination was alive with danger.

Before settling in for a serious attempt at sleep, Kit rose and padded over to the window, shutting it tightly. The room would be stifling, but the sound of the wind rustling through the tamarisk tree made her uneasy, reminding her that an enemy could use that tree for stealthy entrance and exit as well as she could. Kit left the lamp burning when she settled back into bed, like a child hoping that a light, however dim, would chase imagined goblins from the room. It was childish, but it helped. For what seemed like hours Kit lay stiff and alert, starting at every nighttime creak or rustle. Finally, exhaustion overtook her. She sank into a restless slumber littered with nightmares. On she slept, as the house became quiet, as the last servant made his way to his bed. On she slept, until the nightmares became real.

She woke abruptly, choking and panicked. A large callused hand clamped down tightly over her mouth, smothering her effort to scream. Eyes wide with terror, she looked up into the face of Logan Steele.

Kit blinked at the nightmare. He didn't disappear. Instead, his lips curled upward in a scornful smile that convinced her he was real. No nightmare could copy so well the cold glitter of those blue eyes, the cynical slant of his straight heavy brows or small dimple at the corner of his mouth—the one softening grace in that harsh face. Oh, Lord! What was she doing noticing dimples when her fate was at hand? Kit tried to scream again, clawing frantically at the gagging hand that pinned her to the pillows.

Logan shook his head in an almost friendly admonition. One long finger pressed to his narrow lips, cautioning her to silence and submission.

"I'm not going to hurt you, Katarina, unless you force me to." His voice was a mere whisper of sound. The pressure of his hand eased, allowing her to breathe. "I'm going to remove my hand from your mouth. If you scream or struggle, my love, I will make sure that you don't utter another sound for a very long time. Do you understand?"

Kit gave a small nod of her head, and he released her. She was immediately tempted to sound a loud call for help. But something in those cold blue eyes gave her pause. This was not the Logan Steele she had wound around her finger so many times. This was not the Logan Steele whose stern visage would melt into a warm smile at the touch of her hand or a soft word from her mouth. The aura of predatory menace that surrounded this Logan Steele made him a stranger, the frightening climax to her fears, and definitely not a man to be trifled with.

"Get up," he ordered in a low voice.

Kit complied with reluctance, wishing suddenly that she had worn a flannel nightgown this night instead of the flimsy thing that enhanced more than it covered. Before Logan's eyes could feast upon her near-nakedness, she reached for the dressing gown that lay at the bottom of the bed. She was arrested in midmotion by a steely hand clamped around her wrist.

"Faith!" A slow, infuriating grin accompanied his voice. "It's a bit late for modesty between us, don't you think?"

Kit's face heated with shame as his eyes traveled the length of her from the crown of her ebony hair to the bare toes peeking out from the hem of her night rail. She resisted the urge to squirm uncomfortably under his gaze, knowing that the dim glow of the lamp accentuated every soft mound, every alluring curve, every shadowed valley of her body. Logan Steele had in previous weeks caressed every inch of her body with hands and mouth, had plumbed her most intimate depths, had fused his flesh with hers in scorching possession, and never had she felt ashamed. But now he looked at her as though she were a piece of merchandise, a slave being sold upon the block. And she hated him for it.

"You're still beautiful, Katarina." A spark of desire lit the dark recesses of his eyes, and if it was softened by the least portion of tenderness that had once been theirs, Kit did not see it. "I vow it's a crime against nature to put something so treacherous into such a delectable package. You ought to have scraggly hair, warts, and a hooked nose to look like what you really are."

Kit longed to strike with clenched fist against that smug countenance, but she dared not. So she struck with words instead. "Murderer," she flung. "Scoundrel. Slime. I hate you. I wish you had hanged." Each word came out in a vehement hiss of hatred, but their target seemed unmoved.

"I know you hate me, Katarina. No need to elaborate."

His lips curled into a mocking smile. "Besides, my love, it's very unwise to fling insults at a man who has you in his power—and who is about to carry you off to a fate that only a rascally scoundrel like myself could concoct."

Kit's eyes grew wide as he took a step toward her. "You wouldn't dare, you blackguard!" Her voice rose along with her terror. "I'll scream if you touch me! I'll bring the whole house down around your ears if you dare!"

Her jaw was suddenly in his hurtful grasp, the panicky flow of threats choked off in midflow. Logan's free hand clenched into a fist that gently but ominously grazed the side of her head. Kit's eyeballs strained in their sockets to see what that deadly fist was doing, but Logan merely smiled and held her still.

"I warned you, little miss loudmouth. Next time this will be for real. Now, not another word."

He dragged her with him to the wardrobe and hastily pawed through her clothing. Finally he tossed out the breeches and shirt she had worn so often aboard the *Ice Maiden*.

"Get dressed. And be quick about it. My patience is getting short."

With a growing sense of doom Kit turned her back and let the night rail slip to the floor. The heat of Logan's gaze seemed to burn holes in her skin. She cursed her shaking fingers as she fumbled first with the breeches, then the shirt. Once they were donned she felt much safer.

"Stay still," he ordered as she started to turn.

Logan grasped her hands and efficiently bound them behind her back with ribbons that he had found on her dressing table. Her ankles were afforded similar treatment. He turned her around, and noting the rebellious set of her jaw, tested the bonds to ensure their security. She grimaced as much with anger as with pain.

"Ouch! Dammit, that hurts! You tied them too . . . mmmmph!" Her words were promptly muffled as he stuffed a handkerchief into her mouth and secured it with a scarf.

"Tied them too tight?" he asked unsympathetically. "What a shame."

Kit gave a muffled squeal as Logan hoisted her into an

undignified position over one broad shoulder. Adding injury to insult, a hard hand landed a whack upon her upended backside.

"Quiet now," he warned.

Ignoring Kit's indignant struggles, Logan carried her down the stairs and through the dark house. They slipped out the back entrance and, hugging the shadows that were the blackest part of an already black night, skulked through the yard toward the brush. With every step her captor took, Kit thought of a new curse to call down upon his head, and her own head, and the head of every one of the ineffective guards who were supposed to be seeing to her safety. As Logan quickly ducked into a shadow to avoid the searching eyes of one of Bartlett's drivers, Kit considered the risk of trying to screech around her gag. As though he had read her mind, Logan forestalled her attempt with a warning pat on her rump.

"Be still, Katarina, or I'll be forced to do something you won't like at all." The prowling guard turned away. Three more of Logan's long strides took them to the safety of the brush.

Logan laughed softly as he allowed Kit to slide to the ground. To her ears it was a wicked and completely infuriating sound of triumph. "Don't despair, my love," he assured her. "I'm not going to give you nearly the drubbing you deserve. I just intend that you should meet the fate from which I was trying to save you. Of course, that was before you so kindly delivered me up to my enemies."

The smile pulling at his mouth grew into a wickedly satisfied grin. "I've always been fond of poetic justice."

Chapter 19

Kit didn't know that the night could be so long. Like an unpleasant dream that rolled on and on, the misery refused to end. Still gagged and bound, she was hefted over Logan's shoulder like a sack of flour. More than her dignity was bruised on the short trip to the beach. At every step it seemed that her captor's broad shoulder would fairly split her in two, and her every struggle of protest was met with a solid, painful whack on her vulnerable rear. A pleading look at Peter brought only an uncomfortable shrug in response, and that despicable little Irishman Carmody looked as though he was positively enjoying himself.

Finally the jarring procession came to an end. No one said a word as Kit was unceremoniously lowered into the bottom of a shallop that rocked gently on the incoming tide. Peter, Carmody, and Logan scrambled in after her, bringing a small cascade of seawater with them. Kit counted nine others in the boat—John Bonny, Tom Trelawny, Jud Smythe, Gabriel Potter, and five whose faces she recognized but whose names escaped her. They were all the crew who had lived ashore in Logan's house. Several of them, including young Tom, regarded her with cautious sympathy as she lay on the rough plank deck. The others looked at her with hostile stares, or refused to meet her eyes at all.

The single sail was hoisted. Greenhaven slipped rapidly astern. Kit was too angry to be seasick as the little boat plowed its way through the rough chop. She kept her gaze fastened on Logan's broad back, putting all the heat of her anger into a searing glare that could have melted tempered steel. But the scoundrel didn't acknowledge her with so much as a glance, and his indifference only fueled Kit's ire. It was bad enough to be kidnapped and hauled off to some vindictive fate of Logan Steele's concocting, but it was worse still to be ignored.

In just slightly over an hour, Kit was able to make out the faint silhouette of the headland just east of Carlisle Bay. The jut of land slipped slowly past as the sky faded from black to dull gunmetal gray, but it was still dark enough for the little shallop to pass unnoticed under the guns of Wallenghby Fort.

Once past the headland, the helmsman tacked to a different course. The pirates seemed confident of where they were going, and not too many minutes passed before the dim outline of a ship materialized out of the darkness. Even Kit's untutored eyes recognized the *Ice Maiden*. With silent efficiency the shallop was turned into the wind and the sail lowered.

Logan turned from his place in the prow, and Kit felt the full weight of his attention swing around to rest on her. She promptly decided that being ignored was the far safer thing. His eyes swept the length of her, and she felt rather than saw the studied insolence of his gaze. The dark blot of his face revealed nothing of his temper.

"Mmmmph!" She muttered a protest into her gag as he squatted down beside her and tested her bonds with an ungentle jerk.

"Don't tempt my fist, Katarina. There are less pleasant means of ensuring your silence than that gag." His voice was a mere whisper, yet it carried a full measure of contempt. Giving her bonds one last tug, he turned to Tom. "Keep her quiet by whatever means," he ordered in a hushed voice. "She'd have all our necks in a noose if she had her way."

Tom frowned, but nodded silent acquiescence. He sat beside Kit and patted her shoulder in a small offering of comfort while the rest of the crew stripped to pantaloons or breeches and silently slid into the warm waters of the bay. Sir Thomas Modyford was going to lose his ship again, Kit guessed. The man ought to know better than to leave it anchored so far from the other ships in the harbor. Didn't he learn anything from past lessons?

The minutes dragged by and all Kit heard was the measured breathing of the boy sitting beside her and the quiet wash of waves against the hull. Then there was a faint splash, a muffled grunt, a muted thump. More silence, followed by a strangled groan. Moments later a soft hail floated over the water, barely audible above the quiet lapping of waves against the boat. With a triumphant chuckle Tom grabbed a set of oars and began to row toward the silent ship. Not much of a fight, Kit mused. Stupid of Modyford not to leave more of a guard to stand watch.

Kit was hefted aboard the recovered *Ice Maiden* like a piece of cargo and slung once more over Logan's shoulder. She caught a brief upside-down glimpse of Modyford's guards huddled together in a sheepish group by the rail. Then the deck almost grazed her head as she was carried swiftly down the companionway to the deck below. Her indignant, randomly aimed kick was rewarded with a surprised "Oof!" of pain from her captor. Kit smiled in satisfaction, but another furious kick brought a stinging swat on her upended rear.

"Ice Maiden, hell! Firebrand is more like it!"

Logan kicked open the door to his cabin and tossed his burden casually onto the bed. Kit landed with a painful jolt to her bound arms. Her hair, loosened by her struggles, fell about her like an ebony curtain. A furious shake of her head failed to dislodge the strands from her eyes. With a faint smile twisting his lips, Logan reached forward and smoothed the midnight mass back from her face. The touch of his fingers on her skin made Kit's heart jump with alarm, and with something else that should have died days ago, but hadn't. Clear blue eyes mocked her as his fingers slid down to rest on the pulse that fluttered wildly in the hollow of her throat.

"Don't get too comfortable, Miss Fire and Ice," Logan warned in a voice that was soft and menacing at the same time. "I'll return soon. And then we'll settle some things between us, you and I." Ignoring her mumbled protests, he turned and left without a backward glance.

The door slammed behind Logan with an ominous thud. Kit whimpered angrily into her gag and twisted her arms in a frustrated attempt to free herself. A few moments of skin-scraping agony convinced her it was hopeless. She was trussed as securely as a hog bound for slaughter, and doomed to stay that way.

Kit lay back on the mattress and listened to the heavy pounding of her heart. She was afraid, she realized with a hint of shame. Since she had first come awake to the feel of Logan's hand covering her mouth, anger and indignation had kept fear at bay. But now it was creeping its insidious way into her mind, making her want to cringe from the knowledge that her future was a very undecided thing.

The creak of the windlass and the metallic rattle of the anchor chain grated across the peaceful silence. Bare feet pounded on the deck above Kit's head, and the thunderous crack of sail taking the wind signaled their imminent departure. Modyford's ship would sail unhindered under the cannon that guarded Carlisle Bay, while the governor's militia searched for Logan on Barbados. By the time Kit's kidnapping was discovered and the theft of the ship reported, the *Ice Maiden* would be safely out to sea.

Kit groaned in an agony of frustration. The governor was a fool, Modyford was a fool, and, most of all, Kit St. John was a fool. She herself had helped Logan escape, and what thanks did she get? She was being dragged off to God only knew what fate, and her brother's murderer was once again free to wreak havoc on the sea. She was not only a fool, but a monumental fool. Probably a more foolish woman had never been born upon the earth.

When Kit finally dropped into uneasy slumber, her dreams were plagued by twisted memories of Logan Steele, the sweet and the bitter jumbled together in an uneasy panorama of their turbulent relationship. His kindness, gentleness, humor, and rare flashes of ruthless violence paraded before her mind in vivid images that made her toss and sweat upon the bed.

She finally woke from the torture with a cry of pain. Burning agony washed over her hands and wrists and flooded up toward her shoulders.

"Hold still, dammit!" Logan's impatient voice penetrated the sticky cobwebs of sleep. "Do you want these off, or don't you?"

The pressure on her wrists was gone. Her bonds had been cut. The gag was gone as well. Kit lifted herself to one elbow and watched in groggy confusion as Logan slipped his blade between her ankles to cut them free. She massaged her wrists and grimaced in pain, but no sympathy softened the hard glitter of Logan's eyes. He turned to the cupboard by the desk, took down two glasses, and poured them both a portion of wine.

Kit eyed the proffered glass suspiciously. Ripples of midmorning sunlight reflected off the sea and streamed through the stern windows, making the red depths of the wine glimmer like a rich jewel.

"It's not poisoned, I assure you." As if to prove his point, Logan downed his in a single swallow, then poured himself another glass.

"I don't care to drink with you," Kit explained in a frozen voice.

"An uncivilized attitude," he commented, one brow lifted in disapproval. "As I recall, you've done much more than drink with me in the past."

Her hand lashed out in swift retribution, but before it reached his face, Logan's long fingers closed around her wrist in painful restraint. With a single jerk he pulled her from the bed, dragging her forward until her face was only inches from his. "Don't try my tolerance with your witchy ways," he warned in a voice suddenly grown dark. "My patience is never very long, and right now it is shorter than usual."

Kit met his anger with a defiant lift of her chin. She retrieved her hand and tried to massage away the marks of his grip. "Do I try your patience as much as my brother did, Logan? Are you going to murder me the same way you murdered him?"

Logan looked at her for a long moment, his features chiseled out of stone. But he gave her no answer. A chill spread icy fingers down her spine.

"What are you planning for me, Logan?" She tried hard to keep her voice from quivering, but the onslaught of his hard-eyed stare made the task difficult.

"Do you really expect me to murder you?" he asked tonelessly.

"What else should I expect from a murderer? Killing must come easily for you."

"Murderer, is it?" Logan smiled bitterly, dragging his eyes from Kit's face and crossing the cabin to look out the stern windows. "Perhaps it fits. Only God can judge. I've killed a few men, for one reason or another. But killing never comes easily." He paused, a brooding frown pulling his brows together in a dark slash. "I didn't kill your brother, Katarina."

She sneered. "Do you expect me to believe that?"

"I suppose that would be too much to ask, wouldn't it?"

A flicker of doubt clouded Kit's certainty. "If you didn't kill him, then why didn't you reply to my message?"

"I did, if you will remember." He turned toward her, his narrow lips twisting into a bitter smile. "I had a rendezvous that night, and I didn't return until the following evening. As soon as I learned what had happened, I came to your summons—and walked into the welcoming arms of the governor's militia."

Kit lowered her gaze, feeling heat rush to her face. She knew the scarlet flush made her look guilty as sin itself. "I didn't set that trap. The governor did it without my knowing."

"Do you expect me to believe that?"

"I suppose that would be too much to ask, wouldn't it?" she said quietly, throwing his own words back into his face.

There was a long moment of hostile silence before Kit had the courage to persist with her question. "What now, Logan Steele? It appears that I've had my turn at vengeance. Now it's your move. What are you going to do?"

Logan turned away as though to contemplate his answer. Looking at his broad back, Kit remembered the cruel stripes that Oliver had put there. How much could she really blame Logan for killing her brother? she wondered.

"Vengeance...." Logan pronounced the word as though he were weighing its value. When he turned around to face her, his eyes lacked their former icy glitter. They were as unreadable as an empty blue sky. His face showed not a hint of what he was thinking. "I'm not a vengeful man, Katarina. I have no plans for revenge."

She sniffed in disbelief. "What do you call this—carting me off in the middle of the night and leaving me trussed up in this cabin for hours on end?"

He shook his head and smiled. "Perhaps that was unkind of me, my dear, but that wasn't revenge. Revenge is a nasty word, a killing word. I merely plan to educate you in the realities of your life. You've always claimed to be a girl who likes to face up to the real world. I've decided to teach you a lesson in reality. It might do you good."

"What do you mean?" Kit didn't like the tone of his voice one whit.

"I have a surprise for you. I'm afraid it isn't a very pleasant one."

"What?"

"If I told you, it wouldn't be a surprise any longer, would it?" His grin was wicked, and the sight of it whipped Kit's anger into renewed life.

"Don't play games with me, you villainous pirate! If you think to frighten me with this mysterious posturing, then you've sadly underestimated your victim!"

"Victim?" Logan asked quietly, refusing to match her ire. "You're not my victim, Katarina. If I truly wanted to hurt you, my little innocent, I would. There are so many ugly ways a man can hurt a woman."

Kit backed away from Logan's slow advance and flinched as his hands came up to cup her face. For an aching moment of suspended time she thought he was going to kiss her. An undisciplined part of her heart was disappointed when he didn't. "Be grateful that I'm too much of a gentleman to use such methods," he continued softly. "For there is an animal part of me that would like to."

When he released her she was trembling, much to her shame. He left her where she stood and went to the door. Hand on the latch, he turned.

"I didn't kill Oliver, Katarina. Your brother was a barracuda wearing a man's clothing. If I had killed him, I would admit it. I'd even be proud of it."

Kit gripped the bedpost as if she would tear it from the frame and hurl it at Logan's head. She hated him for making her tremble. She hated him for making her weak with desire. She hated him for insulting the dead man who had been her only family. But most of all she hated him for being an arrogant, unscrupulous devil who had his claws in her heart and was tearing her to pieces.

"I hate you," she said in a quiet voice full of loathing.

His eyes flashed with an instant of regret, then became bland and expressionless. "I know you do, Katarina."

The door closed quietly behind him. Kit stared at it for a long time. Then her gaze shifted to the desk. The pencil portrait that Logan had drawn still hung there. Her own face, more beautiful than she had ever conceived it, stared at her out of the paper, mocking her with its saucy smile and its laughing, loving eyes. With grim determination Kit stalked to the desk and ripped the drawing from the bulkhead. Methodically and thoroughly, she shredded it into tiny, meaningless pieces.

Eight days later, a steady breeze propelled them into the Bay of Cayona, the well-guarded anchorage for the Isle of Tortuga. The notorious buccaneer haven was not what it once had been. Since January 1654 it had been ruled by the Spanish, who had ousted its lawless inhabitants to forest camps on the wild northern coast of Hispaniola. Not until a year later when the British fleet gathered to threaten Santo Domingo did the Spanish garrison withdraw, allowing the buccaneers to drift back to the island. Before they left, the Spanish troops had systematically devastated the town and blown the Huguenot tyrant Levasseur's clifftop fortress to smithereens. The buccaneers willingly picked up the pieces, glad once again to have safe haven for their ships and plundered cargo.

Kit stood at the rail with Tom at her side, watching Levasseur's ruined fortress slip by as the *Ice Maiden* sailed slowly toward the forest of masts that crowded the docks. She thought back to the day when she had betrayed Logan to Governor Searle. She had guessed then that the rogue would take refuge in Tortuga. What she hadn't guessed was that he would drag her along with him.

Kit wrinkled her nose. "This place smells like a sewer," she commented to Tom.

"A French sewer," the boy corrected. "There are enough Frenchies here to sink the island. Sometimes Dutch and

English aren't too welcome, so watch your step when we go ashore."

"Go ashore?" Kit asked in surprise. "I'm not going into that filthy, pirate-infested pesthole!"

Tom shrugged. "I don't think the cap'n trusts you enough to leave you here—or the crew to keep you from leaving."

"That's ridiculous! Where would I go?" Kit's mind roiled with uneasy speculations. "I wish I knew what that blackguard has planned for me."

Kit had labored under the weight of Logan's gaze all week. Whenever she emerged on deck, his eyes swung to her as inevitably as a compass needle swings to north. She refused to give the devil the satisfaction of driving her below, so she ignored him with a haughty show of indifference. But the contemplative attention of those sea-blue eyes unnerved her. Kit imagined him cogitating on her fate, not believing for one moment his denials of revenge. She felt like a helpless mouse dangling from a cat's claws, waiting for the feline jaws to snap closed in final, deadly violence.

"Don't worry so much." Tom's cheerful voice brought Kit back from her dark speculations. "Doc told me that Logan has a house here—in the good part of town. You'll be all right there."

A house, was it? It had better have more than one bedchamber, Kit thought sourly. She certainly wasn't going to share a room with Logan!

With cold bravado she had informed Logan on their first day at sea that she would not share his bed, or his quarters, and that if he so much as touched her she would somehow find the means to kill herself—or still better, kill him. Without a word of objection Logan had gathered his things and moved into Peter's cabin, leaving the main cabin with a feeling of stark emptiness almost as great as the emptiness in Kit's heart. But no matter how much her foolish heart objected, Kit had no intentions of relenting.

"Anyway," Tom continued, "we'll only be here for a few days."

"Why are we here at all?" Kit asked in a disgusted voice.

"To get information, I guess."

Kit's eyes narrowed with sudden interest. "What information?"

"The cap'n hasn't told you?"

Kit shook her head.

Tom shrugged. "I guess it won't hurt to tell you. We're trying to find the Jackal, and Tortuga is the best place to start looking. Somebody here ought to know where that devil is."

"The Jackal," Kit repeated in a frozen voice. "Why does Logan want to find the Jackal? I thought he despised him."

"He wants to kill him," Tom replied in a fierce tone.

"He wants to fight the Jackal," Kit echoed incredulously. "The fool! The mule-brained, bloody-handed fool!"

Tom looked at her in surprise, but Kit didn't linger to argue the point. She crossed to the quarterdeck companionway with long, angry strides. As she mounted the steps and made a line toward Logan, the crew took a look at the set of her face and faded as far away from their captain as they could get.

"I demand an explanation from you!"

"Save your display of temper, Katarina." Logan kept his eyes fastened on the docks, ignoring her as completely as one could ignore such a whirlwind of feminine ire. "I'm busy. We're about to drop anchor."

"I don't care what you're about to drop! I demand to know why you are pursuing the Jackal! And why you've dragged me along! What has that rogue pirate to do with me?"

Logan sighed and turned from the rail. The crew hastily hid their snickering smiles and turned curious eyes back to their work. "What has the Jackal to do with you, Katarina? Perhaps nothing. Perhaps a great deal. Why do you ask?"

"If he has nothing to do with me, then why are you pursuing him?"

"Do you think that I do nothing that doesn't concern you?" His smile mocked her. His clear blue eyes laughed. "What a self-centered little witch you are, my love."

Kit's hand itched to make painful connection with his arrogant jaw. In frustrated fury she turned and paced back and forth along the quarterdeck rail. Finally she stopped before Logan and glared at him with a mix of anger and pleading.

"You're insane!" she declared. "You know that, don't you? You are committing suicide and dragging the men and me with you! Why are you doing this?"

Logan leaned back against the railing in a posture of infuriating unconcern. "I've decided that it's time for the infamous Jackal to meet his end. I'm tired of crossing the trail of slaughter that he leaves in his wake."

"You're a fool!"

He smiled. "Guilty as charged. But I'm not inviting death, my love. Even a villain such as I has many things to live for. Making your life miserable is only one of them."

"Ooooh!" Kit's hands clenched into tight fists at her side. She longed to pound both of them into Logan's smirking face. "God save me from bloody, bullheaded fools who think that they can conquer everyone and everything just because they're men!"

"A useless prayer, Katarina." Logan favored her with a smile that was full of promise. "Not even God can save you from me, I think. Now get the hell off my quarterdeck and leave me to my work."

With a furious glare and a despairing attempt to hold her head proudly erect, Kit complied.

The taproom of the Sea Gull Inn was full of noise and smoke and the acrid odor of unwashed bodies. The tankard that sat on the table in front of Kit was less than clean, and the ale that it held was warm and sour. Never having drunk ale, Kit didn't know if the unappetizing drink was supposed to taste like last night's leftover dishwater, or if the quality of the inn was carried over into the quality of the beverages that they served.

"I don't know why Logan dragged us in here," Kit complained to Tom. "Why couldn't we have stayed at the house?"

Tom shrugged, looking around the taproom with eager interest. He lowered his voice to a confidential whisper.

"This inn is a first-rate place. Everybody who's anybody comes here. See that fellow over there?" The boy pointed to a tall, hawkish-looking fellow in a bright scarlet coat and black satin sash. "Doc tells me he's one of the richest buccaneers on the island. He's one of the captains who've helped in transporting the rescued slaves. He was a slave on Barbados for two years, so he knows what it's like to be chained."

The man looked more like an indolent London gentleman than a pirate, but something about the set of his shoulders and the watchfulness of his eyes told Kit he wasn't a fellow that anyone with a scrap of good sense would choose to fight. Most of the patrons of the tavern were of the same ilk—hardened-looking wolves of men who even as they relaxed looked ready for a brawl. Most of them were gaudily dressed in silks and satins and liberally adorned with jewelry. But all the rich fabrics in a king's wardrobe couldn't make these fellows look civilized.

The women were even worse. The ravages of liquor and ill-use were covered with face paint, and blatantly displayed charms left almost nothing to the imagination. Their every movement was calculated to attract a man, and they were remarkably successful despite the fact that many of their charms were sagging and the odor of cheap perfume did not mask their lack of personal grooming. Every man in the room took for granted the right to reach out for the lush flesh that gaping bodices temptingly revealed, or to slide their hands up skirts to fondle saucily swinging hips and willingly parted thighs.

Kit found the whole scene disgusting. Logan had brought her here to humiliate her. There was no doubt about it. Was this one of the realities of life about which he so mysteriously prated? If so, she wanted nothing more than to flee back to the sheltered cocoon of Greenhaven. She wanted nothing to do with this place, and nothing to do with a man who found pleasure in this sort of company.

"You're too young to be in a place like this!" Kit said in an indignant voice. "Logan should know better."

"I'm not too young. The cap'n told me to watch out for

you," Tom returned proudly. "And that's what I'm going to do."

"Splendid," Kit said testily.

She looked around the room, uneasily noting the number of eyes that were turned in her direction. One set of eyes in particular rested upon her with a disconcerting gleam. They belonged to a lean, greasy-looking buccaneer whom Logan had taken great pains to search out.

"Who is that nasty-looking fellow who is in conversation with Logan?" she asked Tom. "I don't like the looks of him at all."

"He's some Frenchman who's supposed to be tight with the Jackal. Not too many in the brotherhood will sail with that villain." For a moment Tom's eyes turned opaque, and Kit wondered if he was remembering his nightmare aboard the *Carrie Ann*.

"But if that fellow sails with the Jackal, why would he reveal his whereabouts to Logan?"

Tom gave Kit a wordly-wise smile that looked out of place on his youthful face. "Among these fellows, gold will buy you anything."

In truth, the gold in Logan's purse wasn't getting him very far in his negotiations with Jean Main de Fer—named "Iron Hand" for the hook that replaced his left hand, and his talent in using it as a weapon. The man was a greedy scoundrel. He would sell his own mother for gold, but on this afternoon he had set his eye on something else of value, a treasure that Logan was not yet ready to yield.

"The girl is not for sale," Logan repeated. "With what I'm offering, you could buy a dozen women with sweeter temperaments and more flesh on their bones. Take my word for it. That one is no bargain."

The Frenchman arched an inquiring brow. "Then why are you so reluctant to part with her, Capitaine? You want to know where Le Jackal is sailing, eh? And your little English lady over there tickles my fancy. It seems to me you are being unnecessarily stubborn, *mon ami*."

"And it seems to me that you are being unnecessarily obtuse. You can name your price for the information I want. But the woman there is not part of the bargain."

"*Eh bien*. Suppose I take your gold and give you what you want, eh? And then we fight over the lady in question." The Frenchman flexed the fingers of his right hand. "A good fight would be entertaining, and I am told you are a worthy opponent for any man."

"I don't fight for what is already mine." Logan fastened the Frenchman with a stare that would have made a sensible man back down, but only served as a challenge for Main de Fer.

"Ah! You are not a sporting man, I see. What a pity."

Logan bitterly regretted bringing Kit to the inn. He should have left her locked securely in his house, despite the fact that the housekeeper was already tut-tutting over his treatment of her and the lads who tended the garden were google-eyed with adolescent awe. Kit could wheedle her way into anyone's affections, and he was reluctant to trust her to others' care. Even young Tom was not proof against her charm. And now this randy buck of a Frenchman was turning his eye her way.

"I will get my information elsewhere," Logan warned. "If you scorn my offer, there are others who will not."

The Frenchman regarded him from under lazily drooping lids. "I think not, Capitaine Steele. You have something I want. If you are too much the coward to fight for it, then I will take it without a fight."

Softly spoken though the words were, they cut across the room and halted all other conversation. Buccaneer ears were finely tuned to hints of a fight. Tom looked up from his conversation with Kit. He sensed trouble in the sudden silence, and even more trouble in the heavy gaze that Main de Fer had turned on their table.

"Miss Kit," he said in a suddenly boyish voice, "I think we'd better get out of here."

"One moment, *mon petit* cockerel." The Frenchman's voice rang out in the ominous silence as Tom and Kit rose from their seats. "Stay. I must have words with your companion once I have rid our island of this upstart."

Buccaneers moved as a group to block the exit. Here was a promise of an entertaining fight, and they didn't want the prize walking away before she could be awarded to the victor.

"Wonderful." Kit sat down, her lips drawn into a tight line of anxiety. She was not concerned for Logan, she told herself sternly. The rogue deserved whatever fate he brought upon himself. She was frightened for herself, and herself only.

Logan and the Frenchman rose from their seats, each measuring the other with the canny regard of experienced fighters. The center of the room was hastily cleared of tables and chairs by eager onlookers. Every man in the room was grinning in anticipation of the blood soon to flow.

The silence was cut by the rasp of two rapiers sliding from their sheaths. The Frenchman whipped a brief salute toward his opponent, and then glanced toward Kit to see if she was suitably impressed by his bravado. Logan took advantage of his distraction and lunged, scoring a shallow bloody trail across Main de Fer's chest.

"Not very sportsmanlike, *mon ami*." The French buccaneer sprang lightly out of reach of Logan's sword. Ignoring the streak of blood on his chest, he smiled tauntingly.

"I don't regard killing as a sport," Logan said in a voice hard as steel. "If you insist that I kill you, I will, my friend. But I would advise you to take my gold and give me what I want, or I will have it from you at the point of a sword."

Main de Fer's reply was a vicious attack that forced Logan back against the crowded mass of tables. "You are bold for a man who did not want to fight. Perhaps this will be entertaining after all."

"Only if you regard death as entertaining," Logan gritted through his teeth, straining to keep the Frenchman's flashing blade at bay.

Kit gripped Tom's arm with a trembling hand. "Can't we do something?"

"I don't think so," the boy replied in a shaky voice. It appeared to Tom that his captain had more than met his match in the adept Frenchman. "We should have brought Mr. Van Halen along. I don't know how we're going to get out of here if that Frenchie runs the cap'n through."

Kit gave the boy a look of wide-eyed panic. "You mean Logan could lose?"

Tom didn't reply. His silence told Kit more than she wanted to know. Logan was as quick and agile as ever, his rapier a flashing, deadly blur that defied the eye. But for all his skill, he was scarcely holding his own. The Frenchman drove him back, keeping him ever on the defensive. A killing gleam was in Main de Fer's eye.

Then fate took a hand. The two combatants crashed through the pile of tables and chairs that had been pushed from the center of the room. Back and still farther back Logan was forced. His lips were a compressed line of concentration. Sweat ran down his brow, into his eyes, and in rivulets down the corded column of his neck. The muscles of his arm and back bulged with the effort of keeping his blade between himself and violent death.

The Frenchman couldn't resist a taunt. "I think *la mademoiselle* will enjoy my favors, *n'est-ce pas*? Then perhaps I will give her to my good friend Capitaine Le Jackal, eh?"

"You may get a surprise if you do that, friend."

Logan stumbled. His hand closed on the leg of a chair. In a last desperate move to save himself, he flung the chair into the Frenchman's path. It tangled in Main de Fer's feet, sending both men into a heap on the cluttered floor, Logan on top.

Logan gasped for breath, not believing his good fortune. He pressed the razor edge of his sword against Main de Fer's windpipe.

"Now, friend, you will give me for free what I offered to purchase with gold."

A rattle of fear was pulled from the Frenchman's throat as the pressure of Logan's blade increased. "Tar Island!" he gasped. "He was . . . supposed to go to Tar Island to . . . careen and scrape his hull. I . . . meet him there in five days."

"I don't think you will keep that appointment."

Logan debated slitting the man's throat. It was the wisest choice in the long run. He tensed his muscles, girding himself to do the bloody deed, when he felt the weight of Kit's eyes. Without turning his head he knew it was her gaze that was sending the chill up his spine.

Logan eased his blade from the downed man's throat. Kit had once accused him of being a murderer. He refused to prove her right. Instead, he thought ruefully, he would prove himself a fool.

The Frenchman looked at Logan in disbelief as he pulled his blade back. He stretched out his hand toward his own blade as Logan rose, then cried out in pain as a heavy boot trod deliberately on his right wrist. Logan smiled in unpleasant satisfaction at the sound of bones snapping.

"That should keep you out of trouble until I can take care of your friend."

He glared warningly at the gathered audience as Tom and Kit scurried toward the tavern door. Kit paused to watch in horror as the Frenchman whimpered and cradled his crushed wrist.

"Did you have to do that?" she asked Logan with caustic disapproval. "Is such cruelty really necessary?"

Logan pushed her urgently toward the door, knowing that it had not been she who had started the trouble, but feeling uncharitable just the same. "Keep that wicked tongue of yours still, Katarina. You cost me a lot of effort today. Don't make me wonder if you're worth it."

Chapter 20

The *Ice Maiden* sailed on the evening tide, straight from the Bay of Cayona into the teeth of a rising storm. It was not a strategy of sound seamanship, but Logan refused to chance his quarry being warned of the fate pursuing him. The Jackal had few enough friends, but all it would take was one buccaneer thinking to curry favor with the most successful pirate of them all. The chance of finding the villain careened and relatively helpless at Tar Island was a piece of good fortune that could not be thrown away. The storm would have to be risked.

But if the storm brewing on the sea was bad, it was a mere passing squall compared to the storm brewing in Kit's mind. Her thoughts were a jumble of confusion and conflicts. Certainties had become doubts, and the stone foundation of her beliefs was turning to quicksand.

She had been so sure that Logan Steele wanted nothing more than to hurt her in return for the hurt she had dealt him. But when the perfect opportunity had come along, he had rescued her from disaster almost at the cost of his own life. And yet he didn't want her for himself. He had raised no objection when she had booted him out of his cabin. Kit had expected some resistance, at least, and the lack of it had left her a tiny bit miffed. She was at war with herself, fighting to douse the fire that still kindled in her veins whenever she saw the rogue. He, apparently, had won his war all too easily. Perhaps, a scornful little voice told her, Logan had never had a fire to douse.

Kit paced the confines of the stern cabin. Every step was a challenge, for in the angrily tossing sea the deck was never where her feet thought it was. She should be on the bed, she told herself, clinging to the mattress, but her restless energy wouldn't let her stop moving. Her life had become a morass of questions and doubts, and a rising tide of queasiness in her belly combined with the uneasiness in her mind to create a maelstrom greater than the one tossing the ship.

Damn Logan Steele! Her mind cursed him over and over. He kept her cruelly suspended in uncertainty, a worse fate than any other he could have concocted. What was the mysterious lesson he promised to teach her? Why had he dragged her from her home if not for some grisly revenge? And why did Peter, Doc, and even faithful Tom look at her with pity in their eyes? What did they know that she didn't? Damn Logan Steele! Damn him!

Finally Kit surrendered to the storm, no longer able to keep her feet beneath her. She collapsed in a heap on the bed and lay there watching the lantern swing in dizzy circles. Shadows lunged and twisted as the dim light rocked back and forth. To Kit's troubled eyes they looked like black demons dancing in the pit of hell. She closed her eyes. Still she could see them twisting and turning, writhing and laughing and mocking.

With a miserable groan Kit lurched from the bed and clawed her way toward the chamber pot. She spent the next half hour kneeling there, her stomach rebelling with every dip and plunge of the ship. That was how Logan found her, green-faced and bleary-eyed, clinging to the chamber pot as though it were her only anchor in life. She raised her head as he stepped into the cabin, cursing herself for a fool. Sick as she was, despicable as he was, her heart still jumped at the sight of him. Why, oh why couldn't she hate him as she should? She lowered her aching head back onto her arms, expecting him to voice some scathing comment that would make her feel even worse. But he didn't say a word. He just stood there dripping seawater onto the plush wool carpet.

"Are we sinking yet?" Kit finally moaned, not really caring. She couldn't be any more miserable dead than she was alive.

Logan seemed to wake from a spell. He reached for the towel that hung on the wardrobe and dabbed at his wet hair. "The ship isn't sinking, but it appears as though you might be."

He wrung the towel into the basin, then folded it into a square.

"You should be on the bed." With gentle insistence he helped her to her feet. Her stomach instantly rebelled and turned itself inside out, but there was nothing more for her to bring up. Logan steadied her while the dry heaves racked her slender frame. Then he pressed the cool wet towel to her face. The nausea subsided a bit, and Kit remembered her anger.

"Get away from me," she rasped through her burning throat. "I don't need . . . I don't want . . ."

"What you need is some of Doc's special remedy for the stomach heaves." He picked her up and, negotiating the crazily tilting deck as though it were rock steady, carried her to the bed. "Stay here. I'll be right back."

"No! Wait, damn you!" Kit raised herself to a shaky sitting position. "How dare you be kind to me after..."

"After what?" he asked, a half smile playing around his mouth.

"After making my life a living hell!"

"Faith, is that what I'm doing?"

His insouciance only goaded Kit to greater anger. Weakened by sickness and tortured by uncertainty, she was easy prey for her riotous emotions. She gave them full rein. Launching herself from the bed, she grabbed for the long-bladed dagger Logan always carried at his hip. With a skill she hadn't suspected in herself, she pulled the knife from its sheath and hurled it. The dagger buried its tip in the deck between Logan's widely planted feet, vibrating from the fury of Kit's toss. Logan stared at it, his only reaction a slightly raised brow.

"Damn you, Logan Steele! Pick it up. Drive it into my heart! Or shoot me!" Kit's ebony hair flew around her in wild disarray as she lurched for the desk and pulled out the top drawer. She grabbed the pistol that always resided there and threw it at her tormentor's feet, not caring that it wasn't loaded. "Shoot me! Run me through with that bloody sword of yours. Kill me, Logan! But don't keep me dangling with these mysterious hints. I cannot stand this! I can deal with death, and loss, and any number of things you might think to do with me! But I can't deal with ghosts!"

She collapsed once more onto the bed, panting with exhaustion and angrily wiping at the tears streaming down her face. Logan bent and picked up the weapons she had thrown at him, placing the dagger back in its sheath and tossing the pistol into its drawer.

"Ghosts, eh?" He gave her a wry smile. "You may be closer to the truth than you think."

"No!" she wailed, covering her ears with her hands. "You're doing it again! Stop!" She buried her head in a pillow, seeking to block out anything more he might say.

Logan sighed and sat himself down on the bed. With insistent strength he pulled Kit from her ostrich position and cradled her against his broad chest. Absently he stroked the wild, luxuriant fall of her hair.

"I never meant to torture you, Katarina." At the same time he spoke the words, he wondered if they were true. Was he really free of the desire for revenge? When he lay at night in his solitary hammock, didn't he taste the need to hurt this woman who had wounded him so? Hurt her not only for not believing in him, for betraying him, but also for refusing obstinately to be driven from his heart. "I would tell you what you want to know, my sad little mouse, but you wouldn't believe me. You will have to see with your own eyes."

"See what?" She raised her eyes to his in a desperate plea. He shook his head in refusal, and her head dropped in dejected resignation onto his chest.

"God! I hate you, Logan Steele. I hate you. I hate you. I hate you." Kit's lips repeated the litany, while her stubborn heart replaced hate with another word entirely.

Logan held the sobbing girl until long after she fell asleep, her face nestled into the hollow of his throat, her breath soft and warm on his skin. She fitted so naturally against him, felt so right gathered into his arms. Everything about her called to him, even through the sticky web of hurt and betrayal they had spun around themselves.

Kit stirred in her sleep. "Logan?" Her hand splayed out over the hard, flat muscles of his chest.

"Yes?" he whispered, knowing that she spoke to a phantom in her dreams, not to him.

"Logan. I love you. I love you." Her voice was a sigh, the words almost indistinguishable.

He pressed a kiss to the top of her shining head. "I know, Katarina. I know."

They were both caught in the trap. Logan disentangled himself from her arms, laying her gently down on the pillows. He should have the strength to drive this minx from his heart, but he didn't, fool that he was. She would never forgive him for what he was about to do, but it was much too late now for him to change the course he had set. He wondered if he would ever forgive himself.

* * *

The storm blew over, and in the brisk breezes left in its trail the *Ice Maiden* skimmed through the swells like a fleet dolphin. Three days of steady sailing brought them to Tar Island, an out-of-the-way retreat frequently used by the buccaneers to refit and careen their ships.

As they approached the lee side of the little island, there was no sign that the treacherous Main de Fer had been telling the truth. No break in the dense green jungle and glaringly white beaches pointed the way to a safe anchorage. The place appeared to be completely uninhabited by either animal, native, or pirate.

"It seems your trip was for nothing," Kit commented to Logan, leaning on the rail and admiring he strip of dazzling white beach. The sea surged onto the sand in quiet waves, then rolled back out over a shallow shelf whose clear waters displayed shifting hues of lavender, azure, cerulean, and aquamarine. The island looked like an unspoiled paradise, not a haven for cutthroats and thieves.

"Wait," Logan advised her with a smile. "There's more here than meets the eye."

Cautiously picking her way among the shoals, the *Ice Maiden* soon ventured around to the windward beaches. This aspect of the little isle was nothing like what had greeted them on the leeward shore. Here the sea staged a relentless attack, rolling over a fringing coral reef in foaming breakers. Behind the reef, a quiet lagoon bordered a narrow strip of beach that rapidly faded into jungle.

Kit declined to comment that this side of the island didn't look any more promising than the other side, for Logan's face was wearing a tensely expectant expression that was shared by the others on deck.

"There she be!" The hail came from Michael Carmody, who was taking his turn at the wheel. He pointed his finger toward a break in the reef that looked far too small for any ship to negotiate.

"Come about," Logan ordered. "Get a man in the chains. I want continuous depth soundings."

Peter began to shout orders through the trumpet of his hands. Carmody swung the great wheel around and men jumped to the ratlines like so many agile monkeys. As the frigate crossed the wind, the sails flapped in thunderous objection.

"You aren't going to cross the reef, are you?" Kit asked, astounded.

"It's safe enough as long as one keeps an eye out. I've done it before."

"But there's nothing here!"

"Wait and see, Katarina." Logan chuckled. "What your uncle would give to know about this place! Luckily, none of the men who enjoyed the hospitality of his fortress knew how to find it."

"I see," Katarina said, although she didn't.

Logan took his eyes from the reef and looked at her instead. The desperate, panicky, too-bright flare was gone from her eyes. Every now and then a smile played around her lips. Apparently since the night of the storm she had found some measure of peace within herself. The perpetual frown had left her face, and Logan had even noticed her talking and laughing with Tom and Doc. Kit's catharsis of anger and frustration had left acceptance in its wake. Logan wished he could find the same measure of peace for himself.

"We're going to make it on one tack," Peter said confidently.

"So we are," Logan confirmed, his mind jerked back to the problem at hand. "Peter, go below with Gabriel and open the weapons locker. I want every man of the crew armed with as much as he can carry—just in case."

It wasn't until the *Ice Maiden* had sailed majestically through the reef that Kit noticed the subtle break in vegetation.

"I suppose now you're going to tell me there is a hidden harbor in there," she said, half in jest.

"That there is, my love." There was a wickedly satisfied glint in Logan's eyes. "And in that harbor is the answer to all your questions."

"Mr. Bonny," Logan barked, "take the wheel. Carmody, I want you on the guns. And God help you if you miss your target."

The Irishman bared his teeth in a wolfish grin as he relinquished the wheel and hurried to the main deck, where the cannon were being primed and loaded.

"What are you going to do?" Kit felt a quiver of apprehension race through her veins at the sight of sand being strewn over the deck and the malevolent mouths of cannon being stuffed with deadly iron.

"I'm going to blow the bastard right off the beach," Logan answered in a deadly voice.

"You're so sure that the Jackal is here?"

"Yes." His eyes never left the slowly passing shoreline as they crept into the hidden cove. "I can feel him as surely as I can feel you here beside me."

"And if he is here, and he blows you out of the water before you can blow him off the beach?"

"No." Logan shook his head confidently. "This time I'm not going to lose. Now get below, Katarina. What's coming is not a sight for a lady's eyes."

Logan turned away. Kit, tempted to make a very unladylike gesture at his back, ignored his order.

The crew uttered not a word as the *Ice Maiden* slipped silently through the crystal-blue waters. Armed with cutlasses, rapiers, knives, and muskets, they stood by the loaded cannon with eyes anxiously scanning the shore. Finally they were rewarded when a sharp twist of the cove revealed the ungainly bulk of a brigantine tilted awkwardly on its side and held there with ropes fastened to sturdy trees. Above its waterline the ship was painted a ghostly gray. It looked like a beached whale, and was just as helpless. The clever Jackal had finally been caught with his pants down.

"I don't see the shore guns," Peter noted in a worried voice.

"They're well hidden." Logan swept the shoreline with a spyglass. "But you can be sure we'll hear from them soon enough."

The beach came alive. Figures ran to and fro, looking like ants in a frenzy of confusion. Shouts floated across the water, along with a noxious odor of the sulfur and pitch that was being used to reseal the brigantine's hull.

"Look alive, lads," Logan called. "We'll have to take the first one on the chin."

No sooner were the words out of his mouth than the jungle belched smoke and fire. Deadly cannonballs hurled toward them. One holed the mizzen topsail. Another crashed into the forward quarterdeck railing, scattering a spray of deadly splinters across the deck. One man screamed and clutched at his thigh, and John Bonny sank to the deck without a sound. His place at the helm was quickly taken by another crewman.

The blast knocked Kit from her feet and flung her headlong against Logan's tall form. He caught her adroitly, gaped at her in surprise, then rained an impressive string of curses down upon her head.

"What the bloody hell are you still doing up here, you damned little fool?"

Kit fought to regain her balance and push him away. But he held her fast.

"Doc!" Logan yelled.

Doc motioned two crewmen to carry Mr. Bonny below, then hurried over to the rail.

"Take this witless female below and put her to work at something useful." He gave Kit a little shake. "If you show so much as a hair abovedecks before it's safe, I'll make you sorry that one of those balls didn't put an end to your misery. Understand?"

He shoved her into Doc's arms and promptly began yelling orders down to where Michael Carmody and his cannon waited on the main deck. Halfway down the main companionway, Kit was almost knocked from her feet by the thunderous belch of the *Ice Maiden*'s starboard guns. She clapped her hands to her ears and scurried below, following Doc to the aft storeroom that had been converted into an infirmary.

"Hah!" Doc gloated. "Those shore guns won't bother us much longer!"

Kit stumbled against the old man as the frigate heeled sharply and swung to port. Doc righted her with a fond pat on the shoulder.

"Don't worry, Miss Kit. We're just turning our stern to those guns so we present a smaller target. Then when they've fired again we'll turn and blast them with our port guns while they reload. Don't you worry, girl. Logan Steele knows what he's about."

Doc was right. It took only one more sweep of the *Ice Maiden*'s battery to silence the guns that the *Jackal*'s crew had hauled ashore. No more wounded came below to be tended. Kit helped Doc attend the deckhand who had a splinter through his thigh. Poor old John Bonny, with a similar splinter through his throat, was beyond help.

With no more work to keep her hands busy, Kit paced restlessly around the little infirmary under Doc's watchful eye. When the *Ice Maiden*'s cannon roared once again, she jumped.

"What's going on now, do you suppose?" Her brows drew together in a V of concern.

"If we were in the stern cabin, we might be able to peek. The captain didn't say anything about not watching through the windows, now, did he?"

The stern windows gave them a good view only when the frigate swung around to make another pass, but that was sufficient. They could see that the jungle where the shore guns had been hidden was smoldering, and now Logan was concentrating his fire on the helpless brigantine. There was nothing that the *Jackal* could do to defend himself now that his shore guns were destroyed. The *Ice Maiden*'s guns spoke one more time.

"That's my boy, Carmody, you blasted Irishman!" Doc crowed and almost hopped around the cabin with glee. "That boy doesn't miss once he's got something in range!"

When the ship next came about, Kit could see that Doc was right. The brigantine would never sail again. It resembled a huge downed beast. A jumbled mass of spars and tumbled masts jutted like ravaged and broken bones from a carcass.

"Did I tell you?" Doc rubbed his hands together in satisfaction. "The Jackal finally gets what's coming to him, and no better man to do it than Logan Steele. He knows what he's about, that boy!"

"What now?" she asked, peering out the stern windows in morbid curiosity.

"Ah, now! Now we could leave them stranded here until the navy can pick them up and give them their just deserts. Or..." He paused, listening to the faint sound of shouted orders drifting down from above. "I thought so! We'll launch the longboats, go ashore, and finish these villains once and for all!"

"Why?" Kit cried. "What if... what if they overpower our crew?" Logan could be killed, her mind shouted in silent agony, or wounded. "They could take the *Ice Maiden* and sail away! Why give them that chance?"

Doc gave her arm a paternal pat of comfort, his eyes suddenly dark with pity. "Logan wants the Jackal for reasons of his own. It's a shame to say it, but our boy has a pigheaded streak. Once he starts something, he likes to see it finished."

Pigheaded! Kit thought furiously. Doc didn't need to tell her about Logan being pigheaded! And arrogant and insolent and high-handed and the biggest fool to ever walk the face of the earth! But Lord, she prayed, don't let that pigheaded fool come to any harm!

"Don't look so glum, my girl," Doc said. "Logan Steele's a man who can take care of himself. He'll come back to you safe and sound."

Surprised, Kit looked at Doc, then sniffed in a fine show of unconcern. "I couldn't care less if the scoundrel doesn't come back at all!"

Doc shook his head and smiled knowingly. "Ah, youth! How glad I am that I'm no longer young."

The Jackal's crew were waiting for them when Logan and his men piled out of the boats and charged splashing and yelling up the beach. Logan's crew were fighting for greed, knowing that the destroyed brigantine most likely held the rich pickings of the Jackal's last prey. But the Jackal's men were beyond thinking about treasure. They fought for their very lives. Logan's crew stood in their way of escape, and survival.

The two groups of men met with a clash of steel. Muskets fired from behind the screen of the jungle, but the balls peppered both groups alike, and an angry order shouted from the Jackal's band silenced the guns. The deadly work was left to clubs and razor-edged steel as both groups hacked and stabbed and pounded at each other with only the curses of the living and screams of the dying as accompaniment.

Logan's concentration was only partially on the man who was presently trying to carve him with a cutlass. He quickly dispatched his foe, then looked up to scan the struggling knot of fighters. Before he found his quarry, another pirate jumped at him, sword raised to cleave his skull in two. Logan ducked beneath the blow, blocking it with one arm, then sent a foot of polished steel into the fellow's gut. Before he could wipe his bloody blade, he was set upon by still another opponent shouting for his blood.

Lunging, dodging, and parrying with automatic skill, Logan kept an eye peeled for the one man he sought above all others—an unmasked Jackal who wore Oliver St. John's face. Logan wanted to see the bastard looking at him down the length of a sword, tasting the bitter ashes of defeat, and knowing who had brought him down. Fate owed him that much, Logan thought.

The Jackal continued to elude Logan's searching eyes, but another set of sharp eyes caught sight of Logan's face and lit with an evil anticipation of revenge. Logan had his hands full crossing blades with two of the Jackal's crew when he recognized Simon Brownlow cutting his way through the crowd on a path headed straight for him. Somehow he wasn't surprised to see Kit's former overseer in the ranks of her brother's cutthroats. A sword had replaced Brownlow's whip, and he was wielding it with deadly ferocity.

Logan dispatched one of his opponents, but the other fought on with untiring determination. With a curiously detached regret, Logan knew he couldn't turn in time to fend off Simon Brownlow's attack, not without inviting his current foe to run him through. He caught just a glimpse of the killing gleam in Brownlow's eye before that gleam was abruptly extinguished by the brutal stroke of Michael Carmody's cutlass. At the same time, Logan sent a length of steel into his opponent's heart.

"Stinkin' bastard!" Carmody spat on Brownlow's corpse and lifted his bloody cutlass in a brief salute to his captain.

"He won't be stuffin' any more slaves into that bleedin' little oven-hole o' his."

The battle was not a long one. Too many of the Jackal's crew had been killed by the volleys from the *Ice Maiden*'s guns, and the others had been ill-prepared for battle. Tar Island had always been a safe retreat. The brigantine's cannon had been hauled ashore as a habitual precaution, but no one expected to be attacked. The Jackal's crew had discarded their weapons to work on their ship, and now they were paying the price. Many of the pistols so hastily grabbed were unloaded, and many blades unhoned.

The white sand of the beach quickly turned to crimson. As the battle moved toward the shattered brigantine, it left behind a trail of bloodied corpses who would never again sail the seas or carouse in the taverns of Tortuga. Some were from the *Ice Maiden*. Most were from the Jackal's pack.

By the time the survivors of the brigantine's crew threw down their weapons and pleaded for mercy, Logan's driving purpose had crested to a tidal wave of frustration. He examined every one of the sullen, defeated men who were being herded together in a group by his own gloating crew, and found that not one of them wore the face of Oliver St. John.

Logan cursed under his breath. "You! Ungalas! Stand guard over these men." His voice cracked like a whip in his annoyance. "Peter, you and Gabriel take the others and search the brigantine for anything of value. Keep it orderly, mind you! Anyone who gets caught appropriating for himself answers to me."

Everyone hopped to his task, eager to find what riches they had won. From the avarice in their eyes, Logan knew that nothing aboard the ghostly gray ship would escape their notice. But his own avarice was for a prize that had not yet been found. With his mouth set in a line of bitter distaste, Logan started his grisly search of corpses to find the remains of the man he sought.

An hour later the Jackal's plundered cargo was laid out on the beach before the greedy eyes of Logan's crew. But the Jackal himself was still missing. Logan's hard eyes swept the sullen group of prisoners, who had been pressed into digging a mass grave for the abundant corpses littering the beach.

"Ungalas!" Logan bellowed in an ill-tempered voice.

"*Sí?*"

"Bring me"—he paused to consider the prisoners—"bring me that villain in the purple sash."

Ungalas grabbed the unlucky fellow and pushed him to his knees in front of Logan. Glassy eyes looked up into Logan's and suddenly lit with fear. The *Ice Maiden*'s captain was an arresting sight, his shirt spattered with other men's blood and plastered by sweat to the hard, flat muscles of his chest; his long, muscular legs planted wide apart in an arrogant stance; his brow banded by a sweat-stained scarf; his hand casually grasping a bloody rapier as if it were an extension of his arm. He looked very much at home among the savage destruction he had wrought.

"Now, friend," Logan said, his voice a quiet threat, "tell me where your captain is."

The pirate's eyes grew wide. He cast a desperate glance toward the group of prisoners. "Don't know," he confessed.

Logan's sword came up to rest at the hollow of the prisoner's throat. "Don't you?" he queried with chilling intensity.

The man swayed back, but the deadly point of steel followed him. "I don't know, goddammit! Ye gots t' believe me! I don't know!"

The prisoner's face beaded with sweat. His eyes pleaded. Logan brought the tip of his rapier to rest below the fearful man's chin and urged his face to tilt upward. The pirate whimpered, feeling his life teeter on the edge of Logan's blade. "You don't know." Logan snorted with disgust. Then with an impatient nudge of his boot, he urged the pirate to his feet.

"Anyone who tells me what's become of the Jackal is free to go about his business," he offered.

The prisoners looked at each other and looked at the corpse-strewn beach. But no answer was forthcoming. It was then that a hail from the *Ice Maiden* floated out over the water.

* * *

When the last of the boats had headed for the beach, Kit cautiously poked her head through the hatch. Seeing the deck populated only by Tom Trelawny, she stepped the rest of the way through. Doc followed her out.

"I thought you would be landing with the rest of those fools," Kit commented to Tom in a relieved voice.

"The cap'n wouldn't let me go," the boy replied, disgruntled. He turned to Doc. "Can I take the spyglass up to the crow's nest?"

"Go ahead," Doc answered. "But I want to hear what's happening, you young imp!"

"That boy has set his sights on becoming just like Logan Steele," Doc said as the youngster scampered up the ratlines.

"More's the worse for Tom."

"Oh, he could do worse for a model. Logan is a very exceptional man."

"Yes," Kit noted caustically. "I've noticed how exceptional he is."

Doc shook his head. "You're too harsh in judging him."

"Rubbish!" Kit replied. "You're a dupe for his excuses, Doc. I can see clear through you."

"Can you?" Doc asked with a knowing smile. "What a shame you can't see through Logan as well."

"Ahoy!" Tom called down from the crow's nest. "We're roustin' 'em good! Five o' the fellows ran into the jungle. The others are diggin' a grave for their mates. We cut 'em to pieces."

"Where is there to run?" Kit asked a frowning Doc.

"Nowhere. This cove goes around the point there and continues up a bit. Other than that..."

"Doc!" Tom was motioning wildly with the spyglass. "Miss Kit! Over there!"

Doc turned in the direction Tom indicated, then cursed. "Damnation! That's where they ran!"

Kit followed his gaze to where an outcropping of sand and jungle hid the upper cove from view. The bowsprit of a tiny sloop was just becoming visible as the little craft sailed around the point. Her single mast was crowded with sail, and even in the light breeze she was making good time.

"Logan!" Doc shouted across the water. "Logan! Look!"

Logan turned at the hail from the *Ice Maiden*. A figure at the rail was wildly gesticulating toward the bow. Logan looked and saw nothing amiss. Then his frown of confusion was replaced by a look of fury as the single mast of a small sloop became visible above the screen of trees that hid the upper cove.

"There's the Jackal," he spat, then finished with a string of curses that impressed even the hardened prisoners who stood watching their captain and officers escape. In the fury of the fight they had all but forgotten about the sloop they had captured and towed into the cove for repair. "They had that thing anchored around the point."

Logan felt like physically kicking himself down the beach as the sloop drew abreast of the *Ice Maiden* and let loose a vindictive shot from the bow gun. He could see Doc and Tom and—God above! Was that third figure Kit?—trying to man one of the port cannon to return fire. Bitter fear clawed at Logan's heart. If any one of those three was hurt, he promised himself, he would personally see to it that Oliver St. John regretted every stinking moment of his worthless, brutal life.

By the time the prisoners and plunder had been loaded into the boats and brought aboard the *Ice Maiden*, the Jackal's little sloop was free of the cove. And by the time the larger frigate could negotiate a safe passage through the reef, the fugitives would be hull down over the horizon.

Logan stood tight-lipped and stiffly angry at the quarter-deck rail, watching the speck of the sloop draw farther and farther away. It would have been useless to try to persuade his crew to greater haste on the island. No buccaneer worth his rum would leave good plunder behind. But that knowledge didn't ease the ache of frustration in Logan's breast.

"Get the men aloft," he ordered Peter. "And keep them on their toes. We're going through that reef under all the sail we can cram on the yards."

Peter did not look comfortable with the prospect.

"And you!" Logan turned furiously to Kit. "What are you doing abovedecks? I told you—"

"You told me not to come up until it was safe," Kit reminded him, ignoring the thunderous scowl on his face. "It seems safe to me, except for possibly the daggers that are shooting from your eyes. Are you not happy to have finally won your war with this Jackal?"

"I didn't win the war," he told her in a disgusted voice. "Just a skirmish."

Kit lifted a brow. "Are the answers you promised me disappearing with that little ship?"

Logan opened his mouth to deliver an acid retort, then closed it. He shot her a look that made her more uneasy than any blast of anger could have.

"He won't get away," Logan said. "I know where he's heading."

"Oh?"

"There's the feel of a storm in the air, one that I'd guess will make the blow a few days back look like a little squall. That sloop can't take the pounding a big storm will deliver. I think our Jackal is headed straight for home."

"Home?" Kit asked uneasily.

"Yes, indeed. Home." He took her arm in a firm, unyielding grip from which Kit suddenly felt a desperate need to escape. "Come below with me, Katarina. I think the time has come for us to have a talk."

Chapter 21

"I don't believe you! I won't believe you! You lying villain! How dare you concoct such a story!"

Kit slammed her fist against the bulkhead, ignoring the pain that shot up her arm. The stern cabin seemed to rock with her indignation. Oliver alive and roaming the sea as the infamous Jackal! What rubbish! What utter drivel! Logan was truly mad if he expected her to swallow such a dose of nonsense!

"You're right," Logan admitted, propped casually against the desk. "I wouldn't dare to invent such a tale. Therefore it must be true."

Kit clenched her fists until her nails bit painfully into her palms. She gazed longingly at the bottle of wine that sat on the desk. She coveted it not to drink, but to break over Logan's loathsome head.

"Oliver is dead. I saw the body for myself. Killed by your bloody hand. Shot with your pistol. Thrown to the sharks in your own twisted anger!"

"Must have been a pretty sight," Logan conjectured grimly. "Kind of the sharks to leave enough for you to identify."

Kit blanched at the memory. "It was Oliver." Her mind reeled anew with anger and loss. "It had to be Oliver."

"Anyone else missing around Greenhaven?"

"No." Yes! her mind countered. George Marshall. He hadn't been aboard Logan's ship. His build was the same as Oliver's, and his hair color also. He had disappeared the same afternoon that Oliver died. "No," Kit repeated, as if denying the possibility would change the facts.

"It would have been most convenient for Oliver to disappear, don't you think, Katarina? And if he could leave a body behind—supposedly his own—and pin the murder on the man who could expose him, so much the better."

Logan did not enjoy the sight of Kit's pain. She had betrayed him and constantly reviled him. By rights, he should relish wounding her with the unsavory truth. But instead he wanted to fold her in his arms and soothe the hurt away until her eyes were clear and her lips could once again smile. Impossible, of course. He was a fool to still love her. And she was a fool also, to be caught in the same trap as he. The bitter truth was tearing her to pieces. He knew it, and he hated it. But there was no way he could stop it.

"You're mad," Kit protested. "You're simply making excuses for yourself. Why would Oliver do such a thing?"

Logan shook his head and laughed bitterly. Arms folded across his chest, he looked completely comfortable, disturbingly confident. "Think, my love. If I shouted to the world that Oliver St. John was the Jackal, few would believe me since everyone thinks I've murdered the man I defamed. And even if I could make a convincing case, no one would hunt down and hang a dead man."

Kit's eyes blazed a hatred scraped from the very depths of her soul. "Oliver wouldn't do that! My brother was not a murderer, nor a pirate. You are the murdering pirate. You and none other!"

"Denying it won't help, Katarina." Logan's eyes softened with a touch of sympathy. "Even now you are beginning to see the truth. I'm sorry. I know how much it hurts."

"Don't you dare look at me that way!"

The last thing Kit wanted from Logan was pity. What she wanted was the truth. The real truth—not these trumped-up tales that the most gullible child would scorn. Logan was a consummate actor, for his voice rang with the conviction of one who believed what he said. But Kit knew better. The tale was impossible, a vile fantasy from the realms of madness.

"What an evil revenge this is!" she said, her voice a low hiss of contempt. "I'm surprised you don't show me some mutilated body from your bloody foray onto the island, then tell me that the poor hapless soul is the Jackal, and Oliver. What do you plan to do? Sail back to Barbados for a hero's welcome after having destroyed the Jackal's ship? Sully an honorable man's memory with this vicious invention of yours?"

Logan sighed and combed his battle-grimed hand through his hair. He wondered what made women so obstinate, and so loyal to the wrong people.

"Is this your idea of revenge, Logan Steele? To see my name ruined and my property confiscated because of Oliver's so-called crimes?" Fists clenched at her sides, it was all Kit could do to refrain from pummeling the wretch into telling her what she wanted to hear. "I tell you I'll not play along with your game. I'm not that easily duped. You killed Oliver. All the servants heard you fighting."

Logan was out of patience. Coming abruptly to his feet, he grasped Kit's shoulders and shook her hard. Her eyes went wild and wide as he forced her to face him.

"You listen to me, Katarina! You listen to me and take the damned blinders from your eyes! Why do you think young Tom mistook you for the Jackal the first time he saw you dressed in breeches with your hair tied back? Do you know how much you and Oliver look alike?"

"That's ridiculous!"

"Then why did Tom recognize Oliver when he delivered my message to Greenhaven?"

"He must have been mistaken."

"And why did we find Simon Brownlow among the Jackal's crew? Tell me that! He's been working for Oliver all along. Can't you see that?"

"Coincidence!"

"Coincidence be damned!" Logan's face was dark and fierce, making Kit want to cringe away. But the unyielding power of his hands held her fast. "Why did Oliver try to kill me when I confronted him with the truth? Because there was no way he could deny what I knew. That's why! I tell you true, Katarina." He gave her another teeth-jarring shake. "I don't care if you believe I killed your brother. Because when I find the bastard I'm going to remedy my past mistake and see that the villain swings from the gibbet on Execution Dock!"

The open-handed blow Kit swept across Logan's face was not a ladylike show of feminine displeasure. It carried all the power of her considerable strength, and all the vicious force of her anger. Logan's cheek turned white and then red from the pounding, but he didn't twitch a muscle, not even when she hit him again with equal vigor.

"Are you through?" he asked with mocking patience.

"No!" she shouted, near hysteria. "Get out! Get out before I commit murder myself!" She cast wild eyes around the room, searching for something substantial to throw at him.

"Your servant, my lady." His sardonic bow was a twin to the insolent gesture he had dared on that first ill-omened day in the cane fields.

"Out! Out! Get out of my sight!"

Logan adroitly dodged the leather-bound volume that Kit hurled in his direction, then sidestepped the pewter mug that sailed after it.

"I hope you hang! I hope you're drawn and quartered! I hope you rot in hell for a thousand years!"

"No doubt Oliver would appreciate the company," Logan noted dryly, ducking beneath a flying tankard that shattered on the bulkhead behind him. "You won't be rid of me this way, you know. In fact, Katarina, I don't think you'll ever be rid of me." He regarded her panting, white-faced, wild-eyed form with sympathy. "You are caught in the same trap as I, loving someone you should by all rights despise. Everywhere you look, everyplace you go, you will see my face and hear my voice. I'll haunt your dreams and torment your waking hours. I'll dog your every step, always a part of your mind, your body, your very soul. Even should I be hanged and cut into a thousand pieces, I will still be a part of you."

"No! No! No! No! No!" Kit shrieked out the denials, tempted for the first time in her life to yield to feminine hysterics. Never had she been torn by such conflicting emotions. A thousand voices in her mind seemed to scream at her, pushing her first one way, and then another, and then still another. And there stood that infuriating rogue, so cool in the face of her anger, so confident in his power, so certain of his strength. She wanted to pummel him, slash at him, and at the same time seek refuge in those strong arms and cry out her agony against the solid wall of his chest.

"Believe I speak the truth, my Katarina." Logan's voice was quiet, but its intense, possessive quality frightened Kit more than any angry blast or threat could have. "I speak from experience, for I am possessed by you in the same manner."

Kit bit her lip until she could taste the warm saltiness of her own blood. "You are possessed by the devil and none other, Logan Steele." Tear-streaked face a mask of iron determination, she closed her hand around the pitcher that sat on the washstand. "Now get out before I send you straight to your infernal master."

She hefted the pitcher above her head like a warrior brandishing a spear. A sad smile playing about his mouth, Logan took the better part of valor and backed toward the door. "I can see that my first estimation was correct. You will be convinced only by seeing with your own eyes. So be it."

The door closed softly behind him as he made his exit. Kit stood still, breathing as though she had raced a mile with the hounds of Satan at her back. Her hands shook, and her stomach was tied into painful knots. Lips pressed into a tight, angry line, she started to lower her unlikely weapon. Then on second thought she raised the pitcher and hurled it toward the door. With hot, tear-filled eyes and a sinking sense of doom, she watched the delicate china explode into shattered ruin—so like her life—and fall in broken, pitiful pieces to the deck.

The seas were beginning to rise by the time the *Ice Maiden* sailed into Half Moon Bay. The eastern headland—that lonely stretch of beach and jungle where Oliver's body had been discovered—was a dark blot against a sullen sky, and the western expanse of the bay was veiled by low-hanging clouds. An angry chop had been whipped up by the wind, and sea spray pelted the deck like salty rain. Logan had been right about a storm rising, Kit admitted, as she stood at the rail like a cold, lonely statue and watched the shoreline slip by. She adamantly refused to acknowledge that he could be right about anything else. Just the same, she was relieved to note that there was no sloop anchored within the confines of the bay.

Kit fired a triumphant, scornful look at Logan as he joined her at the rail. "It seems your quarry has fled elsewhere."

"Do you think so?" Logan's smile was unclouded by dismay.

Kit noted that Logan's eyes were fixed on the outlet of a small river. In its higher reaches that river became the stream that ran beside Greenhaven's mill, and the pond where Logan had . . . Kit jerked her mind from the path it was following.

"That river isn't navigable," she protested, reading his mind.

"Certainly not by anything as large as this frigate." Logan turned his gaze from the shoreline to her face. "But perhaps by a small sloop with a shallow keel, at least in the lower reaches close to the mouth. It would be an ideal place to wait out a storm."

"Rubbish. Empty conjecture. Take your fantasies elsewhere," Kit said wearily.

"I will. But first I will take you home, Katarina. Just as I promised I would." Logan glanced up to where Greenhaven's big coral-stone mansion was just becoming visible through the gray mist and tangled vegetation.

"There is no need for you to take me home," Kit said in a chilly voice. "Just set me ashore, and I will make my own way."

"I wouldn't dream of sending you into the Jackal's den unguarded."

"Greenhaven is not the Jackal's den. And you are not welcome there." The storm gathering in Kit's dark eyes rivaled the one rising on the sea. "Besides, there is no one at the house except the servants and slaves, and," she added with a touch of malice, "possibly a troop of militia, if my kidnapping has been reported."

"I doubt very much the militia is in residence. If they are, my love, then no doubt you will get your wish to see me hang."

"Good!" she replied with gusto.

"On the other hand, if your dear half brother is there . . ."

"He won't be."

"Are you sure of that?"

"Absolutely."

"Then you would not object to a wager."

"I don't play games of chance with the devil," Kit said scornfully.

"Is that what I am?" Logan placed one long finger under her chin and turned her stony face toward his.

"You're close enough," Kit assured him. His touch sent

a small quiver down her spine. She tried to tell herself it was revulsion.

"Tsk!" His eyes were mocking. "Where is your confidence, Katarina? Afraid you might lose?"

"Not at all. Oliver is dead by your murderous hand. How could he be here?"

"How, indeed?" Logan smiled with irritating aplomb. "Since you're so certain that you are right and I am lying, there would be no harm in your promising me something of value if we find Oliver somewhere on Greenhaven."

Kit frowned, instantly suspicious. "What thing of value?"

"Say... a kiss," he ventured.

"I'd rather kiss a snake."

"Sweet Katarina! I thought that was, in your opinion, exactly what I was asking you to do."

"I'm not in the least tempted to invite such a fate."

"What is this?" Logan taunted. "Are you not so certain as you pretend?"

"I'm certain enough. But I trust you not one whit. Just what could you hope to accomplish with a kiss?" Kit nervously noted the devilish light in Logan's eye.

He smiled, and the intimacy of that smile tingled along Kit's nerves with disconcerting warmth. "You would be surprised—or perhaps you wouldn't—by what I might accomplish with a kiss."

Memories of their time together flashed through Kit's unwilling mind. She did indeed know what Logan could accomplish with a kiss. How many times had a simple kiss started their ascent to ecstasy? How many times had the touch of his lips upon hers wooed her from reluctance to passion, from anger to bliss, from stubbornness to sweet acquiescence? But not anymore. Logan no longer had that power over her. Or if he did, Kit thought ruefully, she would never let him know it. That was one victory she would never permit him.

"And if you lose?" she inquired coldly.

"If I lose..." Logan turned his gaze back to where Greenhaven's mansion was now hidden behind the thick rise of jungle. "If I lose and Oliver isn't alive and isn't the

Jackal? Then, Katarina, my love, I will owe you more than I can ever repay."

The shallop that conveyed Kit ashore also carried Logan, Peter, Michael Carmody, and four others of the *Ice Maiden*'s crew. As the shallop pulled slowly away from the ship, Kit waved a desperate good-bye to Tom and Doc, knowing she would never see them again, knowing that they and many other members of Logan's band would leave a hole in her life that would never be filled.

By the time the boat scraped along the beach, Kit's face had turned a pale shade of green. Her queasy stomach and roiling emotions were vying for the privilege of causing her the most distress. She was certainly in no mood to argue with Logan, but it seemed that argument was the only thing left to them.

Logan lifted Kit from the boat and refused to set her down as he turned to Peter.

"You have your task."

Peter nodded grimly. "Aye, Logan. We'll see to it."

Peter and a crewman pushed the shallop back into the surf and leapt aboard. Only when they had rowed beyond the line of breakers did Logan set Kit down.

"Where are they going?" she asked with a suspicious frown.

"To the river mouth."

"So you've sucked Peter into this foolishness also."

"Only you regard it as foolishness, Katarina."

Kit sniffed disapprovingly and started up the beach. Logan followed, taking her arm to help her through the deep sand. She shook him off.

"There is no need for you to come to the house." She was tired of fighting. All she wanted was to reach the haven of her own chamber and her own bed. Even with her feet on dry land, she felt the world was tilting about her. "You are not welcome at my home."

"And if Oliver is there?" Logan shouted above the rising whine of the wind.

"As far as I know," Kit returned, "the day has not yet come for the dead to rise from their graves."

"You might be surprised."

She shook her head silently.

Logan was insistent. "If you are, how shall I collect my bet?"

"Oh, I'll be sure to let you know." Kit raised a mocking brow. "Where shall I send the missive? Tortuga, in care of your refined friends at the Sea Gull Inn? Or perhaps to Wallenghby Fort? You'll surely end up there again unless you get back to your ship and sail as soon as this storm blows over. And this time I won't be fool enough to help you escape."

Logan took hold of her shoulder and swung her around to face him. "I'm touched by your concern, my love."

"It's your crew I'm concerned about, Logan, not you."

"Are you sure about that?"

Kit sighed. She was weary of this sparring match. "Give it up, Logan. Let me go. We simply aren't meant to be together. It was a mistake from the very first."

"Was it?"

His hands moved to cup her face, and his mouth came down upon hers in gentle exploration. Kit felt the old magic begin to melt the hard core of ice she had been so desperately trying to maintain. As his tongue thrust in and out, caressing the recesses of her mouth in a simulation of male conquest—that sweet masculine victory that he had taught her so well—tendrils of fire woke and uncurled in her loins, fire that quickly flooded her veins and raced to every nerve in her body. She felt his hands slip from her face, float down over her shoulders, her breasts, her waist, then pause and grip her buttocks, pulling her roughly against him to feel the heat and the need of his arousal. Her arms stole around him. The feel of taut muscles straining under her hands, thick windswept hair curling around her fingers, steel-thewed strength demanding surrender, taking possession, snatching her very soul. . . .

It took a deafening clap of thunder and the sudden hard pelting of rain to jolt Kit from the spell that Logan was weaving. Who she was and who he was came back to her like a flash of lightning ripping across her brain. With all the strength left in both body and soul, she pushed him away.

"Are you so sure we don't belong together?" His smile was lazy, laced with passion and promise.

Kit drew herself up in haughty disdain, wooden and pale and stiff. "You claim the prize before you've won the wager."

"Just a fair warning of what's to come, my love. Give your brother my regards till we meet again."

"With any luck we won't ever meet again!"

Logan waved a casual good-bye and started back down the beach. Surprised that he had yielded so easily, Kit stood like a sodden statue until the heavy gray curtain of wind-driven rain hid him from view. She stood for a moment longer, her eyes focused on nothing, her mind numb with relief, or was it something else? Finally, picking up her waterlogged skirts and turning up the path toward the house, she walked stolidly on, feeling even more desolate than she had the day that Oliver died.

By the time Kit reached the house the rain was coming down in sheets. She slipped on the veranda steps, knocked off her feet by the wind.

"Raleigh!" Her call was snatched by the wind and drowned in the rain. "Raleigh!"

No one answered. Struggling back to her feet, Kit made her way to the door and pulled it open against the force of the wind. The sudden silence as she gained the entrance hall seemed thunderous. It took a moment for both her ears and her balance to recover from the chaos of the storm. She stood, dazed, dripping on the expensive parquet floor that her father had imported from England, when suddenly it struck her just how very silent the house was. Where was everybody?

"Mandy? Raleigh?" Lord! Had all the servants taken advantage of her absence and gone? Surely not! "Mandy?"

A confused-looking Mandy scuttled out from the direction of the kitchen. She peered at Kit through suspicious eyes.

"Mandy?"

"Oh, my lamb! It's really...? Oh, look at ye! We were all so worried. Where 'ave ye been, miss?"

Raleigh followed behind the plump redhead, looking

pleased to see Kit in his own dour way, and equally displeased with the small pond that was growing around her feet.

"Where is everyone?" Kit asked. "I called and called."

"We was in the kitchen, miss, 'avin' a small meetin', we was. Wait till we tell ye. . . . Oh, but look at ye! Ye'll catch yer death, ye will! Come upstairs right this minute fer a bath an' dry clothes. An' ye can tell me why ye left and frightened us all out o' our wits."

"Mistress Carpenter. . . ." Raleigh said in a mysterious tone.

"Don't ye worry, Mr. Raleigh. Ye just tell those boys to 'op to and 'aul some water fer the mistress's bath. Everythin' will be all right now that Miss Kit is finally 'ome."

Kit did not feel that everything was all right now that she was home. In fact, as she followed Mandy up the stairs, she sensed a definite pall about the house that had nothing to do with her absence.

"What is going on around here, Mandy?" She accepted the towel the maid handed her and gratefully slipped out of her sodden gown and petticoats. "Why all those furtive looks between you and Raleigh?"

"Lord Almighty! The strange goings-on around 'ere! We was worried about ye, miss. Where've ye been?"

Kit sighed. "I've been caught in a nightmare. That's where I've been." She regarded Mandy's face warily, fearing the impossible premonition that had her in its grip. "Somehow I don't think the nightmare is over yet. Will you tell me why the servants are all huddling in the kitchen, and why you and Raleigh look for all the world like you're plotting rebellion? I suppose Mrs. Calloway is in there with the rest of you. Mrs. Simpson, Susan, and Lucy, Harry, and the boys?"

Mandy nodded. "We was all set to leave, soon as the storm blew through. Every last one o' us."

"Leave? Why?"

"The master's back, love, an' we thought you was gone fer good. Risen from the dead, Mr. Oliver is, an' lookin' like a bloody ghost."

Kit's heart stopped for an instant, then pounded furiously.

The rain and wind beating at the bedchamber windows were drowned out by the sound of blood thundering in her ears. It was impossible, ridiculous, ludicrous. It couldn't be happening.

"When did he return?" Kit asked quietly, as if the small remaining portion of her world had not just tumbled down around her ears.

"A few hours ago. 'E didn't give no explanations, an' 'e flew into a fury when 'e saw that ye weren't 'ere. Gave Mr. Raleigh a good cuff—can ye imagine? Then 'e closed 'imself in 'is chamber an' threatened to strangle the first one t' wake 'im. Oh, 'e's in a vile mood. We weren't goin' to put up with it without ye bein' 'ere."

"He has reason to be in a vile mood," Kit said with a sigh. "Why didn't you tell me about this when I first came in?"

Mandy looked unhappy. "It's 'ard to find the words to tell o' such a thing. God 'elp me, it's 'ard to tell what t' think around 'ere anymore! People dead an' then comin' back, lookin' like they've been chased out o' hell; people disappearin' in the middle o' the night; governors an' lords pesterin' us poor servants fer answers we don't 'ave. I—"

"The governor was here asking questions?"

"Oh, aye. A fair pest 'e was, an' that struttin' Sir Thomas Modyford, too. Don't know when t' leave a body alone, those two don't. They fair tore apart Mr. Oliver's study. Just like they suspected 'im o' doin' somethin' wrong."

A knock on the door could hardly be heard above the sound of wind and rain beating at the windows. Kit pulled a dressing gown around her and nodded for Mandy to answer.

"It's yer bath, miss." Four little black boys stood outside in the hall, each carrying a bucket of steaming water.

A bath was the farthest thing from Kit's mind, but she motioned for the buckets to be carried to the bathing room. She hardly noticed when the boys left, or when Mandy clucked impatiently at her dallying.

"Yer water's gettin' cold, love."

"What? Oh, I don't want a bath."

"But—!"

"Mandy, fetch me some paper and a pen. I need to send a

note to the governor. No." She hastily negated the order with an impatient wave of a hand. "I can't do that. I can't. Oliver is my own flesh and blood, my father's only son! What am I to do?"

Mandy frowned as her eyes followed Kit's restless pacing. "Beggin' yer pardon, love, but ye've left me far behind."

The look Kit gave her maid was so full of anguish that Mandy became alarmed.

"Are ye ill, love?"

"No. No. I'm not ill. I . . . I can't explain. Not now." Kit tore off her dressing gown. "Fetch me a dry gown," she demanded. "I must see Oliver, and I must see him now."

"I wouldn't advise it, miss. 'E's not 'imself. 'E surely isn't. An' 'e's not goin' t' like being woke."

"Being awakened from his nap is the least of Oliver's worries," Kit answered cryptically.

Kit left a confused and distressed Mandy moaning over the waste of a good bath and forced herself to walk down the hallway toward Oliver's chamber. With every step she told herself that just because Oliver was alive didn't mean that Logan was right. Her brother—teasing, lighthearted, frivolous, irritating, overprotective Oliver—could not be a notorious pirate who wallowed in bloodshed and torture. Oliver was quick-tempered, it was true. Sometimes he was cruel, often he let power go to his head. But he wasn't the monster who had ravaged the *Carrie Ann*. This was all just a coincidence. Oliver would explain everything and they would both have a good laugh at the ridiculous situation.

Mandy was right. Oliver growled like an angry bear when Kit shook him from sleep, and he growled even more fiercely when he saw who it was had awakened him.

"What the devil!" Oliver shot to a sitting position and reached instinctively for a weapon that wasn't there. He blinked in confusion when he saw Kit standing with arms akimbo and foot impatiently tapping the carpet. "It's you!" he said with some amazement. "Where have you been, Kit? The servants fed me some cock-and-bull story about . . . !"

"I might ask the same of you." Kit's voice had an edge

of steel. She wasn't about to put up with Oliver's bullying on this occasion.

"Indeed?" He cocked a brow at her sharp tone. "No 'Welcome home, brother dear,' no expressions of joy at my miraculous return?"

"You are supposed to be dead."

"So I hear. I didn't learn about my unfortunate demise until I returned." He shot her a wry smile as he reached for his dressing gown and swung his legs over the bed. "Poor Mr. Pettijohn. I do hope they didn't hang the fellow."

"They didn't," Kit supplied in a tart voice. "Do you want to explain what happened?"

"If you insist. Will you be so kind as to turn your back, Kit? I know you're my sister and all, but . . ." He shook out a fresh shirt and breeches and smiled winningly.

Kit obliged and turned, noticing as she did the pile of dirty clothes by the wardrobe. Was that a streak of blood on the sleeve of the shirt? Her stomach twisted.

"Well?" she urged.

"Oh, yes. An explanation for my vexed little sister. It's all very simple. Your friend Pettijohn and I had a mix-up in the study. It was over you, of course. The fellow really has quite a violent temper, you know. I thought he was going to run me through. Even took a shot at him to defend myself. But he got in a lucky blow with his sword. Left me bleeding like a stuck pig."

"And . . ."

Oliver shrugged. "And I was so put out when I came to that I decided I couldn't stay here at Greenhaven another day, even another hour. If I did I would surely kill the chap, and you would never forgive me. So I bound myself up and took the yacht out to meet the *Elizabeth* as she sailed out of Carlisle Bay. You remember she was scheduled to leave that day."

"The servants didn't see you leave."

"Ah, well. It was rather abrupt, I admit. They were probably elsewhere, and I didn't bother to talk to them. But I left you a note explaining the whole thing. Didn't you get it?"

"No." Kit's voice was hard as ice. Oliver wasn't as

skilled at lying as Logan. But of course it appeared now that Logan hadn't been lying at all.

"Must have gotten misplaced. Sorry I worried you. You can turn around now."

Kit turned, her face a frozen mask of anger. "Your story doesn't serve, Oliver. Tell me the truth."

Oliver looked blandly innocent. "That is the truth, dear sister. I know you're vexed, but..."

"I'm more than vexed." Kit went to the wardrobe and picked up the soiled shirt. She turned the bloody sleeve toward its owner. "How do you explain this?"

"As I said, the villain got in a lucky blow."

"Over your ribs, if that bandage across your chest tells the truth. This blood is fresh, Oliver, and smudged, as though it was smeared onto your shirt by contact with another body. And since I see no other wounds, I assume it belongs to some unfortunate who met with your sword."

"I was—"

"And how do you explain the mutilated body that was pulled out of the bay?"

"How should I know who that was?"

"Oliver," she said sadly, "I know."

"You know what?" His eyes narrowed in suspicion.

"Everything. That shot you fired from your bow gun almost put an end to me."

"What?"

For a moment more Oliver held on to his mask of innocence. Then his face changed to a harder, sharper countenance. The brother Kit had known was gone.

"Just how did you come to accompany that rogue to Tar Island?"

"Much against my will, I assure you. But that doesn't matter, does it?"

Oliver sighed, took the shirt from her, and threw it impatiently aside. "I suppose you would have found out sooner or later. Actually, it will be much more convenient not to have to pretend while I'm in my own home."

Kit drew a shaky breath, not wanting to believe it was true. Would the nightmare never end?

"I thought I was rather clever, you know. That fellow

Pettijohn is every bit the scoundrel I am, by the way, but I suppose you know that, too. He knew too much, and the stupid sod confronted me with it. I tried to kill him, but he jumped me before I could aim. Cut me, then knocked me cold. Don't know why the bloody fool didn't kill me."

Kit knew, and cringed to remember all the curses and accusations she had thrown in Logan's face.

"When I came to, he was gone. I decided on a clever plan to discredit anything he might say, and protect myself at the same time."

"So you staged your own murder," Kit said miserably. "Poor George Marshall."

"Yes, well, he was nothing, Kit. Not worth your feeling sorry about. I knew he would be unrecognizable once the currents had carried him down to the eastern beaches. Remember that blackie we saw chewed up over there so many years ago?"

"Yes, I remember."

"Then I had Nick take me across to the *Elizabeth* on the yacht. Nick's been in my employ for some time, by the way. He's done very well for himself dealing in the 'merchandise' I've taken. And he's the one who found safe anchorage for my ghost ship, and for the *Elizabeth* when I'm out on the brigantine. I always leave Barbados on the *Elizabeth*, then switch to my sleek gray beauty. The fat *Elizabeth* is much too slow for adventuring."

"For pirating, you mean. I should have known Nick would be involved."

Oliver chuckled. "Don't frown so, sister mine. It will be easy enough to get another ship to carry on my grand career. And the *Elizabeth* is still quite safe. We're going to be far richer than you ever imagined."

"And how are you going to explain your disappearance, and the body?" she asked dully.

"Simple case of mistaken identity, along with a misunderstanding of where I was. Haven't you learned yet, Kit? People will believe almost anything if you have enough money and influence."

"And Logan Steele?"

"You think of all the loose ends, don't you?" Oliver

laughed, but his face lacked any trace of humor. "He won't be back, sister mine. I arranged for a couple of trustworthy seamen to carry indisputable proof of the rogue's piracy to the governor. Logan Steele is past history. He'll never dare set foot on Barbados again. And when I meet him next time at sea, he'll be food for the fishes. Come now, let's see if old Mrs. Simpson can whip us up a midafternoon meal, eh? I'm famished, and you look all done in. While we're eating you can tell me how you happened to be with that scoundrel when he attacked me."

For a moment Kit simply stood and digested the fantastic story Oliver had just told her, and the cold-blooded unconcern with which he had told it. The facade was gone, revealing a nightmare creature beneath. The last remaining portion of her safe and secure world was being swept away. Had she known the truth about anything in her life?

"I'm rather glad this happened," Oliver continued blithely. "Now we can be full partners in everything. I've been gaining an interest in the plantation, you know. I've an idea about—"

"Wait, Oliver." She put out a hand to detain him as he headed for the door. He looked as though they had been discussing nothing more significant than the weather. "Surely you don't mean to continue this . . . this bloody career of yours."

"Of course." He regarded her as he might a particularly slow child. "Why not?"

Kit closed her eyes, wishing she could open them and everything would be back to normal, wishing, even, that Oliver had remained dead and not risen from his supposed grave as this cruel caricature of the brother she had loved. She must convince him to stop this insanity. Even now it might be too late for redemption. The governor and Modyford already suspected him. Why else would they have searched through his belongings?

"I won't let you continue, Oliver. I've seen the results of your so-called adventures. It's . . . it's inhuman, what you do. I won't let it continue. I can't."

"Don't be stupid, Kit. You're not some fainthearted

female who balks at adventure. You're a St. John. Like me."

Her hand squeezed his arm as if she would hold him back from his cutthroat career by sheer force. "I won't let you go on like this. We can live very well by legitimate shipping and the profits from the sugar. You can run Greenhaven if you want, or continue with the shipping. You can do anything you want, but this piracy has to end. The Jackal must die. Don't let Oliver St. John die along with him."

Again Kit saw a transformation. Oliver's eyes narrowed, his mouth tightened. There was a cruel glint in his eye that convinced her once and for all that this was not simply some monstrous joke.

"Just what do you plan to do if I insist on continuing, sister mine?"

"Oliver," she pleaded, "don't make me threaten."

"Don't make *me* threaten, Kit." His face was dark, his mouth a hard, cruel slash in a stony countenance. "Much as I would regret the need, even a sister is dispensable at times. Survival is everything. Everything. Do you understand?"

Kit did, but she didn't want to admit it, even to herself. "No, I don't understand. What has happened to you? Where is my father's son, where is the boy who . . . ?"

"Don't be a fool, Kit! What do I have to say to make you come to your senses?"

Kit's eyes widened. She suddenly realized that if she gave Oliver cause to doubt her loyalty, he would kill her with as little remorse as he had killed poor George Marshall. He was a madman. Why had it taken her this whole insane conversation to realize it?

"You've said enough," she said in a defeated voice. "I think I just came to my senses."

She grabbed for the pitcher on the washstand, remembering with a painful jolt that she had used the same kind of weapon against Logan when he had tried to tell her the truth. The pitcher missed its target, but gave Kit the time she needed to dash out the door, into the hallway, and down the stairs. She remembered the pistol in her office—too late! She was already past the office door, and Oliver's footsteps were treading the upstairs hallway in a cadence of doom. No sense yelling for help from the servants. He would kill them without a thought.

Kit stopped her headlong flight, swaying first one way then another in her indecision. Oliver was coming—no! Not Oliver. Never again would she think of him as Oliver. He was the Jackal. Monster, cutthroat, madman. Logan had been right all along. Kit had been wrong. And now, she thought with desperation, she was going to suffer for her stubborn stupidity.

A crash of thunder echoed in her ears. A flash of lightning lit the front entranceway windows with a ghastly glare, fit accompaniment to Oliver's sudden appearance at the top of the stairs. Without further thought Kit fled—out the front door, down the veranda steps, and into the fury of the tempest.

Chapter 22

The wind was like a solid wall. Kit leaned against it and fought with all her strength, but it blew her where it would, battering her, drenching her, knocking her to the ground, snatching her up, then knocking her down again. Kit tried to scream and choked as her mouth was filled with rain. The wind howled in her ears and whipped her hair into stinging strands that lashed and cut at her face and eyes. The world was a gray whirling mass of wind and water. The house was gone, the lake, the lawns, the stables—everything had disappeared into the maelstrom. How had she been fool enough to leave the shelter of the mansion?

A voice screeched her name above the shriek of the wind, and Kit was reminded why she had chosen to face the storm. If Oliver dared to follow her, he would be just as overwhelmed as she. She stumbled on, obedient to the storm's whimsy. For what seemed an eternity she lurched here and there, hunching her shoulders against the driving rain and squinting her eyes against her wildly whipping hair. She fell again and again, and each time the struggle to rise was more difficult. Her mud-soaked skirts chafed her legs. Every inch of exposed skin was numb from the wind's battering force. She could no longer feel her hands, her arms, her face, and she imagined them stripped raw and bleeding.

Just when Kit thought she could stand it no longer, the wind shoved her against a rough wall. She spread herself against it, grateful to know that something solid and unmoving still existed in the world. Cautiously she inched her way along the wall until her ribs came painfully in contact with an iron latch. This was the stable, then, and not the house. Inside was shelter and warmth—and safety, perhaps.

Carefully Kit raised the latch, but for all her caution the wind caught the door and tore it from her hand, and then from the hinges. The crash was noticeable even above the howl of the storm. Yanked cruelly from her feet, Kit crawled the last inches into shelter.

"What the . . . ! Miss Kit!"

Adam was there, lifting her to her feet, brushing away the wet hair that was plastered to her face. Kit wanted to warn him. If Oliver should come, he would pay no more heed to Adam than he had to George Marshall. But she was gasping for breath. Her voice wouldn't obey her will.

Then Oliver was there. The crash of the door had guided him to her refuge. Wet and muddy and as bruised by the storm as Kit was herself, he blew in with the wind and rain that howled around the open doorway.

"No!" Kit gasped as Oliver reached for her arm. She pulled away from Adam's solicitous hold and searched for something, anything that she could use as a weapon.

"Sister mine." Oliver's voice was gloating, his smile triumphant. "How foolish of you to wander out into the storm."

Adam looked at them both in confusion, and Oliver motioned to him with an imperious gesture.

"Get back to your room, man. I will take the mistress back to the house."

"You can't go back out there, sir," Adam objected, looking from one to the other. "Not until the storm dies."

"Do as I say!"

"No!" Kit gave the stablemaster a gentle push toward the doorway. "Get help, Adam. I'll explain later. Just . . ."

"My sister has taken ill." Oliver interrupted in a voice of deadly calm. "She's quite out of her head."

Adam frowned, totally confused.

"Do as I say," Oliver repeated, taking a threatening step toward the stablemaster.

"Go, Adam!"

Kit grabbed a hoof pick that hung outside the tack room door. Her brother laughed at the puny weapon, but his humor fled when she threw it with all the force she could muster straight at Oliver's face. Her aim was true.

"Ouch! Dammit!" Oliver wiped at the nick in his cheek and his hand came away bloody. "Bitch!" A deadly light came into his eyes.

Adam took his cue and ran. Oliver lunged after him, but he was too late. The stablemaster disappeared into the fury of wind and rain that whirled outside the open doorway. Face a grim mask of frustration, Oliver turned once more to his defiant sister.

"You've opened my eyes, little Kit." His voice was soft, like a sheath of velvet hiding a sharp dagger. "I thought you would see it my way eventually. I thought you would be glad of the wealth, the freedom, the fine things I could bring you. I thought you would marry Nick Basey, or some other fellow who would be a partner in our venture."

Kit backed toward the aisle that ran between the stalls, wondering desperately what to do, where to run. There was a killing gleam in Oliver's eyes and an obscene joy on his face. He was enjoying this, she realized with a sick heart. He was going to kill her, his sister, his only family, and he was going to enjoy doing it.

"You had to be stubborn, didn't you, Kit? You had to be all holy and outraged. Virtuous ice maiden. You couldn't stop to think like a flesh-and-blood woman for once in your life."

Kit's groping hand found the handle of a rake carelessly left leaning against a stall. She swung it around in front of her as though it were a spear. Oliver laughed.

"I wouldn't laugh, friend."

Oliver turned, his sword scraping from its scabbard. A dripping Logan stood just inside the doorway, Adam by his side.

"Logan!" Kit's voice was a soft whisper of relief. "How...?"

Logan didn't take his eyes from Oliver. "Did you really think I would let you come up here alone, Katarina, into the den of this filthy hyena? I followed you, but would have lost you in the storm, if not for Adam here."

"How noble!" Oliver sneered. "You think to rescue the lady fair. You've just saved me the trouble of hunting you down, Steele. I'm going to enjoy this."

Logan drew his sword. "Enjoy it, then. It's the last thing on this world that you will enjoy." His eyes were cold as death itself, and even Kit shivered at the remorseless purpose she read in their depths.

Adam slipped over to Kit. His eyes were full of questions.

"Go find a weapon," Kit commanded. "A knife, a sword, an ax—anything. Quickly. I'll explain later."

He went, questions unanswered but spurred to haste by the fear in Kit's voice. He came back with the rapier, now rusted and nicked, that his father had used to fight the Dutch.

"Can you use that?" Kit asked doubtfully.

Adam shook his head and shrugged. He was a stablemaster, not a swordsman.

"Then give it here." Kit took the sword and prayed she wouldn't have to use it.

Oliver and Logan were circling warily, like two wolves claiming the same prey. A feint here, a tentative lunge there—each tested the other's speed and skill, biding his time in taking his foe's measure. Both knew that only one would emerge alive from this battle, and neither was in a hurry to die.

Then, as though an invisible signal had been given, both sprang to the attack. Kit watched, her heart and her breath both racing in time to the struggle. Steel met steel, rasped, slipped, blocked, circled, slid. Bodies lunged and dodged, turned and jumped in a dance that would end in death for one, victory for the other. Once Logan dodged not quite fast enough. A line of scarlet appeared on his breast. Oliver grinned. Kit gasped. Her hand tightened on the hilt of her weapon.

The combatants moved farther into the stable, Oliver advancing, Logan retreating, Kit and Adam following. Windwalker whinnied in alarm as Logan stumbled against the door to her stall. Oliver grunted and lunged. The tip of his sword drove into the wood where Logan's heart had been only a second before. But Logan was no longer there. He was two paces away, smiling the smile that Esteban del Vargas had seen the moment before he plunged into death.

Oliver had no time to unstick his blade before Logan was upon him. Grabbing for the rake that had been Kit's defense, he swung it toward Logan with all his might, connecting with his foe's wrist and sending the sword flying from his hand.

"Now we'll see the finish of you," Oliver boasted. He swung the rake in vicious arcs that drove Logan back and still farther back toward the far end of the stable, where he would be pinned against the wall and easy meat for the rake's jagged teeth. Kit discarded Adam's rusty rapier and jerked Oliver's sword from the stall door, motioning Adam to retrieve Logan's blade. In desperate haste she ran to the end of the aisle, where Logan was only two strides from having the wall at his back. Oliver's Arab bay gelding looked curiously over his stall at all the excitement. Next stall down, the untamed red stallion that Oliver had named Demon kicked the wall in vexation at the disturbance.

Dodging Oliver's wild swings, Logan slowly retreated closer and closer to the wall. Death was just moments away, and Kit didn't know how to help. Oliver's wary eye was on her as well as Logan, and her puny sword could not reach beneath the swinging rake.

Then Adam tapped her on the shoulder. He motioned his

intentions. He would distract Oliver and the swinging rake. At the same time Kit should toss Oliver's blade to Logan. Kit shook her head in emphatic refusal. She suspected Adam had the better throwing arm, and they would only get one chance.

Kit motioned to the sword in Adam's hand, then without a second thought or a plan she moved forward, blade at the ready as Tom had taught her so many weeks ago. She leapt back as the rake swung briefly—too briefly—in her direction. That wouldn't serve at all. Oliver could so quickly turn and pin her against the stalls with the rake. He would be distracted, and she would be dead.

Cheat. That was Tom Trelawny's primary rule of self-defense. When in doubt, cheat.

"Oliver!" Kit shouted.

Oliver turned only an eyeball. Kit hefted her blade and threw it like a spear. It clattered to the floor after harmlessly grazing Oliver's shoulder, but the prick was enough to still the rake for the one instant Logan needed. He reached out and deftly caught the blade that Adam had so expertly thrown. Logan lunged forward. Oliver stumbled back, crashing against the door to Demon's stall. The latch splintered and gave, and Oliver's momentum carried him back and down to land beneath the hooves of the agitated stallion. A shriek of anger from the stud, a scream of pain from Oliver, and it was over.

"Oh, my God!"

Kit ran toward the stall but was snatched back into the trap of Logan's arms. He firmly pressed her face against his chest, hiding the drama in Demon's pen. The stallion had not yet finished venting his fury upon Oliver's body. Kit sobbed into Logan's shirt, trying not to hear the sound of hooves connecting with flesh and bone. It was long after the dreadful pounding had ended that she found the courage to look up.

"Is he dead?" she quavered.

"He's very dead," Logan confirmed. "Forgive me, my love, for ever having mocked your style of swordsmanship."

* * *

It was over. Governor Searle and the militia had left. Sir Thomas had left also, taking Logan with him and leaving Kit in peace. Leaving her alone, with silence, with sadness, and a host of painful memories.

Oliver was gone for good this time, buried in the family plot with no pomp and very little ceremony. Kit's image of her brother had died along with him. All the sweet memories had turned bitter, tainted with his villainy. Never would Kit be able to remember the boy she had loved without remembering the man he became.

The parlor draperies were pulled against the bright tropical sunlight. The room was as gray and gloomy as Kit herself, garbed in black mourning, hair pulled back into a severe knot at the nape of her neck. She sat quietly, as she had every day for the past week, pretending to read but not really reading, trying to mourn for Oliver but succeeding only in mourning for herself.

The servants tiptoed furtively about their duties, stunned by the revelations and violence that had shaken the household to its very core. They were half afraid of her, Kit thought. No doubt they looked for her to be revealed as an echo of her fiendish half brother. After all, was she not of the same blood, sprung from the same father's loins?

The only person Kit really wanted to see never came. Logan owed her nothing, Kit acknowledged. So why should he come? And why should she want him still? He had given her all the explanations she desired during those miserable hours they had sheltered in the stable. Kit had been stunned and numb, trying to forget the rough burlap sack that was hidden away from her sight in an empty stall—the sack that held the bloodied and crushed remains of her father's son, her only family, the man who had tried to kill her. But she heard well what Logan had to say, heard and understood and grew angry at the whole world.

Who would have guessed that the scraggly convict Oliver had bought off the auction block was the Earl of Wallingham's younger brother, notorious London rakehell, rebellious black sheep of an aristocratic family whose title and wealth dated back to the days of King Henry II. Tired of his younger brother's unconventional and rebellious troublemaking, the earl convinced him to follow a life at sea, where his energy and restlessness could be put to use.

Deferring to the earl's wishes, Logan readily climbed the ladder of rank and gained a reputation as a first-rate naval officer, until he chanced to serve under a commander so brutal that he had been forced to rebel once again. Mutiny was not a charge that could be dismissed by family influence. Even though a naval inquiry showed the captain unfit to command, Logan was condemned to hang.

The sentence was never carried out. Sir Thomas Modyford had needed an experienced sea officer with nothing to lose, a man with courage, strength, and a conscience not too delicate to overstep the bounds of the law. With Parliament's covert approval, he struck a bargain with the condemned man—life and freedom in return for the Jackal's demise, by the court's hand or by Logan's own, it mattered not. Logan would go to Barbados as a slave and, as others had before him, escape to the lawless freedom of the seas, where he would discover the identity of his prey and bring him either to justice or to death. Part of the scheme would be arranged by Modyford—a ship plus any clandestine support he could give. The rest had to come from Logan's ingenuity and luck.

Logan had fulfilled his grisly bargain, in the process dabbling in his own private little ventures, and also serving as Modyford's eyes and ears on the Venables–Penn expedition. His slave-snatching ring won him the exasperation of his employer, but when all was said and done, Logan had accomplished what he had been sent to do. Modyford had sent a wolf to hunt down a jackal. That the wolf had stolen some sheep along the way couldn't be helped.

Some of the story Kit learned from Logan's own mouth. The rest was supplied by Sir Thomas. It was a story in which she had only a small part, Kit realized. She had been a pawn, a piece of evidence, and perhaps a small morsel of entertainment for the wolf. Nothing more. Kit was left with her life in a shambles, her family name in ruins, and her family's property—Oliver's portion at least—subject to confiscation by Parliament. Oona had been right. Logan Steele was a conqueror who left destruction in his wake.

Raleigh cleared his throat. He stood in the arched parlor entrance with a suitably mournful look upon his face.

"What is it, Raleigh?"

"A caller, miss. Mr. . . . uh . . . Steele."

Logan. How ironic that Logan Steele could now walk in the open with honest people and use his own name without shame, and Kit St. John, once so proud, could not. Suddenly Kit was afraid, tempted to tell Raleigh to turn him away.

"Show him in, Raleigh." Kit's voice was composed. Her mind and heart were not.

Logan breezed into the room like a breath of fresh air. Without a word he pulled the draperies back from the windows and opened the shutters. His eyes swept Kit's black gown with disdain.

"You're not really in mourning for that rogue, are you?"

Kit blinked in the sudden glare of sunlight. "I mourn the brother I thought I had," she said coolly, "not the monster that he was."

She flinched from the force of Logan's vitality. Her mind was not as cool as her voice. Tears were close to the surface, burning her eyes. Not tears for Oliver. Never that. The tears were for herself, because she still loved this brash wolf of a man. Because she had fancied herself so strong and had proved so weak in the face of his very masculine, very persuasive charm. Why would he not finish with her and leave her in peace? She had longed to see him, had haunted the parlor window every day hoping to see him come, but now that he was here she was only reminded that he had used her, had never loved her, had played her for a fool. In the end he had saved her life. But without him that life was hardly worth living.

"I'm sorry," he said unexpectedly. "I know that you loved the man he pretended to be."

She answered only with silence, watching Logan pace the room with the same coiled-spring stride that carried him so fluidly across his quarterdeck. No wonder he was a rakehell and rebel, Kit thought. London society would be too small and too narrow to hold his energy. He was a man who would never bow to convention, or even to the law if he thought his way was better.

"And I'm sorry that I left you alone so long," he continued. "Modyford has kept me busy these last days, but now I'm free of him. And . . . I thought perhaps you needed time to sort things out."

"You have left Sir Thomas's employ?" she asked in a bitter voice.

"We've finished with each other, he and I."

"And what of your crew?"

Logan chuckled. "Gone their own ways, most of them back to lawlessness. They have a pardon for their past if they choose. Most of them do not choose. Doc is returning to England, as are Gabriel and Jud. Carmody is headed back to Ireland to cause trouble there. Young Tom has a post as midshipman on a British ship of the line, thanks to Sir Thomas."

"Eager to emulate his hero, no doubt."

Logan ignored the cutting edge in her tone. "And Peter is taking up legitimate trading out of Jamaica."

Did he come only for small talk? Kit wondered. Why could he not leave her in peace, leave her to put the past to rest? He owed her no courtesies, no gallantry. It was over. They were through with each other. Why not just let it lie?

Logan stopped his pacing and swung to face her. "Do not look at me with such grief in your eyes, Katarina."

Kit had not been aware that she was looking at him, but she was. Hastily, she lowered her gaze. A flush crawled up her neck and warmed her cheeks.

"I am sorry, my love. I had hoped there could be some other way, some way to spare you all of this. I tried, that day in the study, but Oliver would have none of it."

"You but did your duty," Kit said distantly.

"Aye. Perhaps. But I'm sorry for the grief it caused you, and sorry for the part I played."

"It was not an honorable part." She let her eyes lift to Logan's. Let him see the accusation there. Let him feel what he had done to her.

He came and knelt beside her chair. His hands captured

one of hers, and refused to release it when she flinched away. "I never lied to you, Katarina."

"Did you not?" Grief was giving way to anger. A small spark of spirit lit her eyes, as if a guttered candle had been relit.

"No, I did not. Chance alone decreed that I should end up at Greenhaven, meet you, and"—he smiled that devilish, infuriating smile that was so achingly familiar—"become so intrigued. It was young Tom's mistaking you for the Jackal that first made me suspect that Oliver was my man. But believe me, I never intended to use you as a way to your brother. Everything that passed between us, Katarina— everything!—was about you and me, not me and Oliver."

Kit snorted her disbelief. "Is that why you are here—to justify what you have done to me? Do you think that saving my life is not payment enough for my . . . my services?"

Logan rose to his feet, dragging Kit with him. Her hand was held in a gentle vise. She could not escape his grip. Neither could she escape the lure of his eyes.

"There is no need for me to justify anything I've done to you. All that I did I did from a passion that I believe you shared."

Could it be true? No. She would not be fooled again. She would not be weak again.

"I came to collect my wager," he said solemnly.

"Your wager?"

"My kiss. I believe that was the prize."

"Don't be ridiculous."

"Madam." Logan cocked an irreverent brow. "I have been called beast, murderer, renegade, cad, rake, and many other less pleasant things. But I have never been called ridiculous."

"You mock me."

"Never." The smile on his face was echoed in his eyes. Kit cursed herself for a fool, feeling her heart succumb once again to his spell.

"You are a cocky scoundrel, Logan Steele." She could not keep the hint of surrender from her voice. "Just what do you hope to accomplish with a single kiss?"

"I have told you before, you would be surprised what one might accomplish with a kiss."

His smile was lazy, sensual, full of promise. He pulled her to him, drew her arms around his neck, and captured her lips with his own. It was a kiss of affection that quickly became passion, gentleness that progressed to demand, tenderness that escalated to near-savagery. Kit knew she was lost. The ice so painfully, so carefully rebuilt was melting, scorched by her response to this man who was fire incarnate. Logan was right. So much could be accomplished by a single kiss.

"My life," he whispered. "My very soul. I love you. How could you ever doubt it?"

Again his lips possessed hers with aching tenderness. Kit's knees gave way under his assault. His mouth never leaving hers, Logan lifted her and sank down on the settee, cradling her in his arms.

"That was two," Kit objected, gasping both for air and for sanity. "You only bargained for one kiss."

"Aye," he returned with mock seriousness. "I do cheat occasionally." He traced his finger down her cheek. "What is this? Tears?"

More tears followed. Sobs tore at Kit's throat. All the jumbled emotion that she had held in check ran riot in a catharsis of tears. Logan held her against his chest, rocked her, soothed her, whispered reassurances in her ear.

"What have we done to each other?" she wailed softly.

"Hush now. Hush. We have neither one done anything that cannot be repaired."

She clung to him, ignoring the protests of her tattered pride and the dictates of good sense. Finally the flood of tears ceased, the sobs faded into distressed hiccups, then quit altogether.

"I've soaked your shirt," she sniffed, pushing away.

"No matter."

"I'm sorry. I'm"—she made a halfhearted gesture to brush away the strands of hair that had drifted across her face—"I'm a mess."

Logan smiled tenderly. "You were never more lovely."

Liar! she thought. But she loved the lie, and she loved

him. "What now?" Her voice was tentative. She almost didn't want to know.

He released her. She felt bereft. Rising from the settee, he turned his broad back toward her and crossed to the window. The sunlight made a mahogany halo of his hair.

"I've been offered land in Jamaica, but I think that making money from the sweat of slaves does not suit my fancy. Not after having a taste of slavery myself."

She wished desperately that she could see his face.

"There is a colony in New England—Rhode Island, it is called, though it's not an island at all. I've purchased a large tract of land there. It has good lumber, fertile soil, streams running with fish."

"New England! You're leaving." The new spark in her eyes faltered.

He turned. One brow lifted in gentle inquiry. "I'll need a wife by my side. A woman of spirit and courage, strong enough to lend a hand in building an empire in a truly new world. It's a world where people are measured by their strength and their brains instead of their pedigree, Katarina, where a past can be forgotten. Anyone's past."

She caught her breath. "Are you asking me to...to marry you?"

"Did you expect me to leave you behind?"

Kit abandoned all pretense at dignity and threw herself into his waiting arms. He kissed the top of her head, her brow, the tip of her nose, and then finally, in sensuous promise of things to come, her mouth.

"I'll sell Greenhaven," she said breathlessly when lack of air finally dragged them apart. "We'll need money to build your empire."

"Our empire," he corrected. "And you needn't sell anything, my love. My brother has the family title, but not all the family money." His eyes sparkled with mischief. "And then there's all that pirate plunder."

"Then I'll turn it over to Lionel Edmond to run," she insisted. "To save for our children. I want to forget the old and get on with the new."

"You love this place."

"I love you, Logan Steele. Scoundrel, rogue. All I need is you."

"I am the one thing you'll never lose," he assured her. His hands caressed her face, and she sighed with the ecstasy of his touch, the joy that he was her future, that she was his love.

"And to think," Logan said softly, almost to himself, "that those fools called you Ice Maiden. How could they not see the fire beneath the ice?"

She smiled dreamily. The only fire she could see was the one in his eyes, burning there for her.

Passionate western romance from *Virginia Brown*

☐ *DESERT DREAMS*
(D34-806, $3.95, U.S.A.) (D34-807, $4.95, Canada)

A half-Apache beauty and a dashing young captain find adventure on a hunt for hidden gold in 19th century New Mexico.

☐ *LEGACY OF SHADOWS*
(D32-264, $3.95, U.S.A.) (D32-955, $4.95, Canada)

A Celtic beauty aids a heroic Viking warrior and is banished by her people to the snow-swept North where she wins the respect of his people and his reluctant heart.

**Warner Books P.O. Box 690
New York, NY 10019**

Please send me the books I have checked. I enclose a check or money order (not cash), plus 95¢ per order and 95¢ per copy to cover postage and handling.* (Allow 4-6 weeks for delivery.)

___Please send me your free mail order catalog. (If ordering only the catalog, include a large self-addressed, stamped envelope.)

Name _____

Address _____

City _____ State _____ Zip _____

*New York and California residents add applicable sales tax.